# SPECTRE RISING

## A SPECTRE THRILLER

C.W. LEMOINE

This book is a work of fiction. Names, characters, places, and incidents are either products of the author's imagination or used fictitiously. Any resemblance to actual events or locales or persons living or dead is entirely coincidental. The views in this book do not represent those of the United States Air Force Reserve or United States Navy Reserve. All units, descriptions, and details related to the military are used solely to enhance the realism and credibility of the story.

2016 Edition

Cover artwork by Liz Bemis-Hittinger of Bemis Promotions.
www.postscript-media.com

*This book is dedicated to the memory of Linda Martin Lemoine.*
*I love you and I miss you, Mom.*

# AUTHOR'S NOTE

I started writing *SPECTRE RISING* in the Fall of 2009 after returning from my first deployment in the F-16 during Operation Iraqi Freedom. In the four years since then, the story has undergone a few breaks in writing and several major revisions.

I wrote this book because I enjoyed writing and wanted to share some of the insights from the cockpit of the F-16, but didn't feel like my personal story was interesting or heroic enough to warrant its own book. There are plenty of other books from much more interesting people on that front.

I think it's important to remind people that *SPECTRE RISING* is entirely from my imagination. Although some of the stories are based on real events, the narrative is entirely fiction. The squadrons and people in this book are made up, despite sharing similarities to actual operational squadrons and places. I use them only to enhance the realism and credibility of the story.

Unlike Cal "Spectre" Martin, I have been very fortunate in my flying career – having had the opportunity to fly the F-16 and F/A-18 in both the Air Force and Navy. The views in this book are entirely my own, and do not represent those of the United States Air Force Reserve or United States Navy Reserve.

Thanks for reading. It was a pleasure writing this book.

"Fight on and fly on to the last drop of blood and the last drop of fuel, to the last beat of the heart."

— *Baron Manfred von Richthofen*

## THE *SPECTRE* SERIES:

**SPECTRE RISING** (BOOK 1)

**AVOID. NEGOTIATE. KILL.** (BOOK 2)

**ARCHANGEL FALLEN** (BOOK 3)

**EXECUTIVE REACTION** (BOOK 4)

**BRICK BY BRICK** (BOOK 5)

**SPECTRE: ORIGINS** (PREQUEL SHORT STORIES)

Visit www.cwlemoine.com and subscribe to C.W. Lemoine's Newsletter for exclusive offers, updates, and event announcements.

# PROLOGUE

*Basra, Iraq*
*2009*

"Thunder Four-Two, Knife One-One, standby for new tasking." The secure radio hissed and crackled to life. It was the voice of the British Joint Terminal Attack Controller (JTAC) with whom he had been working for the last two hours.

"Knife One-One, Thunder Four-Two, go ahead," he replied, stuffing his water bottle back into his helmet bag. He had been airborne in his F-16 for over four hours, having refueled three times. It was the standard mission in the new Iraq. Takeoff, check in with the JTAC, stare at dirt through the targeting pod for an hour, hit a tanker, check back in with the next JTAC at the next tasking, wash, rinse, and repeat, until the mission window ended six hours later and it was time to land. Not quite as glamorous as the early days of the war when everyone cleaned off their weapons racks on every sortie.

But Captain Cal "Spectre" Martin had never seen that Iraq. It was his second deployment, and despite his air medal, he had always managed to bring his bombs home. He had come close to dropping bombs many times over his thirty combat sorties, usually arriving just as the hostilities were dying down, or being called off because the locals had already taken care of the problem. *The price of success*, he thought.

It truly was a new Iraq. In late 2008, the United States and Iraqi governments came to terms on a Status of Forces Agreement. This agreement defined the withdrawal of coalition forces from major Iraqi cities and laid the foundation for their eventual troop drawdown. It also required warrants for searches of any homes and buildings not related to combat. It was the first step of the United States government handing back the keys of Iraq to the Iraqi people.

As a result of this new agreement, however, the rules of engagement for coalition forces became more restrictive. No longer could a JTAC designate a target for destruction based on enemy activity. Search warrants had to be acquired. Iraqi police had to be notified. The remaining airpower, F-16s doing twenty-four hour patrols over predesignated areas, was relegated to searching for suspicious activity through their advanced targeting pods.

And Spectre had been doing just that. He had checked in with Knife One-One to look for suspicious activity – people placing Improvised Explosive Devices on known supply routes mostly. He was number two in a flight of two, separated by thirty miles working with two different JTACs – standard ops with fewer jets to patrol the skies these days.

"Thunder Four-Two, we have a TIC at MSR NOLA, convoy requests immediate support, contact Whiskey Eight-Zero on Green Ten, how copy?" the JTAC responded in his thick British accent.

He had heard it several times before on his first deployment – TIC, or Troops In Contact, was the magic acronym indicating friendly forces were currently engaging hostiles. Under the current ROE, it was the only way airborne weapons employment was authorized. After hours of lethargy, it was the only phrase that got his blood pumping. Someone on the ground was in trouble, and he was the cavalry. It was his first time hearing it on this tour, and he just hoped he could get there in time to make a difference.

"Thunder Four-Two copies all, will contact Whiskey Eighty on Green Ten, copy troops in contact," Spectre replied in an unshakably cool, calm tone despite the adrenaline now coursing through his veins.

"Cleared off, and happy hunting," the Brit replied.

He checked the cheater card on his kneeboard for the frequency called Green 10 and typed it in the upfront control of the F-16. He typed in the coordinates for the center point of MSR NOLA, the codename for the main highway westbound out of Basra. During daylight hours, it would serve as a busy highway for civilian and military traffic, but now at 0200 and with a curfew in effect, it would only be used by the military and those looking for a fight.

Of course, Spectre knew they weren't really looking for a fight. The people still fighting in Iraq were terrorists. They were looking to create fear and panic, and disrupt the progress of rebuilding Iraq. They wanted the infidels out of their land, so they could create a strict Islamic regime that would ultimately be used to oppress the Iraqi people. They were cowards who couldn't win a head on fight with even the budding Iraqi Security Forces. So instead, they played the asymmetric warfare game: ambush the vulnerable convoy with IEDs, harass the American bases with Indirect Fire attacks, and kill the women and children of those who sought to make their country better. It was all part of the desperate last stand of a defeated group.

With his sophisticated Embedded GPS/INS navigation system now directing him to the hot zone, Spectre sped to the area at nearly 500 knots. He knew in these situations time could mean the difference between life and death for the guys on the ground. They were the real reason things were going so well in Iraq, and he wasn't about to let the cowards they were facing get in a sucker punch.

He keyed his auxiliary radio to contact his flight lead. Despite having flown most of the mission alone, he was still the wingman, and his flight lead would be the ultimate decision maker. He needed to get the information to his flight lead as quickly as possible so their firepower would be available to the convoy in trouble.

"Thunder Four-One, Four-Two on Aux," he said, indicating that he was calling his flight lead on their secondary radio.

"Go ahead Spectre," he replied. Major Brett "Pounder" Van Pelt was an experienced Instructor Pilot (IP) and flight lead. He had been to Iraq three times prior. He had seen the transition firsthand from the "Wild West" to the restricted "look but don't touch" mindset.

"We've got a TIC at MSR NOLA; I'm inbound to contact Whiskey Eighty on Green Ten."

"Copy, go check in with the JTAC, I'm on my way, don't do anything without me," Pounder replied sternly. He was a fast burner in the F-16 community, having served as an operational test pilot testing the latest and greatest weapons for the active duty before joining the reserves. Just prior to the deployment, he was even selected by the Air Force Reserve Command as the alternate to go to the coveted Air Force Fighter Weapons School. Pounder was going places.

The convoy was over fifty miles away, but Spectre arrived on the scene in just over five minutes. He checked in with the JTAC, callsign Whiskey 80, who gave him the on-scene situation. A small convoy had been moving food and medical supplies along MSR NOLA from Basra to a village near Zubayr when an IED exploded, wounding two Iraqi soldiers and severely damaging one of their HUMVEEs.

"Requesting Armed Overwatch while we move the wounded to the MRAP and repair the HUMVEE, go with Fighter to FAC," the excited voice said over the secure radio. It was Whiskey 80, the American JTAC in the convoy. He sounded young – *couldn't be older than 21,* Spectre thought. *What a shame, not even old enough to drink legally in America, but old enough to have people try to blow him up.*

"Roger, we've got one F-16 with one on the way, each jet with two by GBU-12, two by GBU-38, and five hundred-fifty rounds of 20 millimeter, thirty minutes of playtime. Understand Armed Overwatch, confirm you're strobing?" he asked, repeating the instructions and giving the fighter to FAC brief, an abbreviated way for pilots to give Forward Air Controllers on the ground their weapons load out and time on station. Tonight each jet was loaded out with two 500lb GBU-12 Laser Guided Bombs, two 500lb GBU-38 GPS guided bombs, and 550 rounds in the 20MM Vulcan cannon sitting over his left shoulder.

"We are now," Whiskey 80 replied, indicating that he had turned on his Infrared Strobe to mark their position.

Spectre took his Night Vision Goggles out of their case and attached them to his helmet. He had been flying all night with them off. He hated them. Unless there was some tactical importance to wearing them, he avoided it at all costs – they just gave him a headache. If there was ever a time of tactical importance, it was now. After a quick scan, he quickly picked up the bright strobe flashing among the headlights on the highway. He picked out six vehicles, and then slewed his Litening II Advanced Targeting Pod to their position.

Using the Forward Looking Infrared mode of his targeting pod, he could easily make out the vehicles. The first two were

HUMVEEs, followed by three MRAPS – the Army's armored fighting vehicle designed to withstand IED attacks and ambushes, and one HUMVEE at the rear. The black and white pod image wasn't very clear at that altitude, but it appeared that the rear vehicle was the damaged one.

After confirming the JTAC's position, he began scanning the nearby area for threats. He put the jet into a 45-degree bank, right hand turn and set the autopilot to hold that turn so he could focus on the ground. The right hand "wheel" kept the F-16 in an orbit over the target area, keeping the targeting pod that was mounted on the right chin mount from being masked by the fuselage.

Pounder checked in just as he settled into his search. "Do you hear me on secure?" he asked on aux.

"Negative, I'm talking to the JTAC now," Spectre replied.

"I can't hear shit, what's going on?" Pounder demanded.

When he was a Lieutenant, Spectre never appreciated Pounder's attitude, but now it was just flat out annoying. A situation was developing on the ground and for whatever reason Pounder couldn't get his hands in it, so he was being short.

"There's a disabled vehicle and wounded, we're tasked with Armed Overwatch. I'll pass you the coordinates on the datalink, but so far nothing is happening," he said, trying not to show his irritation.

"Sounds like Iraqi standard – hurry up and do nothing. Well, I'm almost at Tanker Bingo, so we'll have to yo-yo, think you can handle it by yourself?" Pounder asked. He was nearing the preplanned fuel state to discontinue whatever tactical operations they were conducting so they could make the tanker or go home with enough fuel to land safely. With yo-yo operations, Spectre would stay on station alone until Pounder could get fuel on a tanker and make it back. Once back, they would complete a hand off and Spectre would head to the tanker alone, ensuring a fighter would always be overhead.

"I've still got 20 minutes until Bingo, I can handle it," Spectre replied.

"Fine, but don't do anything without me. I'll be back in 20 minutes."

Spectre acknowledged and continued with his search. He knew the rules. Ever since a young wingman nearly hit friendlies on a drop while his flight lead was at a tanker, the reigning Operations Group Commander had decreed that no aircraft would drop ordnance as a singleton, no matter what the situation. Flight leads were not supposed to leave their wingmen alone on station, but given the situation, Spectre wasn't about to argue and leave these guys alone on the side of a highway in the wee hours of the morning.

"Thunder Four-Two, this is Whiskey Eight-Zero, we are taking fire!" the JTAC screamed. His voice was cracking. Spectre could hear gunfire in the background. His eyes snapped back to his targeting pod. He could see the friendly troops hiding behind the vehicles on the road. Zooming out the pod image, he picked up two trucks on the other side of the road with several combatants in the back. He couldn't tell what kind of weapons they were holding, but they appeared to be shooting.

"Thunder Four-Two, Whiskey 80, we have troops in contact, danger close, standby for nine-line," he screamed once again. More shots could be heard in the background. They were under heavy fire. The nine-line served as a way for the Forward Air Controller to pass target information in a Close Air Support situation.

Spectre hesitated. He had strict marching orders from Pounder and the rules of engagement – *don't do anything solo*. He could see the friendlies taking heavy fire on the ground. They didn't have the firepower to hold the enemy combatants off by themselves for long, and he had no idea when Pounder would be back. He didn't have time to wait.

"Thunder Four-Two ready to copy nine-line," he replied. *Fuck it.* He was there to protect the troops on the ground, not watch them die while he sat idly by with his hands tied by ridiculous rules to cover some general's ass.

The JTAC screamed the required information to him and then said, "Request you strafe these fuckers NOW! We're taking heavy fire and they are advancing on our position!"

He had all the information he needed. With the proximity of the enemy to the friendlies, the fragments from the bombs would potentially injure them. He had to be surgical, and the 20MM was his choice. Loaded with High Explosive Incendiary rounds, the bullets would disable any vehicles and rain fire upon the cowards who had ambushed the convoy.

He called up the strafe pipper in the Head Up Display and set the aircraft systems up for his strafe pass. He would make his roll-in parallel to the friendlies so as not to shoot over them or toward them.

His adrenaline was now full throttle. Despite that, he remained focused. He rolled in, establishing a 30-degree nose low dive using the pitch ladders and flight path marker in his HUD. He set the gun cross at the top of the HUD on the target. It was the first truck.

"Thunder Four-Two, in from the east, tally target, visual friendlies," he said, his still-calm voice masking the fear and excitement he was feeling.

"You're cleared hot!" the JTAC replied, indicating Spectre was cleared to expend ordnance on the target.

He steadied the boresight cross on the truck as the gun pipper symbology rose to meet the target. The pipper in the F-16 gave a constantly computed indication of where the bullets would go at any given time. It was commonly referred to as the "death dot" because where you shot, death would follow.

As he reached the preplanned range with the pipper on the truck, he squeezed the trigger. The jet vibrated with a metallic rattle as the Vulcan cannon spat one hundred rounds per second. He held the trigger for three seconds, then released the trigger and began a 5G recovery from the dive.

For what seemed like hours, there was quiet on the radio. He reestablished his right hand wheel and picked up the target again in the targeting pod. He could make out very little as the dust settled from where he hit.

"Good hits! Good hits!" the JTAC exclaimed. "You're cleared immediate re-attack on the second truck, you're cleared hot!"

Spectre picked up the second truck visually through his Night Vision Goggles. It was now speeding westbound toward the front of the convoy.

"Confirm the truck is moving to your position," Spectre asked, trying to slow things down so as not to be too rushed and make a mistake.

"That's affirm, he just... oh shit!" the reply was cut off. Spectre's heart sank. He saw the glowing streak of something large and hot shooting from the truck in his FLIR. He knew it immediately. It was an RPG. He watched as the second HUMVEE in the convoy was rocked by the explosion and the infrared targeting pod image washed out from the heat of the blast.

The situation had gone from bad to worse. The radio was silent. He watched helplessly as the truck that had fired the RPG turned back away from the convoy to dig in and continue its assault. He was already risking it, but without a JTAC on the ground, he could not shoot.

"Help!" a scream came over the radio.

"Say again," Spectre asked, hoping it was the JTAC.

"This is the MRAP commander, we are under heavy fire with several casualties, our JTAC is down, request Emergency CAS, my initials are Hotel Sierra!"

Unlike working with a qualified JTAC, Emergency Close Air Support was the most difficult CAS scenario to manage. It referred to a situation in which a fighter provided support with a ground controller who was not a qualified air controller. Someone with no prior training would be guiding bombs and bullets from fighters onto nearby targets. The rules of engagement allowed it, but only at the discretion of the operator in the air, and only in the direst of situations because of the risk of friendly fire.

He called the MRAP commander back. *Time to go to work.* He confirmed that no personnel or vehicles had moved from the highway. The second truck was still the target.

He picked up the second truck visually and rolled in just like the first time, establishing a 30-degree dive and putting the boresight cross on the truck.

"Thunder Four-Two, in from the west," he said, hoping his new controller would respond.

"Do it! Take them out!" the MRAP commander exclaimed.

He exhaled a bit. At least he had positive contact with someone. Once in range, he put the pipper on the truck and squeezed the trigger for two seconds. The bullets spat from the trusty 20mm just has they had done before, until the gun was empty

Just as he began his recovery from the attack, he heard "Abort, abort, abort!" It was the call reserved for discontinuing the attack.

His heart sank.

# CHAPTER ONE

*Homestead, FL*
*Present Day*

Victor Alvarez stood alone in the grass parking lot. It was still dark out, but the horizon glowed orange in the distance as the sun began its upward trek. He hated morning, especially South Florida mornings. The air was almost completely saturated with moisture, and although it was almost fall, it was still eighty degrees.

The parking lot was relatively isolated. It had taken him twenty minutes driving down a dirt road to reach it. It had previously served as a parking lot for field workers to drop off their vehicles, but with the recent recession and the foreclosure of the landowner, it was now just a vacant lot. He was in an area known as the Redlands of Homestead. Only minutes from the Everglades, it was mostly open farmland with a few houses scattered here and there. It was the perfect place to escape the congestion of Miami, or the eyes of an unwelcome third party observer.

Alvarez leaned against his car as a lone pair of headlights approached from the distance. It was almost six o'clock in the morning. He pulled a handkerchief out of his pocket and wiped the sweat away from his brow. Despite having spent his whole life in this climate, he had still never fully embraced it.

The car pulled to a stop next to his. The silver Honda Civic was much louder than he expected. *It must have a broken muffler or something*, he reasoned. Not quite what he was expecting from a man like the one he was about to meet, but in this business, he had learned not to assume anything, especially not when dealing with Americans.

Alvarez ran his fingers through his jet-black hair and casually approached the car. He was holding a small envelope in his left hand and resting his right hand on his holstered gun. The man in the battered Civic was right on time and at the right place, but that didn't make him trust the stranger just yet.

"Are you Victor?" the man in the car asked. It was too dark in the car to make out his face.

"Yes, do you have the documents?" he replied with a thick Spanish accent.

"Here's everything you asked for, flying schedules, personnel files... everything," the man responded nervously, handing Alvarez a thick manila envelope through the car's window.

Alvarez leaned on the roof of the car. He was a tall man, and the low ride height of the car brought the window only up to waist level. He took the envelope from the man and put it on the roof of the car. Alvarez then handed the man the small envelope that he had been holding.

"These are your instructions. The first of the funds has already been transferred. The rest will be delivered upon completion of this operation."

"Oh...ok... uh... But no one knows my name right? There's nothing pointing to me when this is over, right?" The man was fidgeting in his seat.

"Your government will never find out," Alvarez reassured him. "Don't worry."

Alvarez had seen it many times before. He had been an agent with the Cuban Dirección General de Inteligencia for ten years. He had spent most of those years in South Miami. It was easy to blend in there. The majority of the population was Cuban or Hispanic, and almost everyone spoke Spanish fluently. No one even raised an eyebrow. He had used Americans many times before. Occasionally it was for intel, but often it was for assistance. They seemingly always tried to justify what they were doing, whether it was for their families or some political reason. Alvarez didn't care, but he still didn't respect them. He needed them for his operations, but they were traitors to their country, plain and simple.

Alvarez watched as the man opened the envelope and read the instructions. He looked for any signs of hesitation or weakness. He had been assured that his new contact would follow through, but he was more than ready to terminate their arrangement with a 9MM round to the man's temple at the first sign of weakness.

"Do you have any questions?" he asked with a toothy grin.

"No, I can do it."

"Good. Go. You'll be just fine." Alvarez grabbed the files off the roof of the car and pulled out his cell phone as he walked back toward his car. The little Civic sounded like a bumblebee as it sped off into the now rising sun. He dialed the number he had been given by his handler. It was time to check in.

"How did it go?" the voice asked.

"It is done. We have everything we need to proceed." Alvarez knew his cell phone was probably being monitored. The Dirección General de Inteligencia was the main state intelligence agency of Cuba. Since opening for business in late 1961, the DGI had been involved in intelligence and espionage operations across the globe. They had been involved in aiding leftist revolutionary movements in Africa, the Middle East, and mostly Latin America. In the United States, the DGI had been heavily involved with the international drug trade, assisting homegrown terrorist cells, and intelligence gathering operations for third party countries. The CIA, NSA, and FBI all had them on their watch lists.

"Excellent. Select the target and do what is necessary."

"Yes, *jefe*. You won't be disappointed." He hung up the phone and tossed the documents on the passenger seat of his car. This was the first operation he had undertaken without the knowledge of his government. It was going to make him a hero and wildly rich. He had a lot of work ahead of him, and a very short timeline.

# CHAPTER TWO

R-2901
*Four Months Later*

"Rattler Two-One, Thunder One-One checking in as fragged, ready for words," the metallic voice said over the Harris PRC-117F Manpack Radio. The dismounted radio, called a manpack, served as a multi-band, multimode radio that covered the gamut of waveforms. Frequencies covered included VHF, UHF, and UHF SATCOM radio. The unit was also compatible with the Single Channel Ground and Airborne Radio System, an Army system. It served as a lifeline for any JTAC to support assets in the air.

"Roger, Thunder One-One, Rattler has you loud and clear, situation is as follows: we have several wounded friendly forces holed up in the urban village. They are unable to move at this time and are surrounded by multiple hostiles in pickup trucks," he replied, looking up at the jets circling over their position. From his observation position, he could barely hear the two F-16s in a right hand orbit high above, but with the overcast sky, he could clearly see two dark specks speeding across the clouds like ants on a blanket.

The two men were set up on the roof of a metal building overlooking a series of tin buildings just a quarter mile away. The terrain was relatively flat, and from atop the two-story building, they had a relatively unobstructed view of the village. Even for a village, it wasn't much. A dirt road running north from their observation position was split by fifteen tin buildings before intersecting another dirt road that led out to a narrow tree line.

"Do you recognize the voice?" he asked, turning to the man standing next to him. The man was about six feet tall with a narrow frame and muscular build. He wore khaki 5.11 Tactical pants with a black Survival Krav Maga t-shirt. Oakley Half Jacket mirror tinted sunglasses masked his deep set, blue-gray eyes, and a desert camouflage boonie hat covered his light brown hair. His square jaw clenched as he pondered the question.

"C'mon Joe, you know I don't fly with those assholes anymore," the man replied with a grin.

Tech Sergeant Joe Carpenter laughed and turned back to his Toughbook Laptop and PRC-117 radio. He was wearing the standard issue Air Force ABU digital camouflage uniform complete with flak vest and ballistic helmet. A former Army Ranger, he had been a JTAC for three years after going Green to Blue in search of a more aviation-oriented career. Unable to fly because of a color vision test, his search landed him right back with the Army, as an embedded JTAC.

Perhaps one of the most physically demanding jobs in the Air Force, JTACs were frontline battlefield airmen. They were embedded with ground forces to advise the ground commander on Air Force air power capabilities, and in the heat of battle, to control aircraft during Close Air Support scenarios. Of course, it was just Carpenter's luck that he'd get out of the Army just to go right back in a new uniform, but he didn't mind, he was at the tip of the spear and he loved it.

To Carpenter, though, the best thing about working for Mother Blue was the toys. He knew the Army had the same technology and capabilities, but in the Air Force, he always seemed to have the latest and greatest at his fingertips. At the moment, the latest and greatest happened to be his Toughbook Laptop equipped with the newest Precision Strike Suite for Special Operation Forces software – PSS-SOF. With PSS-SOF, he could pass airborne operators high fidelity GPS coordinates of his own position or the enemy from the comfort of whatever foxhole he happened to be operating out of.

"Damn Spectre, still no love for the Gators?" Carpenter asked sarcastically. The Gators were the 39th Fighter Squadron stationed out of Homestead Air Reserve Base in Southern Florida. One of only two fighter squadrons remaining under the Air Force Reserve Command, the Gators had been Spectre's squadron until the aftermath of his final flight that night in the skies over Iraq.

"None. Don't you think you should pass them a nine line and get this party started?" Spectre was never known for his tact. It was one of many reasons he and Carpenter got along so well.

Carpenter nodded and keyed the microphone as he read from his Toughbook. "Thunder One-One, nine-line is as follows: items one through three are NA, line four: one hundred twenty feet, line five: group of trucks, line six: One Six Romeo Mike Lima Nine Three Eight Four Four Eight Zero Six, line 7 NA, Line 8: five hundred meters southeast, nine-line as required, remarks: final attack heading 270 plus or minus 10 degrees. Call in with final attack heading and expect clearance on final. Read back lines four, six, and restrictions."

The fighter repeated the nine-line perfectly as the F-16s maneuvered into position overhead. By using the standard nine-line format, Carpenter had given the fighters all the information they needed to take out the target, including elevation, coordinates formatted in Military Grid Reference System, distance from friendly positions and restrictions on attack direction.

"It's Magic," Spectre muttered.

Carpenter turned and gave Spectre a puzzled look.

"Magic? No man, it's science. We give them the coordinates of the bad guys with this fancy laptop, they plug it into their system, and the bad guys go boom."

"No shit, smartass, I mean the guy flying. It's Magic Manny," Spectre fired back. Lt Col Steve "Magic" Manny was the Director of Operations for the Gators.

Carpenter picked up his binoculars with one hand and the handset of his radio in the other as he watched the F-16 roll in on its target.

"Thunder One-One, in heading 275," announced the tinny voice of Magic over the PRC-117.

"You're cleared hot," Carpenter replied, clearing the pilot to employ ordnance while ensuring that the fighter's nose was pointing at the right target.

Spectre watched as the F-16 rolled in and hurled itself toward the ground. Seconds later, two objects fell as the jet turned back skyward. He winced in anticipation of the impact only to be greeted by two barely audible thuds.

"Good hits! Good bombs!" Carpenter exclaimed on the radio.

"Inerts are so anticlimactic," Spectre sighed.

"What do you expect? They drop two five hundred pound pieces of concrete that are shaped to look like real bombs. It's way better than when they roll in and just 'simulate' without anything coming off the jet. Now *that* is boring." Carpenter always had a way of putting a positive spin on things.

Just as Spectre was about to explain the merits of training without any ordnance on the aircraft, his cell phone rang. It was his boss.

"I have to go Joe, thanks for letting me spot for you," he said as he hung up the phone.

Carpenter gave him a nod and turned back to the target. He had invited Spectre to make the drive from Homestead to Avon Park to catch up and observe the Forward Air Controller side of Close Air Support. They had been friends since college, but aside from an e-mail or phone call here and there, they rarely got to see each other nearly ten years later.

Spectre picked up his backpack and climbed down the Conex container to begin the mile hike back to his truck. His boss had been brief but the sense of urgency was apparent in his voice. It was time to quit playing and get back to the office – *something new had come up.*

With the boss as vague as he was, Spectre was forced to wonder what could be going on until completing the three-hour drive back to Homestead to find out. *Was the store finally going to be bought out by a bigger chain? Did some new, rare find show up that needed an immediate appraisal?* These were the new questions that weighed heavily on his mind since his transition to civilian life.

It wasn't a very easy transition to make. When Spectre was told by his superiors upon returning from Iraq that he'd never fly an Air Force Reserve aircraft again, he refused the non-flying staff job they tried to force on him. For him, flying the F-16 hadn't been about the adrenaline rush or the need for speed. It was about serving a higher purpose. In the current world climate, that meant providing Close Air Support for boots on the ground. When the powers that be decided he was no longer fit to do that, he decided his services could be better used elsewhere.

Unfortunately for Spectre, the economy he escaped to wasn't conducive to his unique skill sets. And after several rejected applications to a myriad of three-letter agencies and private contractors, he found himself quickly burning through his savings.

That was until he met Marcus Anderson. The gruff Mr. Anderson had been a classmate of Spectre's in their Survival Krav Maga class. And although Marcus was nearly twenty years his senior, the two became fierce sparring partners. The former Marine versus the former fighter pilot, each did a good job of keeping the other on his toes. A black belt himself, Marcus had helped Spectre earn his black belt in Krav Maga.

Through their training and constant ribbing, the two became good friends. And when Marcus learned that Spectre was down on his luck, he didn't hesitate to bring him into the family business.

Anderson Police Supply in Florida City, FL was established in 1981 by the late John Anderson. A former Miami-Dade County detective, John Anderson had retired to the more rural Florida City to escape the explosive expansion of Miami and Ft. Lauderdale, while still being close enough to visit. What originally started out as a hobby of collecting rare and unique guns soon became a fairly lucrative business for John. His buddies from the force appreciated the discounts on firearms and supplies, while the locals enjoyed having a full service firearms dealer with a huge inventory right down the street.

After returning home a decorated Marine Recon Sniper in 1999, Marcus decided to leave the Corps and join his father in running the store. By the time his father passed away in 2001, Marcus had watched the store grow from the back corner of a bait and tackle shop to a 20,000 square foot facility equipped with an indoor shooting range and a fully configurable electronic shoot house.

When Marcus learned that Spectre had a business degree and extensive web design experience from college, he didn't feel so bad about giving Spectre a chance. And after only a year, Anderson Police Supply had become one of the foremost online dealers in firearms and tactical gear.

Spectre arrived at the store well after business hours, but the parking lot was still full. *Something must really be going on*, he thought. He had spent the three-hour drive going over the possibilities in his head, but none of them seemed likely enough to cause Marcus to be so tight lipped. He really had no idea what to expect.

He swiped his access card and opened the heavy metal door when the lock clicked open. The access control system had been installed shortly after the latest renovations, allowing better control and tracking of those employees who were able to access the building after hours. He then proceeded inside the large showroom, complete with multiple glass showcases. Handguns of all calibers and types were proudly on display inside each case, organized by manufacturer. Rifles of varying calibers and sizes were mounted behind each of the showcases on the wall. It was a gun lover's heaven.

Spectre noticed the staff crowded around the range rental counter of the store. He could barely make out Marcus's gray hair standing behind it, apparently talking to the staff. He threw his backpack onto one of the showcases without slowing down and continued to where the others were gathered around.

"No, it does not mean you'll lose your job," Marcus continued, apparently already midway through his speech. He paused and nodded as he noticed Spectre joining the crowd.

"Then what does it mean?" one of the junior salesmen asked.

"Would you let me finish? Do you think I won't tell you?" Marcus barked. The junior salesman retreated, his face red.

Spectre chuckled. *That was Marcus.* Patience and diplomacy would never be his legacy.

"What's going on?" Spectre whispered to the girl next to him. She was barely five feet tall with long brown hair and bright blue eyes. To Spectre, and to most of the males in the store, she was probably the most attractive girl there. Were it not for his pending engagement, he might have made a move on her. Perhaps even more successfully than the hundreds of guys that were being shot down on a daily basis.

"The boss just announced that the store is downsizing," she replied.

"Downsizing how?"

She replied with a finger to her mouth and pointed to Marcus, who was still staring down the junior salesman. Even at five foot nine inches and just over 170 pounds, Marcus was an expert in creating the fear of God in just about anyone.

"As I was saying," he continued, "we're not downsizing staff for now. We're going to move a lot of the floor salesmen... err... salespeople to the corporate accounts, internet sales, and range. We're also going to be cutting back on the store hours. I don't want to have to let people go, but you're all going to have to work with me. This is the best I can do with the shit sandwich we've been given."

Marcus made it a point to make eye contact with every man and woman standing around that counter as if he were readying the troops for a final charge into battle. To Marcus, that wasn't very far from the truth. For his business, this was do or die time. They had to either pull themselves out of the red and adapt to a changing economy, or face extinction.

"That's all I can say for now, folks. Just know that we're going to work together and pull this through. Cal, can I talk to you in private?"

Spectre nodded and walked behind the counter. He followed Marcus into his office and closed the door behind them. Marcus collapsed into his big leather chair and rubbed his temples.

"Nice speech, boss. The troops are ready for war," Spectre poked with a grin.

"War is a lot easier than this shit. *Way easier.* You have a target. You have an objective. You kill him. This? This is a cluster fuck."

"What's going on? When I left yesterday, things weren't so doom and gloom. Sure, we had a bad quarter, but nothing we haven't seen before," Spectre replied. He was referring to the quarterly financial reports their accounting staff had put together the day prior. As expected, gun sales were down across the board. The only thing doing well was the internet sales department.

"We were doing fine. Until this morning, and I got this," he said as he handed Spectre a letter.

Spectre took the letter and started reading. He couldn't believe it. It was a non-renewal notice from the local Customs and Border Protection branch. One of their largest government contracts for supplying firearms, ammunition, and tactical gear was being terminated.

"I've got a buddy at CBP; I'll ask what's going on."

"Don't bother, I already talked to the Air and Marine Branch Chief in Homestead," Marcus said, eyes closed as if what he was saying was also physically painful. "The President has cut funding to all Customs Air and Marine branches nationwide. He thinks this one might be closing altogether."

"It can't be! This is one of the busiest branches in the country!" Spectre was beside himself. The Homestead Air and Marine Interdiction branch of CBP was the front line in the country's battle against smugglers, drug runners, illegals, and terrorists. With a fleet of Blackhawk helicopters, AStar helicopters, Dash-8 surveillance aircraft, and trained interdiction agents, it was second only to the Tucson branch in activity.

"I know. Fucking Democrats," Marcus said with an exaggerated sigh.

# CHAPTER THREE

*Homestead, FL*

"I love you, I'm just not *in love* with you anymore," she said. Her eyes were watering, but her tone was unwavering and she looked him right in the eyes. There was nothing left for interpretation.

"Chloe, I don't understand. Where did this come from?" Spectre was sitting on the couch right across from Chloe Moss. He was leaning forward, hanging on every word and every gesture from the woman he loved. The woman who, until just seconds ago, he thought loved him too.

"I've been thinking about this for a long time, baby. It's just not the same anymore. You're not the same anymore."

He leaned back on the couch. *Where did this even come from?* They had been together for nearly five years, the last two of which they had been engaged. And despite no firm date for their wedding, he had never questioned their mutual resolve to be together.

"What do you mean I'm not the same anymore? I'm the same man you fell in love with when you first showed up to the squadron. What's going on?"

From the moment they first met, Spectre thought Chloe Moss would be the only girl he would ever love. With her curly light brown hair and bright green eyes, Spectre was entranced by her the very first time they met at his desk.

"Excuse me, can you tell me where Life Support is? I need to drop this stuff off."

Spectre looked up from his computer in what he'd later describe as a sensory overload. Even in the standard issue flight suit, she was beautiful. Her voice was angelic. She even smelled pretty.

"Huh?" he replied. He was gawking, and a single syllable grunt was about the best he could have hoped for, given his surprise.

"Hi, I'm the new pilot here. Lieutenant Chloe Moss," she said, extending what amounted to her free hand as she struggled to hold her G-suit, helmet, and harness with both hands.

He sat there for a second, staring at her barely outstretched hand, and then realized what was happening. She was the new Active Duty exchange pilot everyone had been talking about. After regaining his senses, he shook her hand and grabbed the falling harness from her arm.

"Here, let me help you, Life Support is this way. I'm 'Spectre' Martin. But you can call me Cal. Or Spectre. Or Captain Martin. Or 'Hey You,'" he said with a sheepish grin. *Smooth. Real smooth, Cal. Want to go ahead and tell her the names you just picked out for the children you're going to have too, while you're at it?*

Accepting the help, she followed him to the Life Support shop where pilots kept their flying gear.

"Thanks, Captain Cal 'Spectre' Martin. You can call me Chloe. Or Eve since that's technically my callsign," she said with a wink.

From that point on, their relationship progressed at record pace. Within a few months, just as Spectre was about to deploy on what would be the last deployment of his career, the squadron caught wind of their relationship.

Despite the fact that they were essentially the same rank, and no undue influence existed in their relationship, the leadership was whole-heartedly opposed to their relationship. To them, if it wasn't bad enough that she was the first female fighter pilot, it was worse that one of their own Reservists was dating her. *It could not stand.*

And that began Spectre's downfall with the Gators. As the leadership pushed back, he refused to yield. What he was doing wasn't illegal, and they had determined that they were in love. To Spectre, separation was not an option. The squadron leadership even threatened to have her reassigned, and they would have too, if not for a political favor called in by her mother, a former Congresswoman.

Despite the squadron pushback, their relationship seemed to press on stronger than ever. Spectre deployed with the squadron that had become very much against him while Chloe stayed home and continued her initial upgrade to become a Combat Mission Ready Wingman.

After being sent home early from Iraq, Chloe and Spectre even took it a step further, opting to move in together with their two dogs. Their relationship continued to speed along as they became more and more committed to each other.

And although Chloe continued to fly and slowly make progress with her career while Spectre awaited the outcome of his now famous strafing incident, the two never let it get between them.

Spectre supported her as she struggled through the upgrade program. The squadron seemed to have it out for her, determined to make it painful for her to upgrade. She had re-flown several of the upgrade rides and her instructors had threatened a few times to have her pulled from the upgrade program to give her more time in the jet before trying again.

Spectre helped her prepare and study for every flight, giving her advice on how to deal with the squadron that had turned its back on him, while Chloe listened patiently and gave him advice while he relived his own life changing moments over and over.

It had been a tough decision to let it all go, but with his career behind him and the generals giving him a firm "hell no" on returning to the jet, Spectre decided to move on to civilian life. He would not lose Chloe and his career. He could manage moving with her every three years. He liked the stability the relationship gave him. So he finally proposed.

Now he was sitting on their couch staring at the ring he had given her as she twisted it around on her finger. It had been his mother's ring. He had kept it after his parents had been killed in a car accident. It had been his grandmother's ring before that. It was the greatest gesture of love he could think of at the time.

"Cal, I love you, but the spark is just not there anymore. You and I have grown apart, and I don't think you even know who you are since you quit flying," she said. She was no longer looking at him, but staring at the ring as she twisted it on her finger.

"So what does this mean? You're done? It's over? You're the one! We can make this work!" His eyes were starting to water.

"I'm sorry baby, but I just don't think so," she replied with a tear rolling down her cheek.

"I thought I was your symbolon, remember? Doesn't that mean anything to you?" Spectre pleaded. It was a nickname Chloe had called him since the day he proposed. It was a term coined by Plato referring to two halves yearning to be joined as one. However, as Spectre asked the question, he realized she hadn't called him that in a while. *Maybe they really were growing apart after all.*

Chloe frowned. She pulled off the ring and looked at it. Time seemed to stand still as she offered it to Spectre.

"Just like that?" he asked. His face felt flush and his heart sank as he took the ring from her.

"I'll sleep in the guest room until we figure out what we're going to do with the house," she offered as she wiped away the tears. Her tone had suddenly turned very business-like. She got up and walked past him, pausing to touch his shoulder. He grabbed her hand.

"It's for the best," she said. She withdrew her hand and walked into the bedroom, her Golden Retriever following, and closed the door behind her.

Spectre sat there, head in hands, trying to digest what had just happened. Zeus, his 100 pound German Shepherd, slowly approached and nudged his elbow with his nose. The dog sensed the pain, and was trying to cushion the blow the only way he knew how.

"What the fuck just happened, Zeus?" But there were no explanations for Spectre, not even from the incredibly perceptive former military working dog.

❋   ❋   ❋

"Mom, I did it. It's over," she said, holding the cell phone to her ear as she collapsed on the bed. Her voice was trembling as she tried to hold back the flood of tears.

"Good for you sweetheart. He wasn't good enough for you," Maureen Ridley responded. Her voice was flat and unemotional.

Chloe sat up and rubbed her bloodshot eyes with her free hand. Her mom had never liked Cal, but Chloe had always thought she'd eventually come around, especially after Cal solidified their relationship with his proposal.

"Mom, I know you didn't like him, but this is still hard," Chloe said. "*Everything* is hard right now."

"Sweetie, you're young. You will find the right guy," Maureen responded reassuringly.

Chloe hesitated for a minute. Part of her wanted to let her mom know about her secret, but she still wasn't quite sure what was going to happen and she was afraid of what her mom might say. *It was all such a blur.*

"Thanks, Mom. I just feel overwhelmed," Chloe finally responded after a long silence.

"Is the squadron still giving you trouble?"

"Every day is a new battle, just like you told me it would be," Chloe replied. As a Congresswoman, her mom had seen firsthand what it was like to be a successful woman in a male dominated profession. It was a constant uphill battle.

"Do I need to make more phone calls?" Maureen asked.

"No, Mom, it's fine. They're just doing it because I'm the first female fighter pilot. I won't let them get to me. I'll show them."

"That's my girl," her mom responded. "You'll get through this like you've gotten through everything else. I'm proud of you."

# CHAPTER FOUR

*Hialeah, FL*

Victor Alvarez waited patiently in his car as he prepared for his next meeting. It was completely dark out, except for the orange tint of the streetlights lining the street. He was parked across from the Hialeah U-StoreIt complex, a two-acre lot of climate controlled storage buildings. He had been very careful in arranging the meeting, reminding his contact to take random routes and ensure no one was following him.

Alvarez watched as the main gate opened and the white truck gained entry. It was the late model Ford pickup he had been expecting. Just as he had instructed, the bed of the truck was filled with furniture so as not to draw attention. Alvarez would wait for the man to unload the furniture in the storage building he'd secured for them and then, when he was sure no one had followed them, he would meet the man in the alley behind the storage building.

"My old friend, how was your journey?" he asked as the man rounded the corner into the alleyway. He was 5'8" and average build. He had short black hair with a thick mustache and dark skin. He was sweating from the combination of the South Florida humidity and his recent exertion. He was wearing a Members Only jacket and gray slacks.

"Victor? I am well, thank you for getting me here," he replied.

Alvarez approached him with a file jacket in left hand and offered a handshake with his right. The man grasped his hand and pulled him closer into a hug.

"No need for it, Abdul, it was easy," Alvarez lied. Getting Abdul Aalee into the United States had been anything but easy. It had taken much time and patience to get everything perfectly into place without drawing the attention of the Americans, and even then, everything had almost been jeopardized at a marina in Marathon Key, FL.

Getting Aalee out of Iraq had been the easy part. The DGI had contacts in Iran that made it easy for them to get people out of the Middle East once clear of American forces. With the drawdown of forces, there just weren't enough patrols and surveillance to watch every square mile of the border between the two countries. Once across the border, the DGI agent on the ground in Iran escorted Aalee to Tehran, where travel was arranged under a fake alias and passport to Saudi Arabia. He stayed in the belly of the cargo ship carrying railway carriages produced by Wagon Pars to Cuba, where the DGI held him out of sight of the American spy agencies.

With a new identity and passport, he flew to Mexico and then to Bermuda. From Bermuda, his hosts had arranged a 65 foot Azimut yacht to take him to America. They used the yacht to blend in with the hundreds of ships celebrating the regatta off the coast of Southern Florida, and then went to port in Marathon Key, FL.

Despite cutting his hair and trimming his beard except for the bushy mustache, a boater in the marina had managed to spot him. The boater had been retired Army intel, and had recognized the man from the daily threat briefings while deployed in Iraq. The boater alerted local police who stopped Aalee to question him. With convincing American credentials and many threats of filing suit for harassment, Aalee and his handler were able to convince the Americans that they were just boaters enjoying the beautiful weekend weather.

"It was Allah's will. So, tell me, what have you in mind to strike back at the great Satan?" Aalee asked with a sinister grin.

Alvarez smiled. He didn't buy the great Satan rhetoric, but he enjoyed the enthusiasm of those that did. His driving factors were money and service to his country, and at the moment, he had been recruited for a mission that could both make him rich and increase his country's standing in the world.

"Your unique skills will be useful here," he replied, handing him the file jacket.

"What is this?" Aalee took the jacket and opened it, pulling out several photos and documents.

"It's a personnel file, along with some surveillance information we've gathered."

"Do you wish them dead? What is their significance?" Aalee asked, studying the glossy photos.

Alvarez took the pictures from Aalee. "This is former U.S. Representative Maureen Ridley," he pointed to the woman in the picture standing outside, watering her flower garden.

"The second picture is her husband, Jack Rivers, and the third is of their 18 year old son Evan. The man is old. He shouldn't pose much of a threat, and the boy is retarded. Their information is all in the file. We need you and your men to take them as hostages."

Aalee frowned as he scratched his chin where his full beard once was. Allah would certainly forgive him for altering it. After all, it was the will of Allah that he go to America and strike a blow to the great Satan.

"Hostages? What good could these people be to you? They will not fetch much of a ransom." Aalee's frown deepened. He had served five years as one of Saddam's top interrogators in the Republican Guard before the regime fell in 2003. He could make anyone talk, and had done so many times to root out those disloyal to the regime. After the collapse in 2003, Aalee turned to Al Qaeda. Working closely with Al-Zarqawi, he instilled fear in the hearts of those who would help the Americans. Anyone he found to be loyal to the coalition or the West was tortured in front of their families and killed.

"I do not want to go into detail here. The Americans may be listening, and this is too big to jeopardize our operation. Just know that you are doing your part to deal a major blow to their military. The ransom is bigger than you can even imagine." Alvarez smiled reassuringly.

"And if the ransom fails? The Americans don't negotiate, remember?"

"Then you will send a message to the Americans that not even their political leaders are safe, and we will still prevail."

Aalee's frown finally broke into a wry smile. He enjoyed taking the fight to the Americans. They had killed his parents with their senseless bombings during the first war in Iraq. They were non-believers, and Allah's will was to cleanse the world of their filth. He hoped whatever scheme the Cuban had come up with would fail, so he could show the pigs exactly what they had brought upon themselves with their evil ways. Maybe once the Cubans got whatever they wanted, he would do that anyway.

"All the information is in the packet in your hands." He reached in his pocket and pulled out a prepaid flip phone. "This is the only phone you will use to contact me. You will use the code included in the packet when speaking on it, and you will not make any other calls on it. Do you understand?"

Aalee nodded and took the phone, studying it. "Do not insult me with your condescending ways. I am perfectly aware of how to conduct myself."

"I am sorry. This is very important to everyone. I must go. Thank you again, old friend."

"It was nice to see you again. Allahu Akbar."

# CHAPTER FIVE

*Homestead, FL*

The sound of his office door opening startled Spectre out of his daze. He had been sitting at his desk in his lone corner office thinking about the events of the day prior. In just a few hours, he had gone from job stability and a happy home life to turmoil and love lost. No matter how much he tried to figure it out, he still couldn't discover where he'd gone wrong.

"You ok, big guy?" Marcus asked, cup of coffee in hand.

"Chloe dumped me," he said, looking up from his monitor. His eyes were puffy and bloodshot. He didn't even try to sleep the night before. Instead, he just stayed awake, trying to relive every moment he'd been with Chloe, desperately searching for the moment he'd gone off course. But despite knowing their relationship, like most, was never perfect, he could find no reason for what happened.

"Holy shit, are you serious?" Marcus nearly choked on his coffee as he sat in the chair across from Spectre.

"Yeah, it's pretty much the first thing she did when I came home last night," he said, pulling the ring out of his pocket and tossing it onto his desk. He then went over in detail everything that had happened the night before. He told Marcus how she was sitting in the living room, with the TV off, waiting for him when he finally got home. How she broke the news to him, gave him the ring back, and then locked herself in the guest room. He had even tried to talk to her through the guest room door, but all he heard was her talking to her mom on the phone.

"You sure it was her mom?" Marcus was suspicious. His standard response to any relationship problem was that the girl was obviously cheating on him.

This made Spectre smile slightly. "Well, either that or she's calling the dude 'Mom.'"

"I'm sorry buddy, I know it's tough. But she didn't give you any reason at all?"

"She's not in love with me anymore, and I'm not the same person since I stopped flying," replied Spectre as he rubbed his bloodshot eyes.

Marcus hesitated for a bit. Everyone that knew Spectre acknowledged that he had become a changed man since being forcibly removed from the cockpit. Some knew the change was for the best. It opened up many new opportunities and friendships that he wouldn't have otherwise had. Despite the good that had come from the incident, others still said he was a shell of his former self. He just didn't seem to have the drive and confidence that he used to have. He went through the motions of everyday life, but he wasn't the Spectre that people had known and loved. Marcus, however, was a firm believer in that former self.

Marcus had known Spectre, both before and after his flying career ended, and he knew a significant change had occurred. Although they hadn't been close friends before they started working together, Spectre had confided in Marcus many times that he was frustrated with his squadron. He complained that there was just too much inertia, too many lazy people, and no work ethic. Change was nearly impossible for the Gators of the 39th, and Spectre hated it. To Spectre, organizations that refuse to adapt and grow, even in the military, often were left behind.

Although Marcus had his own selfish reasons for believing that Spectre was better off in the civilian world, Marcus felt as if Spectre was a lot happier and less cynical since they'd first met. But he couldn't ignore how he'd benefited from Spectre's change in status. Spectre had single-handedly changed Anderson Police Supply into a viable Twenty-First Century business. He had given them a web presence and business model that was sustainable and realistic.

"Do you really think that's true? Are you sure she's not fucking someone else?"

Even in times like these, Spectre appreciated Marcus's candor. He knew that a guy like Marcus didn't get to where he was by sugar coating things. He was a man that spoke his mind. While some people would be horribly offended and turned off by it, Spectre always felt like it offered perspective.

"The thought crossed my mind, but I don't believe it. She's not that kind of girl," Spectre replied.

"There's no such thing as 'that kind of girl,' Cal," Marcus said cynically. "Weren't you in here just the other day complaining that she was acting differently?"

"Yeah, but that's because she had been stressed out about her flight lead upgrade," Spectre said, shaking his head. "The Gators have been making it incredibly painful for her to get through it."

"And your sex life?" Marcus asked with a raised eyebrow.

"What? Dude, that's none of your business," Spectre shot back.

"I'm just saying man, that's the first thing to go when they're cheating," Marcus offered, holding his hands up.

Spectre considered it for a moment. Their sex life had been pretty sparse in the last few months, but he had attributed it to the stresses of her job and the fact that he spent most of his time working at the gun store. They just didn't have time anymore.

"I appreciate the concern, but I don't think that's it. She's probably just worn down by the harassment program the Gators have been putting her through and taking it out on us. I guess I have been here a lot lately too, so that's probably part of it. Hopefully she'll come around when she finally finishes her upgrade and is under less pressure."

"If you say so, bud," Marcus said. "But there are plenty of better women out there if she is cheating."

"She's not cheating on me," Spectre replied firmly.

"Alright, enough girl talk." Marcus shrugged. "Let's get back to work. You and I are going to take a ride up to the base to talk to Director Browning about that letter. If you're a good boy, they might even take you for a ride in the Blackhawk."

"Jeepers do ya really mean it, Mr. Anderson? That would be so swell," Spectre answered, doing his best Wally and the Beav impersonation.

"Let's go," Marcus rolled his eyes.

Marcus opted to take the slightly longer route to avoid the Florida Turnpike, or as he liked to call it, the IdiotPike. Except for his time in the military, Marcus had lived in South Florida his entire life. Throughout it all, he had noticed the quality of driver go from mediocre to downright awful.

Marcus likened the local drivers to "Iraqis doing jumping jacks" referencing the famous YouTube video of the Iraqi soldiers who couldn't quite master the basic exercise. He loved everything about living in South Florida, except driving. He firmly planned on buying a houseboat, living on the water, and never driving again when he finally retired. It couldn't come soon enough.

As they made the long sweeping left hand turn on 137th past the Homestead-Miami Motor Speedway, a flight of F-16s made their final approach to land.

"Is that your ex?" Marcus asked.

"Well, she was supposed to be flying this morning. Could be." Spectre couldn't quite get used to referring to her as the "ex." He was still very much in denial that their relationship had become unrecoverable.

Arriving at the south gate of the base, Marcus showed his retiree identification and the military gate guard waved him through.

Once a major Cold War era Air Force base, Homestead Air Reserve Base was a shell of its former self. Prior to Hurricane Andrew in 1992, Homestead Air Force Base, as it was then known, was a major base, home to several F-4 and eventually F-16 basic training squadrons. The base was ideally suited for a large infrastructure with a huge runway that was over two miles long and two hundred feet wide that could support the largest of aircraft. After Hurricane Andrew and the devastation it left in its wake, however, the base nearly shut down.

It was the Air Force Reserve Command that saved it, keeping a lone F-16 squadron on base. The over water airspace was ideally suited for the F-16's air-to-air training missions, and with the Florida Air National Guard on site for homeland defense, the base served strategic purposes as well. Being the gateway to South America, Homestead ARB also served as home to Special Operations Command South, the US Coast Guard, and Customs and Border Protection's Air and Marine Branch for South Florida.

Marcus drove the white Tahoe down Coral Sea Boulevard toward the Customs Air Branch Operations Building. The entire base was under a renovation project to modernize the buildings. Those that weren't surrounded by construction equipment were severely run down, most likely original from the days that the active duty ran the show.

As they parked in front of the Operations Building, they could hear the rhythmic gunfire of the firing range right next-door.

"Sounds like home," Marcus said, holding the door open for Spectre.

Director David Browning was waiting for them in the lobby when they walked in. He was a short, slightly heavyset man in his mid fifties. He was wearing a khaki flight suit with police utility belt and a USP .40 holstered on his right hip. A gold US Customs federal agent badge was velcroed to his left breast.

"Marcus, it's good to see you," he said, extending his hand.

Marcus gave Browning a firm handshake without breaking eye contact. It was his signature greeting that few could forget.

"Thanks for meeting with us, Dave; I know you're a busy man. You remember Cal," he said, nodding to Spectre.

"I do. Cal, how are ya? Wish we could have hired you, but we've had a lot of cutbacks lately, as you can about imagine."

"No problem sir, I'm doing ok," Spectre replied.

After signing into the visitor registry, Spectre and Marcus followed Browning past the sea of cubicles to the director's office.

Browning offered them coffee as they sat at the conference table in the large office. Spectre declined as Marcus graciously accepted.

"Marcus, I'm going to be honest, we're hurting right now," Browning explained as he handed Marcus his coffee.

"You mentioned that on the phone yesterday," Marcus replied dryly.

"We didn't cut you out because we found someone cheaper. We cut you out because there's no money," Browning explained. "We've been cut off.

"This fiscal year's budget has completely gutted us. The hours we have allocated for the Blackhawks have been cut in half. The Dash-8s aren't even 24-hour operations anymore. They're telling us that when people retire or move away, to close out that position. And this is just another step. That contract we had? The one you bid on with all the other local companies. Well, that's done. If it's equipment or a firearm, we have to get it from another branch – and that's only when the original becomes completely unserviceable. Ammo? Well, our training round allotment has been comingled with our real world bullets. So it's either shoot paper targets or bad guys, but not both. If guys want to stay current, beyond their yearly qualifications, it's on their own dime."

"We can work out a deal for that," Marcus interjected.

"I know you can, Marcus, and you have been great for us in the past. This goes much higher than my level. Much, much higher."

"Democrats," Marcus grumbled.

Spectre tried his best not to laugh, but sometimes Marcus could be hilarious, even when he wasn't trying to be.

"Whatever the case may be, it's above my pay grade," Browning responded, attempting to veer the discussion away from the impending political train wreck.

"Is it really that bad?" Spectre asked.

"This doesn't leave the room, got it?" Browning asked, waiting for a nod from both men across from him.

"The answer to your question is yes. Just last week, we were tracking this guy, Abdul Aalee," he responded, pointing to a picture on the wall of an Arab man with dark hair, deep set brown eyes, and a full black beard. "Heard of him?"

"Sounds familiar." Spectre pondered the name. "Iraq?"

"He calls himself Abdul Aalee, or servant of the Most High. A couple of three-letter agencies were tracking him for several months in Iraq earlier this year. He was suspected of orchestrating the suicide bombs attack in Ramadi that killed nearly two hundred people. With the new Status of Forces Agreement, they could never get a warrant to go in and get him. Last month, he completely fell off the grid. No one had any idea what happened to him. Some even thought he was killed."

Spectre leaned forward in his chair. Aalee was the kind of asshole he had twice been to Iraq to stop. He had seen the name in intel briefs before his flights. The man had a history of ruthless violence against those sympathetic to the West. He had been behind a few Improvised Explosive Device (IED) attacks and had sent countless suicide bombers to their death in the name of Allah.

"Our informants told us the new player in town was there to take over the Brothers of Freedom, a group the FBI had been watching based in Hialeah," Browning continued. "So they handed his case file off to us and told us to keep an eye out for him. We've got some cool toys to find people with, so we did. We tracked him. Cell phones are a funny thing, these days, even sat phones. We found him in a regatta peeling off to Marathon Key."

"So you got him?" Spectre asked anxiously.

"Ha," Browning replied. "Not quite. The air asset tracking the boat had to go home for fuel, so we put a high priority request in for additional assets due to the target. It was denied! 'Use what you have,' they said.

"We even got lucky. Some boaters were spooked by an obviously foreign man on their not so foreign dock, so they called the cops. Cops show up, can't do anything, so they call us again. Since the cops can't detain him, we are left holding the bill. No air assets available. No tracking. Now he's here. Guess who takes the blame?"

"So you're telling me there's a terrorist asshole on US soil right now, and you guys don't know where he is?" Spectre asked incredulously.

"There's always a terrorist asshole on US soil, Cal. The problem is we're stretched too thin. That safety net we set up after 9/11 is becoming more and more porous. We'll catch this guy, I'm sure of it, but you see my point? We're only winning because the bad guys are dumber than we are lucky. I just hope our luck doesn't run out."

"Democrats!" Marcus replied.

Browning rolled his eyes and looked at his watch. "Anyway, we've got a Blackhawk going up in twenty minutes for a local area orientation for a new pilot. You guys want to tag along? When you said you were coming, I cleared it through Division. Cal, I think you might even know the pilot."

# CHAPTER SIX

A s they walked out to the Customs ramp, the large rotors of the Blackhawk helicopter were already turning. Even with earplugs, the sounds of the turbine engine and rotors beating the air into submission were deafening. An Aviation Enforcement Officer stood waiting outside the black and gold unmarked helicopter with two pairs of David Clark aviation headsets. He handed them to Marcus and Spectre as they climbed aboard.

"Spectre, is that you?" a raspy voice said over the intercom. As Spectre took his seat, he saw the pilot in the right seat turn to face him. Despite the Nomex helmet and visor, he could still see that it was one of his former squadron mates from the 39th.

"How the hell are ya, Elvis?" replied Spectre, reaching out to shake his hand.

Tim "Elvis" Breuer had been one of the lucky new hires of CBP in the last three years. He was among the last in the pool of applicants that did not possess both fixed wing and helicopter ratings. He had been hired and immediately sent off to school to get his helicopter add on, and then to learn the Blackhawk helicopter. Throughout his training and new career, he still maintained his currency as a Reservist F-16 pilot with the Gators a few times per month. He was living Spectre's dream.

"Flying fighters and this bad boy, I can't complain," Breuer tapped on the center console.

Spectre was genuinely happy for the guy. It was good to see nice guys like Elvis doing so well.

Elvis put the Blackhawk into a hover just a few feet off the ground and did a pedal turn to orient them with the taxiway. They had been cleared to hover taxi down Taxiway Alpha, but to hold short of the runway for an eastbound VFR departure.

As they proceeded down the taxiway, Spectre looked out the left side to see the twenty-five F-16s sitting on the ramp. Except for the newly installed conformal fuel tanks on the spine, they looked exactly the same as the last time he had flown them. But he knew that the similarities stopped there. These jets were completely different internally from the ones he'd flown.

With the F-35 slipping further and further to the right and getting more and more expensive, the Air Force was finding itself losing in the technological war with China, a country whose ingenuity was only surpassed by its espionage capabilities. So when the newly appointed Chief of Staff of the Air Force testified before Congress that the Air Force would be unable to guarantee total air dominance in a potential proxy war with China over North Korea or Taiwan, the men holding the purse strings took notice.

The Chief of Staff argued that it could be done under the cost of a squadron of the $200 million apiece F-35s. His solution? A new breed of F-16 called Titanium Vipers.

The F-16 Block 60 production line in Fort Worth, Texas was still very active producing the latest Block 60 "Desert Viper" for export to the United Arab Emirates. Due to military export control laws and the funding dumped into the project, the US Military couldn't just start buying Desert Vipers off the line. That would have been too easy, despite the fact that the Active Electronically Scanned Array radar, advanced electronic warfare and electronic countermeasures suites, and weapons systems were more advanced than any F-16 in the US inventory. In order to buy the new F-16s rolling off the showroom floor, they had to be renamed. So the Block 70 "Titanium Viper" was born.

But the Chief of Staff didn't stop there. Within his budget, he was only allowed to add two squadrons of new iron. So instead of sending the older jets to the bone yard, he ordered that the rest of the remaining F-16s, including Guard and Reserve, be upgraded to Block 70 capabilities under the Semper Viper program.

The mechanically scanned array and slower-than-a 1986 Apple II-Processor APG-68 radar had been replaced with the newer AESA. The old hardwire data buses had been replaced with state of the art Ethernet and high capacity solid-state hard drives. All of the gauges were replaced with digital displays, and the two color MFDs had been swapped in favor of high definition LED displays. And that's just what Spectre had seen in the technology demonstrator simulator he had been given the chance to sit in before he left the Air Force. He was sure there were more cool toys in that jet now than even he could imagine. It would've been awesome to be stepping to that jet to fly right now.

But as they passed the flight line bustling with crew chiefs and maintainers preparing the jets for the next event, Spectre knew that those days were behind him. Maybe it had changed him, but for now, he had a lot more on his mind. He was riding in a Blackhawk, which was cool and all, but it didn't answer the lingering questions about Chloe, or give him solace that his position at the store wouldn't eventually be eliminated.

He tried to shake it off. Enjoy the ride, he told himself. At least you're not staring at the "Guns-a-palooza" ads on the website right now.

After holding short of the runway waiting for an orange and white Coast Guard HC-144 "Ocean Sentry" to complete its touch and go, they were cleared to depart to the east.

They flew low to the southeast past the Nuclear Power Plant over Homestead Bayfront Park and into Biscayne Bay. There were many boaters out on the crystal clear, blue waters of the Atlantic taking advantage of the calm waters and beautiful sunny day. Heading south along the bay, they passed the Ocean Reef Club, an exclusive resort for the richest of the rich equipped with its own private airport for jet-setting guests and residents.

As they flew south along the Florida Keys, their backup radio came to life with a call from the CBP Operations Desk. A Coast Guard Law Enforcement Boat was attempting to intercept a "Go Fast" boat with suspected drug smugglers and requested air support.

"You guys up for it?" Elvis asked over the intercom. "It could get dangerous."

"Yes, we promise not to sue," Marcus responded, eager to see some action.

"Only if you let me shoot the SCAR," Spectre joked. He was referring to the FNH SCAR-H Rifle chambered in 7.62 x 51mm the AEO was carrying. It was the Mk 20 Sniper Support Rifle version based on the Mk 17 rifle. It included a longer receiver, a beefed up barrel extension and barrel profile to reduce whip and improve accuracy and an enhanced modular trigger configurable for single-stage or two-stage operation together with a non-folding precision stock.

"This baby's mine," the AEO replied. He was specifically trained in airborne sniper interdiction missions, from either a sling harness while sitting on the skid of an AStar helicopter, or through the side door of any Blackhawk.

"Hold on fellas," Elvis said, maneuvering the Blackhawk into a tightly banked turn. From Spectre's vantage point, it looked like the rotor blades were only a few feet away from hitting the water and ruining their day, but Spectre trusted Elvis. He'd flown with him in combat, and he knew Elvis only pushed aircraft within his own limits.

The Blackhawk sped along only fifty feet above the water at nearly 140 miles per hour. Spectre had flown low levels at nearly 600 miles per hour in the F-16, but never lower than 500 feet, and never with this kind of a sensation of speed. It was eye opening. *It was just fun.*

As they neared the intercept location, the Fast Boat was easily recognizable, being trailed a few hundred feet by a 33 foot Coast Guard Law Enforcement Special Purpose Craft struggling to keep up. The Fast Boat was small and light, with two high horsepower outboard motors. It was specifically designed to outrun the authorities or other smugglers.

Elvis put the aircraft in another high-banked turn to parallel the Fast Boat's path. He used the turn to bleed off the excess airspeed down to 60 miles per hour, easily pacing the boat.

"Slow him down," Elvis said to the AEO in the back. The AEO readied himself out the right door as they pulled up alongside the Fast Boat. Using his Leupold sight, he set up for the shot.

Despite the David Clarks and the steady thump of the rotors, the shot was easily heard by Spectre. He couldn't see where it had hit, but he could see the boat start to slow as the Coast Guard SPC-LE gained distance. The men on board the Fast Boat were starting to panic and began throwing bags overboard.

Elvis used the opportunity to gain altitude and slow to match the boat's new pace. He wanted to give his AEO a better angle for the second engine. The AEO again readied himself. Just as the first, the second shot was true and the boat slowed to a coast.

The SPC-LE initially passed the boat and circled around. Elvis brought the helicopter to a hover while the AEO in the back kept a watchful eye on the boat's occupants, ready to take out the two smugglers in the event they turned hostile. Once back alongside the disabled boat, the men in the SPC-LE boarded and arrested the two men at gunpoint.

"Not bad," Spectre said over the intercom.

"Believe me, this is the most action we've seen this year. You're just lucky," Elvis admitted.

"Yeah...*Lucky*," Spectre replied sarcastically. If he were lucky, he certainly didn't feel like it.

# CHAPTER SEVEN

*Winter Haven, FL*

The three-acre plot of land was small by their neighborhood's standards. In this part of Florida, though, it wasn't much of a neighborhood. The large ranch homes were all separated by no less than a quarter of a mile, visible to each other barely during the day, and only by their lone streetlights at night. Neighbors rarely saw each other except at the occasional social gathering.

For Maureen Ridley, it was the perfect place to retire and enjoy life. She had spent her entire life moving from major city to major city in pursuit of her very successful career as a corporate litigator. She had raised her children with almost nonexistent yards in the tightest of neighborhoods. She had always looked forward to the day she could stretch out and enjoy the secluded life.

The four-bedroom ranch home on ten acres was exactly what she had been looking for. It had plenty of room for their two horses to roam free from their custom stables. The single-story home had been built twenty years previous with solid construction – the kind strong enough to withstand several major hurricanes, something even the so-called "hurricane proof" houses that had been built in the recent years couldn't boast. The backyard featured a large dual level below ground swimming pool equipped with a stone waterfall feature from one level to the next. As the years clicked by, the pool became less about the beauty it added to the property and more about the therapeutic value it held.

At age 65, Ridley had achieved a fruitful life as both a public servant and devout mother of two. She had retired as a three term Representative of Florida in the US House of Representatives, championing education and healthcare reforms. In her mind, her biggest accomplishment in life, however, had nothing to do with her career, but in balancing that while raising two children, one of whom had cerebral palsy.

Evan Rivers was thrust into the world with the deck stacked against him. To the doctors, it was a miracle he had even survived birth, much less to the age of 18. Born premature and with the umbilical cord wrapped around his neck, Evan was deprived of oxygen long enough to cause permanent brain damage. Like every parent of a special needs child, it was always Jack and Maureen's hope and prayer that Evan would one day develop and grow to lead a functional and normal life, but after therapy and treatment after treatment, it became clear that Evan would never develop more than a fourteen month old in a man's body. While he was ambulatory, he could only make cooing noises like a baby or cry in pain. He could not feed himself or use the restroom on his own. He would forever require twenty-four hour care.

Maureen walked into the living room of the spacious ranch home from the kitchen. The shiny marble tiled floors reflected the light of the 60 inch plasma TV that Jack was especially proud of. It had been his homework to design an entertainment room for their dream retirement home, and with the combination of the oversized high definition TV, seven speaker Dolby Digital Surround Sound system, and Blu Ray disc library, he was pretty sure he had nailed it.

There were two large leather chairs in the center of the room, with an ottoman on one side and a leather couch on the other. Jack was planted in the near chair with remote in hand in his Bermuda shorts, t-shirt, and socks, while Evan sat quietly playing with his Tickle Me Elmo in the other. They were watching Wheel of Fortune – Evan's favorite TV show. The spinning wheels and colors kept his undivided attention.

"Dianne, can I get you anything?" Maureen asked. Dianne Jennings sat on the couch. She was Evan's evening caretaker. She shared the duties with two other women who alternated days, nights, and weekends among themselves.

"No, ma'am, I'm fine, thank you." She smiled shyly.

Maureen walked in and sat on the ottoman, joining the family in their evening ritual. It was part of the routine they'd grown into in their quiet life. They would spend their evenings doing yard work or hanging out by the pool, then settle in with Wheel of Fortune before getting ready for bed. After years of twelve and fourteen hour days at work for both Jack, who was a retired futures trader, and Maureen, it was a welcome paradigm shift.

Their peaceful evening was interrupted by the growling of their two-year-old miniature dachshund named Scooby. Scooby's growl turned into a bark as a loud thump was heard outside. Jack's attention suddenly snapped from the TV to the door behind him.

"Did you hear that?" he asked as he put the remote down and slowly rolled out of the chair. At the age of 70, he was in excellent physical condition and health, but his arthritis often made it difficult to get moving again after sitting for long periods.

"It was probably just the neighbor's cats knocking over the trash can," Maureen replied casually.

"I'll go check it out," he said as he slipped his sandals on over his socks and grabbed a flashlight out of the closet.

As he walked outside, it wasn't quite completely dark. The sun had just set, leaving an orange afterglow over the horizon. He walked around the side of the house, finding an overturned trash can just as Maureen had predicted. He cursed the cats and picked up the overturned trashcan, replacing the full garbage bags that had fallen out.

He walked out to the edge of their long driveway. All was still quiet. Just as he was about to end his investigation, he noticed a dark colored minivan parked on the gravel road tangent to their property line. It was unusual to see anyone on that road, especially this late in the evening. He decided to walk over and investigate before going back inside.

Jack used his flashlight to look into the windows of the minivan. Except for a few McDonald's bags and fountain drinks, the van was empty. There was no one in it or anywhere around it. He originally thought it may have been just a couple of high school kids looking for a place to get some privacy, but now he wasn't sure what to think. The local sheriff could probably help out.

He caught something moving in the corner of his eye just as he started the walk back to the house. It was immediately followed with a brief but intense pain, and then everything went dark.

\* \* \*

As much as Spectre hated mandatory fun nights with the Gators, he hated the idea of losing Chloe even more. So when Chloe asked him to accompany her as her guest at the squadron boat party, he reluctantly agreed.

Over the past two weeks, Spectre had done everything he could to rebuild the burned bridges of their relationship. He had spent hours talking and listening, trying to rekindle the spark they once had. Chloe had agreed to try to work things out, but she refused to guarantee anything.

In fact, to Spectre it seemed like she had been the one that changed. She had gone from being physically affectionate to cold and withdrawn. Her greeting in the mornings and in the evenings when he came home felt cold and unemotional.

But as much as the warning signs were there that it was completely unrecoverable, Spectre pressed on. He even sat through couples counseling sessions in which she confessed that she wasn't even sure she wanted to give it another try.

This night was just another attempt to right the sinking ship. He knew she hadn't yet told the squadron about their break up for fear of the "I told you so" mafia bearing down on her. It wasn't really a genuine attempt to make things right, but deep down Spectre thought maybe a night out with him could relight the spark.

So they spent the evening on the water with the Gators, laughing and joking as if nothing had ever happened. They were a team again, sharing with each other in the ridiculousness of the Gators. Spectre was pleasantly surprised.

With the boat finally back in its slip, Spectre was ready to take Chloe and go home. A night spent hanging out with the Gators could be fun, but tiring. It was hard to stay patient with people that completely lost control when drunk.

As the two walked down the dock to the parking lot where they'd deposited their car, Spectre saw one of the Gators standing on the pier looking out into the water. He had seen the man previously walking with another, much larger Gator whose callsign was Ox. The same intoxicated Ox who had fallen over into a trash can much earlier in the night. *It couldn't be good.*

Spectre was about to ask what was going on as he approached the scene, until he looked down into the slip and saw what had happened. There he saw Ox holding on for dear life to a mooring attached to the boat in the slip. He had somehow stumbled and fallen in and was now dazed and completely clueless on how to get out. All he could do was yell in a slurred speech. "Arrrgh, I'm all right."

Spectre sighed. "I need to get him out of there before he drowns himself."

"Be careful. I'll go see if I can find more help," Chloe responded.

"I'll be fine." Spectre began disrobing. No one else was sober enough, or competent enough in his mind, to save the large man. He handed Chloe his shirt, wallet, and cell phone and began to assess the situation. *Good thing he had opted to wear a swimsuit.*

The man on the dock protested at first, trying to talk Ox to safety. The large man yelled incoherently and tried to drag himself to the front of the boat using the rope. It was all to no avail, as there was no exit. The only option he had was to swim under the dock and to the boat in the next slip. There he could either climb the ladder back onto the dock, or use the back deck of the adjacent boat to climb out of the water. He currently possessed neither the wherewithal nor motor skills to perform such a task.

Spectre jumped in the water. Ox thrashed and kicked, having no idea what was happening. Spectre tried to calm him and wrapped his right arm around the large man's chest. He convinced the man to let go of the mooring and began swimming. Spectre was relieved that they were in salt water and despite his mass, the man was mostly fat. The buoyancy helped.

Grabbing onto the ropes and crossbeams of the dock as he swam along, Spectre guided them the requisite twenty feet to the ladder. Once there, he faced his second challenge – getting the large man up the ladder. He sized up the situation, realizing that the bottom rung was only at chest level for him. It would have been easy for a sober man, but nearly impossible to get the overweight drunk up without assistance. Or a large crane.

He coached the large man into grabbing the ladder. Once on, Spectre pulled himself up and positioned his right thigh to create a makeshift step. In his condition, the man had very little upper body strength, but Spectre was sure he could at least push up with his legs.

He was right, and the man slowly began climbing as more people began to show up to help from the dock. Spectre heard another splash as another drunken Gator jumped in to help. *Great.* This guy was nearly falling off the boat on the ride back, and now he too was trying to save the large Gator. *Excellent.* The newcomer hero tried to take over the situation, attempting to push Spectre out of the way and force the large Gator up the ladder himself. Since the large Gator was almost up the ladder, Spectre swam back a bit to get out of the way, until he heard a thump and yet another splash.

Another Gator had made his way into the water. This time, it was another Good Samaritan Gator who had been helping above but had lost his balance in his drunken state. He had fallen backward off the dock and into the water while hitting his head on the boat behind him. Spectre's eyes grew big as he heard the splash and saw nothing emerge from the water. He raced to the Gator's last known position, finding only an arm of the flailing man and pulling it to the surface.

The man's head finally reached the surface as he gasped for air. "I'm ok!" he said with a laugh. "I just fell in." Spectre helped the man reach the ladder with less assistance than the first. This guy was in much better shape and a little more coherent. By the time all the victims had made it up the ladder, the newcomer hero still remained. He was convinced that Spectre had also fallen in, and was not going to go anywhere until Spectre went first. Spectre refused and insisted that the newcomer hero go first. He finally agreed and stumbled his way up the ladder, where everyone thanked him for saving the two distressed Gators. Spectre followed the man up the ladder with everyone now safely out of the water.

Upon seeing that Spectre was ok, Chloe rushed over to him with a towel. "I'm so glad you're ok, when I couldn't see or hear you, I thought they had dragged you under or something," she said as she gave him a hug. He kissed her on the cheek and accepted the towel.

"I told you not to worry about me," he winked.

As the Gators congratulated the newcomer hero for his bravery, one of the senior Gators approached Spectre laughing. "Did you fall in too?"

Spectre planted his forehead firmly in the palm of his right hand. "I can't win with these idiots," he mumbled.

After driving a few of the Gators home, Chloe and Spectre finally made it back home.

"I had a great time tonight, even though it was with the Gators, thanks for inviting me," Spectre said as he started to head toward the master bedroom.

She stopped him before he could turn around and kissed him. It was the first time he had any physical contact with her since the breakup, and it was as if a spark had been sent up his spine. His heart was now racing.

"The night's still young," she said seductively, kissing his neck.

"You're drunk," he said stopping her. As badly as he wanted her, he didn't want it to be like that. Not after all they'd been through in the previous weeks and her drunk. She'd reached the drunken stage of horniness she called "Stage 2." It had been good for him so many times before.

"So?"

"So," he said pushing her away, "I want you so bad right now, but this is not right. Not with everything we've been through."

"Ugh. Fine. Good night." She was pissed, but he knew she wouldn't last much longer. She had maybe two or three minutes left before she would pass out on her bed. He wanted to take advantage of the situation so badly, but he really loved her, and he wanted it to be right. He didn't want her to only want him when she was drunk. *He wanted the old spark back.*

At least that's what he told himself as he banged his head against the door after she'd stumbled back to her bedroom.

# CHAPTER EIGHT

*Warning Area 465*
*100 miles Southeast of Homestead, FL*
*2058 Local*

"**S**wamp Three-One, check," the female voice crisply said over the radio.

"Two," he responded sharply. Lt Col Jeff "Pistol" Pitre had been flying the F-16 for fifteen years. He had seen it evolve from a day, clear weather fighter to a day or night all weather fighter with some of the most amazing technology. A seasoned flight lead, Pistol was an airline guy – a traditional Reservist. He did the requisite six flights per month in the F-16 only to turn around and fly the masses around in his company's Airbus A320. *Not a bad side job for an old guy*, he thought.

Pistol maneuvered his F-16 into a tactical formation behind his flight lead. Despite his thousands of hours, tonight he was flying off Eve's wing, the newest flight lead in the squadron. It was only her second time leading at night after her upgrade, and Pistol had been assigned to fly with her as her "seeing eye wingman." He would try to keep her out of trouble. For now, she would only be flying with more experienced pilots.

She had cleared him to fly wedge, a fluid position varying from a one to three miles and thirty to seventy degrees swept aft. Through the monochrome green Night Vision Goggles, he could easily see her covert strobe flashing at three miles as if they were right next to each other. Although NVGs didn't turn night into day, it was pretty damned close.

Despite the advantages NVGs gave, Pistol was still gun shy about flying with them. In the last five years, he had been one of three Gators to eject out of an aircraft, and his was perhaps the scariest.

He had been flying as a simulated aggressor - red air - just as they were tasked tonight. His job had been to simulate the enemy aircraft as a training aid for the other four-ship. They simulated enemy weapons, tactics, and maneuvers. But while executing those tactics over the Gulf of Mexico three years ago, he lost his orientation with the horizon. With no discernible references outside and a dimly lit cockpit, he couldn't tell which way was up or down. He entered a graveyard spiral, eventually realizing he was in an unrecoverable situation and ejecting just moments before the F-16 impacted the water. The whole night was a blur, but he was so thankful the seat had worked as advertised, and that his wingman was able to find him and direct the rescue helicopter to his position.

Beyond his goggles, the sky was completely dark. The moonrise wasn't anticipated for another three hours, and over the water, there was no cultural lighting whatsoever. Not that it would have mattered. There was a thick undercast deck of clouds at five thousand feet. Due to the weather and illumination, they were operating under strict training rules to prevent the loss of another aircraft.

In front of him, Pistol had two multifunction displays. On his left, he had his radar displayed, showing him where the blue four ship was, and on his right, he had his datalink with blue circles denoting where each member of the flight was. Since tonight he was only number two of a two ship, there was only one other circle shown just a few miles in front of the fixed aircraft that represented his ownship position.

His radio crackled to life. "Swamp Three-One, Gator Two-One, fights on, fights on." The voice was the gruff old voice of "Magic" Manny who was leading the blue air. They were over fifty miles apart, at separate predesignated points of the training airspace. The call signified that it was time to point at each other and begin the exercise.

"Swamp Three-One, copies fight's on," Eve replied coolly. As the wingman, Pistol had no speaking role. His job was to just be in position, shut up, and say "Two" when appropriate.

Over his secondary radio, Eve directed, "Swamp flight, Action." It was her command for them to execute the maneuver she had briefed beforehand. He was to turn forty-five degrees away from the blue four-ship for thirty seconds and then turn back toward them, while she would roll one hundred thirty-five degrees nearly inverted and pull, executing a sliceback. It was the maneuver that made him most nervous, since it was doing exactly that only a few years ago that tumbled his head so much that he could no longer control his aircraft. At the end of the flight brief, he warned her to just be careful. They couldn't afford to lose another jet or worse yet, a pilot.

Pistol executed his check away as he watched the datalink circle representing Eve's aircraft make the one hundred eighty degree heading change and descend. His focus turned to his radar as he attempted to lock up the blue players to simulate launching missiles at them.

After a few seconds of driving forward, the blue players called a kill at his bullseye position. Pistol acknowledge with a "Copy, kill," and turned back toward their starting point. It was then that he realized that he never heard Eve call her turn inbound.

As he rolled out south toward their starting point, he looked down at his datalink display. To his horror, only his ownship position was displayed.

"One, two, aux," he said, indicating he was talking on their auxiliary frequency.

There was nothing but silence.

"Swamp, Gator Two-One, Picture." It was the blue flight lead making the standard call to ask for the position of any hostile aircraft in the area.

There was still silence. It was the red flight lead's job to respond. Eve had dropped out of communication.

Pistols face became hot as he considered what might have happened. *Dear God no. Not again. Not to her.*

"One, two, aux." His voice was shaking. He was growing more nervous.

*Silence.* There was no reply. He hoped her radios had just failed or something simple. He scanned the horizon in his goggles looking for her flashing beacon. *There was nothing.* With the solid undercast deck, she would've been easily recognizable several miles out.

"Knock it off, knock it off," he screamed on the radio. *This was not good.*

"Gator Two-One, knock it off," the blue flight lead replied.

"Gator Two-Two knock it off."

"Gator Two-Three knock it off."

"Gator Two-Four knock it off."

"Swamp Three-One, Gator Two-One, say reason for knock it off," the blue fighter queried.

Pistol stopped for a second to compose himself. He was shaking. He didn't know what could've happened to her, but he suspected the worst, and he had to act on the worst.

"Gator Two-One, this is Swamp Three-Two, we've got a possible aircraft down. Last contact during maneuvering. Swamp Three-One is no longer on the link, and I am *negative* contact."

"Gator Two-One copies, we'll relay to Miami Center, confirm you're not hearing a beacon?"

His heart sank. She wouldn't just fly off without trying to rejoin and give him night flashlight signals if she simply lost her radios. If she ejected, her seat's emergency beacon would be transmitting on the UHF frequency 243.0, the universal emergency frequency.

He frantically switched his radio to 243.0. *Complete silence.*

"Gator, Swamp Four-Two, negative. There's no beacon."

# CHAPTER NINE

*Haditha, Iraq*
*2009*

The steady click of the exhale valve on his mask was almost hypnotic as Spectre stared listlessly out the canopy at the barren desert. He was only on the third hour of his four-hour airborne reconnaissance mission, and he had already depleted his supply of Rip-It energy drinks and Power Bars.

Equipped with a canoe shaped Theater Airborne Reconnaissance pod strapped to the underbelly of his F-16, it was amazing to Spectre how much things had changed since Vietnam. Gone were the days of the F-4 screaming over treetops avoiding flak and small arms fire while taking pictures at nearly 500 knots. In Iraq, it was all about the autopilot and flying point to point at medium altitude while the computer did all the work. *Bummer.*

That serenity was suddenly interrupted by the shrill sound of a female voice saying *"Warning! Warning!"* over his headset. Named for the authoritatively nagging, yet attractive, female voice of the onboard Voice Warning System, Bitching Betty was the result of an early human factors analysis. In it, scientists determined pilots were more likely to pick out female voices in stressful situations in a flurry of radio chatter. As time progressed and women took more of a role in aviation and air traffic control, this reasoning became less valid, but the name stuck.

With no loss of thrust noted, the audible warning forced his eyes to the "eyebrow lights" on the top of the dash. It was here that Spectre's heart sank. The HYD/OIL light glowed an ominous red. He was either dealing with a hydraulic failure of some sort or low oil pressure. In the middle of bad guy land with no suitable airfield within at least thirty miles, he prayed for the former.

His eyes shifted to the engine gauge cluster below the eyebrow lights. Starting with the oil pressure, his fears were confirmed. The gauge was fluctuating between 10 and 15 psi - well below normal operating limits. As he worked his way down, all other instruments seemed normal. His Front Turbine Inlet Temperature, RPM, and hydraulic pressures were all in the green. It was definitely an oil system problem.

While not a critical action procedure in which regulations dictated the steps had to be memorized, oil system malfunctions in the F-16 were one of those things pilots just had to know. There was no time to dig through the checklist and read all the notes, warnings, and cautions. It was expected that the pilot would know that the decision tree depended on the current oil pressure – above 10 psi and you were using everything the motor could give you to make it to the nearest field; below and you were minimizing throttle movement hoping the current power setting would be enough to get you home without seizing the engine.

In as much as a person with engine trouble over a country with people determined to cut your throat could be lucky, Spectre was lucky that his oil pressure was sitting just above 10 psi. His training immediately kicked in. All of the emergency procedure simulators and quizzes he had undergone through training would be put to the test.

As Spectre selected afterburner and started climbing, he hit the LIST button and pressed seven on his Upfront Control Panel. This gave him the nearest suitable airport within a 50 mile radius on his display. He was east of Haditha, 40 miles from Joint Base Balad. The math on the F-16 was easy: technically, it was capable of 7 miles for every 5,000 feet of altitude, but the pilot math was a 1:1. At 40 miles, he needed 40,000 feet of altitude to safely glide to land with room for error.

Spectre turned east and continued climbing through 20,000 feet. At 40,000 feet, if the engine were to quit, he wouldn't have enough hydrazine to power the Emergency Power Unit through the descent. Without the EPU, there would be no power to the completely electric fly-by-wire flight control system. He needed a little tailwind and a lot of luck.

Dubbed the "OG's doorbell," the Stores Jettison button was aptly named because the doorbell-like button would immediately result in a visit from the Operations Group Commander once on the ground. Without hesitation, Spectre used his left index finger to press the button labeled EMERGENCY JETTISON and held it. The wing rock and subtle thunk from the jet indicated that the two 370 gallon external fuel tanks and two 500 pound bombs had been jettisoned from the aircraft. Once gone, Spectre released the button and hit the MARK button on his Upfront Control Panel.

If he made it home, the bosses would want to know where he'd dropped his stores.

With his wings completely clean except for the lone air-to-air missiles on his wingtips, the rate of climb increased slightly as Spectre desperately tried to make it home. The canoe on his centerline, however, was still firmly attached, having not been carted by charges to separate it from the jet. His jet was as slick as it was going to get.

"Thunder Three-Two, Three-One on Aux," Spectre said keying his auxiliary radio. He had cleared his wingman off for his own separate reconnaissance tasking after the last tanker. The datalink now showed they were 90 miles apart. There was nothing he could do to support except start heading toward him in case he had to jump out.

"Go ahead for Two," his wingman replied. It was First Lieutenant Danny Stewart, a brand new wingman fresh out of the upgrade program.

"I've got a HYD/OIL light, I just punched off my stores and I'm RTB, you're cleared to rejoin if you can," he said. There was no panic or rise in his voice. Despite the prospect of being minutes from swinging in the chute, his radio transmissions portrayed ice-cold professionalism.

"Confirm you've run the checklist?"

"Affirm," Spectre pulled the checklist out of his helmet bag. He would look at it if he had a moment, but right now, he knew he had run everything.

As Spectre climbed through 25,000 feet, the situation went from bad to worse. The swinging oil pressure gauge caught his eye as it fluctuated between zero and ten. He knew the normally reliable GE engine only had minutes left in its life.

"Looks like the oil pressure's about to dump, can you mark my location?" He was instructing his wingman to use the datalink and moving map to get a geographical fix on his position.

"I think so," the wingman replied. There was doubt in his voice.

With the oil pressure now below 10 psi, Spectre instinctively moved through the next step on the checklist. He found the EPU switch beneath the throttle, flipped up the red guard, and pushed it forward. The green EPU ON indicator light illuminated as the EPU whirred to life. The light showed AIR, indicating the EPU was running off engine bleed air. As long as the engine stayed running, the EPU wouldn't deplete his limited supply of hydrazine.

Spectre switched his primary radio to the Supervisor of Flying frequency at Balad. He explained that he had jettisoned his stores and was currently flying with an activated EPU, allowing the fire and rescue crews to prepare for the toxic ammonia-like exhaust gases they would be experiencing if he made it home.

Just as he was about to discuss his plan of action, the GE finally let go. It started with a vibration so violent it shook his HUD and ended with a thump. The engine had finally seized due to oil starvation.

Spectre checked his altitude. He had just hit 30,000 feet, but he was still 35 miles from his base. It was going to be close. Having built up speed from being in afterburner, Spectre traded his excess speed for altitude, reaching his desired airspeed at 33,000 feet and 32 miles. Even with better than a one to one glide ratio, it was still going to be close. That canoe on the centerline added a considerable amount of drag.

Spectre's MFD showed his wingman still 40 miles out. He was gaining ground, but not fast enough.

"I'm engine out now, save your gas." It was nothing more than a heads up for his wingman. There was nothing Stewart could do for him right now except be there and orbit for support if Spectre did have to eject.

"2"

Spectre's F-16 was gliding over the desert. The good news was that it was daylight; at least he wasn't trying to find a blacked out Balad on NVGs. The bad news was also that it was daylight. If he ended up short, every bad guy with an AK would see his jet crash and his parachute. His decision to carry extra 9MM magazines for his Beretta M9 wasn't looking so excessive anymore.

As Spectre got closer, he could barely make out the field behind the steer point diamond in his HUD. He could make out cultural features, but couldn't quite make out the runway.

The SOF called him on his primary radio. Not to pile on to the already bad day, but the visibility was down to ¼ mile due to a sandstorm. All fighters were being diverted or sent to the tanker to wait it out. The recommendation was to press on and then eject in the bailout area so Special Operations Forces could pick him up.

Spectre was now sweating behind his visor. He'd have to make a decision soon. If he continued on, he'd be over the populated area of Balad. At that point, there was no turning back. He had to make the runway. If he decided to bail out, he would have to turn north. There would be no chance to make the runway if the weather changed, and although the Special Ops guys would be on their way, there were still several factions of potentially hostile groups in the area.

He dialed in the ILS on his HUD and HSI. He was perfectly lined up with Runway 12 just 15 miles out. He still couldn't make out the runway due to the dust storm, but he knew the steer point diamond sat exactly on the end of the runway from his checks on takeoff.

The wind on the ground appeared to be gusting. The dust storm was only a hundred or so feet in height, but enough to cover the runway. The gusts made the runway barely visible. Spectre decided to go for it. If it looked bad, he'd dump the jet in the open area to the north of the runway, away from any people or structures.

Relying completely on his instruments, Spectre continued gliding toward the runway. The former Soviet base had two intersecting runways, nearly two nautical miles each in length. If he could stay on runway centerline and get to the diamond, he'd have plenty of room to stop. If that didn't work, he could drop the hook and take the departure end cables.

At seven miles, Spectre was still doing 240 knots, carrying extra speed to compensate for the drag of the TARS pod. He waited until the diamond was between the 10 and 15-degree pitch ladders at the bottom of his HUD at four miles and lowered the gear handle. With no hydraulic pressure, the gear did not lower, but the action allowed the flaps to lower under EPU power. After putting the gear handle down, Spectre grabbed the alternate gear extension handle and pulled, using pneumatic pressure to lower the gear.

The two main gear lights turned green, but the nose gear remained unsafe. The nose gear wouldn't be able to extend until he slowed below 190kts. Spectre needed the airspeed. He'd worry about the nose gear later.

With the gear lowered, Spectre shifted his aim point short of the diamond. Normally, he would have put the flight path marker a few thousand feet short, into the overrun, but Spectre was flying blind. He had to guess based on the diamond. The runway was still obscured. Tower cleared him to land, advising that the fire crews were standing by.

Spectre used the radar altimeter to time his flare. If he waited too long, he would hit short of the runway at high speed. Too soon and he'd sink and stall into the runway. Neither would be very survivable for him or the aircraft. At 100 feet, he shifted his aim point to the diamond, letting his speed bleed down to 180 knots. The nose gear extended with a clunk.

As he descended to 50 feet, he shifted his aim point again. He put the flight path marker just below the horizon, indicating that he was just barely descending. He could now make out the runway lighting in his peripheral vision. At least he was somewhere on the runway.

Spectre winced as the radar altimeter leveled off at 10 feet. He tried to hold it off as long as he could, keeping the angle of attack indicator at 11 degrees while the aircraft slowed. With a thud and a slight bounce, the main gear touched down. He held the nose up in the aerobrake until reaching 100 knots, then lowered the nose and applied full brakes.

With no hydraulic power, Spectre relied on what was left in the hydraulic accumulators to power the brakes. Not knowing how much runway remained, he dropped the hook, but the aircraft rolled to a stop as Zeus started growling.

Spectre sat straight up in his bed as the knocking at the door became more apparent. He tried to shake off the dream he had been having. It haunted him night after night, just like the strafing incident. He convinced himself he wasn't in Iraq anymore. He was in Homestead, and someone was knocking at his door at 11 PM. Chloe had been night flying, maybe she forgot her key.

# CHAPTER TEN

*Homestead, FL*

When Spectre opened the door, he was overcome with extremely conflicted emotions. On one hand, he wanted to punch the man standing on his doorstep, but on the other, he was absolutely horrified by the potential reason the man was even standing there.

Colonel Ross "Coach" Louhan was the Operations Group Commander for the 39th Operations Group. Although Coach had taken command of the 39th well after Spectre separated from the Air Force, Spectre detested the man with all of his being.

The wretched, vile little man had been the Air Expeditionary Group Commander during Spectre's last deployment. While only an Active Duty Lieutenant Colonel at the time, the evil little troll with salt and pepper hair and crooked nose had been in charge of both the active duty and reserve squadrons deployed to Joint Base Balad during Spectre's deployment.

It had been Coach that had met Spectre at the jet after his engine out experience. It had been Coach that grounded him for a week for not ejecting instead of trying to land in the dust storm. It had been Coach that had grounded him for strafing without his flight lead and without a qualified JTAC. And worst of all, it had been Coach that sent the scathing, slanderous email to the head of Air Force Reserve Command filled with outright lies about Spectre's lack of airmanship, flight discipline, and regard for the rules.

That e-mail had cost him his flying career. The three star general, wanting to save a delicate Active Duty and Reserve Coalition, responded with a simple, "He won't be flying my airplanes anymore. Thank you for bringing it to my attention." And with that, Spectre was pulled from the cockpit and sent back to the states. No formal hearing. No chance to plead his case. No looking at the facts of the last flight of his career. He had been administratively reassigned to a non-flying staff job and given a formal letter of reprimand.

With the steady drizzle outside, Spectre seriously considered pushing him into the nearest puddle and slamming the door. The pure sight of him made his jaw and fists clench in unison. But Spectre knew there was a reason Coach and the chaplain were standing on his doorstep so late at night, and it wasn't good.

With a forced smile, Coach asked to come in. Spectre ushered them in and sent the growling Zeus to his bed.

"Cal, this is Chaplain Moise," Coach said as they sat. The two were dressed in their pressed Air Force service blues. *This was definitely not a social visit.*

Before Spectre could ask what was going on, Coach began explaining. "Cal..." he began. It was an obvious jab in Spectre's mind, refusing to address him by his callsign. Coach always considered himself above everyone, but those not flying were especially beneath him.

"As you probably know, you're Captain Moss's emergency contact as her next of kin," he continued. Chloe apparently had never updated her Record of Emergency Data after the breakup, or she still believed, as he did, that there was hope for their relationship.

Spectre's eyes began to water. He knew what was coming, and Coach was dragging this out.

"What happened?" Spectre interrupted impatiently. He knew the routine. *Get to the point already.*

"As you may know, the Gators have been night flying this week. During maneuvers tonight, we lost contact with Captain Moss. Search and rescue efforts are underway, and right now she's listed as missing, but we have not heard anything from her."

Spectre looked away. He didn't want to show weakness in front of the man he hated so much, but the news was crushing. Coach was giving him the press release version, but he could read between the lines. No contact usually meant no ejection attempt. He had seen it far too many times before, but this time, it had happened to the woman he loved - or used to love. *It all seemed so trivial now.*

"Cal, we're doing everything we can to find her, but the weather has hampered our search, and there's a lot of water to cover."

"Was there a beacon?" Spectre was referring to the emergency beacon in the F-16's ejection seat. When set to AUTO, it would automatically begin broadcasting on UHF frequencies, allowing search and rescue teams to locate the survivor in the event of incapacitation.

"There will be a Safety Investigation Board convened—"

Spectre immediately cut him off. "Don't give me that horse shit, Coach. The least you can do is tell me what you know. You owe me that."

"Fine," Coach yielded. "Captain Moss was leading a red air sortie tonight. During a preplanned maneuver, she was to execute a 135-degree turn with a rapid descent to a lower altitude block. Pistol lost contact with her on the datalink sometime after that. He tried to find the wreckage, but with the undercast solid weather deck, he couldn't find anything. There was no chute, no flares, no calls on the primary or backup rescue freqs, and no beacon."

Spectre sat back in resignation. "It's almost the same thing that happened to Pistol."

"It's too early to tell. We're still looking for her, and we're hoping she managed to eject like Pistol did, but it's looking like a possible controlled flight into terrain scenario."

"What happens now?"

"We keep looking for her. If we can't find her in a couple of days, it will become a recovery effort."

Spectre had developed a thousand yard stare. He was in complete disbelief. Just a few weeks ago, the two had been planning the rest of their lives together. Everything was happening so fast. First the breakup, now she could possibly be gone forever. He was living a nightmare.

"Cal, I have to get back to squadron. Chaplain Moise can stay here with you and talk to you as long as you need."

Spectre said nothing. He didn't think any amount of talking would do anything. He felt helpless, and wanted to be in the air, circling the waters of the Atlantic looking for Chloe as part of the rescue effort.

Coach stopped himself as he started for the door. "Oh, almost forgot. She listed you as the person to notify her parents for something like this. She probably just never updated it since you left the Air Force, but technically, you're that person. I'd go myself, but it's a pretty far drive north, and I really have to get back to running the rescue operation. Can you do it? I'll send the chaplain with you if you like."

"Of course I'll do it," Spectre barked. The smug bastard just didn't get it. Everything about him felt fake and forced, and even in a time like this, he just couldn't manage a genuine gesture.

"Great. I'll have someone at the Ops Desk call you if anything changes."

Coach got up and walked out, leaving the chaplain behind without waiting for a response. Spectre watched through the nearby window as he got in his car and sped away. The car sounded awful – way too loud for such a little car. He would have expected a colonel to be driving something much nicer.

"Let me get changed, do you want to go with me or do you want me to take you back to base?" Spectre asked, trying to refocus. Coach always seemed to bring out the worst in him.

"Whatever you need me to do. I'll gladly ride with you and help you talk to her family," the chaplain responded.

Spectre appreciated the offer. Her family never really liked him, and breaking the news to her overbearing mother would probably be something better left for the chaplain anyway.

# CHAPTER ELEVEN

*Winter Haven, FL*

T he pain started as a dull throb and accelerated to a sharp pain as Jack Rivers regained consciousness. His brain seemed to be starting its own reboot cycle, as more and more nerve centers seemed to come online and send signals of sharp pain to his brain. He tried to open his eyes, only to realize his left eye was swollen shut. He had no idea where he was, only that his last memory was walking back inside from that van. At least, he thought it was a memory. *It could've just been a dream.*

But the pain Jack was feeling was no dream. He strained to see anything with his right eye, but wherever he had ended up was completely dark, or he had also lost vision in his right eye. As more of his senses came online, he heard what sounded like a soft whimper somewhere near him. It almost sounded like muffled crying. He started to pick up his hands to his face, only to realize that he couldn't move them. His hands were bound to the chair he was sitting in. As he struggled against his restraints, he realized that he'd found another source of pain. The rope used to tie him down was digging into his skin, causing even more pain as his brain cycled through the nerve centers of his wrists, face, and ribs. He found it hard to breathe.

His eye finally adjusted to the darkness. There was just enough light from under the door to his right to make out shadows in the room. There were two silhouettes lying on the floor in front of him. He could barely make out the up and down movement from the one closest to him. It was a female sobbing. He couldn't tell whether it was Maureen or the live in nurse, Dianne. The other silhouette lay motionless beyond the first. It was too dark to tell if whoever it was could still be breathing or was sleeping or unconscious.

He slowly looked around the room. The more he regained his senses, the more he realized his breathing was labored. He must've broken or at least bruised a few ribs at some point. He felt like he had been in a car accident or heavyweight fight. None of it was adding up. As the shadows started coming together, his location started to make sense. He was in the utility room near the north end of the house. He could make out the washer and dryer off to his side, and the coat rack in the corner. He was tied to a metal folding chair near the back corner of the room.

He tried to talk. His jaw was also incredibly stiff and sore. Whatever had hit him hadn't stopped at the initial strike.

"Maureen?" His voice was barely above a whisper. The muffled sobs increased and he saw the nearest silhouette roll over. *That answered nothing.*

"Maureen, is that you? Are you ok?" The sobs were replaced by a muffled "Oomph." She was gagged. There would be no conversation.

Jack was desperate for answers. *Who could've done this?* He had heard of a burglary a few miles up the road last month, but they just stole the valuable stuff and took off. *This wasn't a burglary,* he reasoned. They would've tried to come when they weren't around, and during the day like the other burglary. *Maybe it was the work of that new gang in town. A gang in Winter Haven, Florida of all places.* It made his blood boil. *If this were a bunch of spoiled gangbanger wannabe kids, they'd have hell to pay.*

The door opened. The hallway light was blinding until the shadow of the man entering hovered over him. A man entered, leaving the door open. The light was now enough to see that it was Maureen lying on the floor. He tried to look around Maureen at the other figure on the floor. *Evan!* His heart started racing. He could see Evan lying there on the floor, his arms tied behind him. He wasn't moving. His blood boiled even more. *Who would tie up a handicapped child? Who would even touch a special child like Evan?* Jack struggled against his restraints, only to exacerbate the pain in his chest and wrists.

"Who are you? What the fuck are you doing?" he demanded of the dark figure standing before him. He wasn't very tall. Even seated, Jack was almost at chest level with the man.

"Such language Mr. Rivers. You Americans are all alike. So demanding and vulgar, even in a position of disadvantage." His accent was thick, but his English was perfect. *A Middle Easterner? Nothing made sense.*

"What do you want from us? Let us go! Untie my wife and son!"

"Your son is weak. Allah has cursed you."

Jack's face grew flush. *He wanted to kill that son of a bitch.* He had never felt so angry and scared in all of his life.

"Fuck you!"

The man wound up and backhanded Rivers. The blow itself wasn't painful, but his jaw and head were now screaming in pain from earlier. He could barely think.

"You will not speak to me in that manner." The man had no emotion whatsoever in his voice. "Mr. Rivers, your predicament requires no action. You will sit there and cause no trouble for us until we are done with you. If you do this, we may let you and your family live. If you do not, I will kill your son first. It will be slow and painful, and you will watch. Your wife will follow, and then I will kill you. Your lives mean very little to me."

"Why are you doing this?" he said feebly. The image of his son at the hands of this madman was horrifying. His will to resist was instantly snatched from him.

"What we are doing and why is not of your concern. Concern yourself with your family's survival. That involves cooperation."

"Where is Dianne?"

"The fat one's services were no longer required, and that miserable little rodent you had as a pet as well."

He killed Dianne and Scooby. *What an animal! Poor Dianne.* She had just gotten engaged a month ago, and now she had been slain at the hands of a madman.

"You didn't have to kill them. Please don't hurt my family!" Jack pleaded.

"The fat one tried to alert the police. She was of no value to us. Now, as you Americans say, smile." He held up a camera in front of Jack. The flash was blinding. The man walked over to Maureen, who gave a muffled grunt. He slapped her and then, grabbing her by the hair, he picked her head up and snapped a picture of her face.

He then walked up to Evan, who was still unconscious and kicked him in the ribs. Evan moved slightly and groaned. As he woke, he gave a blood-curdling scream in pain. The man backhanded him and snapped a picture. Evan grunted with the blow and continued to cry. The man kicked him in the stomach, knocking the wind out of him and walked out of the room, closing the door behind him.

# CHAPTER TWELVE

*Winter Haven, FL*

It was nearly 4 AM by the time Spectre and the chaplain made the final turn, down the long country road to Chloe's parents' house. After Coach left his house, Spectre had made several attempts to call Chloe's mom and Jack using their individual cell phone numbers and their house phone. He even tried calling Dianne's cell phone. All attempts were met with voice mail, or in the case of Mrs. Ridley, a notification that her voice mailbox was full. He figured as much. Even in retirement, she was still being bombarded with phone calls.

The news media had done a good job of keeping the incident quiet, only making a brief statement that there had been an incident with an F-16 in the Atlantic during a routine training mission. Despite that, Spectre figured it was only a matter of time before the news became more widespread and reporters started showing up. After talking it over with the chaplain, Spectre had decided that since he was unable to reach the family, it would be best to notify them in person, before the media could get to them.

Nearly four and a half hours and two Red Bull energy drinks later, Spectre and the Chaplain were nearly there. Spectre had gone through what he might say in his mind over and over. Her mom had been "reserving judgment" about him since the moment he and Chloe first started dating, and he had his suspicions that she had played a key role in Chloe's sudden change of heart. He never quite understood why, other than perhaps her unrealistic standards mixed with his sudden fall from grace in the military, but her distaste for him was evident every time they interacted.

Jack, on the other hand, was a completely different story. Spectre and Jack seemed to get along just fine. They were both gun guys. Spectre respected the man living his life in the shadow of such a strong and outspoken woman. He had been by Maureen's side for over twenty years, and had suffered through several of her campaigns in the House of Representatives. Spectre was sure that came with its own challenges, being just far enough into the spotlight that he could never quite relax. And then there was the ridiculousness of the last name issue, something he had been dealing with as he prepared to marry Chloe.

Chloe Moss was born to David and Maureen Moss. When the two split, Maureen retook her maiden name of Ridley. With that, she established herself as an attorney and eventually a corporate litigator where she eventually met Jack Rivers. Having established herself as a professional, she kept her last name when the two were married a few years later. When Evan came around, the two decided that he should share Jack's last name. So it became that the family of four, Maureen, Jack, Evan, and Chloe had three separate last names.

Of course, this mattered very little to Spectre until the discussion of their wedding came up. Spectre had grown up in the South, and while mainstream chivalry and decorum might have been dead to most, to him it certainly was not. Chloe, at the behest of her mother, was intent on keeping her last name. In fact, she even wanted Spectre to consider taking hers, if he were so intent on them sharing a last name. It was a blow to his ego, especially with all that had been going on with his employment status, but before she had dropped the hammer on their relationship, he thought they had worked it out. She finally seemed agreeable to going along with the traditional route, despite her mother.

Spectre was still deep in thought over his past with Chloe as they made the final turn onto the winding two-lane road toward the house. He shook it off as the GPS alerted them that their destination was ahead on the left in half a mile.

As Spectre and the Chaplain reached the lone row of houses on the dark country road, Spectre pointed out the gravel road next to the house and told the chaplain to pull into the driveway past it. With the moonless night, the property was completely dark save for the fluorescent streetlight illuminating the driveway.

The chaplain pulled up in front of the garage and parked. A few lights were on inside the house, and Spectre was pretty sure he saw someone walking around.

"They're up early," the chaplain commented, pointing at the kitchen window.

"Yeah, I think Jack gets up around this time. Maybe he's just having his morning coffee," Spectre replied. Although there was no way Spectre could see himself waking up at 4 AM every morning in general, much less in retirement, he had to respect a man disciplined enough to stick to his routine, even with nowhere to go.

"How do you want to do this, Chaplain? Do you talk first or do I? At the very least, you should walk up first, since you're in uniform. Jack's less likely to shoot you." Although a joke, Spectre wasn't really sure how Jack felt about him since the breakup. Seeing the chaplain in his Air Force service dress uniform would probably disarm him enough to let Spectre break the news gently. *At least he hoped.* Jack was still a card-carrying NRA member with an impressive arsenal, so anything was possible.

"Based on what we've talked about for the last few hours, it would probably be best if I did the talking at first. You can help explain some of the more technical stuff. What they need now is a familiar face, and despite your past, you're still someone they can trust."

Spectre nodded and they exited the blue government sedan. With the garage door closed, the two followed the sidewalk to the front of the house.

Spectre stopped halfway down the path. "Shit. I forgot the teddy bear I was going to give Evan. Just wait on the front porch, I'll be right back."

Spectre turned and started a half jog back to the car. He had found a teddy bear dressed in a flight suit at one of the truck stops they had stopped at on the way, and he knew Evan would love it. As he started to open the Impala's door, he heard the house door unlock and open.

"I thought you were going to wai—"

The unmistakable sound of the gunshot left Spectre's ears ringing. It took him a moment to even register it as he instinctively dropped to the ground. It had been the last thing he was expecting, but it was enough to get his adrenaline pumping. *Had Jack finally lost it?*

Spectre low crawled around the car and leaned against the left front tire, hoping to shield himself if Jack decided to start shooting in his direction.

"Jack! What are you doing?" Spectre pleaded. Another two shots registered, hitting the side of the government vehicle. Spectre drew his own weapon. As a licensed concealed carry holder, he never left home without his Glock 36, a sub-compact semi-automatic handgun chambered in .45ACP. He certainly didn't want to use it, especially not on someone else's property, but with shots fired and the chaplain presumably down, he was left without a choice.

"Jack! What the fuck!" Spectre crouched behind the driver's side door and peeked over the windshield. In the darkness, he could make out a figure, someone a lot taller than Jack.

Another shot was fired. The bullet zipped past Spectre's head. He ducked back down. His hands were shaking. He had done shooting from concealment scenarios hundreds of times in the store's shoot house, and he had been shot at from the comfort of his F-16 in Iraq, but he had never been this close before.

Gathering himself, Spectre stayed crouched and moved toward the rear of the car. The front passenger window shattered as he reached the driver's side door. Apparently, he wasn't low enough. He reached for his phone to dial 911. *Not a single bar of coverage. Fuck you AT&T. More bars my ass.* Maybe a neighbor would hear the gunshots and dial 911, but Spectre knew he couldn't count on that. They were in the middle of nowhere and the nearest house was nearly a quarter mile away. There were no guarantees anyone would wake up at four in the morning.

As Spectre reached the rear bumper of the car, he repositioned himself for a better look, keeping his weapon low and ready. His assailant was now out of concealment, standing next to one of the decorative columns on the front porch. It was clearly not Jack. Spectre leaned around the taillight and took aim.

# CHAPTER THIRTEEN

"Tariq, do you hear that? Someone's here."

He had only dozed off for a second, but it took a moment for Tariq to regain his senses. They had been left by Aalee to guard the hostages. It was not a glorious job, but Tariq knew it was for the greater good. Aalee would not lead them astray. It was Allah's will and part of a bigger plan.

"Find out who it is!" Tariq jumped, trying to appear in command. He got up out of the recliner and followed Kasim to the nearby window. A dark blue car had pulled into the driveway.

"Do you think it's Abdul?" Kasim queried, looking anxiously out the window.

"At this hour? I don't think so. He said he wouldn't be back until tomorrow." Tariq watched as the dark sedan pulled up to the garage and turned off its lights. It looked like an official vehicle. It was not the van that Aalee had left in, so it couldn't be him. Besides, Aalee had faith in him. *He wouldn't need to check up on them.* Tariq had the situation under control, and strict orders on how and when to report in.

"There are two of them! They're getting out!" Kasim exclaimed. For Kasim, it was his first real mission as a soldier for the cause. He was convinced that Aalee would fulfill the promise of jihad against the infidels in America, punishing them for their greed and imperialism. *Trespassing the Holy Lands could not go unpunished.*

Tariq drew his Glock 17 9MM upon seeing the uniformed man exit the car. It was certainly not Aalee, and the man with him carried himself like a police officer of some sort. *Had Aalee been captured? Surely they would send more than just two men if that were the case.*

"Kasim, take your weapon and go to the hostages. Make sure they stay quiet. I'll deal with these two."

Kasim nodded and hurried to the laundry room where the hostages were being held. The smell was absolutely horrid as he opened the door. *They were nothing more than animals, defecating on themselves. Disgusting.* He looked forward to putting an end to their miserable lives when this was all over.

Tariq walked to the front door holding his Glock behind his back as the two men approached. He planned to talk his way out of it. They were just hired help. The homeowners were asleep and should not be bothered. It was obviously all just a big misunderstanding that could be dealt with at a more reasonable hour.

Suddenly one of the men turned and ran back to the car. *He must have found something.* There was no time to talk them away.

As Tariq opened the door, the man in uniform began to speak, but Tariq didn't give him a chance to finish. Pulling the Glock from behind his back, he fired it at waist level, hitting the man in the gut and dropping him to the ground. He had caught the man completely by surprise. If it weren't for the other man Tariq now had to worry about, he would have taken a moment to enjoy the surprised look on the infidel's face as he clutched his stomach and fell to the ground.

Tariq stepped out onto the porch. The other infidel had apparently fled back to the car, losing his will to fight at the last moment. *It was typical of these cowards. They never stood to fight, instead using fighter jets and drones to fight their battles from far away.* He could not let the man escape.

Tariq fired two rounds at the car, hoping to get a lucky shot. With just the street light and no moon, it was very dark out. He could barely make out the figure leaning against the car. The man yelled something, but Tariq couldn't make out what he was saying. *Was he trying to surrender?* He had heard many stories of the infidels surrendering from Aalee in Iraq, but had never seen such a thing first hand. He had no use for more hostages. *The coward was better off to him dead.*

Tariq saw the coward's head pop up once more above the hood, and he fired again, barely missing. He could see the feet moving underneath the car and as he once again popped his head up, Tariq fired. This time the glass shattered right where the silhouette had been.

Tariq waited for return fire. There was none. *Had he hit the other man?* He looked back at the man lying on the front door step, clutching his stomach and gasping for air. He would be dead soon. He had seen that uniform before. It was some sort of military uniform. They both must have been unarmed; otherwise, there would have been return shots by now.

Tariq stepped out onto the sidewalk, keeping the car in his sights. The coward was probably dead, but he didn't want to take any chances. He needed to make sure of it and get rid of the body. Abdul Aalee was going to be pleased. *It was another victory in the fight for Allah.*

As Tariq walked toward the car, his confidence vanished as quickly as he had gained it. He had made a horrible miscalculation. The muzzle flashes were the last thing he saw. The pain was extreme, but short lived as the world went dark.

# CHAPTER FOURTEEN

**T**wo *in the chest, one in the head. Two in the chest, one in the head.* The mantra that had been ingrained in him since his first formal trip to the firing range was suddenly at the front of his mind. It referred to the Mozambique Drill, a shooting method made famous by shooting legend Jeff Cooper, whose student found himself facing an advancing adversary at close range during the Mozambican War of Independence. When the first two center of mass shots with his Browning HP35 handgun failed to stop his opponent, Mike Rousseau adjusted his aim for a final headshot, ending the fight then and there. The drill later became known as the Failure to Stop Drill and became the standard by which military and law enforcement personnel were trained with handguns.

Spectre's first two shots were in quick succession, hitting just left of the man's heart. The third shot, after a brief pause, went right through his Adam's apple. If the first two shots hadn't done it, the third ensured that the chaplain's attacker was dead before he hit the ground.

As the man's lifeless body fell to the ground, Spectre rushed to the chaplain with his gun low and ready. He had no idea how many more, if any, were in the house. *It still didn't make any sense why any of this was happening.*

On the way, Spectre approached the attacker and picked up the Glock 17 9MM next to his lifeless hand. The man appeared to be of Middle Eastern descent. Given her past, Spectre wondered if this had something to do with Congresswoman Ridley as some sort of act of terror.

Moving toward the house, Spectre found the chaplain lying on the ground, struggling for air. A pool of blood surrounded him as he held pressure with his right hand against his wound. He wouldn't last much longer without medical attention.

"Hang in there Chaplain, we're going to get you help," Spectre said, examining the wound. It had been years since he sat through the mind numbing Air Force mandated Computer Based Training slides on Self-Aid Buddy Care, but he knew the basics. The chaplain's airway was unobstructed and his breathing was labored, but the biggest threat was the abdominal gunshot wound and subsequent bleeding. The chaplain was at extreme risk of shock and Spectre had no way of knowing what, if any, vital organs had been hit by the bullet.

Spectre reached for his phone again, hoping for a better signal. Again, he was disappointed. He vowed to pay the ridiculous early termination fee and cancel AT&T as soon as he got home. *Fucking ridiculous.*

"Chaplain, do you have your phone on you?"

The chaplain nodded and with his free hand, shakily pointed to his inner coat pocket. Spectre reached in and pulled it out. *Thankfully, it wasn't AT&T, and it had full signal strength.* He quickly dialed 911 and pressed the green SEND button.

The 911 operator answered almost immediately. Spectre explained the situation, careful not to implicate himself, and requested an ambulance. The operator attempted to talk him through some basic first aid for the chaplain, but it was nothing Spectre hadn't already done. The wound needed to be cleaned and the bullet removed.

"There's another inside," the chaplain said weakly as Spectre hung up the phone.

Spectre leaned in closer. The chaplain barely had enough strength to form the words.

"Another man...I...saw him running...when the door opened."

*Another attacker and possibly more.* Spectre couldn't wait any longer for the police. There was nothing more he could do for the chaplain, but hope the paramedics showed up. He hated the idea of leaving the chaplain alone to die, but Chloe's family might still be in the house and in danger. *He had to act.*

He handed the attacker's weapon to the chaplain. If he could muster the strength to defend himself, he would at least be armed.

Unlike the movies, Spectre had no reason to check his mag or rack the slide of his Glock 36. He shot three rounds. He had six in the magazine and one in the chamber when the night started. It was basic math, but he was regretting not carrying a second magazine as he considered that the next attacker, or attackers, might have as much or more firepower as the first. His philosophy had always been that carrying a concealed weapon would result in firing a few rounds at most, not getting into a shoot out. He made a mental note to rethink that later.

Spectre walked into the house, keeping his firearm close as he cleared left and right. He had hundreds of hours practicing in his store's shoot house, but nothing could prepare him for the real thing. He had just shot a man, and now he was facing an unknown enemy with unknown numbers and no backup.

As Spectre cleared the living room, he turned left toward the kitchen and laundry room.

"Don't shoot!" screamed a heavily accented voice. Spectre raised his weapon and pointed it at the direction of the scream. He watched cautiously as the door to the laundry room opened and a man emerged.

"Hands! Show me your hands!" Spectre barked. The man quickly raised his hands high above his head. He was scared shitless.

"Don't shoot! I surrender!" he pleaded.

Spectre held his position, front sight lined up on the man's chest. "Keep your hands up, turn around, and get on your knees." Spectre was winging it now, but he had watched enough COPS to look like he knew what he was doing.

The man complied, leaving his hands in the air as he reached his knees.

"Please don't hurt me! I didn't touch them!"

"Touch who? Where is the family?" Spectre demanded, slowly approaching the attacker. He ordered him to interlock his fingers behind his head as he moved closer.

"They are all in there, but I didn't kill the fat one, that was Abdul! I swear it."

Spectre's mind raced. *The fat one? Who was the fat one?* As Spectre approached the man, he searched the kitchen for something to bind the man's hands with. With his right hand pointing his Glock at the cowering terrorist, he quickly opened drawers as he passed, searching for something – *anything* – that would allow him to secure his newfound prisoner and clear the rest of the house.

"Are there more of you in this house?"

"No! No! Abdul left last night. It was just me and Tariq, but you killed him!"

Spectre found a roll of duct tape in a drawer. He grabbed it and walked up to the man kneeling in front of him. Holstering his weapon, Spectre shoved his boot into the small of the man's back, causing him to face plant into the tile floor. There was a crack as the man's nose broke against the hard floor. He screamed in pain.

With the man on the ground, Spectre planted his left knee into the back of the man's neck, holding his face into the tile and preventing him from getting up. He grabbed the man's right wrist and pulled it behind his back, then did the same with the left, duct taping his wrists together. With his hands secure and groaning in pain, Spectre released pressure on the man's neck and taped his ankles together.

"If you even try to move, I'll shoot you," Spectre warned. The man didn't respond. Blood was gushing from his nose and he was groaning in pain and muttering something in Arabic.

Spectre unholstered his weapon and proceeded into the laundry room. As he turned on the lights, he saw Chloe's family bound and gagged on the floor. The room smelled of urine and feces. *It was awful.* He holstered his weapon and, starting with Evan, he removed the restraints and gags and checked his condition. He was breathing, but unconscious.

With Evan safe, he moved to Jack and helped him out of his restraints. *Maureen could wait. She never liked him anyway.*

"You ok, Jack?" Spectre said as he cut the last rope with his Gerber knife. Jack quickly went to Maureen and started to work on her restraints. Spectre handed him his knife.

"Yeah, I'm fine. They killed Dianne and the dogs. Cal, there was another one here – the leader."

*That must have been whom he was referring to as the fat one. Now it made sense. Dianne. She never hurt anyone.* Spectre couldn't imagine why anyone would want to hurt her. She had always been so upbeat and happy-go-lucky around the house, especially when taking care of Evan.

"I'm sure the police will find him. What's important is that you're ok."

"No, you don't understand, I think they're going to go after Chloe," Jack said as he stood. The lights from the police and EMS vehicles arriving lit up the kitchen as they pulled into the driveway.

Spectre's heart sank. The action of the night had nearly made him forget what brought him there in the first place. The family had obviously been tortured, and a long time friend and employee had been killed. Chloe's death would absolutely crush them.

"Jack, that's why I'm here. We need to talk," he said grimly.

# CHAPTER FIFTEEN

*Hialeah, FL*

Victor Alvarez hated public meetings. He originally wanted to meet with Abdul Aalee in a secluded location where no one would be able to see or identify either of them. With his preplanned locations, he always knew where a surveillance van would park or where listening equipment could best be set up because he had done it time and again. Public locations, while nice for blending in, especially in South Florida, were at risk for just about every fear he could think of in a meeting. Anyone could be listening, anyone could be watching, or any of his enemies could be nearby, ready to strike without warning. It went against all of his training.

And yet there he was, exposed to all threats in the little Cuban Café outside of Hialeah, Florida. It had been Abdul Aalee's idea to meet there. He had stayed in the nearby safe house the night before, and contrary to Alvarez's fears, he thought the noise of the rowdy little Cuban diner would give them privacy from any potential listeners. Alvarez was not pleased by the location, but the fact that Aalee had left the two morons behind to guard the prisoners was an even bigger concern.

Normally, Alvarez would not have budged on such an important tactical issue, but in the recent months, Alvarez found himself compromising more and more. He chose to believe that it wasn't complacency, but a firmer grasp of the big picture and the important battles. *Maybe Aalee knew his men better than Alvarez thought.*

Aalee was the ultimate narcissist. He had come from a world where people followed him without question. He was brutal and merciless to his enemies, and no one dared question or challenge him. Although Alvarez did not share this fear of his associate, he knew that the man would not work for him without a healthy dose of coddling.

As he sat in the crowded, smoke-filled diner, he was reassured that the location wasn't a battle worth fighting. The dull roar of the patrons laughing and talking, mostly in Spanish, would serve as cover for their conversation. As long as Aalee didn't get too boastful about what he had done and speak directly about the operation, Alvarez reasoned, they could maintain the security of their operation even if the Americans were listening. And as for leaving the hostages alone, well, there was nothing he could do about it now.

He sat facing the door in a booth in the corner of the cramped diner. It gave him a good view of anyone entering or leaving. The booth was away from the window, but he still had a good view of the outside and any cars in the small parking lot. It was there that he watched the minivan park in front of the window across from him.

Abdul Aalee emerged and walked casually to the front door. *For a man who had spent years being hunted by the Americans,* Alvarez thought, *he didn't seem to fear capture even in the belly of the beast.* It was either a case of extreme arrogance or stupidity. He wasn't yet sure which.

Aalee walked in and sat down across from Alvarez.

"Hello, my friend," he said casually.

Alvarez smiled and handed Aalee a menu. "It's good to see you again. I've heard you have been doing good work. I must admit I'm a little surprised by your decision to have breakfast with me here."

Aalee rubbed his chin and grinned. His facial hair was starting to grow back in patches.

"It was not much of a challenge. I had to kill their servant for trying to alert the police. The old man put up no fight. They will be fine with my men."

Alvarez winced at the thought of Aalee and his men killing indiscriminately. It was the price of using him to do the heavy lifting. But he had hoped, that with the simplicity of the operation, the collateral damage would be minimized.

"It's unfortunate that you had to do that. Hopefully there are no further complications."

Alvarez was interrupted by the Hispanic waitress. They spoke to each other in perfect Spanish. When it was Aalee's time to order, he spoke in heavily accented English. He was proficient in Spanish, but had no desire to make the attempt. When she was gone, Alvarez leaned forward and continued.

"Remember, old friend, you are not to kill them. They are very valuable to this operation. Do you have the photos?"

Aalee frowned. He reached into his pocket, pulled out the SD card from his camera, and put it on the table in front of him. "You mean this?"

Alvarez nodded, his eyes focused on the memory card in front of him. It was the key to moving the operation forward.

"Everything you have asked, I have done. The family is not harmed, for now. When this is over, though, I will use them for our cause." Aalee slid the SD card across the table.

"I don't care what you do when we get what we want and the operation is complete, but for now you have to do this cleanly. There can be no mistakes." Alvarez picked up the card, examined it for a second, and put it safely into his pocket.

Aalee slammed his fist on the table, causing the patrons next to him to stop their conversation and look at them. "Do not tell me how to operate!"

Alvarez smiled nervously at the two men staring at him and tried to reassure them that everything was ok. When he was satisfied they were no longer paying attention to them, he leaned in and apologized in a low voice.

Aalee leaned back and smiled. "Have faith, my friend. You will get what you want. When you do, I will continue to carry out the will of Allah."

Alvarez nodded. He hated having to put up the front that he actually believed any of that nonsense. Despite having grown up with a background laced heavily with strict Catholicism, Alvarez considered himself a strict atheist. The world he had seen left no room for a god.

They finished their breakfast and discussed the next steps of the operation. Aalee would return to the house and ensure that the hostages were ok, and then once he received word from Alvarez that the operation was complete, he would be free to execute them for his propaganda.

As Alvarez sent for the check, his phone rang. It was Special Agent Jay Leon, his long-standing asset within the Miami office of the FBI. Almost six years ago, he had turned Special Agent Leon from a newly assigned agent with a gambling problem to an effective and well-paid asset. The current phone call was just one of the many dividends he had enjoyed from turning him.

Aalee watched intently as Alvarez's face grew more serious.

"Jay, are you sure?" he asked. The man responded and Alvarez hung up the phone. He was using every bit of self-control to avoid pulling out his weapon and shooting Aalee right in the head in the middle of the café. His instincts had been spot on. *Leaving those two idiots alone had been a bad decision.*

"What is it?" Aalee had been leaning in, trying to hear the largely one-sided conversation.

"It is no longer safe here, we must go," Alvarez said, turning to smile at the waitress returning with the check. He pulled two twenty dollar bills out of his pocket and put them on the middle of the table.

"Where? What is happening?"

"Do you remember how to get to Daytona Beach?" It was their code for the secondary meeting location at Flamingo Park in Miami.

"Yes, it's…"

"No need to tell me, old friend," Alvarez interrupted. He really was going to have to shoot him. *It was amazing a man so careless had managed to make it this far in this business.* "Just nod."

Aalee nodded. His expression had turned from concern to anger. He did not like to be patronized.

"I am going to get up and walk out the front door. I want you to wait five minutes and then exit through the side entrance over there. Go to Daytona Beach and wait. I'll call you and let you know when I can meet you. Do you understand?"

Aalee nodded again. As Alvarez began to stand, Aalee grabbed his arm and stopped him.

"What has happened?"

Alvarez removed Aalee's hand as he leaned in close.

"Your people were discovered," he whispered, "and it's not safe to go back."

Without waiting for a response, Alvarez turned and walked out through the front door. He put his sunglasses on as the bright morning sun blinded him. He had a lot of work to do, and with the recent events, the timeline would have to be sped up dramatically.

# CHAPTER SIXTEEN

*Winter Haven, FL*

It had been nearly a decade since he had been to the Air Force's Survival, Evasion, Resistance, and Escape (SERE) School, but the training seemed to be instinctively coming back to him. The memories of sleep deprivation, questioning, sensory deprivation and the subsequent loss of the sense of time were all coming back to him now. He had hated the training, but always knew he'd be grateful if he needed it and it worked.

But Spectre wasn't quite sure why he would need it now. He had saved three lives. He had acted within the boundaries of Florida Law in using lethal force to defend himself and another during a forcible felony. And it definitely was a forcible felony. A former US Congresswoman and her family had been kidnapped at the hands of very dangerous men. Their housekeeper had been brutally murdered. And to top it off, they had shot a US

Air Force Chaplain, which led to the firefight that killed one and led to the surrender of the other.

He had been in between the holding cell and the interrogation room all night and into the morning. They had taken his valuables, including his watch, when he checked in. There were no clocks on the wall and no windows to the outside world. His sense of time had been taken from him, and at first, he had been made to sit and wait what seemed like forever in the white fluorescent lighting of the small interrogation room. The temperature of the room was cranked up, causing him to sweat. Spectre recognized it for what it was – textbook interrogation techniques. *He was being treated as a criminal.*

The first detective to question him had been fairly polite. He offered him water and a snack and appeared to make no judgments as Spectre told his story. He only briefly interrupted Spectre's narrative a few times for clarification as he took notes. At the end, he merely thanked Spectre for his time and left. He made no mention of the road ahead. Spectre had already waived having an attorney present. He was hoping to be out and on his way home soon.

Spectre was exhausted. He had been up at least twenty-four hours straight. Probably a lot more, but he had no way of knowing. The crash from the adrenaline high wasn't helping matters either. The bottle of water hadn't been enough. He felt dehydrated and had a headache. He was starting to regret his decision to waive the attorney. Maybe an attorney might have been able to get him out of there more quickly, but he technically wasn't under arrest. He was only being questioned.

A few minutes later, two men walked into the cramped interrogation room. The first was slightly heavyset, a surprise to Spectre given the FBI badge clipped to his belt. Spectre had considered applying to the FBI after separating from the Air Force, and the physical fitness standards seemed pretty challenging. He reasoned that it must be part of the screening process, but not an annual requirement.

The agent sat down in the chair across the interrogation table from Spectre. He looked to be in his mid forties, slightly balding with salt and pepper hair on the sides. He was wearing a beige suit with no tie.

The second man walked in behind him carrying some files. He looked much younger. Spectre guessed he was in his late twenties or early thirties. He had on a white polo shirt with an OSI badge embroidered on it and khaki 5.11 Tactical pants. He also had an OSI badge clipped to his belt.

Spectre frowned as the second man sat down. The Air Force Office of Special Investigations was the investigative branch of the Air Force. In Spectre's experience, they usually investigated airmen selling drugs in dorm rooms or sexual assaults, not a high profile kidnapping and murder.

Spectre said nothing as the two men sat down across from him. He felt like he had talked for hours with the last guy. No point in wasting more energy. They could watch the tape if they wanted more information.

"Mr. Martin," the portly agent began, "I'm Special Agent Thomas, and this is Special Agent Baxter. We're with the Miami Joint Terrorism Task Force. We're really sorry for the delay, but as you can imagine it took us a while to get here."

The Joint Terrorism Task Force was a multi-agency group designed to tear down interagency walls and work together to stop terror attacks on US soil. They were each agency's best and brightest chosen to combat terrorism.

The JTTF had offices set up in each region around the country to bring federal agencies together to share information, resources, and skills to help bring those that would do harm to Americans to justice. With so many immigrants and people of every culture, Miami in particular was a hotbed for activity. Terrorist Mohamed Atta, leader of the 19 terrorists who hijacked four aircraft on 9/11, trained and operated in Southern Florida. In 2009, seven homegrown terrorists were arrested in Miami in a plot by Al Qaeda to blow up the Sears Tower in Chicago. It was an easy area to access and operate without anyone raising an eyebrow.

Spectre still didn't see the connection though. He had gone over and over in his head the events of the last twenty-four hours during the torturous waiting games, but despite the backgrounds of the men he encountered, he was not convinced it was terrorism. US Representatives were just likely targets for kidnappers.

Spectre said nothing. He could only stare at the two men. He simply nodded and waited for an explanation of why they were here.

The younger agent broke the awkward silence. "Mr. Martin, I understand you've been through a lot in the last twenty-four hours, but could you tell us what happened last night?"

"Ok," Spectre's voice cracked. "You've had me here for, what six to nine hours? I just spent the last however long reliving this nightmare to the detective from the Sheriff's Department, on tape, with him taking notes, and your first fucking question is what happened last night? You have got to be shitting me!"

The portly agent's face grew flush. "Sir, you don't have to be rude about it. We're conducting a federal terrorism investigation here. It is important for both you and us that you cooperate here."

"What the fuck is that supposed to mean? Am I being charged?"

"That's not out of the realm of possibility," the portly agent responded smugly.

"Fine. I want a lawyer," Spectre replied, folding his arms.

"Sir, we're not here to charge you," the younger agent interjected. "We have a very specific interest in this case, and we would be grateful if you could help. I have read Detective Worley's notes, and I'm sorry for asking such a vague question."

Special Agent Thomas glared at the younger OSI agent. In his mind, there was no need to kiss this disrespectful prick's ass. If he wanted to do things the hard way, they could oblige. He hadn't gotten as far as he had by letting suspects walk all over him. Baxter was just a rookie. He wasn't running this show.

Spectre nodded. He was tired of the bullshit, but realized he had probably taken it a little far.

"I'm happy to try and help. What would you like to know?"

Agent Baxter pulled out the file he had carried in. He pulled out three pictures and laid them out on the table in front of Spectre.

"Do you recognize these men?"

Spectre leaned forward and examined each one. They appeared to be surveillance photos of three Arab men. He picked up the first one and studied it for a minute.

"This is the guy I shot."

"That's Tariq Al Ansari, a Saudi national and fairly low-level figure in an Al Qaeda cell we had been tracking," Baxter explained.

"Do you recognize the other two?" Agent Baxter prodded.

Spectre put down the first photo and picked up the other two side by side.

"This is the guy that pissed his pants and surrendered," Spectre said, waving the picture in his left hand.

"And I have no idea who this guy is," Spectre said, motioning with the picture in his right hand. "Care to fill me in?"

"We'll ask the questions here," the portly agent replied tersely.

Spectre wasn't sure if the guy was kidding or just an idiot. He was contemplating how many insults he could launch before landing himself in real trouble. *Maybe he could even choke the fatty out. Gitmo is probably nice this time of year. It isn't worth it though,* Spectre thought. Instead, he just stared the man down without saying a word.

"We don't know much about the man in custody. His name is Kasim Razvi, and we're pretty sure he's from the tribal regions of Pakistan, but he seems to be a relatively low-level player," Baxter explained, ignoring the growing tension between Spectre and Agent Thomas.

Spectre was starting to like this Baxter guy. He wasn't sure if they were doing the Good Cop, Bad Cop routine on purpose, or if Crisco was just a dick. He assumed the latter, but either way the OSI agent seemed pretty sharp.

"The other picture you're holding," Baxter continued, "is of a man who calls himself Abdul Aalee, or servant of the Most High."

Spectre leaned forward in his chair. He remembered the name from his visit to Customs and Border Protection with Marcus. His CBP friend had told them about the current state of affairs and mentioned Aalee's name.

"I've heard of him, but you think he's behind this?"

"Well, this kidnapping fits perfectly with Aalee's modus operandi," Baxter replied.

"What do you mean?" Spectre asked.

"Aalee was pretty big on high-level kidnappings in Iraq. Government officials, judges, anyone with money. Sometimes he would ask for a ransom and then kill the hostages, others he would just kill the hostages for propaganda. Really nasty stuff."

"Yeah, I remember the intel briefs," Spectre replied. "I supported Special Ops guys a couple of times trying to save hostages. What do you want to know?"

"You were dating the Congresswoman's daughter, correct?"

The question brought back a flood of memories. He had almost forgotten what had brought him to this town in the first place. The woman he had loved until a few short weeks ago, and maybe even still loved, had gone missing in an F-16. She was probably dead. Spectre still couldn't believe it.

"Yeah, we dated," he mumbled.

"Did she ever mention any of these men? Talk about any threats her parents might have gotten?"

Spectre rubbed his eyes with his hand and cleared his throat as he held back the tears.

"There were always threats when her mother was in office. Some asshole hates this policy, or another asshole wants her dead. That's politics, but nothing actionable that I'm aware of. And there was never any mention of Al Qaeda. Besides, she's been retired for a while now."

"Have you ever seen any of these men before tonight?"

Spectre picked up the pictures again and studied them. He was so tired, but he wanted to help as best he could. He knew at least Baxter was well intentioned.

"No, last night was the first time."

"This man," Baxter continued, holding up the picture of Kasim, "did he say anything before the police arrived?"

Spectre thought about it for a minute. "Yes, he did. He said he didn't kill the fat one. He was very adamant about it. He said it was Abdul."

"Did he say anything else?"

"When I asked if there was anyone left in the house, he said this Aalee guy had left the night prior, but that's it."

Baxter was busy taking notes as Agent Thomas interjected, "The report says you and the chaplain went to notify the family."

"Correct," Spectre replied. He really had hoped Crisco would have just kept his mouth shut. Things were going so much more smoothly without him.

"Notify them of what?"

"You didn't hear? Their daughter went down in an F-16," Spectre replied, hanging his head.

Baxter looked up from scribbling notes, his eyes wide. "Oh man, I'm sorry to hear that. Somehow we missed that."

Agent Thomas didn't share Baxter's compassion. "So you took the chaplain and a loaded gun to tell a former US Congresswoman that her daughter is dead in the wee hours of the morning?"

Spectre could feel the vein in his neck throbbing. He was pretty sure he could crush tubby's windpipe from where he was sitting. He didn't want to have to deal with Baxter. He seemed like a nice enough guy. He liked him, but it was his own fault for associating with this waste of oxygen. He would just be collateral damage.

"The chaplain and I felt that it would be best to tell the family as soon as possible, and since they weren't answering their phones, we decided to drive up." Spectre's jaw was clenched.

"And so you brought a gun?"

"I always carry a weapon. I have a valid concealed carry permit in the State of Florida, check my wallet," Spectre replied.

"You didn't answer my question. Why did you bring a gun?" Thomas was leaning on his forearms, trying to intimidate Spectre.

"Because if I didn't, you wouldn't have anyone left to question," Spectre shot back.

Baxter stood, handing Spectre his business card. "Ok, I think we've covered everything. Mr. Martin. Thanks for your time. Here's my card. If you think of anything else that might help us, please give me a call."

"There is one more thing," Spectre said.

"What's that?" Baxter replied. Thomas was standing, but still staring Spectre down.

"How is the chaplain?"

Baxter shook his head. "He was in surgery a couple of hours ago. The doctors say it's a long shot."

"Thanks," Spectre replied.

The two men walked out with Baxter leading the way.

# CHAPTER SEVENTEEN

*Homestead, FL*

T he drive back to Miami with Agent Thomas had been awkward for Special Agent Sean Baxter. Thomas was obviously flustered by the interaction with Martin and his inability to control the tone of the interview. He had spent most of the drive home making excuses and complaining about the lack of respect. Baxter thought the ranting had been a huge waste of time. Instead of going over the case and trying to put together the missing pieces, he had to sit there and listen to his senior associate exercise his narcissistic inadequacies.

But compared to the older FBI agent, Baxter was a rookie. He had only been with the Air Force Office of Special Investigations for two years and had been assigned to the JTTF a few months prior. At 26, Baxter was fairly young in comparison to other civilian OSI agents, many of whom had transferred from other agencies or been active duty enlisted airmen prior to becoming agents.

The only son of a decorated Secret Service agent killed in the line of duty, Baxter had known he wanted to be in law enforcement his entire life. As soon as he was out of high school, he joined the county sheriff's office and worked his way through college. After college, with the economy in shambles and federal government cutbacks, he couldn't find a way into the Secret Service to follow in his father's footsteps. They just weren't hiring. So he became a Texas State Trooper, hoping to join the elite Texas Rangers.

But after three years of working the highways of Southeast Texas and achieving the requisite rank of Trooper II, the Rangers weren't accepting applications. So Baxter continued his search, until one of his old buddies from high school serving in the Air Force recommended OSI.

He knew nothing about AFOSI, other than assuming it was probably similar to the TV drama NCIS, being a military investigative agency and all. After a little research and a visit to the local field office, Baxter was convinced that would be the path for him. So he applied for a civilian agent position and a few weeks later was notified he had been selected to go to Federal Law Enforcement Training at Glynco, Georgia to become a federal agent.

Baxter's first assignment after FLETC and the subsequent AFOSI training was Homestead Air Reserve Base in Florida. Despite having lived all over the country during most of his childhood while following his dad's career from assignment to assignment, Baxter considered himself a Texan. So Homestead and the surrounding area had been a culture shock for him. He didn't have time to care, however, as it kept him busy doing exactly what he wanted in counterterrorism.

The rookie had been picked for the AFOSI representative to the JTTF by sheer luck, but it was exactly the kind of work

Baxter had been hoping for. Miami was a hotbed for counterterrorism and counterintelligence. In the few short months he had been part of the JTTF, he had seen several very troubling close calls.

Less than a few days prior to tagging along with Agent Thomas, four Syrian men were arrested in a foiled plot to use a rental truck to blow up Land Shark Stadium, home of the Miami Dolphins. But when the lackey of the group paid using the stolen identity of a deceased Mr. James Smith, a streetwise clerk alerted authorities. The FBI and members of the Miami-Dade Sheriff's Department served a warrant at the address the man used to register the truck, uncovering enough ammonium nitrate to level the entire stadium. Better off lucky than good, the lead ATF agent in the case mused.

But Baxter wasn't a fan of luck, especially when it came to terrorism. His father had instilled in him the value of attention to detail. With it, his father always said, luck wouldn't be necessary. People, especially criminals, can seem highly unpredictable on the surface, but when you look at the details of a case, patterns and trends start to emerge. The skilled investigator always looks for the proverbial fine print during an investigation.

As he sat in his small office in the AFOSI building in Homestead, the details of the Martin case were bothering him. He had only ridden along with Agent Thomas to get a better glimpse into investigating a suspected terrorism operation. Thomas had an excellent reputation in the counterterrorism community, and Baxter had been told by several other agents that there was no one better in the business to follow. Thomas had been the lead investigator on several successful cases. His conviction record was impeccable.

So why, then, had he spent the entire drive back complaining like a petulant child who had been chastised? Why weren't they discussing the details? Specifically, what was the connection between the Congresswoman's daughter and this kidnapping?

There were several unanswered questions. Baxter flipped through his copy of the case file. They were only able to interview Martin and retrieve the detective's notes. The family had been too busy at the hospital with their handicapped son, who required emergency surgery due to his injuries. The boy's condition had turned to critical, and his parents were unwilling to talk more. So while none of the witnesses were able or willing to talk, the only suspect in the case had been transferred to Miami-Dade County for federal custody just before they arrived. *Maybe that's why Thomas had been in such a bad mood.*

Baxter rubbed his eyes as he sat at his desk. It was nearly 7 PM, but he wanted to read through the case file once before locking it up and going home. If he didn't, the whole thing would eat at him. His instincts told him to look for more details.

He flipped through the transcript of the detective's interview with the Congresswoman. She focused mostly on the murder of the housekeeper and dog, and the beatings of her son. She wasn't sure how they even got to the house or what happened before they dragged her husband into the laundry room.

She did mention Martin, but only that she had been surprised to see him. She had never really liked him nor thought him capable of any heroics, but she was thankful he showed up. She still couldn't believe her daughter was missing. It was all simply overwhelming to her.

Baxter put aside the transcript and picked up the interview with Jack Rivers, Congresswoman Ridley's husband. It was much more detailed. Mr. Rivers had obviously had some level of training, probably from his time in the Army in Vietnam based on his profile. He described the men in great detail. The two that were left behind were low-level henchmen. The real leader had left the night prior after taking pictures of their faces.

As Baxter continued reading, Rivers explained that he had tried to listen in on the leader's phone call, but it was in Farsi or Arabic, he wasn't sure. What bothered Rivers was that he heard their daughter's name. He had been sure. There was no mistaking it.

Baxter reread the line from Mr. Rivers. "He took the picture, walked out of the room, and I think he was on his cell phone. I'm not sure what he said before. It was in another language. Farsi. Arabic. I'm not sure. But I know I heard 'Chloe Moss.' And I worried. I thought maybe they were going to get her too or they had her. But then, when it was all over, Cal told me what happened. Do you think they did it?"

Baxter put down the report and turned to his computer. He opened up the Air Force database and began searching. The Safety Investigation Board that investigates all mishaps probably hadn't released its report on the incident yet, but he could probably get the preliminary report. After a few clicks, he was staring at the report.

//AT 0105Z F-16 LOST CONTACT IN WARNING AREA W465. WINGMAN REPORTED LOSS OF CONTACT ON PREPLANNED MANEUVER. SEARCH AND RESCUE EFFORTS INITIATED BY AIRBORNE AIRCRAFT. NO BEACON NOTED OR COMMUNICATION ATTEMPT MADE BY DOWNED AIRCREW. COAST GUARD AND AIR NATIONAL GUARD ASSETS DEPLOYED TO ASSIST RESCUE EFFORTS. DUE TO STRONG WINDS AND ROUGH SEAS WRECKAGE HAS NOT BEEN LOCATED. INITIAL ASSESSMENTS INDICATE NO EJECTION ATTEMPT MADE BY PILOT. CAUSE OF MISHAP UNKNOWN AT THIS TIME. SEARCH AND RESCUE WILL TRANSITION TO RECOVERY IN 72 HOURS. //

Baxter picked up the phone and dialed Agent Thomas' cell phone.

"Sir, it's Agent Baxter, I'm sorry to bother you, but-"

"Baxter?" Thomas interrupted. "It's almost eight, is there something wrong?"

"No, sir, it's about the Congresswoman's case," Baxter replied.

"What about it?" Thomas barked.

"Sir, I was reading the transcripts of the interview, did you get a chance to read them?" Baxter decided to take a more submissive approach. After all, he was just the rookie, and he was already seeing that Thomas had a bit of a temper. Better to ask "cool questions" as his dad called them, than to come off as the know-it-all rookie.

"Yes, I read them. Get to the point."

"Yes, sir. Well, I was just reading through Mr. Rivers' statement, and the thing about the daughter, Chloe Moss, raised a red flag."

"The daughter? The one killed in the crash two days ago?"

"That's correct, sir. I pulled up the crash report, and-"

"Let me stop you right there, Baxter," Thomas interrupted. "The crash report and whatever happened to the daughter is your prerogative, and I get that. But we've got a former US Congresswoman who has been kidnapped by known terrorists. We've got more important leads to follow up on with that front."

"But sir..." Baxter was trying to keep his humble tone while pleading his case. "Mr. Rivers specifically mentioned thinking the terrorists might have had something to do with the crash."

"Ok, Baxter, I'll bite. You have the report? What does it say?"

"It says no ejection attempt was made and no wreckage has been found yet," Baxter replied, reading the report as he scribbled notes.

"So you think the crash didn't happen? Is that what you're getting at?" Thomas' tone changed from subtle to full-blown condescension.

"No sir, I'm not saying that—"

"Do you think the terrorists shot it down with a missile, and it vaporized mid flight?" Thomas interrupted.

"No, not at all," Baxter was starting to lose his cool. This prick was dismissing everything without even hearing him out.

"Look, Baxter, I know you're new at this, but you're chasing a bad lead. Fighter jets crash. It's the cost of doing business. Have you ever been fishing offshore? The ocean can get pretty nasty. I'm not surprised they haven't been able to find the wreckage yet, but I doubt these guys have the technology to just vaporize a jet in mid air. Give it a few days, and I'm sure, when the weather gets better, they'll find it. But for now, we've got a known terrorist on the run, and I'm not about to let this asshole get away. If you want to keep tagging along and help, that's fine, but don't waste my time unless you have something solid, are we clear?"

"Yes, sir," Baxter replied meekly. He had been scolded like a child. He hated it, but he was far too new to rock the boat. Thomas had completely deflated him.

"Good. I'll see you at the JTTF tomorrow morning. I'm working on a few leads right now so bring your A game."

Thomas hung up without waiting for a response. Baxter felt embarrassed. The senior agent had completely discredited him without so much as hearing him out first. He leaned back in his chair and closed his eyes. His father lived and worked in a different time. It was a time before 9/11 and the constant public scrutiny involved with counterterrorism. But he wondered what advice his father would have in this case. Then it hit him.

The truth is always in the details.

And with that, Baxter knew what he had to do.

# CHAPTER EIGHTEEN

*Joint Base Balad, Iraq*
*1000 Local*
*2009*

"**S**CRAMBLE! SCRAMBLE! SCRAMBLE!**"** It was the sound of the duty officer's voice over the intercom system as the corresponding klaxons screamed from above.

Spectre had been sitting in the Lay-Z-Boy recliner, G-suit and survival vest on, playing Call of Duty on the 50 inch Plasma TV with his flight lead, "Pounder" Van Pelt, when the scramble order was given. They instantly jumped from their chairs and ran for the door.

They were sitting 15-minute alert at Balad Air Base in Iraq. In their role as the Air Sovereignty Alert fighters, they were the first line of defense against foreign airspace violations from neighboring countries. But, until now, Spectre had never been scrambled. He had been scheduled for alert over a dozen times, but had never gotten the call. His tour had been fairly quiet so far. *Something real must've been happening.*

The two ran out the wooden alert shack to their respective F-16s in their hardened shelters. Spectre's crew chief, the young Airman responsible for assisting with the launch, ran right past him from the maintenance shack at a full sprint toward the jet. Their pre-briefed contract with each other was simple – from the time they got the scramble order, they had only fifteen minutes to be airborne – Spectre had told him to do what he had to do to make the launch happen. He would handle the rest.

As his crew chief plugged in his headset and began his checks, Spectre put on his harness and zipped up his G-suit. The jet was already pre-flighted and postured for a quick start, so there was no need to do a walk around or check anything. With his harness on, he hurried up the ladder, hopping into the F-16's reclined ACES II ejection seat.

Spectre had already briefed his crew chief at the crew changeover. As soon as the young Airman pulled the ladder, Spectre would fire the Jet Fuel Starter and begin the startup process. The JFS spun to life as the crew chief removed the ladder and set it aside. Within seconds, the JFS had spooled up and Spectre moved the throttle to idle, starting the powerful General Electric F100-110 engine. Spectre lowered the bubble canopy as the engine and electrical systems came online.

The crew chief ran out of sight performing his checks as Spectre ran through his alert launch checklist. Most of his systems were already set up, requiring him only to power them up and run their respective Built in Test modes. A few minutes later, he gave the crew chief the signal to pull chocks.

With the chocks pulled and the crew chief ready, Spectre released the brakes and taxied the F-16 forward. It was loaded for combat, with two 500 pound laser guided bombs, two AIM-

120 air-to-air missiles, and two AIM-9 air-to-air missiles. Their mission called for flexibility. They could either be tasked to support troops on the ground, or a possible, but less likely, air threat.

As Spectre taxied forward, he looked out to the adjacent Hardened Aircraft Shelter and saw Pounder taxi his jet out as well. He tuned to the mission frequency on his UHF radio and listened in.

"Snake One-One check secure." Pounder's voice sounded hollow, as if he were talking through a tin can. It was a secure frequency to ensure no enemy could listen in.

"Two," Spectre replied crisply.

Pounder checked in with the controlling agency and they were given their tasking: investigate an unknown aircraft near the Iraq/Iranian border, slow moving. Pounder acknowledged.

Spectre wrote down the clearance and followed his lead to the runway. "Investigate" was not clearance to engage. That would require positive enemy indication and some sort of hostile act from the aircraft. Essentially, they were just going to Observe and Report, like mall cops.

Within seconds, Pounder's F-16 was in full afterburner hurtling down the 10,000 foot runway. Fifteen seconds later, Spectre selected full afterburner and followed, holding low on the runway once airborne until reaching 400 knots, and then starting an aggressive climb to follow Pounder. It was standard procedure to avoid any small arms threats that might be waiting on the other side of the base's fence by climbing quickly to stay out of range.

Spectre rejoined to a combat formation as they climbed out. They were holding 400 knots as they made their way to the area of the bogey aircraft. Spectre wondered what they might expect to find. The last time he had heard of jets being scrambled on an air-to-air mission was years prior when an Iranian UAV had been shot down after crossing into Iraqi airspace. He figured it was probably something similar, especially being a slow moving target.

As they checked in with the controlling agency for that sector, they were given their tasking.

"Snake One-One, investigate BRAA 090/50, 1000, track west, bogey, slow mover, maintain block 10-15," the female voice directed. The aircraft was fifty miles due east of their position, tracking toward Baghdad at a slow speed. They were given clearance to maintain between 10,000 feet and 15,000 feet. *It's probably an Iranian UAV*, Spectre reasoned. The aircraft was not squawking the appropriate IFF transponder code or talking to anyone.

"Snake One-One copies," Pounder responded and then keyed up their interflight radio. "Ok, Two, game plan will be eyeball, cover. You have the top two thousand feet of the block; I'll take the bottom two thousand feet. I'll go in and get the visual ID while you cover from the wheel. Green'em up."

Spectre's head tilted in the cockpit. "Green'em up" was a directive to arm the aircraft's offensive weapons. It was usually reserved for times when ordnance would be employed, to prevent an inadvertent drop or accidental firing.

"Confirm going green?" Spectre asked.

"Affirm," Pounder replied. "Aircraft type is unknown. Could be Iranian attack helicopters."

"Two," Spectre replied. Now wasn't the time to argue, but he decided not to flip the Master Arm switch from SAFE to ARM. If he needed it, he could do it later. There was no reason to end up on CNN for accidentally dropping a 500 pound bomb on a village. Pounder's attitude bothered him a bit. They had only flown together a few times, but he seemed to be chomping at the bit for action much more than other pilots he had flown with.

"Snake One-One, radar contact 080/20," Pounder declared. He had picked up the unidentified aircraft twenty miles ahead.

Spectre shifted his attention to his radar screen. He rolled the radar antenna lower and found a return 20 miles off his nose. When the aircraft locked the contact, Spectre studied the data. It was moving 100 knots directly toward them. He looked up and maneuvered into position as Pounder offset for the visual identification.

"Snake Two targeted," Spectre announced. It was an informative call to let his flight lead know he also had radar contact. Pounder could spend more time getting the VID than trying to talk his wingman's eyes onto the target.

As the range decreased, Pounder requested a lower block to get a visual ID.

"Negative, Snake One-One, unable," the female controller responded.

"Say reason," Pounder snapped.

"Multiple UAVs block 4-8 BRAA 080/15, maintain block 10-15," she responded. Spectre didn't like it. *Why didn't they get the drone traffic out the way?*

Pounder acknowledged and switched back to interflight. "Two, the game plan will remain the same. We'll set up a five-mile wheel over the target and get a targeting pod ID."

They would set up a five-mile orbit around the target aircraft and use the advanced targeting pod to get a visual. It was a fairly standard technique, and since it was still daylight, they would be able to use either the Electro Optical or Forward Looking Infrared sensors of the targeting pod.

Spectre pulled up the targeting pod on his right Multi-Function Display. It was slaved to the radar lock, immediately giving him a black and white image of the target. He zoomed in. At this range, the targeting pod was good enough to give them a general idea of what they were looking at. *It was a helicopter.*

Helicopters made Spectre nervous. It wasn't because they were dangerous. They could be. Although many attack helicopters carried air-to-air missiles, most fighter pilots weren't overly concerned about being shot down by a helicopter. Instead, the real threat in this theater was friendly fire. It was a fear reinforced by history and the blood of American serviceman.

In 1994 during Operation Provide Comfort in Iraq, two F-15s had been scrambled on a very similar mission. Like the helicopter Spectre and Pounder were orbiting, two American UH-60 Blackhawk helicopters had failed to squawk appropriate IFF codes as they flew over Northern Iraq. The F-15s mistook the Blackhawks for Iraqi Mi-24 Hind gunships, and shot both down, killing all 26 aboard. It was one of the deadliest friendly fire incidents in US history and resulted in disciplinary action for both pilots and the controller that failed to properly identify the target.

Pounder relayed the identification to the controller as they set up their orbit. The controller told them to monitor the aircraft as she cleared the airspace for them to get a better look.

"It looks like an attack helicopter, maybe a Toufan," Pounder said over aux. The Toufan was the Iranian version of the AH-1 Cobra. It was a two-seat light attack helicopter produced indigenously by the Iranian Aviation Industries Organization.

Spectre said nothing. He maintained his formation position and switched between the TV/EO mode of the pod and the FLIR mode. He was hoping to get a better look before confirming anything. It was definitely an attack helicopter, but country of origin would be hard to determine without looking at the markings up close.

"Snake One-One, you're cleared surface to ten thousand block, previously called traffic no longer a factor," the female controller advised.

Pounder acknowledged and then updated the plan, "Two, you've got from six to ten, I'll get an ID. This is an attack helicopter that crossed the border. Any hostile act and take it out with a heater. I don't want to be the F-16 guy that gets shot down by a helicopter."

"Two," Spectre replied. He wasn't sure why Pounder even mentioned that. What would an Iranian Toufan be doing alone in Iraqi airspace? That would be a suicide mission and clear act of war. No way. It was probably just an American Marine AH-1 Cobra with a bad transponder or something.

As they descended to their respective altitudes, Spectre set up his orbit. The helicopter wasn't deviating from its route of flight as it steadily headed west.

Spectre watched as Pounder rolled in on the helicopter from the east. It was still mid morning, so the sun would be at his back, making it more likely for an unobserved ID. It also kept Pounder behind the helicopter in an offensive position, but it would be much harder to identify markings. From his altitude, Spectre could only make out the fact that it was a helicopter when he looked outside, so he kept his focus on the MFD with the targeting pod image.

"Snake One-One in from the east," Pounder declared. Spectre kept his eye on the targeting pod. Suddenly the helicopter made an aggressive left hand turn as Pounder neared. Spectre's targeting pod lit up as a string of self-protection flares, designed to decoy IR missiles, came off the helicopter.

"Target maneuver, Snake One is defensive, missile in the air!" Pounder screamed over the primary frequency. "ID hostile, Two, status shot?"

Pounder wanted Spectre to shoot. He must have mistaken the flare for a missile. *This was starting to go downhill.* Spectre could see the situation deteriorating.

"Snake One-Two, negative, knock it off," Spectre replied. He hoped that "knock it off" would allow Pounder to pause and realize that the situation was much different than it seemed.

"Negative!" Pounder screamed "Snake One-One is in for immediate re-attack, hostile! Hostile!"

Spectre could feel the pit in his stomach. They had no idea if this helicopter was friendly or hostile, but Pounder was running on adrenaline and ego. He wanted a kill and thought he had fulfilled the rules of engagement. Spectre had to act fast.

"Snake One-One, abort," Spectre replied, directing his flight lead to discontinue the attack, "Snake Two is in."

He knew Pounder wouldn't risk the midair as Spectre rolled in, so he took the opportunity to roll in on the helicopter. It was still in a left hand turn away from their flight.

He watched as Pounder discontinued his turn and climbed. At least he wasn't so caught up in his blood lust that he was completely ignoring basic safety of flight concepts.

Spectre transitioned to looking completely out the window. The targeting pod image showed great detail, but it was almost useless when it came to identifying markings.

As Spectre neared the helicopter with his F-16, he strained to see the markings. The left turn made it easier for him to see the side of the helicopter and its tail rotor. He could barely make it out, but when he did, it all clicked. It said MARINES.

"Friendly! Friendly!" Spectre said as he climbed his F-16.

"Say again?" Pounder replied. The doubt in his voice was clear.

"That's a Marine Cobra, do not engage!" Spectre replied.

"Marine? No that Cobra fired a heater at me, it's hostile," Pounder said, referring to the flares they had seen. It was obvious Pounder had developed a sort of channelized attention. He was convinced that the flare had been an air-to-air missile, and that the helicopter was Iranian.

"Negative, Snake One, that was a flare. Recommend knock it off and we shadow."

"Snake One copies," Pounder replied. There was almost a bit of disappointment in his voice. Moments ago, he thought he was fighting a foreign attack helicopter. Spectre only hoped he realized he had nearly shot down a friendly.

Pounder took up his position and they shadowed the helicopter as turned back on course to the west.

They flew in silence as they orbited the Cobra. It continued west for ten more minutes, until it landed at a Marine Forward Operating Base just east of Baghdad.

As it landed, Spectre's face felt wet. He awoke to Zeus licking his face and putting his head on Spectre's chest. It was nearly midnight. He had been asleep for only a few hours since getting home from the Sheriff's Department. He had been home from Iraq for nearly five years, but it all still seemed very real.

# CHAPTER NINETEEN

*Homestead, FL*

rolled out of bed and let Zeus out. He had gone straight to bed without changing or showering when he got home. He just wanted to sleep the horror of the last couple of days away.

As he shuffled through the house like a zombie, Spectre thought about the vivid dream he had just been through. It seemed more and more he was reliving his last deployment in Iraq, like a ghost haunting him.

This particular dream was a first. Like the others, it felt so very real. He could feel the mask on his face, hear the static of the radios, and see the F-16's avionics in front of him. He remembered landing and going toe to toe with Pounder over nearly shooting down a friendly helicopter.

Spectre wanted Pounder to fess up for what he had done. Just admit his mistake and let everyone else learn from it. But

Pounder wasn't buying into it. Instead, he wanted Spectre to drop it, and when Spectre pressed him, he threatened to block Spectre's upcoming upgrade to Instructor Pilot.

Spectre regretted his reaction. In the heat of the moment, as they were discussing this on the flight line walking back into their alert shack, Spectre turned to Pounder, got right in his face and said, "With all due respect, you can go fuck yourself."

He then turned around and walked off, not talking to Pounder the rest of the day. This was the first stone in an avalanche that would eventually end Spectre's flying career. When the leadership found out, specifically Coach Louhan, he was grounded for a week and was downgraded from flight lead to wingman for the rest of the deployment.

Later, when Spectre decided to argue the case, the Digital Video Recorders from the flight from both aircraft had somehow been erased, leaving no record of Spectre averting a friendly fire disaster. It was his word against Pounder's, and Coach wasn't interested in Spectre's side.

With all that had been going on, Spectre wondered why the dreams were just starting now. He made a sandwich and sat down at his dinner table. He knew he probably wouldn't be able to go back to sleep. His mind was still racing, thinking about everything that happened.

He was dealing with the shootout fairly well. He had never killed anyone up close before. Sure, he had killed people in combat, but that was remote. He felt disconnected from them. They were little more than blurry images in the targeting pod, blurred out by dust from the 20MM bullets or 500 pound bombs. It was impersonal. The personal connection was with the friendlies on the ground. They were the ones that mattered. They were the only ones that were real.

Shooting someone was different. There was a different feeling to it altogether. *It was personal.* He watched the asshole die, but he wasn't sad. He had no regrets. It was as primal as it could be. Kill or be killed. He just happened to kill. Spectre only wondered if he should feel more guilt.

Instead, he felt guilt for the chaplain. He wondered how he was doing. He hadn't heard anything since he left the Sheriff's Department. The chaplain had gone through major surgery, and they weren't sure if he'd ever walk again, even if he survived through the night. *It was horrible.* Spectre felt responsible, as if there were more he could've done.

He looked around the empty house. It was dark and quiet, but he didn't feel alone. He could almost feel Chloe. It was as if she were still there. The reality of her death hadn't set in yet. Their relationship had changed so quickly. One minute they were the happiest couple on the planet, the next, she wanted nothing more to do with him. And then she crashed, leaving him to question everything.

Spectre couldn't wrap his head around how she could just give up on them so abruptly. He had seen it before in friends, and usually the girl was cheating on the guy, or vice versa. He had counseled his friends many times before. Spectre refused to believe that. Chloe just didn't seem like the type. He knew she had been cheated on before. *It just wasn't possible.*

After finishing his sandwich, Spectre decided to take a shower. He needed it and after thirty minutes of warm water, he felt like his batteries had been recharged. Walking back to his room, he passed by the open door of Chloe's room and stopped.

It had been a weird arrangement. What was once their guest bedroom had now become her room since she first announced they were done. They had gone from lovers to roommates almost instantly.

He turned the light on. An old flight suit was still hanging on the closet door, and her jewelry box was open on the dresser. The room still smelled like her. The bed was unmade, with her laptop sitting open on the nightstand.

With the flood of emotion the sights and smells caused, he thought back to the advice he had given to his friends. *Chloe wasn't the type. Was she?*

The laptop was sitting there. He knew the passwords. They knew each other's passwords for everything. She had never hidden anything from him.

"Chloe, forgive me," he said as he sat down on the bed and turned on the computer. He didn't know why he was doing it, but he wanted closure.

Spectre didn't really know what he was looking for either. As he entered the password and logged on to Windows, there was nothing that jumped out at him. The only thing he could think of was her e-mail account. *But would she really be e-mailing a lover?*

As he opened up her e-mail webmail account, he scrolled through the e-mails. Besides the daily flying schedule that the squadron schedulers e-mailed out every day, there was really nothing of interest. The more he scrolled through her inbox, the cheaper he began to feel.

Convinced he had been foolish to even think of searching her computer, Spectre started to sign off. Before he reached the sign out button, the Drafts folder caught his eye. The link showed two new drafts.

Curious, Spectre clicked on the link and opened the folder. It contained two messages, each with no subject. He had a glimmer of hope as he considered that it might have been a draft to tell him she still loved him. He read the first one.

"Baby, I miss you. I can't wait to be with you again. Love, C."

It was dated two days before the crash, but she had never sent it. It was addressed to no one. Spectre's eyes watered. *Had she really been considering getting back together?*

He pushed back the tears and opened the second draft. Maybe she had written more, explaining what was going on in her heart.

"Everything is ready. We will be together tonight. Don't worry. – Victor"

Spectre's stomach turned. He was confused. He didn't understand why she would sign Victor to an e-mail. *Who was Victor?*

He looked at the date and time the draft was saved. It was written at 12:41PM on the day she crashed.

# CHAPTER TWENTY

*Everglades, FL*

**A**bdul Aalee sat alone in the living room of the small farmhouse. He had been there less than a day, but he was already starting to get cabin fever. He was not a man for sitting and waiting. He wanted action. *He wanted revenge.*

The day prior, he had gone to Flamingo Park and waited as he was instructed by Alvarez. He had waited for over an hour in the heat and suffocating humidity on one of the park benches sitting between the rows of palm trees. As he watched the children playing in the park, he wished he had one of his suicide bombers or a remote detonated bomb. *It would have made a great target against the Americans. They could never be allowed to feel safe again.*

The man who approached him had not been Alvarez. Instead, it had been some lackey. He said his name was Jose. Aalee was prepared to end his life on the spot, but Jose knew their code word. He gave Aalee the address of the small farmhouse in the Everglades and told him to hide until they could regroup.

But the man couldn't tell Aalee what had happened. He had seen on the news that the kidnapping had been discovered. One man had been killed and another was in custody, but neither had been identified. The police also mentioned the search for a third suspect, but also did not identify him. That was good, for the time being. Flamingo Park was a careless choice. He would have to talk to Alvarez about such poor choices later.

He didn't trust the Cuban. He was useful and had done well getting Aalee into the country, but his usefulness was quickly coming to an end. The operation had been a failure. Alvarez had achieved his objectives, but the greater goal had been lost. The infidels still lived. There had been no public execution as he had planned. There had been no glory for Allah and no advancement of their cause.

Aalee plotted his next move as he looked out the window. It was a small two-bedroom farmhouse located off a dirt road. Thick trees and vegetation surrounded the small house on all sides, with a dirt field beyond that. It wasn't a terrible place to hole up. The vegetation would make it harder for traditional surveillance.

With Americans, it wasn't traditional surveillance that bothered him. It was the drones. He had seen many of his brothers in arms killed by drone strikes. He had narrowly escaped a strike himself. The idea kept him on edge. The drones were hard to hear, and nearly impossible to see. They orbited above, only to rain down death and destruction. *They were truly the instruments of the devil.*

That had been Iraq, though. In America, Aalee had never heard of any drone strikes. The Americans would never allow it against their own people. They would rather send their terrorists to trial, or arrest them and let them go later. *It was their weakness.* Aalee smiled.

Despite having armed security patrolling the front and rear, Aalee felt alone. Tariq and Kasim had been low-level players in his operation, although Tariq showed promise. He wondered which one had been killed. He hoped it had been Kasim. Kasim was a good fighter, but he wasn't smart. The Americans would have no trouble breaking him. He was glad neither of them knew the details of their operation in America, but it really wouldn't matter anymore.

Since he had been in America, he had not found the glory he had hoped for. The Brothers of Freedom lacked structure and leadership. It was nothing like the operations he had led in Iraq. He had no one he could confide in, and no one he could really trust. He needed a lieutenant.

Aalee was lost in thought when he was startled by a loud noise. The sound of gunfire was unmistakable. He could almost name the caliber based on the sound alone. As he dropped to the ground, a gunfight erupted outside. He could see the heads of his guards as they ran left and right past his window, firing their MAC-10 compact machine guns. The Americans were attacking.

Aalee scrambled to his bedroom as windows shattered and his men screamed in Arabic outside. He had to arm himself to fight. *He would not be taken alive, and it was the will of Allah to take as many of the infidels with him as he could.*

He pulled a chest out from under his bed and opened it. His men had told him about the chest when he first arrived. It was filled with all of the weapons he needed to make a last stand. He grabbed the fully automatic AK-47 and shoved the four spare magazines in his pocket. Then he grabbed two frag grenades and closed the chest.

Running back into the living room, Aalee slapped a fresh magazine in and chambered a round. He flipped the fire selector to the center position from SAFE to select fully automatic. Glass was still shattering around him as the gunfire was ongoing outside. His men were putting up a good fight.

He ducked behind the nearest window and peeked out. He noticed two of his men down on the ground in the front yard. Aalee spotted two men dressed in black tactical gear in the nearby tree line and began firing. Within seconds, the AK-47 was empty and he slapped in a fresh magazine.

As he was reloading, the incoming gunfire stopped for a moment. Aalee noticed the gunfire from his men had stopped as well. He knew his men hadn't stopped fighting. They were either captured or killed. He was alone. It didn't matter. *This would be his last stand.*

He chambered the round and stood up yelling, "ALLAHU AKBAR!"

He began to fire into the tree line when he was disoriented by a loud bang behind him. His ears were ringing and he couldn't see anything but white light. As he turned to fire, he felt a sharp pain in his chest and he struggled to catch his breath. He fell to the ground, grasping his chest.

As he did, he pulled the rings from the frag grenades in the inner pockets of his coat.

"Allahu Akbar," he repeated.

# CHAPTER TWENTY-ONE

S ean Baxter's binoculars confirmed what the satellite imagery in their briefing had told them. The lone farmhouse was surrounded by thick trees and vegetation. There was no clean approach.

Baxter had arrived early that morning at the Joint Terrorism Task Force building. Agent Thomas was grinning ear to ear as he relayed the news. An anonymous tip had come in overnight. Someone had identified Aalee going into the farmhouse. Satellite imagery confirmed men armed with automatic weapons outside and at least one heat source inside. They acquired a warrant from a federal judge and were given the green light to proceed with the operation.

Baxter sat in the large briefing room as Agent Thomas briefed the plan. FBI SWAT would be backed up by the Miami-Dade Sheriff's SWAT team. The first team would do a rapid deployment from their SUVs off the lone dirt road and use the vegetation for cover and concealment. The second team would fast rope from the Customs Blackhawk helicopter into the opening behind the house, and the helicopter would then provide sniper support. Any resistance would be responded to with lethal force, but the goal was to take Aalee and his men alive.

The three black GMC Yukon XL SUVs and two Sheriff's cars were parked in a row alongside the county road. Baxter, Thomas, and Agent Gus Spencer from the ATF were huddled over a map behind the second SUV, discussing the assault plan. They were all wearing navy blue Rapid Deploy body armor vests with FEDERAL AGENT written across the back in yellow. The Level III armor vests had anti-trauma panels and were rated for rifles up to .308 caliber. The vests could defend against both rifles and knife attacks.

"Our guys really have no cover if they start shooting," Baxter said, handing the binoculars to Agent Spencer. Spencer was easily a half-foot taller than Baxter and Thomas.

"That's why we have to move quickly," Thomas replied. "Once the first SUV drops off the Miami SWAT guys, the Blackhawk will come in and drop off our guys. If they start shooting, the Customs sniper will pick them off. We'll go in with the second SUV and enter the house from the side. It's a pretty basic layout. There are only four rooms total including the kitchen, and it is open to the living area."

"The latest imagery we have only shows five people total, including the person inside," Spencer interjected. "It should be a pretty clean operation."

Thomas turned to Baxter. His balding forehead was sweating. The weight of the body armor over his plus-sized body was causing him to exert himself in the heat.

"Baxter, I know this is your first takedown, but stick with me and you'll be fine," he said. It was the first glimpse of decency he'd shown since they had been working together on this case.

Baxter nodded as Thomas gave the lead Miami-Dade SWAT officer the thumbs up. He and his team were wearing full black tactical gear, each with an M4 hanging from their chests and a Sig Sauer P226 in a drop leg holster. Two SWAT officers on each side grabbed the handholds on top of the lead SUV and stood on the running boards.

Baxter and Thomas climbed into the second SUV. Spencer would stay behind and monitor communications from the road with the third SUV and local police. They would drive in to assist with prisoner transport once the area was clear.

"Alpha One ready," the Miami SWAT leader announced over the tactical frequency.

"Bravo One is one mike out," the FBI SWAT leader replied, indicating the helo was one minute away from dropping them off.

"Green light," Thomas directed over his radio.

The lead SUV took off, kicking up dust as it turned right and sped down the quarter mile long dirt road. Baxter followed a few moments later. The lead SUV slowed as it neared the edge of the vegetation. The four SWAT officers of Alpha Team jumped clear and disappeared into the tree line.

Baxter stopped short of the tree line and positioned the massive SUV into a roadblock. After Alpha Team was clear, the lead SUV turned around and joined them. They would block any attempted vehicle escape from the target house. With the house surrounded by fields and marsh, the dirt road was the only path of vehicle escape.

"Alpha One, in position," came the call over the radio. Alpha Team had made their way through the vegetation uneventfully. "Two armed individuals, north side."

Baxter could hear the thump of the Blackhawk in the distance. He strained to see it coming in from the southwest as he and Thomas exited the SUV. He found the black dot on the horizon as he met Thomas at the rear of the SUV. Within minutes, they would be storming the farmhouse.

The calm before the storm was broken as the black and gold Blackhawk came in over the tree line and gunfire erupted. One of the guards had gotten spooked and started firing at the helicopter. Alpha Two took down the guard out in the open with a carefully placed bullet to the temple, but the other guard had already taken cover. The firefight had begun.

The Blackhawk aborted the drop and circled around as the Customs sniper took aim. With his SCAR-17S rifle chambered in .308 and a Leupold high-powered scope, he was well equipped for the task, taking out the remaining guard in the open on the southern side of the house. That left two guards hiding and shooting back.

With little concealment, Alpha Team took up prone positions and started firing back. The guard at the southern end of the house was using a three-foot high stack of wood and trying to shoot at the helicopter as it passed. The guard on the northern end of the house hid behind a flipped over table under the front porch and was blind firing into the tree line, leaving Alpha Team without a shot.

The Blackhawk made another orbit around the farmhouse. With the southern guard in his sights, the sniper took a deep breath and squeezed the trigger. The bullet ripped right through the exposed guard's neck.

"Southern tango down," the sniper called on their tactical frequency.

"Let's move up," Thomas said, motioning to Baxter. Baxter drew his issued Sig Sauer P228 chambered in 9MM from his tactical drop leg holster and followed. They proceeded up the road into the vegetation, staying low and out of sight.

With the southern area of the farmhouse clear, the Blackhawk pulled into a hover over the farmhouse. The four

FBI SWAT members of Bravo Team in black tactical gear and olive drab flight suits fast roped down from the helicopter before it cut the large rope and climbed back into an overhead orbit. They met at the back door near the pile of wood.

"Bravo One, in position, stacking up," the team leader said. They were preparing to breach and enter through the back door.

"Bravo One, hold position," Thomas directed. The team leader acknowledged.

"Alpha One and Two flanking west, Three and Four hold position with covering fire," the Alpha Team leader directed. They began moving to the right using the vegetation for concealment as the other two team members on the opposite side of the road laid down covering fire to keep the guard's head down.

"Let's go," Thomas said to Baxter. He motioned for him to follow, and he waddled his way through the thick brush, attempting to follow Alpha Team moving west.

More gunfire erupted from the house, this time from inside. It appeared to be coming from one of the windows. It was much louder than the MAC-10s had been, and a different cadence. Alpha Three and Four returned fire, shattering nearby windows.

Reaching the flank of the northern guard, Alpha One took aim with his Trijicon 4 x 32 ACOG scope. The northern guard popped up after reloading to continue shooting into the tree line. Alpha One had his opportunity. A smooth pull of the trigger sent the round ripping through the guard's chest.

"Tango down," he announced. The AK-47 continued firing wildly in the vicinity of Alpha Three and Four, but it didn't appear to be aimed.

Thomas and Baxter followed the two Miami SWAT members to the western door. Despite the firefight, they were relatively close to some semblance of the original plan.

"Go nonlethal," Thomas directed over the tactical frequency as they reached the door. The lead SWAT members of both doors pulled out their shotguns. Their rifles had been using live rounds, but each team had two members with shotguns loaded with nonlethal beanbag rounds. The rounds would be enough to incapacitate or stun, but not enough to kill. Thomas wanted no mistakes to ensure at least Aalee was taken alive to stand for his crimes and for possible intelligence into other attacks.

Alpha One looked back and gave Thomas a thumb up. Based on the layout of the house, Bravo Team would enter first, having more ground to cover, followed by Alpha Team. According to the plans of the house, the back door led through a bathroom and into the main living area. The western door opened into the attached kitchen. The original plan did not involve the agents entering the house before the hostiles were secured, but Thomas had gotten impatient during the firefight. He wanted Aalee alive.

Baxter adjusted his grip on his Sig P228. His heart was racing, and the adrenaline was in full effect. He had no idea what waited on the other side of the door. He hoped Thomas knew what he was doing.

"Bravo Team, bang and clear, Alpha Team five seconds," Thomas said into his radio, directing them to throw a flash bang into the main living room and clear the room. Alpha Team would enter and assist clearing five seconds after the flash bang.

Both team leaders acknowledge. Bravo One opened the back door as Bravo Two stepped in and threw the flash bang grenade into the living room. With a loud pop, the grenade detonated, disorienting any within its radius. Bravo One then entered the room, sweeping left and right as his team followed covering his flanks.

On the western door, Alpha Two opened as Alpha One entered with his shotgun ready. He immediately saw Aalee stumbling, covering his face with one hand and clutching his weapon with the other. As Bravo Team entered the living room,

Alpha One fired a beanbag round directly into Aalee's chest, knocking him back.

"Clear," the SWAT leader called. Thomas pushed him out of the way as he headed for Aalee.

Baxter still hadn't made it through the kitchen when he heard someone yell, "Grenade!"

He dove to the ground behind the kitchen bar and covered his head as the two blasts rocked the small house. Time seemed to stand still for Baxter, but the sound was deafening. He hit the ground and then saw nothing but darkness.

# CHAPTER TWENTY-TWO

*Homestead, FL*

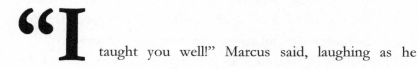taught you well!" Marcus said, laughing as he

slapped Spectre on the shoulder. They were standing behind the counter of the large indoor range as Spectre had just finished retelling the story of his trip to Chloe's parents' house. The store wouldn't open for two more hours, but Spectre had decided to go in early since he couldn't sleep. He knew Marcus would be there. He wasn't sure Marcus ever left.

Spectre nodded with a forced smile. He hated to admit that Marcus was right. He had plenty of training with the Air Force and its 9MM M9 qualifications, but he didn't really start to learn until he met Marcus. The former Marine Sniper and Certified NRA Firearms Instructor was an expert. He had taken Spectre under his wing and taught him everything he knew with a steady diet of fear, sarcasm, and ridicule to emphasize his teaching points. Spectre had gone from an average gun enthusiast who qualified by the Air Force's standards, to earning his NRA Firearms Instructor certification and giving Marcus a run for his money during their monthly run-throughs in the company's reconfigurable shoot house. The training had saved his life.

"So what did her bitch mother say when you untied her, or did you leave her tied up for the cops?" Marcus asked. He found the mental image of a former politician bound and gagged to be highly amusing.

"She didn't say anything," Spectre replied.

"Fucking figures. She probably thinks you were responsible for it."

Spectre shrugged. "But what bothered me was what Jack said when I untied him. He was very concerned about Chloe. He had no idea what happened, but he wanted me to see about her. He thought she might be in danger." Spectre suddenly got quiet.

Marcus glanced over at him. "I know we haven't talked much about it, but I'm sorry about Chloe. Unfortunately, it's a risk in the business we all accepted at one point or another."

Spectre was lost in thought. He had been lost in his thoughts for a couple of days. The e-mail had sent him over the edge. He could deal with the breakup, and Marcus was right, aviation was a deadly business. He'd lost friends before. He was even starting to compartmentalize the shootout, but the e-mails were too much. *Who was Victor? How could she keep a straight face while he busted his ass to work things out?*

Marcus attempted to drag Spectre out of his daydreaming. "So what did the Feds tell you? Who were the terrorist assholes?"

"The guys in the house were low-level guys. I think one was from Pakistan, but do you remember that guy Director Browning was talking about back at Customs?"

Marcus raised his eyebrows. "Aalee? The asshole they didn't have enough money to track?"

"Yeah, that's the one. They think he's behind the whole thing. I couldn't believe it." Spectre realized what he said a few seconds after the words left his mouth. He knew he had just triggered another one of Marcus's political rants. There was nothing he could do, but wince and hope he was wrong.

"I knew it! I fucking *knew* it! Those fucking Democrats, the party of which Representative Ridley was a card-carrying member, did this! They started with handcuffing the military. Then that wasn't good enough, not enough servicemen and women were dying, so they stopped advanced interrogation techniques. Terrorists had to have lawyers. They were cutting off soldiers' heads, but they deserved rights!" Marcus was fuming.

"Marcus, breathe," Spectre said, holding his hands up to try to calm him down. It was no use.

"Then this new prick gets into the big house in Washington, and they all hold hands and sing the song of unicorns and rainbows. The seas would part! Wars would be over! And Ridley was at the front, singing right in tune. She voted for the budget cuts! She *voted* for it! Ha! Look what happens, bitch!"

"Marcus, please, let's take this to your office." Spectre was trying to usher Marcus into the back office. They had been chatting for a while and the first of the other employees began to arrive.

"It's just so poetic, Cal," Marcus said, finally catching his breath. "You think there's no karma, no bigger system, but then this happens. Congresswoman votes to cut Homeland Security and gets herself kidnapped by a piece of shit terrorist. You just can't make this shit up!"

"Hey, easy there. She's still human. She just lost her daughter. Her handicapped son is in ICU, and she and her husband both got the crap beat out of them. It's more than just politics, Marcus."

As they entered Marcus's office, Spectre took a seat on the couch against the wall as Marcus sat in his executive leather chair. Various shooting awards and antique firearms lined the walls of the spacious room. Behind Marcus was an old World War II recruiting poster with a Marine in dress blues that simply said, "READY" and directed applicants to their nearest recruiting station.

"I know, and it sucks that it happened, but come on. Elections have consequences. The world is a dangerous place."

"Ok, politics aside," Spectre was trying to get the conversation back on track, or at least away from giving Marcus an aneurysm. "The guy took off before the chaplain and I got there. Jack told me he had taken some pictures of them or something."

"Standard ransom, probably needed proof of life," replied Marcus.

"Yeah, but proof of life for whom?" Spectre leaned forward on the couch, bracing his elbows on both knees.

"What do you mean?"

"Abdul Aalee is a terrorist, right? Does some high-level kidnappings, blows shit up, whatever. But he does it to prove a point. It's not about money, so why does he need proof of life? Why not just make a video cutting their throats and post it on Al Jazeera?"

It made him sick to think about it, but it was what Spectre expected from terrorists like Aalee. Most famously, Spectre recalled American businessman Nick Berg, who had been beheaded at the hand of Al Qaeda terrorist Abu Musab Al-Zarqawi in Iraq in 2003. The video had been uploaded and spread throughout the internet reportedly in protest of American treatment of prisoners at Abu Ghraib. It was brutal and sickening.

"Maybe he wanted something. Sometimes they request the release of their terrorist buddies, or some other asinine demand like the Jews packing up and moving out of Israel."

"I guess you're right. It's just weird," Spectre said, leaning back.

"You look like shit man, you sure you don't want to take a few days and get your head right? I promise I'll even pay you for one or two," Marcus said with a wink.

"Yeah, I'm fine. I just need to get some sleep. I was out for a couple hours last night before the dog got me, then I couldn't get back to sleep so I came in. I figured you'd be here. Do you live here?" Spectre smirked.

"Only when I'm married," Marcus replied. Spectre knew Marcus had been married at least three times, maybe more. He had only known one of Marcus's exes, and she was tough, but then, exotic dancers in Miami generally were.

"Any of your exes ever cheat on you?" Spectre asked, thinking back to the laptop and the e-mails.

Marcus laughed. "Don't they all?"

"I'm serious. Did you ever find out one of them was cheating on you?"

Marcus stopped smiling. His forehead wrinkled as he considered the question.

"Yeah, my first wife cheated on me with a Navy asshole from the base. A fucking seaman! Do you believe that shit? I was a goddamned trained killer, and she picked some admin weenie who shuffled papers."

"How'd you find out?" Spectre still felt bad about going through Chloe's laptop. The whole sequence of events just made him feel dirty, like he was violating her right to privacy. But the result was even more disturbing.

"I walked in on them doing it on my bed. He was wearing my fucking boonie hat! I still don't feel bad about the beating I gave him. But back then, I only had non-judicial punishment and a forfeiture of pay. A slap on the wrist, all things considered. I can't imagine what would've happened today. I'm sure some kind of pussified sensitivity training and counseling."

"Wow, holy shit. Well, I think you might have been right about Chloe," Spectre admitted.

"She was cheating on you? Yeah man, I'm sorry, but chicks just don't fall out of love like that. She was boning someone else."

"Ok, I get that, but here's what I don't get, why would he have access to her e-mail address?"

Marcus gave Spectre a puzzled look. Spectre explained how he happened upon Chloe's laptop sitting on the nightstand. He described how he found the e-mails in the draft folder, talking about her feelings for him and the e-mail she signed with the name "Victor."

"You found these in the draft folder?" Marcus looked very concerned.

"Yeah, there was nothing in the inbox, sent items, or her deleted folder. I felt kind of stupid, but then I saw two drafts. One of them was signed 'Victor' and talking about seeing each other that night. That was the night of the crash." Spectre was shaking his head. He still couldn't believe Chloe might have cheated on him.

"You sure that wasn't a guy named Victor talking to her?"

"Why would he have her login info and be sending her e-mails from her own account?" Spectre was still very sleep deprived. He couldn't see where Marcus was going with this.

"I was just reading a book about this. Apparently, it's something spooks do. E-mails can be traced and tracked through IP addresses and other digital footprints. So they got around it by creating the modern day equivalent of cold drops.

One party would create a draft on an account with a common logon, and then the other party would respond using the same method. Since no e-mail was ever sent, it made it more difficult for cyber monitors to trace."

Spectre considered it for a moment. "But it was her personal e-mail account, why would they care if someone intercepted it anyway? I'm not NSA or CIA. Just a pissed off fiancé."

"Maybe it wasn't you they were trying to hide from," Marcus replied.

# CHAPTER TWENTY-THREE

*Everglades, FL*

**H**is senses came back online like an old computer booting up. First, he felt his head. It was throbbing worse than any migraine he had ever experienced. His body ached. It was as if he had just been hit with a semi truck. His ears were ringing, but amidst the constant pinging, he could hear a voice.

"Baxter, are you ok?"

Baxter tried to open his eyes. The sunlight was blinding. It took him a moment for his brain to process his surroundings. He was outside, lying in the grass. He could see trees around him, and a large black man standing over him.

"Hold on buddy, the medics are on their way." Baxter finally recognized the man. It was Agent Spencer from the ATF.

Baxter tried to speak. At first, he could produce nothing but a cough. His lungs felt like they were full of soot and ash.

"What happened?" he finally managed. He didn't remember anything. The last thing he remembered was driving the lumbering SUV down the gravel road. Everything after that was a blur. He had no idea where he was or how he had even gotten there.

Baxter tried to sit up. His ribs were killing him. He rubbed his forehead and noticed blood on his hands.

"You're ok buddy, don't try to move," Spencer said, nudging him back down.

The paramedics arrived and started tending to Baxter. They stabilized his neck and checked him for any life threatening wounds.

"I'm ok," he said, trying to sit up.

"Sir, don't try to move," the lead paramedic said.

He pushed him away. "No, really, I'm fine."

Baxter sat up, pushing the lead paramedic back. He saw a small farmhouse in front of him and people running everywhere. The windows had been blown out and the walls looked charred and peppered. Paramedics were tending to other people on the ground nearby.

"What happened?" Baxter repeated.

"Why don't you tell me, buddy?" Spencer replied. The paramedics were still busy checking his pupils, taking his pulse and other vital signs.

"Last thing I remember is driving the Yukon down the road with Thomas. Where's Thomas?"

Spencer frowned.

"Seriously, what the fuck happened?" Baxter asked impatiently. The paramedics were unstrapping his body armor. The outer fabric was torn and frayed. The FEDERAL AGENT on his back was barely readable anymore.

"There was an explosion of some kind. We got here as fast as we could. I dragged you out here. It was really bad in there..." Spencer trailed off, looking at the tattered farmhouse and wounded SWAT members everywhere.

"Where's Thomas?" Baxter insisted.

Spencer shook his head. "He didn't make it. The blast had to have killed him almost instantly. He was the closest one to it."

Baxter slumped. He was struggling to remember details. He had a faint image of Thomas pushing forward into a room, but he couldn't put it into context. Baxter looked over at the other medics tending to the injured. They were SWAT members.

Baxter could hear the rotors of a helicopter in the distance. He recognized it from earlier. The memory of the Blackhawk and firefight started coming back to him. It had delayed the operation, but Thomas wanted to push forward anyway.

"Jesus Christ," Baxter responded. It felt like a war zone. "What about those guys?"

"The CBP chopper is about to land in that field. We've got three critically wounded. They're being taken to the hospital. There were also two killed in the explosion. Three total, but come on, we've got to get you to the helicopter."

"I'm ok," Baxter replied, pushing Spencer away from helping him up. He struggled to his feet on his own. The paramedic hawked his movements, worried he might become disoriented and fall.

"You're not ok, Baxter."

"I'm not like those guys," he said, pointing to the men carrying two litters toward the ambulance. The Blackhawk was waiting in the clearing on the other side of the tree line near the dirt road.

"Maybe not, but you can't remember shit and you're pretty banged up. Helicopter or ambulance, your choice, but you're going to the hospital." Spencer left no room for interpretation in his voice. He meant what he said. The large man could be very persuasive. Baxter was glad he was on their side.

"Fine, I always wanted to ride in a helicopter anyway." Baxter pushed him out of the way and started walking toward the tree line.

"Hey buddy, wait for a second," Spencer said.

"Yeah?"

"The helicopter is that way," Spencer was pointing the opposite direction with his giant arm.

# CHAPTER TWENTY-FOUR

*Miami, FL*

**B**axter stood staring into the interrogation room through the one-way glass. He was watching Kasim Razvi sitting at the small interrogation table. The man looked nervous. He was fidgeting as his eyes darted around the room. Sweat was beading down his forehead onto his bandaged broken nose.

Baxter's forehead was also bandaged, covering the cuts he had received from the blast. He was still sore, having only been released from the hospital a few hours prior. It was late in the evening. The helicopter ride had been only fifteen minutes to the hospital, but one of the FBI SWAT members in critical condition had died en route.

As a non-critical case, he was triaged and sent to wait before doctors assessed his condition. He had a few cuts and bruises and a minor concussion. It was nothing major. His memories of the assault on the farmhouse and subsequent explosion were starting to come back to him. He was given a few painkillers, stitches, told to rest, and sent home.

But Baxter couldn't rest. He was new to the Joint Terrorism Task Force and his assignment in Homestead, but he wasn't new to law enforcement. He still needed answers. He wanted to close the case, for himself and for the brave men Aalee and his men had just murdered.

Agent Thomas was one of those men. Despite some of his methods, Baxter respected Thomas. He was an experienced agent. Baxter didn't necessarily agree with his techniques, and as Baxter pieced together the memories of the assault, he wished Thomas had been more patient and not tried to barge his way into an unsecure building.

All that didn't really matter to Baxter, though. The bottom line was that good men had fallen in the line of duty at the hands of a piece of shit terrorist thug. He didn't know the SWAT members of Alpha and Bravo Teams personally, but he knew Thomas had an ex-wife and two little girls.

"So are you going to talk to him or just watch him sweat?" the female voice from behind asked. Baxter turned around. She was a very attractive blonde with the bluest eyes he had ever seen. She reminded him of the stereotypical Dallas Cowboys Cheerleaders he loved watching during football season in Texas.

"I'm sorry?" Baxter replied. He had no idea who this woman was, but he was still dumbfounded at how hot she was. Her black pantsuit really fit her well.

"I'm Special Agent Michelle Decker from the FBI," she said, extending her hand. "I've been assigned from the Miami field office to continue Agent Thomas's investigation."

Baxter shook her hand. He recognized the name from an earlier phone call. She had contacted him to let him know she would be working the investigation and that Kasim would be in the Miami Federal Detention Facility that evening after being treated for his broken nose. She had set up the interrogation for him.

"It's nice to meet you," he finally replied. He shook off his moment of teenage sheepishness. He was a federal agent, not some high school senior, he told himself. *Attractive woman or not, he had work to do.*

"Thank you for letting me speak to him on such short notice," he said, tilting his head toward Kasim.

"No problem, but it works better if you're in there with him," she said with a smile. "It is getting late, you know."

"Right. Well then, let's get to it," Baxter replied.

"Do you want me to go in with you? In case things get rough and you can't handle it?" she asked with a wink.

"I'll be fine," he said as he walked out, closing the door behind him.

Baxter walked out of the observation room and into the hallway. He took a deep breath and exhaled slowly. He had been through several interrogations before, but never with an emotional tie. He would have to compartmentalize it. As much as he wanted to walk in and hit Kasim with a phone book, he knew that wouldn't yield results. He also wasn't sure anyone even used phone books anymore.

"I want to talk to my lawyer," Kasim said, looking up at Baxter as he walked in.

Baxter said nothing. He walked in calmly, pulled out the chair, and sat across the interrogation table from Kasim. He sat in silence, studying Kasim.

Kasim had beads of sweat dripping off his forehead. He was tapping his foot nervously on the ground, and his eyes were still darting around the room. The longer Baxter said nothing, the faster Kasim's cadence became. He was a nervous wreck.

"Mr. Razvi, I'm Special Agent Baxter from the Air Force Office of Special Investigations and the Joint Terrorism Task Force," Baxter finally said, breaking the silence.

"I said I want to speak to my attorney," Kasim replied defiantly. "I don't care to know who you are. I have rights in this country."

It took every ounce of patience Baxter had to not reach across the table and slam his head into the table. He took another deep breath.

"Mr. Razvi, I understand your concerns, and your attorney will be here soon, but I just have a few questions for you, and I won't bother you anymore," Baxter replied calmly.

"No. I want my attorney. You have to give me an attorney. I have rights!" Kasim shook his finger at Baxter.

"Mr. Razvi, you are a citizen of Pakistan here on an expired Student Visa. You are being held in connection with terrorist activities. You do not have rights. You will get your attorney, but you will be tried by a military tribunal and sent to Gitmo." Somehow, Baxter was still managing to keep his calm demeanor.

"You lie, Mr. Air Force Agent. You lie! Gitmo was closed by your President. I have rights in this country, Aalee told me so." Kasim's eyes were wild with a mix of fear and indignation.

"Abdul Aalee is dead," Baxter said flatly.

Kasim's expression changed to panic. Baxter allowed the news to sink in for a minute. He could almost see the hamster spinning the wheel in Kasim's head as he considered the gravity of the news.

"You lie again, Mr. Air Force. Aalee is not dead. He escaped before the infidel arrived," Kasim finally said rebelliously.

As if on cue, the door opened. Agent Decker walked in with a folder in hand. Baxter saw that it was marked "Aalee Report" and nodded. She placed it in front of Kasim on the table, winked at Baxter, and walked out. He couldn't help but stare at her butt as she walked away. *It was just wonderful.*

"What is this?" Kasim demanded.

"Open it," Baxter replied.

Kasim slowly opened the folder. In it were pictures, taken at the farmhouse, of Aalee's mangled body and face. There wasn't much left. Half of his bearded face had been obliterated by the blast. It was barely enough to identify him.

"We received a tip last night as to Aalee's whereabouts. One of your buddies ratted him out, and now this is what's left of him," Baxter said. He intentionally left out the details of the tip being called in anonymously and that Aalee had taken his own life. He didn't want to give Kasim the satisfaction that his hero might be a martyr. He wanted Kasim to feel like the network had been infiltrated and turned on itself.

Kasim said nothing. He sat in silence, his shoulders slumped, staring at the pictures. His foot tapping grew louder and increased in intensity.

"Now, Mr. Razvi, there's no reason for you not to help us. Aalee is dead. Help us put together the missing pieces and finish this. Cooperation will be very beneficial to you when you go before a tribunal."

Kasim put the pictures down and closed the folder. His eyes darted between Baxter and the one-way mirror. He knew he was being backed into a corner.

"No!" Kasim shrieked. "I have rights in America! You cannot make me talk. Allah will give me strength! We are Allah's soldiers. Abdul died a fierce warrior!" Kasim puffed out his chest and shook his fists defiantly. His foot tapping stopped as he began to feel he had gained the upper hand. He knew the Americans were weak and their freedoms and rights were their greatest weaknesses.

Baxter considered his options. As much as he wanted to, he knew beating the little coward to a bloody pulp would solve nothing, and would probably end his involvement in this case.

Kasim was obviously not responding to the kinder, gentler approach. His patience had finally run out.

"Look, you little shit," Baxter growled, standing from his metal chair. Kasim cowered as if Baxter was about to hit him. "I have tried to reason with you, but you are obviously too stupid to take the hint, so here's the truth. You are a terrorist. You were involved in the kidnapping of a former US Representative and the murder of an American on American soil."

Kasim said nothing as Baxter towered over him. He was still staring defiantly at Baxter. Baxter put both hands on the table and leaned closer to Kasim.

"Have you ever heard of ISI?" Baxter's voice softened.

Kasim's eyes widened. His defiance instantly melted away. He tried to look away.

"That's right, asshole. Pakistani intelligence, or more accurately, Inter-Services Intelligence. You've heard of them?"

Kasim said nothing.

"I'll take that as a yes. You see, Kasim, as I mentioned earlier, you're a citizen of a foreign country. Pakistan, right?" Baxter didn't wait for a response. "Well, in Pakistan, you don't have the same rights as you think you do here, would you agree?"

Kasim nodded nervously. He had heard of people being detained by the ISI and never coming home, or worse, returning with missing fingers and toes and a permanent limp. They were ruthless in their interrogation methods, perhaps even more so than he had seen in his fellow Brothers of Freedom.

Baxter stepped back and folded his arms, letting the question hang in the air for a bit as Kasim considered the implications.

"Now, I know you're not too bright, just being a low-level guy and all, so let me spell it out clearly for you. It just so happens, we have an extradition agreement with Pakistan. Know what that means? It means I have a ticket on a CIA transport with your name on it straight to Islamabad if you don't start cooperating. And I hear they're not quite as concerned about rights of suspected terrorists as you think I am."

Kasim started shaking his head.

"Or, you can cooperate. You'll get your lawyer and a nice air-conditioned jail cell. I'll even put in a good word for you. Choose carefully."

"What do you want to know?" Kasim was almost pleading with him. He couldn't stand the thought of an ISI agent pulling his fingernails off with a pair of pliers, or cutting his toes off. He would be tortured and die in a rotten jail cell.

"What were you going to do with the Representative and her family?"

"I don't know!" Kasim screamed. "You have to believe me! Abdul never told me anything. He only told us what to do and how and when to do it. He kept everything secret! I swear!"

The threat had worked. Kasim was scared shitless. Baxter knew he needed to calm Kasim down. At this rate, the nervous little man would give himself a heart attack before he produced useful information.

"Ok, I believe you Kasim, but if you lie to me, our deal is off," Baxter explained. "Do you understand?"

Kasim nodded.

"Let's start from the beginning. How did you meet Aalee?" Baxter pulled out a notepad from his cargo pants pocket and began taking notes.

Kasim explained how he had been recruited by a cleric in Pakistan. He received training in the Tribal Region of Pakistan in a camp near the town of Razmak. It was there he received indoctrination training, learning basic armed and unarmed combat, bomb making, and English.

Baxter scribbled notes as Kasim described the operation in Razmak. It wouldn't be useful for his case, but he knew it would pay dividends when passed on to the intelligence community later.

Kasim continued, explaining how he had made it into the US on a Student Visa, and had to work and attend classes until activated. Initially, he had no idea when his cell would be activated. He and Tariq lived together in a small two-bedroom apartment. They only knew each other, and Tariq kept contact with their handlers in Miami. He had no idea how they communicated, but he suspected it had something to do with the computer.

Then a few weeks before the kidnappings, Tariq came home one day and announced that they were finally going to do Allah's work. Kasim explained that Tariq briefed him on Abdul Aalee, the great warrior for Allah, and that they had finally received their directions.

Kasim explained how they picked up Aalee from the Marathon Key marina. He was hard to recognize using a picture because he shaved his beard except for a mustache. He was on foot, and had just convinced the Americans that he was there legally. He was still concerned about them though. He thought he was being chased, but they never encountered any roadblocks or other authorities.

"So Aalee stayed with you?" Baxter asked, still scribbling notes on his notepad.

"He slept in my bed, and I slept on the pull out sofa. I thought he would have something for us immediately, but if he did, he didn't tell us. He had several cell phones that he talked on constantly. Mostly in English, but not always."

Baxter's eyebrows arched. "Not always?"

"Sometimes it was in Spanish. At least I think it was. That's what Tariq called it."

Baxter continued his note writing and underlined SPANISH on his notepad. "So he got his instructions on a cell phone?" he prodded.

"No, I don't think so. A few days after he arrived, he made us load furniture in a truck, and then he went to a storage building in Hialeah. Can I get some water?"

Baxter made a drinking motion to the mirror and continued writing his notes.

"Who was he meeting?"

Agent Decker walked in and handed both men water bottles. Baxter made it a point not to stare this time as she walked out.

Kasim took a sip of water and continued, "I don't know. They never told me anything, but I did hear him say Victor when he was talking to Tariq."

Baxter wrote down the name and underlined it as well. It was a solid lead, but finding a Victor that spoke Spanish in Miami was a pretty broad search. It would be easier to find a Victor that didn't speak Spanish.

Kasim continued, explaining how Aalee gave them their instructions. He knew how many people would be in the house and where they would likely be. He even knew how many animals they had. Kasim remembered being impressed by the level of detail Aalee had. He was a great leader.

Kasim described their approach to the house. They parked the minivan down a gravel road out of sight of the main road near the house. When they reached the house, they split up and surrounded the house. Kasim had been told to enter the house from the side, Abdul would enter from the front, and Tariq had the back.

"But then I tripped and knocked over a trash can," Kasim admitted. "The old man came out and found our van, so I hit him on the side of the head with my gun when he came back near where I was hiding. I thought I killed him. Then I heard a gunshot and ran back inside. Abdul killed the fat woman. I don't know why."

The men tied up the hostages then went back outside and dragged the old man back in. They put all of the hostages in the laundry room. Kasim described the ruthlessness of Aalee and his brutality with the handicapped boy.

"So did Aalee use his cell phone while you were waiting?" Baxter asked.

"Yes. He made several calls, and then took pictures of the hostages before he left and put Tariq in charge."

"Did you happen to hear anything at all? Any names? Do you know who he was talking to?"

"I think it was the same person from the meeting at the storage place. I only overhead him a few times, but I know one time he said Moss."

Baxter stopped writing. He remembered reading the old man's statement. It said that Aalee had mentioned his daughter's name over the phone, and that's why he feared for her safety as well.

"Chloe Moss?"

"I don't know. I only heard Moss... It was right before he took the pictures and left."

Kasim then described the assault by Martin, and Tariq being killed. He thought the CIA had found them and was going to kill them for kidnapping the woman. He was very glad to be arrested.

Baxter thanked Kasim for his cooperation and walked out. Agent Decker was waiting for him in the hallway.

"That was some good work in there," she said, putting her hand on his shoulder.

"Thanks, but I have a lot of work to do," he said, waving his notepad.

"Yes, *we* do," she replied. "I'll get started on tracking down any locals we've been tracking with aliases by the name of 'Victor.'"

Baxter rolled his eyes. "Yeah, in Miami? Good luck with that."

"Gotta start somewhere. Anyway, hey, the last part, about Moss."

"What about her? The father said the same thing," Baxter replied.

"She's Air Force, right?"

"Yeah, she was killed in the crash off the coast a couple days ago," Baxter replied, remembering his interview with Martin.

"I read the transcript of your interview. Maybe you should try talking to Martin again. I think he might know more than he's letting on."

# CHAPTER TWENTY-FIVE

*Homestead ARB, FL*
*Air Force Office of Special Investigations, Det 9*

S pectre arrived at the OSI building just before 10 AM. He had been called a few hours earlier by Special Agent Baxter, asking for a meeting to discuss new developments in the case. Baxter had been intentionally vague over the phone, causing Spectre to wonder if somehow he had become a person of interest.

He backed his truck into the parking space and got out. The airfield was eerily quiet. All of the military aircraft were still grounded after the incident. There weren't even jets turning for routine maintenance. *At this time of the day on a weekday, it was just weird.*

Spectre walked into the main entrance of the tiny, windowless building. The reception area was small, with only a

few chairs and a magazine rack. He walked up to the one-way
mirror where the receptionist would normally be and rang the
buzzer. The building seemed empty.

A few minutes later, the door made a metallic click and
opened. Spectre was expecting Agent Baxter, but instead found
himself face to face with a stunning blonde, dressed in a gray
pantsuit.

"Mr. Martin?" she asked, only opening the door halfway.

"Yes, ma'am," he replied awkwardly.

"Have a seat. We'll be with you in a moment. We're just
going over a few new notes."

Spectre nodded and sat down. He had no idea who the
woman was, but she certainly had his attention. It was almost
distracting. He hoped she wasn't planning to question him. He
was sure he would end up saying something inappropriate if she
did.

Spectre grabbed the latest copy of Sports Illustrated from
the nearby magazine rack and settled in. He flipped through the
pages, but was paying no attention to what he was looking at.
His attention was still on the startlingly hot blonde that had just
walked off.

Closing the door behind her, Decker walked down the
hallway past the empty OSI offices and made a left into the
conference room where Baxter was still going over the notes.

Special Agent Michelle Decker had been on the fast track in
the FBI since her first assignment. A law school graduate,
Decker had briefly worked for her county's District Attorney's
office before deciding she wanted to be on the frontlines,
investigating rather than prosecuting.

She had been an agent for nearly five years, first working
counterterrorism in Boston before picking up her follow-up
assignment to the Miami field office. A Georgia native, she
found the South Florida climate much more appealing and was
eager to jump into one of the nation's busiest offices.

"Martin is here," she announced, resuming her place at the conference table. Her notes were scattered everywhere, among empty Red Bull cans. They had been going over the case for three hours.

Baxter ignored her. "So you were saying you've got a lead on this Victor guy?"

"Well, sort of," she said, pulling up the legal pad that she had been taking notes with. "The guy that just called was our lead analyst down here. He searched every database we have, narrowing his search to activity within the last three months. As you can imagine, it was still quite a big list."

Baxter nodded, hoping she would just get to the point. He didn't like to keep people waiting. It was one of his biggest pet peeves, but he needed for them to be on the same page before talking to Martin.

"Anyway, trying to cross reference them with known Al Qaeda or Brothers of Freedom associations was a big goose egg, surprisingly enough. So he called his contact at the NSA and tried referencing it against foreign intelligence aliases."

"What did he come up with?"

"Five names. He's e-mailing them to us now with dossiers from the CIA. Should be on the secure side." She was referring to their classified network, designed specifically to handle message traffic classified SECRET or higher. CIA intelligence usually required sensitive handling, and despite The Patriot Act and improved cross talk among agencies, it was still a miracle to even get cooperation from the spy branches of the government.

"Great. Can you go download them and print them off? I'll start with Martin," he said, standing up to walk out.

Decker picked up some of the empty cans and threw them away on her way out. The classified computers were located in the vault at the end of the hallway. Since Baxter's boss was gone on paternity leave for his second child, the office was virtually empty. Baxter was the de facto boss.

"Mr. Martin," he said, opening the heavy wooden door, "thanks for coming out on such short notice. Can I get you anything?"

Spectre shook his head as Baxter gestured for him to follow into the conference room. He asked Spectre to have a seat and offered him water as Spectre took his seat at the head of the conference table.

"Your new partner is a lot better looking. What happened to the other guy? Sale on doughnuts this morning?" Spectre joked.

"He was killed yesterday," Baxter replied somberly.

Spectre's face turned red. Joking probably wasn't the best approach at a time like this, but this was much worse.

"Holy shit, I'm so sorry. I had no idea. Can you tell me what happened?"

"He was killed yesterday during the attempted apprehension of Abdul Aalee. You might remember him from our previous interview," Baxter replied.

"Yeah, I remember. Attempted? Is he still at large?" Spectre noticed the bandages on Baxter's forehead and put the two together. *The terrorist piece of shit had somehow gotten the best of them during their attempt to apprehend him.*

"No, he killed himself in the process. Took out several good men."

"I'm really sorry," Spectre offered.

"We brought you here today to discuss your association with Chloe Moss in a little more depth," Baxter said, changing the subject.

Agent Decker walked in with files in hand, as Spectre started to explain their previous history. He was struck again by her beauty. She carried herself with a high level of professionalism mixed with grace and attractiveness. She also seemed to have a "don't fuck with me" air about her, something Spectre was sure many men had experienced firsthand.

She handed the files to Baxter and sat down across from him. Baxter nodded at Spectre to continue.

"We were engaged, until a couple of weeks ago, when she just abruptly broke it off," Spectre explained.

Both agents scribbled notes as Spectre explained how she ended their relationship. He felt like he had told the story a hundred times in the last few weeks, but it never stopped being painful. He still didn't quite understand any of it. He thought about the laptop, but decided to leave that detail out for the time being.

"Tell me about the day of the crash, did she say anything before she went to work?" Decker asked, her deep blue eyes almost penetrating Spectre.

"I didn't see her. We slept in separate rooms after the breakup. She was on a night schedule, so I went to work before she was even awake. When I got home that night, I went straight to bed."

"Did her behavior change leading up to the crash? Do anything out of the ordinary? Talk to anyone new?" she asked.

"You mean was she cheating on me?"

"I'm not suggesting anything, Mr. Martin, just wondering if her associations changed," she replied.

"Yes. She stopped associating with me. Otherwise, I don't know. I work at a range that's open until nine. A lot of nights, I wouldn't get home until ten or later. Her car was always home when I got home."

Baxter separated the pictures from the dossiers and pushed them to Spectre. "Do any of these men look familiar to you?"

Spectre flipped through the pictures. They were all Hispanic men in their mid thirties to early forties. Each picture seemed to be some sort of high fidelity surveillance shot.

"No, should they?" Spectre replied, handing the pictures back to Baxter.

"What about the name, 'Victor?'" Decker asked.

Spectre froze. He thought back to the laptop. He had intentionally left it out because he was embarrassed that she might have cheated on him. Despite Marcus's paranoia that they were hiding from the government, Spectre didn't think it was relevant to a case about a kidnapping. Chloe was probably dead. The rescue efforts had long since turned to recovery, despite being hampered by rough seas. There was no need to tarnish her memory.

Decker leaned forward. She could see by Spectre's facial expressions that she had struck a nerve. *He knew something.*

"Mr. Martin, anything you can tell us, no matter how insignificant you think it may be, could help us out in this case," she prodded.

Spectre told them about the laptop he had searched through two nights prior. He explained the e-mails he had found in her draft folder, and how she had been seemingly corresponding with a man named Victor.

"How did you know about Victor?" Spectre asked as he finished his story. "I didn't think it had anything to do with the kidnapping."

"The man you subdued told us about him. He overheard Aalee mention the name on the phone," Baxter replied.

"You don't think Chloe was involved in kidnapping her own parents, do you?" Spectre asked incredulously.

Baxter sat back and pondered the question. Chloe's relationship to the kidnapping was puzzling. She had seemingly no motive to be involved in the kidnapping of her parents, and more importantly, she was presumed dead. But the e-mail draft didn't sit well with him. He knew it was a technique of intelligence agents and terrorists developed in the wake of cyber monitoring. *She was trying to hide something.*

"You said her last message was time stamped the day of her mishap?" Baxter asked.

"Yeah, she must have sent it from work," Spectre replied.

Baxter was still mulling the possibilities over in his head. She intended to meet with this Victor person that night. *She had at least a personal relationship with him. Had he been using her to get to the family? Or were they in it together?* His mental block was still the crash. *Had she been planning to meet with him after the flight?* And then it hit him.

"You flew F-16s, is that correct?" Decker shot from across the table.

"Yes, I had just over one thousand hours in them," Spectre replied.

"Is it possible to fake a crash?" she asked, tapping her notepad with her pen. Baxter looked at her from across the table. She had beaten him to the punch. *She was sharp.*

Spectre's eyes widened. He hadn't considered the possibility before. He had been so caught up in the breakup and the events of the last couple of days that he had never stopped to consider the possibility that she hadn't crashed at all.

"Possible? Yes? Probable? No," Spectre replied. The e-mail and the lack of wreckage were fairly damning pieces of evidence in the case for Chloe faking her own accident, but it just didn't seem like something she or any other U.S. Military pilot would do. She just didn't seem like the type to betray her country. But then again, weeks prior, he didn't think she'd be the type to break up with him either.

"I see. Thank you for your time, Mr. Martin. That's all I have for now. Do you have anything else, Agent Baxter?" Decker asked as she finished writing the last of her notes.

"Not at this time," Baxter said as he stood to walk Spectre out. "Well, Mr. Martin, you've been more than helpful, if you think of anything else—"

"Wait! Mind if I make a phone call? I think I know how we can find out," Spectre interrupted.

# CHAPTER TWENTY-SIX

*Homestead ARB, FL*

**E**quipped with the latest ASR-11 Digital Airport Surveillance Radar (DASR), Homestead Air Reserve Base's Terminal Approach Control Facility was among the most advanced in the country. With Primary Surveillance Radar coverage out to 60 miles and Secondary Surveillance Radar Transponder coverage out to 120, the facility could track targets far beyond the capabilities of most facilities.

Spectre stood at the entrance of the Homestead control tower with Agents Decker and Baxter. He had called his friend Chris Fritz after the earlier questioning session with the two agents. Chris happened to be working in the office that morning and not on a shift as Tower Supervisor, so he was available to meet with them.

The door buzzed open and Chris appeared. He was wearing khaki shorts and a Florida Gators polo shirt with sunglasses hanging around his neck and flip-flops. Spectre always admired the casual dress code the tower guys strictly adhered to when he used to sit in the tower as Supervisor of Flying. Chris did not disappoint.

"Hey Spectre, long time no see, bud!" he said, reaching out to shake Spectre's hand.

"Good to see you too, Chris, thanks for letting us visit on such short notice," Spectre said as the three walked in.

Chris led them to the elevator and they all piled in. The radar room was located on the fourth floor of the fourteen-floor control tower.

"It's no problem, man. Listen, I'm sorry about your girlfriend," Chris said apologetically.

"Thanks, Chris." He didn't feel like correcting him and getting into the same discussion about the breakup he had been involved in seemingly hundreds of times over the last few weeks.

"Who are your buddies?" Chris asked, obviously eying Decker. She shot him the "don't fuck with me" glare Spectre had been expecting, causing Chris to look away toward Baxter.

"Chris, this is Special Agent Baxter with OSI and Special Agent Decker with the FBI," Spectre said. "I have no idea what their first names are, but it's probably not 'Special Agent.'"

"Well, it's nice to meet you guys anyway, I hope my buddy Spectre is not in too much trouble," Chris laughed.

The two agents looked at each other, creating an awkward silence as they rode the elevator up the remaining floors.

As they exited the elevator and walked toward the radar room, Chris turned to Spectre. "You said you wanted to see the new radar facility, but what's this really about?"

"I'll tell you when we're inside," Spectre said, motioning for Chris to keep walking. They made their way to the double doors and stopped. There was a sign warning of the federal penalties involved with interfering with active air traffic control operations on the door, as well as a no cell phones sign.

"Cell phones can go in these boxes," Chris said, putting his cell phone in a slot on the wall. The three followed suit. Baxter pulled out a pager and put it in as well.

"Holy shit, I didn't know people still owned those. Do you deal crack on the side?" Chris joked as he swiped his badge and the magnetic door lock clicked open.

The group entered the dark room. There were two controllers sitting at radar screens, working approach and departure control for the airport. They both nodded as the four walked in. Spectre didn't recognize either of them. Not surprising since he hadn't been back in the tower in many years.

"We need to look at the radar tapes from the other night," Spectre said. His voice was low so as not to disturb the controllers.

"The other night? You mean from the crash? Whoa!" Chris said, putting up his hands. "You know I can't do that. The Safety Investigation Board has those locked down. Safety privilege and all that. You'll have to ask them."

Decker leaned over to Baxter. "We can get a court order if we need to," she whispered.

Spectre held up his hand. "That won't be necessary. Chris, I know you're not supposed to, but I also know you keep backups in here of everything."

"We do, for a month a time, then it gets purged, but everything is recorded on the fifth floor," Chris said.

"Listen, man, I know this is not your thing, but it would mean a lot to me if you could help us out. *For Chloe.*" Spectre gritted his teeth as he said it. He hated playing the false widower card, especially knowing that she might have been cheating on him all along.

"Look man, you know I could lose my job if someone found out," Chris pleaded.

"You're aiding with a federal investigation," Baxter offered. "You won't get into any trouble for helping."

"Alright, Spectre, I'll help, give me a minute," Chris said after a long sigh. He walked off to a vacant terminal and went to work, loading the recording and cueing it up to the night of the crash.

"Good work, Martin," Decker whispered. Spectre looked back and nodded. She was grinning. It made him feel like a high-schooler whose crush had just acknowledged his existence.

"Alright, what are you looking for?" Chris said, readying the playback.

"According to the initial report, the crash was at 2100 local, so let's start there," Baxter interjected.

Chris cued the playback for 2100 and stopped. He explained what the icons and symbols meant. The display had the airspeed, altitude, and transponder code of each aircraft displayed next to it.

"Play it real time," Spectre said. They watched as four aircraft on the north side of the airspace maneuvered toward the two aircraft in the south. The two aircraft in the south started in formation, but then the two blips separated. One maneuvered forty-five degrees to the east, while the other turned away to the south and began a rapid descent.

"That's Chloe," Spectre said, pointing at the blip turning away. His heart began racing. It was the first time he had seen any depiction of the crash. They watched as the blip descended from twenty thousand feet as the airspeed increased. After a few seconds, the blip vanished. Chris stopped the playback.

"I'm so sorry, Spectre," he said solemnly.

"Can you rewind it just a few seconds? Last known position," Spectre said, pointing at the screen.

Chris sighed softly. He felt bad for Spectre. "Sure thing, man."

"Stop!" Spectre said just as the blip reappeared. The altitude showed five hundred feet, and the airspeed read five hundred knots.

"Why wouldn't there be more data past five hundred feet?" Decker asked.

"This radar is good, but that's the last known transponder position, and it lags a bit," Chris responded.

"Can you turn off the secondary transponder read out on here and just show primary radar returns?" Spectre asked.

"It's too far out for a primary, bud, that's over a hundred miles from here," Chris replied apologetically.

"What about the feed from Key West? Aren't you guys integrated with their feed now?" Spectre asked. He was hopeful that they might get some proof one way or another. Maybe they could get a primary return lower than the last known transponder position, or if their theory was correct, a primary return of her flying away.

Chris navigated through a few menus to find the Key West Primary Surveillance Radar and then decluttered the screen. The radar blips were replaced with jagged lines to indicate their source. The screen no longer displayed altitude or airspeed information. Chris returned the playback to the start of Chloe's maneuver and hit play.

The jagged lines maneuvered as before, but with more lag, using the four-second refresh rate of the radar instead of the high fidelity reporting from the aircraft's own transponder. Her aircraft maneuvered like before, and then disappeared. Chris stopped the tape.

"I know what you must be going through, this is tough for all of us that knew her as well," Chris said.

"Keep playing," Spectre prodded.

Chris sighed and hit play. He couldn't imagine what he would be doing in the same situation if his wife were in that plane. He figured he would have been in denial too.

A few seconds after the jagged line symbolizing Chloe's jet disappeared, it reappeared a few miles farther south.

"Holy shit!" Chris said, stopping the playback.

"No, keep playing!" Spectre said, tapping Chris on the shoulder. Chris hit play. The jagged line flew a few more miles and then disappeared.

"Wait, where did it go?" Baxter asked.

"Seventy miles," Chris replied. "That's as far as this radar can see. I'm surprised it even saw that far with her as low as she was. Good thing it was over water, but holy shit!"

"Thanks Chris, but we need to go," Spectre said as he turned to walk out.

"No problem, I can't believe she's still alive. Where did she go?" Chris asked frantically.

"That's what we're going to find out. Promise me you'll keep this to yourself?" Spectre asked, turning back to Chris and putting both hands on his shoulders.

"Yeah man, no sweat, but when you figure it out, you have to tell me, ok?"

"I just hope we figure it out," Spectre replied.

# CHAPTER TWENTY-SEVEN

*Castro Field, Cuba*

The room was dark and warm. There was no furniture and nothing to sit on except for a rug laid out in the corner of the room. The walls were plain, with no windows or decorations of any kind. But despite all of that, it didn't look like a prison cell. It was just an empty room, like a large utility closet or office that had never been furnished. She didn't think it was a prison cell, but the locked door and lack of exit options suggested otherwise.

She sat in the corner, her curly light brown hair frizzed by the heat and humidity. It was hot, much hotter than she had expected. She was wearing a gray t-shirt and jeans that had been given to her when she arrived. They didn't quite fit.

For Chloe Moss, nothing about her situation quite fit. She had been in her makeshift prison cell for God knows how long.

They had told her to change when she arrived, then locked her in this room with only a honey bucket in the corner for relieving herself. It was not exactly the level of treatment she expected.

She had done everything they asked of her, landing her F-16 at Castro Field in the dead of night. The airfield wasn't even lit, yet she managed to make a smooth landing with the help of her Night Vision Goggles. It was something she had never even tried before, but if the A-10 pilots could do it, so could she. And in her opinion, she did it well, contrary to what her upgrade flight grade sheets from the Gators had said. *It was too bad they couldn't see what she had just pulled off.* She could've shown them that she was anything but "Slightly Below Average."

Northwest of Corralillo in Cuba, Castro Field was a relatively unknown airbase to most Americans. Officially, it did not exist. Constructed in the farmlands between La Teja and Corralillo, the base had been started as part of a strategic agreement with the Russians in 2008. It was part of a Russian effort to reestablish itself as a world superpower in the Western Hemisphere and place TU-95 strategic bombers as a deterrent in the region.

The airfield's 13,000 foot runway, and many of its hangars and support buildings, were completed in 2009, but the base never became operational. The funding and negotiations fell apart after Fidel Castro announced that he would be stepping down. The Russians pulled out of the deal and the base sat empty, used only by DGI agents and other intelligence services for field operations.

For that purpose, it was ideal. DGI and friendly intelligence agencies could use it as a staging area. It served as a gateway to both South America and the United States. Its long runway and spacious hangars could support all types of aircraft, from large military cargo transports to light civilian aircraft. The Russians had given the Cuban intelligence community a great gift.

Chloe landed under the cover of darkness, but when she taxied in, she was greeted by armed men in civilian clothing. They met her at the jet and told her to leave all her gear with it. Then they escorted her to the offices of the main hangar as they towed the F-16 inside.

She had expected to see Victor when she landed. He promised to meet her at the jet, but he was nowhere to be found. Instead, she had been treated as an American spy, shuffled into a new pair of clothes, and then locked into this room. She was hoping it was all just a misunderstanding and that Victor would show up any minute to clear things up.

She sat with her knees against her chest and wondered what Spectre was doing. She had no way of knowing how long it had been since she landed, but she figured Spectre had been notified by now. She wondered if they knew that she had flown to Cuba, or if the plan had worked and Spectre was getting notification of her death. She pictured him collapsing to the ground and sobbing.

She still felt bad about him. She loved him, but the relationship had long since grown stale. He didn't look at her the same way anymore, she could tell. They had just been keeping the relationship going on life support for months. Spectre wouldn't even commit to a wedding date.

Victor was exciting, alluring, and exotic. He was all the things Spectre had never been. He treated her like a princess and made her feel like she was the only girl in the room. He was very passionate.

Her short time with him had been a blur. It seemed so serendipitous that he had even come into her life. She had been out with some of the wives from the squadron when they happened to run into each other at a bar. She had accidentally spilled her drink on him and apologized profusely, but his accent and kind smile had been intoxicating.

They snuck off into the corner and talked. She hadn't planned on doing anything with him. She was engaged and even wearing Spectre's mother's ring, but she loved the attention. It was exciting. She was slightly tipsy from one too many margaritas, and she couldn't help herself. She was drunk on the moment.

She thought it would be over when her friends started to leave. She planned on following, hoping no one had seen her, but he pulled her aside and pushed her against the wall. His eyes had been so full of passion and energy. She couldn't even feign resistance as he kissed her.

They exchanged numbers and decided to meet in secret. He taught her how to communicate using e-mail drafts without worrying about her fiancé finding out. The attention and fear of getting caught was so erotic. She was living out her deepest fantasies. They had managed to have sex in places she never imagined. They found bathrooms, parks, and dumpy motels. The whole thing had been a thrill ride, and her fiancé had been none the wiser, making it even more exciting.

And then Victor propositioned her. They could run away together. His father was a wealthy businessman in Cuba with many connections. He knew people who would pay over fifty million dollars for the latest F-16 technology. She would have a brand new life.

She thought she had been a hard sell. Becoming a traitor to the country she loved was a tough pill to swallow, but she didn't really feel like a traitor. She was merely cashing in her chips and starting over. She had served her country for nearly ten years. Surely, the last ten years of her life had been worth that. Hell, the torture they put her through in the Air Force Academy was easily worth that. Or her Instructor Pilots in pilot training. Or the Gators with her upgrade flights. *No one seemed to appreciate her talent. Misogynists. All of them.*

And Victor made it so much easier. His plan made so much sense. She could fake her death so no one would even know what happened. Her family could grieve and not wonder what happened to her. Spectre would move on. She had tried to start the separation process with him early, but he was just too hard headed to listen. He kept trying to make things work. It was sad, really.

It wasn't like she was selling high-level state secrets or anything. The F-16 Block 70 was really just the Americanized version of the Block 60. Plenty of foreign countries were already flying it. The US was just giving them away as part of foreign aid packages anyway. *It wasn't like troops on the ground would die because of what she did.*

Her conscience was clear, and for now, the only thing bothering her was her reception. She should have been on the private jet to her own private island with Victor by now. She had pictured sipping Mai Tais in her hammock all day and making love on the beach all night. She was growing impatient.

Suddenly the door opened. It was one of the armed men that had brought her to this room in the first place. He still had an AK-47 slung from his neck.

"Please come with me," he said with a thick Spanish accent.

"Where are we going now?" she demanded.

"Someone wants to see you. Let's go," he replied, grabbing her arm.

Despite the rough way he was grabbing her, she was excited. She was finally going to see Victor. Her moment had arrived. She planned to give him an earful about not meeting her at the jet, but then she would kiss him passionately. *Her fantasy had come to life.*

# CHAPTER TWENTY-EIGHT

C hloe Moss was ushered by the guard out of her temporary holding area. She still felt she was being treated more like a prisoner than a willing participant, as the guard's grip on her arm was fairly tight. He walked her out through the hallway of the small office and into the hangar where her F-16 had been towed.

The hangar door was partially open, allowing daylight to creep into the huge hangar. Everything on the jet was exactly as she had left it when she was greeted by her armed escort. Her G-suit and harness still hung from the captive-carry training AIM-9 air-to-air missile on the right wingtip. Her helmet was still sitting on the canopy rail with the canopy open. She hoped one of these low-level guys didn't try closing the canopy without moving it first. The Joint Helmet Mounting Cueing System in her helmet would make for a very expensive crunch.

Well, it would have been expensive if she were still a card-carrying member of the US Military. Those days were long gone now. *There was no turning back.* They could destroy the nearly quarter million-dollar helmet and visor for all she cared now. She would still be retiring to her private island very soon.

As they walked closer to the F-16 in the huge hangar, she saw three men standing near the aircraft's 370-gallon drop tank on the right wing. There were two shorter men surrounding a much taller man. The shorter men were dressed in business suits. The taller man was in a colorful button down shirt that was not buttoned. She instantly recognized him.

"Victor!" she screamed, wrestling her arm away from her escort. She took off running in Victor's direction as he turned to face her.

Victor pardoned himself from his two associates and walked forward. She ran directly into his arms and jumped on him, wrapping her arms and legs around him. He looked into her eyes and kissed her quickly, then put her back down.

"I'm glad you made it," he said coolly.

Chloe looked at him sideways. He didn't seem as excited to see her as she was to see him. A hint of doubt crept into her mind, but she quickly pushed it away. She was tired and hungry. *That's probably what was wrong.*

"Why weren't you here when I arrived last night?" she asked, putting her arm around his waist.

"I'm sorry, my dear. I had other matters to tend to. I got here as quickly as I could," he said, kissing her on the forehead.

"When do we leave?" She didn't want to wait any longer. It was time to begin their lives together. The first thing she would do was buy new clothes. *These rags were too big and not very fashionable.* She thought of what she would wear on the beach – something casual, but classy. She didn't want people to know she was extremely rich, but she wanted them to see she had class.

Victor shifted uncomfortably while keeping a straight face. "Soon," he replied.

"How soon? I thought we would be on the beach by now!" she replied impatiently.

"It won't be long, my dear," he said reassuringly. "We just have some business to finish before we can be on our way."

Chloe looked at the two men still standing at the jet. She pulled Victor away from them so they couldn't eavesdrop.

"Who are these men?"

"These are the people that we've made the deal with."

"They're Asian? I thought you said your father had found some Venezuelans?" There was concern in her voice. Victor had told her that his father had found Venezuelan businessmen to fund their getaway. They wanted the jet to cannibalize parts for Venezuela's aging fleet of early block F-16s. She knew Venezuela would never be a threat to the United States, which made it that much easier to justify her defection.

"Chinese," Alvarez replied.

"Chinese!" she shrieked. This was even worse for her. The Chinese had an active espionage and reverse engineering program. She had seen the intel briefings. They had stolen F-35 technology through hacking US contractor databases, reverse engineered F-22 technology for their indigenous J-20 fighters, and sold their new fighters to North Korea and other countries hostile to the United States. *This development was very bad.*

"Lower your voice," he said, trying to calm her down. "These men are willing to pay a lot more than our original offer. This is a much better deal." His accent and deep voice were very calming to Chloe. She knew it was a bad idea, but she couldn't argue. It was hard to argue with his charm.

"Are they spies?" she asked, keeping her voice low.

"No, they are businessmen. They work in the aerospace industry. You know, China is a capitalist country. They're not all bad."

"But—" she began.

"Come," he interrupted, turning her away from them and putting his hand against the small of her back. "Let's go into the office and finish the deal."

Alvarez guided her away from the F-16 and through a door on the opposite end of the hangar. They walked through the hallway and into another series of offices. He turned left and pushed open one of the office doors, revealing a large office. This one was fully furnished, with a large executive chair and stained wooden desk. Across from it were two chairs.

"Have a seat," he said, pointing to the large executive chair. *This was more like it.* She was finally being treated like a real person instead of a criminal.

"I have to go get our associates. They will be here shortly to finish the deal," Alvarez said as he turned to leave.

"Wait," she said, stopping him halfway through the door. "I'm hungry."

"You haven't eaten?"

She shook her head.

"I am so sorry, my love. I will get you something to eat and drink. It may not be much. We don't exactly have a cook here. Is water ok for now?"

She nodded.

"Ok, I will be back with your food in a minute, just sit tight." He flashed his charming smile and left. It was enough to make her melt. The excitement and adrenaline rush had come back. She couldn't believe what she was doing. *It was all so romantic and dangerous.*

She leaned back in her comfy chair and looked around the office. Like the room she was in before, the walls were plain. There were no windows, like every other room she had been in. *The Cubans must have had something against windows,* she imagined. She wondered what all of the money would look like in cash. *Would they have a suitcase like the movies? A duffel bag? Maybe they would just wire the money to an account in the Caymans.* Victor had been handling all those details. She trusted his judgment.

Suddenly the door opened. A small Asian man walked in, carrying a leather attaché in his right hand. Chloe recognized him from the hangar. She wondered where his other friend was.

Chloe brushed away the hair from her face and sat up straight as the man sat in one of the chairs across from her. She leaned forward to shake his hand, but he didn't reciprocate. She awkwardly put her hand back down on the desk.

"Captain Moss, my name is Jun Zhang," he said. He had a very thick Chinese accent. It was almost hard for Chloe to understand him.

"Mr. Zhang, it is a pleasure to meet you, but I would like to wait for Victor to get back before we continue our deal," she said.

"I'm afraid that won't be possible, Captain."

Chloe gave him a puzzled look. Every ounce of intuition was telling her things were about to go horribly wrong. She had a very bad feeling deep in her gut.

"I need information from you," he said, pulling out a voice recorder.

"What kind of information? I would really be more comfortable if we waited for Victor."

"Captain, your cooperation will be most appreciated. Let's start with the aircraft. What are the codes for the combat modes of the radar?"

Chloe's face grew flush. *That was never part of the deal.* She hadn't considered the possibility of having to divulge secrets. Her part was to deliver the aircraft, get the money, and run away with Victor. Giving secrets to the Chinese wasn't part of her plan.

"Mr. Zhang, is it?"

He nodded.

"I'm sorry, but that wasn't part of the deal. For the price Victor has negotiated, I've given you a fully functional, flying F-16 Block 70," she said.

"Captain Moss, I'm afraid there is no such deal," he replied.

"What the fuck does that mean? Get Victor in here," she demanded, slamming her hand on the desk.

The man pulled up his attaché from the floor and opened it. He pulled out a manila folder, closed the attaché, and put it back on the floor next to him. He leaned forward and put the manila folder on the desk, pushing it to Chloe.

"What the hell is this?" she asked angrily as she opened the folder. It was full of pictures of people bound and gagged, their faces badly bruised and beaten. They were barely recognizable.

"Who are these people?"

"That's your family, and if you don't answer all of our questions truthfully, they will die," he replied casually.

# CHAPTER TWENTY-NINE

*Homestead ARB, FL*

Spectre, Decker and Baxter sat in silence on the short drive back to the OSI building. They were all too preoccupied with the latest development in the case to make small talk or throw around theories. The three walked into the OSI building where Baxter swiped his badge, and they shuffled into the conference room.

Spectre sat at the head of the table and Decker retook her previous seat while Baxter opted to pace around the room. They had to work this problem out.

"So what do we know so far?" Baxter said, breaking the contemplative silence.

"Moss's aircraft disappeared from radar just after nine o'clock, and then reappeared heading south before she flew outside of radar coverage," Decker answered.

"Her transponder stopped transmitting," Spectre said, correcting her. "She was always on radar."

"Ok, so how does she get away without anyone noticing?" Baxter asked.

"Night time. She was separated from her wingman on a preplanned maneuver. I think there was a low cloud deck that night, probably four to five thousand foot ceilings. She descends down, turns off her IFF—"

"IFF?" Decker asked, interrupting Spectre.

"Identification Friend or Foe, it's military talk for transponder," Spectre replied. "So she turns off her transponder as she's descending. She had to figure that with the radar lag, people would assume it was just the last known position. Christ, I can't fucking believe it."

Spectre leaned forward and buried his head in his hands. It was all a big nightmare. He didn't know what to believe anymore. Both of the possible scenarios were unsettling. On one hand, the girl he had loved could be dead. On the other, the girl he loved was possibly a defector and a traitor to the country he loved so much. He felt sick.

Decker leaned over and put her hand on his shoulder. Spectre looked up. She gave him a comforting smile, patting his shoulder. "I know this must be hard for you," she said.

"But can't the jets see each other using their own radars or something?" Baxter asked.

"She was too far away from the other aircraft for them to see her," Spectre replied.

"What about her wingman?"

"You mean datalink?" Spectre thought about the question for a minute. "Same as the transponder, she just turned it off to make it look like she had gone lost contact. Probably turned them off at the same time. With the cloud deck, even if she had ejected, finding the wreckage in the middle of the ocean with no beacon would've been difficult. She knew that. She was counting on it."

"Just playing devil's advocate here," Decker said, twirling her pen, "but this is all very circumstantial. Is it possible she crashed and the radar return was just a coincidence?"

"It's possible, but not likely. That was a pretty solid return for quite a few frames before it went out of range. Besides, no wreckage and no emergency beacon. We have more proof that she's alive now than we do that she's dead." Spectre's voice sounded tired. He felt defeated. It was nearing lunchtime, but he felt like he had been up for forty-eight hours straight. Except for a few hours of restless sleep, he had been.

"But why? What motive would she have? Was she in trouble?" Decker asked.

"Money, power, attention, or coercion. That's usually what drives a defector," Baxter said.

*Defector.* The word resonated with Spectre. The girl he had loved so much had seemingly turned on her country. *It just didn't make sense.*

"Mr. Martin —"

"Please, call me Cal," Spectre said, interrupting Decker.

"Cal, did Moss have anything going on at work that you knew of? Anything to push her over the edge?" she asked.

Spectre couldn't imagine Chloe reaching the point of betraying her country. He had always seen her as a strong woman, despite having been through a life of hardships. She had survived living with her real father who had been a complete drunk until her mother remarried, and she moved in with her mother and new stepfather. She had told him of many times she had fought off sexual advances and outright assaults at the Air Force Academy, but said nothing because she didn't want to be seen as "that girl." Her whole life, she had been told she wasn't good enough and would never amount to anything by people intimidated by her successes as a woman. Yet she just smiled and pressed on, graduating number one from her Air Force Academy class and managing to get fighters out of pilot training. She had struggled through her flight lead upgrade, but always seemed to have a positive attitude no matter what the Gators threw at her. Spectre couldn't see how someone so resilient could suddenly snap.

"She was always fighting uphill in her career. Hell, the squadron fought tooth and nail to keep her from even getting this assignment, but she fought back. She won. They made it hard on her to upgrade in the jet. She never held it against anyone, and always had a good attitude," Spectre replied.

"So she had enemies?" Decker asked with a raised eyebrow.

"Don't all strong women in male dominated professions?" Spectre asked, holding eye contact with Decker.

Decker blushed. "I guess so, but had it gotten worse recently that you know of? Did she seem frustrated?"

"No, actually she had been in a pretty upbeat mood until she broke up with me, and even after that when she finally passed her flight lead upgrade checkride," Spectre said.

"Ok, we can get to the why later," Baxter interjected. "So where did she go?" He was still pacing around the room as he tried to make sense of the whole thing.

The room fell silent as they all pondered the question. The obvious answer was somewhere south based on her last known radar track, but the options seemed endless.

"Victor," Spectre said, breaking the silence. It hurt him to say it. *She was fleeing to another man.*

Baxter bolted out of the room without saying a word. A minute later, he returned with folders in his hand. He placed them on the conference table.

"That's a good start. Now, which one?" he asked.

Spectre pulled the first folder off the stack and opened it. "Victor Leon, Venezuelan national, probably not." Spectre tossed the folder aside.

"How can you be so sure?" Decker asked.

"Venezuela is a little far to fly unrefueled, and I think the Venezuelans don't even have tankers without drogues," Spectre said, moving on to the next folder.

"What makes you think she would fly to their country of origin?" she asked.

"I think he has a good point," Baxter intervened. "Aren't most of these guys foreign intelligence agents? If she's defecting, they're probably bringing her straight to their own country to avoid any attention from other governments."

Spectre ignored them. "Victor Cruz, Colombia... nope"

Spectre tossed the second folder and moved on to the third. "Victor Alvarez, Cuba, DGI operative. This is your man." He held up the picture for the two to see.

"Don't you want to look at the other two? What if they're from Cuba?" Decker asked.

"Doesn't matter. She's in Cuba. Look at a map, it's the only logical answer, assuming she did defect," Spectre replied.

Decker picked up the remaining two folders and flipped through them. "Honduras and Peru, he's right," she said.

"Cuba is not a small island. She could have landed anywhere," Baxter said, leaning against one of the conference chairs.

Spectre thought about it for a minute. He was confident that if she were still alive, she had gone to Cuba. It only made sense, but figuring out where she had gone would be a lot tougher. He thought about what he would have done in her position.

"You can rule out any civilian fields or runways shorter than six thousand feet," he began. "They would want maximum security and minimum exposure. Do you have a computer with JMPS?" The Joint Mission Planning Software served as a common mission-planning suite for both Navy and Air Force. It included high-resolution imagery and maps, as well as navigation and combat flight planning tools.

"Yeah, back in the vault, but I've never used it," Baxter said.

"It's a pain in the ass, but I'm pretty sure I still can," Spectre responded. They walked down the hallway and through the heavy vault door into the secure area. Spectre sat down at a computer terminal as Baxter logged him in. Spectre pulled up a map of Cuba. He selected an overlay of all military airfields. Three red dots populated the map.

"Well, I think we can safely rule out Guantánamo Bay, or we might have heard about it by now," Spectre said. Decker and Baxter were huddled over his shoulder.

"And San Julian Air Base is over 300 miles away from the airspace she was flying in," Spectre said as he used the straight line distance measuring tool.

"Too far?" Decker asked.

"It is if you're trying to avoid unwanted attention. It also means she would have flown right by Key West as well. Her last track had her headed south," Spectre replied, rubbing his temples.

"Well then San Antonio de Los Baños Airfield is out too, since Havana is southwest," Baxter said, pointing at the final red dot.

"So she didn't go to Cuba after all," Decker said.

Spectre stared at the map. He was sure that his theory was correct. If she defected, she had to have gone to a military base in Cuba. There was no way she would risk overheating the F-16's below average brakes and running off a short runway after going through so much trouble. And defecting to a civilian airport was just stupid.

"I agree with your logic on those bases, so where did she go?" Baxter asked.

Spectre thought back to his flying days. Cuba had never been much of an area of concern, except right before Castro stepped down. That's when the Russians were stepping up their Global Reach initiative and building strategic bases everywhere. *That was it!* He remembered the intel briefs over Drill Weekends as they discussed the possible threat. The Russians were building a strategic base in Cuba for their bombers. *But where?*

Spectre put down a marker on the map in the Atlantic Ocean. "This was where we last saw her, heading south," he said.

Spectre selected the measuring tool and drew a line from that position one hundred and fifty miles to the south.

"Do you remember when the Russians built that strategic base in Cuba?" Spectre asked.

"Vaguely. It was all over the news," Baxter replied.

"Can you look it up?" Spectre asked.

Baxter sat down at the terminal next to Spectre and pulled up the Secret database. He did a search for Russia and Cuba. The first result was Castro Field. He pulled up the page.

"Give me those coordinates," Spectre said, looking over at Baxter's monitor. Baxter wrote them down and passed them to Spectre. He typed them into the mission planning software and set up a marker. It was twenty-five miles west of the line Spectre had just drawn. *They had found her.*

# CHAPTER THIRTY

*Castro Field, Cuba*

Chloe Moss lay in the fetal position, sobbing softly in the corner of the room. She was back in the room she had first been in before being reunited with Victor. She hadn't been sure before, but now she was certain. She was definitely in a holding cell. *She was a prisoner.*

Except for her white cotton underwear, she had been stripped of the clothes she had been given when she arrived. She was cold and shivering, naked and afraid. Her body ached. Her cheeks felt swollen and sore. She smelled like urine. She hadn't eaten since leaving American soil, but she wasn't hungry. She felt nauseous and weak.

Her refusal to answer any of Jun Zhang's questions were met with a look of disappointment. She demanded proof of life and refused to say anything without it. Zhang didn't say a word as he left the room. She had hoped that was the end of it. She imagined Zhang conferring with Victor, who would have undoubtedly stood up for her and demanded her release and better treatment. *They had a deal after all.*

She wondered if Victor knew about the kidnapping. It seemed plausible, but rather unlikely. Victor knew she was a willing participant in the whole ordeal. He had no reason to try to up the stakes. *No, this was all the work of the Chinese.* They had gotten greedy. They wanted more than just the technology. They wanted inside her mind and all the American secrets it contained.

But Chloe had done her best to resist. *Selling state secrets was never part of the deal.* Anyone could get F-16 technology, even the latest American version. She was sure of it. *But to hand over the keys and everything the government had trusted her with over the last seven years? That was just too much.* She had to draw the line somewhere. Her service and hardships might have been worth fifty million or so, and a new life on the beach, but it wasn't worth giving away the whole playbook and costing American lives.

But the man who replaced Zhang was far less diplomatic. She had recognized him as the other man talking to Victor when she was escorted into the hangar. He was slightly shorter than Zhang, with a very noticeable scar across his left cheek. He and one of the guards had stripped her down to her underwear and tied her to a chair. She was afraid they were going to rape her, and the look in the Cuban guard's eyes seemed to suggest just that, but what they had in store for her was much different.

"My name is Ling. If you cooperate, you will be treated as a human again," he said. His voice was heavily accented like Zhang's, but much deeper. It was much more sinister.

"But if you do not," he continued, "you will wish you were dead. But I won't let you die. Death would be a welcome release from the pain you will feel. Do you understand?"

Chloe nodded. She had to dig deep into her training. It had been years since she had gone through SERE school in Washington and learned resistance techniques. She knew she would eventually break. Everyone broke, they told her. Even the best and most skilled in the intelligence community broke eventually. It was just a matter of holding out as long as possible. In her case, she just hoped to hold on until Victor could settle the obvious misunderstanding and they could be on their way.

They had stripped away her clothes as a way of tearing down her ego and self worth. The more naked a person felt, the more vulnerable they would be, especially women. They wanted Chloe to fear rape. They wanted her to be afraid. *It was working.*

"What is your name?" he asked. As she began to answer, he connected with a strong backhand across the face. Blood oozed from her lip.

"What the fuck!" she screamed. He hit her again with his other hand.

"You will think carefully before answering my questions," he replied.

Tears began to trickle down her face. She was in over her head. She wasn't even sure how she got wrapped up in everything. *It had all seemed so exciting and romantic.* She had confided in Victor all that she had been through. Her life and career had just been fucked up. *Everyone had been against her.* Everyone except Victor. Victor gave her hope. A hope that, despite his best efforts, Cal Martin could have never given her. He was far too set in his ways and too wrapped up in his own drama to give her what she needed. Victor showed her the possibility of a new life.

As more tears rolled down her cheeks, she knew she wouldn't make it out alive. Victor was probably being tortured and questioned the same way in another room. These men, Zhang and Ling, were in control. Once they had what they wanted, they would kill the two lovers. *Victor had been a fool for trusting them.*

"Your name?" he asked impatiently. She flinched in response. She knew that was what he wanted, but she couldn't stop it. He had gotten to her already.

"Chloe Moss," she replied.

"What squadron are you with?" he asked calmly.

She paused for a moment, waiting for another backhand. When none came, she said, "39th Fighter Squadron."

"Good, now how many pilots are in the 39th Fighter Squadron?" he asked.

"I don't know," she replied. "Twenty? Thirty?" She was trying to be intentionally vague. Lying was not an option, but presenting herself as someone with little to no knowledge might prolong the questioning.

Ling wasn't buying it. He knew all of the methods of the trade. He punched her in the stomach, instantly knocking the wind out of her. She gasped for air.

"You disappoint me," he said, moving behind her. He leaned in close to her ear as she was still gasping for air. "I know all of your tricks. You only make this harder on yourself."

"Fuck you," she said defiantly.

Ling nodded at the guard who exited the room. Moments later, he returned with a bucket of water and a rag.

Chloe recognized what was about to happen. Ling was resorting to water boarding. She had been through it before in training, but nothing like the pain she was about to experience. Ling was much more violent than her instructors had been.

The routine went on for what seemed like an eternity. Ling asked more questions, probing deeper into classified subjects, and Chloe evaded. She gave vague answers or none at all, each time finding herself being held down while water was poured over the rag covering her mouth, or being hit by Ling. The water boarding made her feel like she was drowning. The pain and fear were debilitating. Ling continued to threaten her family, but Chloe refused, each time demanding proof of life. *If they were really captive, they were probably already dead.*

After three iterations, Ling untied Chloe and had the guard drag her into the holding cell. It was a small victory, but she had made it through round one at least.

Ling pulled out a pair of pliers from his back pocket and held them in Chloe's face before he left. "This is just the beginning," he said. "You will talk. We'll start with nails first. You will have twenty chances. Then I will bring out the shears and you will have twenty more. I will be back soon. Consider your cooperation carefully."

# CHAPTER THIRTY-ONE

Victor Alvarez stood looking out into the hangar bay. From his second floor office, he had a perfect view of the Chinese technicians working quickly in and around the jet. An external power cart could be heard through the double pane glass, powering the jet's avionics as the technicians gathered classified information from the F-16's avionics.

"You said she would cooperate," a voice behind him said. Alvarez didn't need to turn around to see who it was. He recognized Zhang's voice. It had the kind of shriek to it that made him cringe every time he heard the man speak, but he couldn't complain too much. The man was giving him the biggest payout of his career.

"And you said you wouldn't need Ling," Alvarez replied without turning around.

Zhang walked up to the desk and sat down. Alvarez didn't want to be having this conversation. He wanted the men to take their new jet in however many pieces they needed and be on their way. The longer they waited, the more likely an American intervention would become, and with Cuban-American relations slowly improving since the Russians backed down from their strategic base deal, it was something his country couldn't afford.

Alvarez thought about what his government would do if they found out about his current operation. The DGI had given him considerable leeway over the years, and most within the agency had no idea what he did. For the most part, they just knew he achieved results. That's the way he wanted to keep it, but this was something too big for them to miss. He only hoped they found out after the dust had settled and the Chinese were long gone.

"Losing the hostages was a major setback," Zhang replied.

"I took care of Aalee for his incompetence," Alvarez said, turning to face Zhang. He had called in the "anonymous tip" as soon as his contact confirmed Aalee was in the safe house. His informant in the FBI had told him that Kasim had already said too much. Aalee was a loose end that needed to be tied up quickly. He knew Aalee would never let himself be captured. He was far too arrogant. He wanted to die a martyr.

"I told you he was a risk," Zhang said condescendingly.

"He served his purpose, and now we're here," Alvarez replied.

Alvarez turned and sat in his leather executive chair. He crossed his feet on the desk and opened a drawer, pulling out a cigar box. "Cigar?" he offered, opening the box.

Zhang shook his head as Alvarez pulled out his gold cigar cutter and cut off an end. He lit it with his pocket lighter and took a long drag. Zhang frowned.

"Relax, it's not Cuban," Alvarez said with a puff of smoke in the air.

Zhang said nothing. He was not impressed by Alvarez's laid-back demeanor.

"How much longer will it take your men?" Alvarez finally asked, changing the subject.

"If she talks, they can have everything downloaded by tomorrow afternoon," Zhang replied. "And then it will take another day to disassemble for shipping."

This caused Alvarez to raise an eyebrow. The original deal did not involve any human intelligence gathering from the girl. Once the plane arrived, Zhang's team would dismantle it into many pieces and ship them all separately to Beijing. The kidnapping had been intended as an insurance policy to ensure she followed through.

However, after establishing Moss as an asset, Alvarez didn't think she required any further leverage. The American girl had serious issues that had been very easy to exploit. She was so completely unhappy with her job and bored with her love life that she was almost begging Alvarez to do whatever he wanted. And she had been great in bed to boot. The crazy ones were always the best in bed. It had been a deeply pornographic experience. Alvarez smiled.

"Why are you smiling?" Zhang demanded with a furrowed brow.

Alvarez snapped back to reality and the angry Chinese intelligence operative staring him down across his desk. "I'm sorry. How long will it take if she doesn't talk?" he asked.

"One way or another, she will talk, but if we get no useful information from her, it will take another two days for my technicians to hack the systems," Zhang replied.

Alvarez considered the delay for a moment. He had been watching the American news agencies, and so far, they were still searching for the wreckage. The bad weather over the Atlantic had severely hurt their efforts while helping his cause, but he needed these men gone before the Americans realized there would be no wreckage. Another two to three days was just unacceptable.

"Perhaps I should try to talk to her," said Alvarez as he waved his cigar in the air.

"You?" Zhang laughed. "You have betrayed her, why would she talk to you?"

"She will talk if she thinks I am still in this with her," he replied. "Relax! I know what I'm doing."

# CHAPTER THIRTY-TWO

*Homestead, FL*

**"I**'ve never even heard of an American pilot defecting in the last twenty years," Spectre said shaking his head. He was back in Marcus's office after telling the story of his morning with Baxter and Decker, and their realization that Chloe was likely still alive.

"Dude, she's just a fucking whore," Anderson replied abruptly. "It doesn't have to make sense."

Spectre shot Marcus a disapproving look. "I don't know what I believe anymore."

Spectre had spent the short drive back to the store going over everything in his mind. Chloe had been acting strangely in the weeks leading up to the crash, but at the time, he figured she was just stressed about her upgrade flights and other work related stresses. She just didn't seem like the type to cheat on him or betray her country and defect.

"I know it's tough, Cal, but I knew that chick was bad news. Military chicks are crazy."

"Probably so, but I still don't see why she would defect. She wasn't that crazy," Spectre knew he sounded like a man strongly in denial despite overwhelming evidence, but he just couldn't seem to wrap his head around it.

"Nah, I remember a guy defected with a trainer back in the 60s from here. It was all over the news, but his family was Cuban. He was also Air Force," Marcus said. "Here, I'll Google it."

After a few minutes of hunting and pecking on the keyboard, Marcus squinted at the screen as the search results came up.

"Right here," Marcus said, pointing at the screen. "In July of 1963, Airman First Class Roberto Ramos Michelena defected to Cuba with a T-34 from the Tyndall AFB Aero Club. Ramos had been on a routine flight from Pensacola to Miami in the Club's private T-34. When he failed to arrive in Miami, a search was initiated until Havana Radio announced that the Airman had deserted and returned to Cuba."

"Damn you're old," Spectre shot back with a grin.

"Fuck you, I just remember hearing about it as a kid. This ain't just a hat rack," he said, tapping his head.

"Whatever you say, old man," Spectre replied. "But anyway, what would make her just lose it and steal an F-16? I'm not buying it."

"Didn't another one of your Air Force guys do something similar in '97 with an A-10?" Marcus asked.

"You mean the guy that crashed an A-10 in Colorado?" Spectre replied.

"Yeah, that one. I was at MCAS Yuma working CAS with the Harriers down there when they started the search. He took off from Tucson to go to the range with live bombs, but ended up crashing in Colorado. They sent us looking for the bombs, because they never recovered them at the crash site."

Spectre remembered the story quite well. It had been taught in his human factors classes in both pilot training and when he was in F-16 school.

On the morning of April 2, 1997, Captain Craig Button took off loaded with four live Mk-82 five hundred pound bombs out of Davis-Monthan Air Force Base in Tucson, Arizona. After air refueling near Gila Bend, Button broke formation and headed northeast, turning off his transponder to prevent identification. Nearly two hours later, he was last spotted 100 miles west of Denver before impacting terrain fifteen miles southwest of Vail, Colorado. The cause of the mishap was never fully determined, but many believed his death to be a suicide. A psychological autopsy revealed that Button had been suffering from mental anguish over his former girlfriend's unrequited love and his mother's Christian Pacifist Faith. The four bombs that he had been carrying on his A-10 were never located.

"You think she killed herself somewhere else?" Spectre asked.

Marcus shook his head. "No, I'm saying that even you superhuman, zipper suited sun god fighter pilots can be batshit crazy and do things that don't make sense. Sometimes it's best not to even try to delve into the mind of someone who goes off the reservation like that."

Spectre stared off into space, deep in thought. He had to admit to himself that his relationship with Chloe hadn't been as passionate in the last six months as it had started, but he chalked that up to being part of love. Infatuation was only a temporary aspect in relationships. Settling into a comfort zone was to be expected. Spectre had always thought they had settled into a strong relationship. Besides Marcus, she was his best friend.

He was coming to terms with the probability that the woman he loved had left him, but the why of the equation was still bugging him. Crazy or not, Chloe wasn't the type to be the first defector in modern U.S. history. He thought back to his discussion with Agent Baxter. And then it hit him.

"Remember how you said the e-mail drafts were meant to hide stuff from outside agencies?" Spectre asked.

"Yeah, I remember," Marcus replied.

"So what if you're wrong?" Spectre asked.

"I'm never wrong, but go on."

"What if whoever wrote them wanted them to be seen?"

"Whoa, that's reaching man," Marcus replied, putting his hands up. "I think you need to get some rest and stop trying to jump through your own asshole to figure this out. You'll drive yourself crazy."

"Hang on, hear me out," Spectre replied. Marcus saw an intensity in Spectre's sky blue eyes he hadn't seen before. It was apparent Spectre truly believed he was on to something.

"Go on," Marcus said, sitting back.

"The OSI agent said people defect for a lot of reasons. Money, power, attention, or coercion. Their theory is a combination of money and attention. In a vacuum, I would agree. Money makes the world go 'round and the e-mail makes it look like she was getting attention from this Victor asshole. But what about coercion?"

Marcus sat up straight. Spectre was on to something. He could see the fighter pilot coming out in him, making quick, high order calculations. He had seen brief flashes of it before as Spectre revamped the store with great success.

Spectre didn't wait for an answer. "Her fucking parents and brother were kidnapped! Everyone keeps treating it like they were separate incidents, but what if they weren't? What if whoever is behind it did it to force her to steal the jet?"

"Holy shit," Marcus mumbled.

"Yeah, holy shit is right," Spectre said standing up. "She might have done this thinking her family would be killed if she didn't. Which means right now she's in trouble."

Marcus stood as Spectre turned to walk out. "Wait, what are you doing?"

"I've got to talk to Baxter about this. They have to send a team in to get her back," Spectre replied.

"Cal, hold up a second. It's just a theory. It's decent, but it's not airtight. What if they don't do anything with it?"

"Then I'll do it myself," Spectre replied. Without waiting for a response, he turned and walked out the door.

# CHAPTER THIRTY-THREE

*Castro Field, Cuba*

The sudden appearance of light was blinding as the door to her makeshift holding cell was flung open. There was a loud grunt followed by a figure stumbling in and falling to his knees. After the door slammed shut, it took Chloe a few moments for her eyes to adjust to the low light conditions of the room. She was still curled up in the fetal position in the corner.

When her eyes finally adjusted, she could make out a man on his knees. He was naked except for a pair of light colored boxer shorts. It was too dark to see his face, but she could tell he had a slender frame.

The man groaned as he collapsed on the floor. He took a moment to gather his strength and roll over onto his back.

"Chloe?" the voice strained. The sweet accent that accompanied her name was unmistakable.

"Victor!" she cried as she struggled to crawl to his limp body.

Victor sat up and put his arm around her. As she got closer, she could see his face was bruised and his lip was bleeding. He appeared to be in pain. She had been right. He hadn't betrayed her. She felt relieved and horrified at the same time.

"My love, I am so sorry, I did not mean for this to happen," Victor said, pulling her close to him.

"It's ok," she said, kissing him. "I knew you wouldn't do this. I was so worried. I thought you were dead."

"What did they do to you?" Victor asked, trying to look her over.

"Nothing I couldn't handle," she lied. It had been all that she could handle. She had found herself going right to the breaking point several times during Ling's interrogation, only to barely stop herself. Her training had paid off, but as her teachers had warned, everyone breaks eventually. She knew it was only a matter of time.

"We're going to get out of here together," Victor replied, squeezing her.

A tear rolled down Chloe's cheek. "They're going to kill us."

Victor groaned and pulled her closer. "No, my love. We are going to get out of here together, like we planned."

She didn't believe him, but his words were reassuring. He always had that way about him. He could be so persuasive without saying too much. It was still hard to believe, however. She knew that the Ling would not stop until she gave him the answers he was looking for, or killed her in the process.

"Do you think we can escape?" she asked.

"No, he has too many men. We must cooperate," he replied.

Chloe let the idea roll around in her head. She was cold and hungry. She was still in a great deal of pain from her last encounter with Ling. Giving up seemed so easy, but it went against every fiber of her being. The line in the sand she had drawn for herself had been giving secrets to a rival country. But that line kept getting blurrier.

"Baby, you know I can't," she pleaded. "I won't."

Victor let out a sigh and then looked Chloe in the eyes. His brown eyes seemed to penetrate her soul. She could see the anguish he was feeling. It hurt more than the interrogation.

"Then we will die together," he said gravely.

Chloe suddenly felt guilty. He looked badly beaten. She could tell he was in immense pain. They were doing this to get to her. Ling had probably done this to him. He would kill Victor in front of her if he had to. She was sure of it. She could barely withstand more of the torture, but seeing Victor badly hurt or killed was unbearable.

"I won't let that happen," she said.

"What are you going to do?"

"I'm going to get us out of here. I have an idea," she responded confidently.

# CHAPTER THIRTY-FOUR

*Homestead ARB, FL*

The dull roar of idle chatter was interrupted by a loud voice calling the room to attention. On cue, everyone in the room stood as a group of high-ranking officials walked in. The group was led by a tall, lanky man in a business suit with gray hair and a crooked nose, followed by a two star general, a portly one star, a short colonel, and Colonel "Coach" Louhan. Spectre recognized the short colonel. It was "Cajun" Buchannan, the Wing Commander. Spectre had flown with him in the F-16 Basic Course at Luke. He had never met the two generals before.

"Take your seats," the man in the business suit said as he walked to the center of the room. It was a large conference room with a U-shaped conference table in the center surrounded by theater seating. Several high-ranking Air Force officials sat around the table, with the two generals and Cajun taking seats nearest the man in the suit who was now standing alone in front of the high-ranking officials. Spectre noticed Coach Louhan sitting near Cajun Buchannan. His fists clenched. He still hated the man with all of his being.

Spectre sat in the front row of the stadium seating behind the conference table with Agent Decker. He had driven straight to Agent Baxter's office from the gun shop, arriving just as they had finished briefing the Director of AFOSI on a teleconference.

Although his visit had been a surprise, Spectre wasted no time in explaining his theory to the two agents. He didn't believe Chloe was the type to defect on her own. The kidnapping had been the catalyst. He was almost sure that she had been coerced by the Cuban Intelligence Agent Alvarez and was likely doing it to save her family. It was the only explanation. Chloe just didn't seem like the type to snap like that.

To Spectre's surprise, Baxter was on board with the theory, or at least felt it was plausible. There were logical leaps, as he put it, required to believe that she had willingly given herself up to the enemy just to save her family without contacting the authorities. But Baxter reasoned that people backed into corners could do unreasonable things, and it was entirely possible that the ruthless kidnapping of her family warranted taking no chances in meeting their captors' demands.

Decker wasn't as easily convinced. In fact, she didn't buy it for a second. Chloe Moss was a traitor, plain and simple. There was no gun to her head. She had plenty of opportunities to get help and get herself out of the situation. A highly intelligent woman like Chloe Moss wouldn't just be a naïve victim and play along. She was complicit.

The argument went back and forth for over an hour, mostly between Spectre and Decker. Baxter only played the referee, taking both sides into equal consideration, but leaning toward the kidnapping being the root cause.

Before they could come to a consensus, Baxter received another phone call. Secretary of Defense Kerry Johnson was en route, having been at CENTCOM at MacDill AFB on other business, and would be landing in an hour. After hearing that a brand new F-16 had possibly defected, he wanted a full briefing in person. Baxter invited Spectre and Decker to attend, as long as they promised to sit quietly in the back and not argue with each other. If the SECDEF had any questions about the events at Chloe's parents' house or Aalee, it would be helpful to have them there.

"Gentlemen, I think we all know why we're here, so let's get to the point," the elder statesman began. Spectre couldn't quite place the accent. It was very aristocratic with a touch of Bostonian. "Now who's going to explain to me how we went from suspected mishap to whatever it is you're calling this? Defector?"

Secretary Johnson took his seat at the head of the conference table as Baxter stood from his chair at the far wall and approached the podium in the corner of the room. A large projector screen descended from the ceiling as Baxter brought up his PowerPoint presentation.

"Sir, I'm Special Agent Sean Baxter with AFOSI Detachment 3 here in Homestead. I am the lead investigator on what we are now calling the disappearance of Captain Chloe Moss," he said as he advanced to the next slide showing a timeline of events.

"At approximately 2100 on the night of the crash, Captain Moss was leading a two ship of F-16s from the 39th Fighter Squadron in Warning Area 465 over the Atlantic Ocean during a routine training mission. At 2101, she executed a preplanned maneuver with her wingman, Lt Col Jeff Pitre, in which the aircraft would turn away from each other and descend. At 2102, Lt Col Pitre reported losing contact with Captain Moss—"

"I've read the initial reports, Agent Baxter, get to the point," the SECDEF interjected.

Baxter nodded and advanced to the next slide and hit play. It was the radar feed from the Key West site.

"This is the radar feed from the Key West approach radar," he said, starting the video playback. "As you can see, we lose contact at approximately 21:02:15, around the time Lt Col Pitre lost radio and datalink with Captain Moss. At 21:02:22, however, we see another track south of that position headed due south at low altitude. Based on the speed and relative position, we think that is Captain Moss' jet."

"So where did she go?" the SECDEF interrupted again.

Without missing a beat, Baxter again advanced to the next slide. It was a satellite photo of an airfield.

"This is Castro Field. It is a non-operational military airfield built by the Russians during their push to build up their presence in the Western Hemisphere a few years back. The project was completed in 2009, but when Castro died, the Russians abandoned the project. Foreign intelligence agencies, as well as the DGI have used it as a staging area for South American operations since then."

Baxter advanced to the next slide, showing a map of the area and a plot from Moss' last known position to the airfield in Cuba.

"Based on her last known heading and ties with Cuban Intelligence operative Victor Alvarez, we believe that it is most likely that she landed at this base."

"Let me stop you for a second, before we continue down into this rabbit hole," Secretary Johnson began. "Colonel Louhan."

"Sir?" Coach stood. He was wearing neatly pressed Air Force blues.

"What is the latest on the search and recovery efforts?"

Coach shifted for a moment and picked up his notes. "As of noon today, we have searched a fifty square mile area around the last known position of the aircraft. Due to high winds and rough seas hampering search efforts, we have been unable to locate a debris field of any kind."

"Is it possible the aircraft crashed outside your search area?"

"Without a beacon, survivor communications, or a mark from one of the overhead aircraft witnessing the crash, it is almost impossible to know for sure where the crash actually happened. We have done a grid search with the Coast Guard and Navy, but have so far come up empty handed."

"Do you think the scenario Agent Baxter has briefed is plausible?"

"Sir, I'm not sure I'm qualified to comment on that," Coach responded.

"Sure you are," the SECDEF replied. "Don't you know your own pilots? Do you think one of them would steal a fighter jet?"

Coach looked away, trying to hide his embarrassment. Finally, he said, "The lack of a crash site definitely makes it possible. However, the environment has not been conducive to search and recovery, and we are essentially looking for a needle in a haystack. Captain Moss was an exemplary officer and pilot. Bottom line, no sir, I do not think one of my pilots would do this."

Spectre rolled his eyes. Coach was standing in front of the Secretary of Defense in denial of the evidence and outright lying about his opinion of Chloe. Spectre remembered Chloe coming home crying one day after Coach outright told her during a flight debrief that she was a below average pilot who shouldn't be flying anything in the military. "You would probably be better off working in a USO," he had told her.

But yet, after Spectre's strafing incident, Coach was the first to e-mail a three star general, outright lying about the events of that night to make Spectre look guilty of fratricide. He had even said that one of the friendlies had died of bullet fragmentation wounds during the strafing run, implying that Spectre's bullets had killed him, while neglecting to mention that those bullets were from an enemy AK-47 and that countless others would have died if Spectre hadn't acted. Spectre wondered what the answer would have been had he been the one flying the jet instead of Chloe.

Secretary Johnson turned his attention back to Baxter and nodded for Coach to take his seat. "Agent Baxter, right now what you have amounts to circumstantial evidence. I understand the radar image, but I've spoken to the Secretary of State and the Director of Central Intelligence, and we have no credible information that the Cubans have our aircraft or pilot. What is this Alvarez connection?"

Baxter advanced to his next slide with the profile of Victor Alvarez. He was getting a bit frustrated. He had heard that the SECDEF had a habit of interrupting speakers and going off on tangents, but he didn't think it would be this bad. *If the man would just let him finish, his questions would be answered.*

"Victor Alvarez is a known Cuban Intelligence operative in the Miami area. During our investigation, we interviewed Mr. Martin, who is with us to answer any questions. He gave us copies of correspondence between Moss and Alvarez indicating a meeting on the night of the crash. Mr. Martin was living with Captain Moss at the time of the incident."

Secretary Johnson turned around to look at Spectre who was sitting directly behind him. He looked him over for a second, and then said, "You're the guy she dumped right? And you were still living together?"

Spectre nodded without saying a word. He didn't like the guy already, but he knew he would need him to authorize a rescue effort for Chloe. It was probably better just to say nothing.

"How did you get this alleged correspondence, son?" the statesman asked condescendingly.

"It's complicated," Spectre replied flatly.

"It's complicated? So let me get this straight. Jealous ex-lover comes up with an e-mail and this is your proof that one of our own airmen stole an F-16?" Johnson scoffed.

"She was forced to do it," Spectre replied.

"Forced? Someone put a gun to her head and made her come up with this elaborate way to fake her own death and fly a fighter jet into a shitty third world country? Are you people seriously wasting my time with this?" the SECDEF replied indignantly.

Spectre shifted in his seat. He ran through a few scenarios involving punching the smug bastard right in his aristocratic nose, but none allowed him to escape without having to take down a few friendlies in the process. This whole briefing was starting to become a huge waste of his time.

"Sir, if I may," Baxter interjected. The SECDEF turned around and nodded for Baxter to continue.

"Thank you, sir. As you may know, Representative Ridley and her family were kidnapped a few nights ago by Abdul Aalee. Ridley is Captain Moss' mother. On the night of the mishap, Mr. Martin and a chaplain drove to the Congresswoman's home to notify her of the incident. At that time, Mr. Martin discovered two of the three hostage takers, and after a shootout, was able to secure one of the suspects. After questioning, the suspect gave us the name 'Victor' as Aalee's handler."

Baxter paused, took a sip of water, and then continued, "Mr. Martin has played a key role in this investigation, not only in saving the Congresswoman and securing a key witness, but he also led us to the radar information and a possible location where Captain Moss may have gone."

Agent Decker flashed a smile at Spectre and poked him in the side. Spectre was too focused on punching the old man in the throat to notice the attractive blonde flirting with him.

"Ok, let's say someone did coerce her into doing it. Are you sure it's this Alvarez guy?" Johnson replied.

"Sir, based on the correspondence given to us by Mr. Martin and the statement by Abdul Aalee's man, as well as his status as a Cuban Intelligence operative, we believe so."

"So the jilted ex-lover gives you this information, as well as magically shows up to save the day, and points you to an elaborate scheme in which the first female fighter pilot in this squadron, and Air Force Academy graduate, is forced into stealing an F-16 and flying it to Cuba?" he asked incredulously.

Decker grabbed Spectre's arm. His jaw was clenched and his face reddened. It was clear to Decker he was about to do something he would later regret.

"Sir, are you suggesting Mr. Martin is a suspect?" Baxter was beside himself.

Secretary Johnson snapped his fingers and motioned for Coach to hand him a file. He put his reading glasses on and opened the file folder.

"Captain Cal 'Spectre' Martin, reassigned to non-flying status after a friendly fire incident, given a letter of reprimand and honorably discharged from the Air Force Reserve six months later. Listed as next of kin to Captain Chloe Moss, who we now know dumped him a few weeks ago," the man looked up from his folder. "Is this information correct, Colonel Louhan?"

"Yes, sir, that is accurate," Coach replied with a smug grin.

"I'm not telling you how to do your job, Special Agent Baxter, but before I'd risk alerting the press and starting a media frenzy that one of our own servicewomen has gone off the reservation by stealing a jet, I would at least consider the source.

Do you know what kind of black eye that would give this administration?"

"Then where is the jet, asshole?"

There was a collective gasp as the room fell silent and every head turned to Spectre. He was now standing, his knuckles white from his clenched fists. Decker tried to grab him to make him sit back down, but he shrugged off her attempts.

"Excuse me?" Johnson asked.

"You're so worried about how the media will spin this that you can't see what's going on here," he said. He made no attempts to hide the contempt and anger in his voice.

"Mr. Martin, you've wasted enough of our time in the last couple of days. If you don't sit down and shut up so the adults can talk, I will have you removed. Do you understand?" Johnson looked at his security detail. The two men were slowly approaching Spectre from either side.

Spectre contemplated his next move. He calculated that he could probably deal with the approaching security detail, but the long-term ramifications would be more than a little unpleasant. He didn't need jail time right now. He put his hands up.

"Ok, just hear me out, sir," Spectre said in a disarming tone.

Johnson waved the two guards off and motioned for Spectre to proceed. "You have thirty seconds, the floor is yours."

"I didn't believe it either, but when I freed Chloe's stepdad, he was worried that something had happened to Chloe before I had even told him anything. He had overheard the men who kidnapped him mentioning her name. These assholes knew her. They were doing this to get to her. And Victor Alvarez was orchestrating the whole thing. Now you have an F-16 on foreign soil being exploited by God knows what country. Probably the Chinese, given their track record. And an American Airman being held captive. What kind of media frenzy do you think that will cause for your precious administration?"

"Mr. Martin, your time is up, this is all very circumstantial. As I mentioned before, we have no credible intelligence suggesting anything beyond a simple crash," Johnson dismissed, motioning for his security detail to remove Spectre.

"So you're ok with the idea that an American Air Force Officer is potentially in enemy hands right now, being interrogated by foreign intelligence agents?" Spectre asked disgustedly.

"If that is, in fact, the case, then we will work it through the State Department, but she knew the risks when she signed up. Thank you for your time, Mr. Martin, good day."

Spectre turned to walk out. The guard in front of him tried to grab his arm as the other guard approached from the rear. Spectre rotated his arm out of the guard's grip and pushed him away as he continued past him to the door.

"Don't do anything stupid, Mr. Martin," the SECDEF warned as Spectre stormed to the door.

Spectre stopped at the door and paused for a minute as he reached the door. "The only thing stupid I've done is waste my time with you incompetent assholes," he said as he walked out, slamming the door behind him.

# CHAPTER THIRTY-FIVE

"**C**al, wait!" Spectre stopped and turned to face the female voice behind him. He had barely made it out the door past the SECDEF's security detail to the parking lot. It was Agent Decker.

"What?" Spectre said tersely as she caught up to him. He was still fuming from the confrontation with the SECDEF, but her deep blue eyes were disarming. He was sure people had fallen victim to her attractiveness many times before and had probably fallen over themselves to give her whatever she wanted. *It was hard to resist.*

"Listen, I know you're upset, but there's really nothing we can do right now," she pleaded.

"You stopped me to regurgitate the talking points from the dipshit in there? *Seriously?* I don't have time for this." Spectre turned back to his truck.

Decker grabbed his arm gently as he tried to walk off. "Cal, please, just stop for a second. You've been through a lot in the last couple of days. You and Baxter both. But you have to let the system work. If she's alive, State will negotiate her release."

Spectre turned back and shrugged off her grip. Disarming or not, she represented the establishment. She was part of the system that had destroyed his flying career and was now doing nothing to save the woman he loved. Or had once loved. He still wasn't sure what to believe.

"Were you just in the same meeting I was in? They don't even believe the jet is still in one piece. They're not going to negotiate anything. If she's alive, she'll rot in some prison and no one will ever know it. I can't just sit back and wait, knowing that something could have been done."

"You're not planning on going to the press with this are you?" she replied with a look of concern.

"Rule number one, never talk to the media," Spectre shot back.

"Then what are you going to do?"

"Special Agent Decker, I appreciate your concern, but I really don't have time for this. If I think of anything else that may be beneficial to your investigation, I'll give you a call." Spectre pulled his sunglasses from the top of his head and put them on. He didn't wait for a response before getting into his truck.

Spectre replayed the day's meetings over and over in his head on the drive back to the store. The store was the only place that made sense to him. He didn't want to go home and he needed to talk to Marcus about what the government's official position was. He still didn't know what he was going to do.

The Secretary of Defense, although a total asshole, had been partially right. There was no concrete evidence or proof of life. But the thought of her sitting in a holding cell, scared and alone, was just too much.

Spectre didn't believe in coincidences. It was pretty clear that the kidnappings and e-mails were related. Alvarez had orchestrated the whole thing. It was a pretty smart plan from his perspective. He made her defect by using her family as leverage. But there were still questions hanging in Spectre's mind. *Why didn't she tell him? Did she break up with him to make the pain easier? What about those e-mails she sent to Alvarez?*

The more Spectre thought about it, the more the situation bugged him. The questions were muted by the overarching reality. He had to do something to at least try to get her back. He would never be able to live with himself knowing he did nothing when he could have done something.

Spectre arrived at the store to find Marcus in his office. He was surprised to see Joe Carpenter sitting on the couch chatting with Marcus as he walked in without knocking. Carpenter was wearing faded blue jeans, flip-flops and a Superman t-shirt.

"Joe?" Spectre asked, cocking his head to the side. "What are you doing here?"

"Spectre! Dude, I've been trying to call you," Carpenter said, standing to greet Spectre. "As soon as I heard what happened to your woman, I drove down. Marcus has filled me in. Are you ok man?"

Spectre shot Marcus an inquisitive look. "What did he tell you?"

"He told me about the crash," Carpenter said using air quotes, "and the shootout with the tangos."

"I told him everything I knew, Cal," Marcus finally said.

Spectre shrugged and sat down in the big leather chair across from Marcus. "Then I guess I won't have to repeat anything. You'll never guess who I just met."

"Kate Upton?" Marcus replied with a grin. It was the kind of perverted old man grin that made Spectre cringe.

"No, but close," Spectre replied, turning to Carpenter. "I met your boss."

"Lt Col Samson?" Carpenter asked.

"Much higher. Kerry Johnson was on base today. And I got to sit in on their conference."

"You met the SECDEF? Wow, this must be pretty serious for him to show up in person," Carpenter replied.

"That fucking Democrat? Did you punch him in his crooked nose?" Marcus replied. Spectre wondered what Marcus would have done in that conference room. He was glad he didn't get to find out, although the entertainment value might have made it completely worth the wasted afternoon.

"The one and only. And no, I didn't punch him, although the urge was definitely there."

Spectre related all the events of the day. From the debate with Baxter and Decker to the conference with the Homestead brass and eventually storming out, Marcus and Carpenter absorbed every detail.

Before Spectre could get to the part with Agent Decker in the parking lot, Carpenter interrupted abruptly, "I'm in."

"You're in for what?" Spectre asked.

"Whatever it is you're planning. I'm in. Fuck those guys," Carpenter replied without missing a beat.

"Me too," said Marcus.

"I'm not planning anything. This isn't the movies. I'm not even sure what we could do or how to even get to Cuba."

"Just head south. You'll get there eventually," Marcus replied sarcastically.

"No shit, but that's a pretty big operation for three people," said Spectre. His mind had been racing through scenarios all day. It sounded like a great idea – to do what the government wouldn't and rescue her, and it was what Spectre wanted to do. But it was a logistical nightmare. Even for a trained team, getting in undetected and getting her out would be a challenge. For three lightly armed civilians with no three-letter agency support, it would be impossible. They would all end up captured or killed.

"How would we even get there?" Spectre asked. "It's not like we can just take your fishing boat and cruise on down to Cuba."

The room fell silent. Marcus sat back in his chair and thought about it for a minute.

"What about a helicopter?" Marcus finally replied.

# CHAPTER THIRTY-SIX

*Castro Field, Cuba*

**"A**s I told you before, you will have twenty chances to tell me what I need to know. Are you ready?" Ling was twisting a pair of pliers in his hands. His voice was calm and emotionless. His only interest in this was information. Her refusal to talk to this point seemed to have little effect on him. He made it seem like nothing more than a minor inconvenience to him.

Chloe squirmed in her chair. She was back in the same office, tied to the same chair she had been in some time before. She still had no idea what time or even what day it was. Her watch had been stripped from her along with the rest of her clothes. She felt cold, naked, and vulnerable.

She wasn't even sure her plan would work. Victor had been pulled from the cell moments before they dragged her back into the room with Ling. She could only imagine the torture he was facing. Nothing was going the way she had originally planned. She was supposed to be living her new life by now. She prayed that this plan, although admittedly weak, would be enough to at least get them out of there with their lives.

"Please, this wasn't part of the deal," she pleaded. "I don't know as much as you think."

"Well, we will find out," Ling replied as he moved closer.

As he reached down to grab her right index finger, Moss screamed, "Wait! I will tell you whatever you want. We can make a deal!"

Ling hesitated for a second and took a step back. "I'm listening," he said.

"I can show you how to boot all of the systems up, give you all the codes, whatever you want, but..."

"You are in no position to make demands, Captain Moss."

"I'm giving you everything! I just want you to let Victor and me go. Please! Just don't hurt him." Tears were rolling down Chloe's cheeks.

Ling stepped forward with his pliers and grabbed Chloe's right index finger with his free hand. She tried to resist, but his grip was too strong. She twisted against the restraints.

"Wait! What are you doing?" she screamed.

Ling jabbed the open pliers into the nail bed and clamped down. With a single motion, he ripped the nail off, sending blood everywhere as Chloe screamed at the top of her lungs. Ling stepped back and held the fingernail in front of Chloe's face.

The screaming soon turned to sobbing as he stood over her.

"This is not a game," he said as he flicked the nail into the nearby trashcan and shoved the pliers into his pocket.

\* \* \*

"What's her plan?" Zhang demanded. They were sitting in an adjacent office watching Ling's interrogation on a video feed on his laptop.

Alvarez cringed as he watched Ling rip the fingernail from Moss' index finger. It was brutal and bloody, but Alvarez knew it was necessary. A detainee could not be allowed to feel in control. She had to be made to second-guess every thought of resistance. The pain was horrible, but not life threatening. Those techniques would come much later, but Alvarez hoped it wouldn't be necessary.

"She didn't say," he responded, turning away. "But I suspect it has something to do with the deal she's trying to make."

Ling walked in, wiping the blood off his hands with his handkerchief. He tossed it in the trashcan and walked up to desk where Alvarez and Zhang were sitting.

"She is convinced that Alvarez is being tortured. I think the fear of your death is worse than the fear of her own harm," he said, looking at Alvarez.

Alvarez responded with a toothy smile. "You hired me because I am good at what I do."

"Indeed," Zhang replied. "We still don't have the information though. Do you think she's trying to escape, or does she really care that much about you?"

Ling pulled the pliers out of his back pocket. "I can make her give us the access codes we need. She's already starting to break."

Zhang held up his hand and looked at Alvarez. "You've worked with this asset for many months now. Do you think she will comply? We are running out of time."

Alvarez considered the question for a moment. Moss had been sold on the idea of a new life since day one. She was convinced that Alvarez was not only her lover, but could give her the new life she seemed to desperately want. It had been clear in the prison cell, and it was even clearer in the interrogation room.

"Let her sit in isolation for a while and then give her the deal she thinks she wants. When it is time, take her to the jet using me as leverage. If she fears for my life, as Mr. Ling says, she will not risk it. Besides, my men will not allow her to escape."

# CHAPTER THIRTY-SEVEN

*Cutler Bay, FL*

Tucked away in the Black Point Marina off Biscayne Bay, sat Black Point Ocean Grill, a small bar and grill. It offered live bands and lots of outdoor seating, perfect for tourists and local boaters after a long day on the water.

It was Spectre's favorite local restaurant, serving the best Mahi Burger he'd ever had. He and Chloe used to hang out there after a long work week to relax on the water and enjoy the live music. But on this evening, his plans were much different. Marcus had told him to meet him there after work, presumably to talk about whatever plan he'd thought up in his office earlier that day.

Spectre hadn't seen Marcus since he'd mentioned the helicopter. It was almost as if he had a light bulb moment. Marcus vanished soon after, leaving him to catch up with

Carpenter and bury himself in some work he had left unfinished since the events of the last few days had unfolded.

Spectre still wasn't sure there was anything they could do. Even if they could come up with a way to get in country, pinpointing her location and gathering intel would be tough. It was a noble gesture, but seemed like a surefire way to get all of his closest friends killed.

But the idea of Chloe being tortured was still eating at him. He had seen in training what foreign intelligence services could do to get information out of people. It made him cringe to think that someone would be using such techniques on the woman he once loved.

At the back of his mind lay the doubt that she might be complicit in the whole thing. The draft folder e-mail still didn't make much sense. She seemed to be looking forward to seeing Alvarez, as if he was a lover. Spectre's gut told him something wasn't right, but his heart told him that she was in trouble and she needed him. *He had never really stopped loving her.*

Spectre had chosen the table on the pier farthest from the main building and live band. It was a typical South Florida evening. A few scattered thunderstorms loomed in the distance, but otherwise it was just humid and hot with a light breeze. Spectre was used to it.

Spectre ordered water and thanked the waitress. He was the first to arrive, but only a few minutes later he saw Carpenter walking down the stairs of the restaurant. The band had already started its evening of mostly rock and a few country music cover songs.

"Any idea what this is about?" Spectre asked as Carpenter ordered a beer and sat down. He was wearing a Hawaiian shirt, cargo shorts, and flip-flops.

"Nope, I got the same text message you did. It said to be here at seven. It's 6:55. Everyone else is late."

As Carpenter sat down, Spectre noticed three more men walking down the stairway to their table. In the lead was Marcus, dressed in his usual cargo pants and a polo shirt, followed by two men Spectre did not immediately recognize from the distance.

As the men neared the table, Spectre stood to greet them. He immediately recognized Elvis, his former squadron mate from the Gators, and Director Browning of the Customs and Border Protection Air and Marine branch at Homestead close in trail. Marcus seemed to have a plan.

"You're late, Marcus," Carpenter announced as he shook the old Marine's hand.

"A retired Marine always arrives whenever he goddamned feels like it," Marcus shot back.

"Are you a wizard now too, Marcus?" Spectre quipped.

Carpenter picked up on the Lord of the Rings reference and rolled his eyes. Marcus and his two guests sat down as the waitress took their drink order. He introduced Elvis and the Director to Carpenter. Spectre was forced to wonder what plan Marcus could have possibly come up with.

"I'm really sorry about Chloe," Elvis offered as they each placed their orders. "She was a good pilot. We still don't really understand it."

Spectre gave Marcus a confused look.

"Cal, I invited Elvis and Dave here because I thought they would rather hear it first hand from you," Marcus explained.

"So you didn't tell them?" Spectre asked.

"Tell us what?" Director Browning asked. "Marcus just invited us out for dinner. We heard it's been a rough week for you and figured we'd hang out a bit. What's going on?"

Spectre looked around to make sure no one was eavesdropping and then leaned in. "Chloe didn't crash."

Elvis leaned back with a disapproving look and sighed. "C'mon Spectre, I heard what happened at the wing conference room. You have to come to terms with this."

Director Browning gave Elvis a confused look. Elvis explained what he had heard through the rumor mill about Spectre's confrontation with the SECDEF. The prevailing story was that Spectre had lost his mind in a desperate spectacle with a half-cocked theory about how Chloe had faked her own death and was still somehow a POW in a foreign country.

Spectre listened to the whole story and then calmly said, "You really think I would just pull something like that out of my ass?"

"Listen man, I know you've been through a lot, and your reputation isn't the greatest on the base, so I don't doubt that most of what's been said isn't one hundred percent true. But you can't possibly believe she's still alive after this long," Elvis replied.

Spectre paused for a moment. He considered getting up and walking out. He had known Elvis since his early flying days. The man was a straight shooter and could be sucked into squadron drama at times, but he had never known him to be anything but fair. He still didn't know where Marcus was going with this, but it was clear he had some semblance of a plan in mind.

"Director Browning, do you remember the man you guys were chasing when we last spoke? Aalee?" Spectre asked.

Browning shifted uneasily in his chair. It was clear he didn't like talking about it in public. He knew he probably should not have mentioned it at all to Spectre and Marcus. He simply nodded in response.

"And did you know I was involved in a shootout with his group?" Spectre asked.

"Aalee was killed in a suicide attack," the Director replied frankly.

"You guys are really still this bad at sharing information, aren't you?" Spectre asked rhetorically. "No, before that, he kidnapped Chloe's family. When I went to notify them with the chaplain, I just happened to find them."

Spectre was interrupted by the arrival of their food. He waited for a minute for the servers to leave, and then continued. He explained the e-mails between Chloe and Alvarez, and his subsequent assistance in the investigation by Baxter. He told them how they had discovered the radar track heading south from the radar tapes, and then connected the dots with intel of the abandoned airfield used primarily by Cuban intelligence agencies.

"So this is what you told the SECDEF?" Elvis asked.

"Yes, and he said it was inconclusive," Spectre replied with a look of disgust.

"Well, what motive did she have?" Browning asked as he cut into his seared tuna.

"Alvarez used Aalee to kidnap her family and make it look like a terrorist plot. They were using them as leverage to ensure she followed through. Now it's likely she's being interrogated by a foreign intelligence service."

"Cubans? Really?" Elvis asked.

"Well, they are probably a middle man. You know as well as I do there are plenty of governments trying to get their hands on our technology. The Russians, the Chinese, Iranians, North Koreans, you name it," Spectre replied.

"Spectre, if you're right, then we essentially have an American with sensitive technology being detained in a foreign country. That's an act of war," Elvis said.

"Which is why this pussified administration won't do a fucking thing," Marcus interjected. "Fucking Democrats."

"Politics aside," said Director Browning, "what's your end game? Media? Politicians?"

"We're going to go get her," Carpenter piped up. He had been silent the entire conversation, but now he seemed motivated.

"Spectre, you're not seriously thinking about doing this yourself, are you?" Elvis asked. "You don't have the training!"

"I don't know, but I can't let her die while knowing I could have at least tried," Spectre replied solemnly.

"He won't be doing it alone," Marcus said, nodding at Director Browning.

"What did you have in mind?" Browning asked.

With the band covering "Purple Haze" by Jimmy Hendrix, Marcus went over his plan in great detail. It was something he had done many times as a Marine Sniper, and even with limited resources and information they had, he was certain it could be adapted and applied quickly to their purposes.

They all listened intently as Marcus meticulously explained his elaborate plan, covering every aspect from infil to exfil. He had even come up with contingencies for several different scenarios. It wasn't necessarily air tight, but Spectre thought it was a decent plan.

Marcus had barely finished before Elvis said, "I'm in. The government might be turning its back on an American fighter pilot, but I won't."

Marcus looked at Director Browning for his answer. He simply nodded and took a long swig of his beer.

"The branch is probably going to get shut down, and I'll be forced to retire anyway, might as make it worthwhile," he finally replied as he slammed the empty beer glass down.

# CHAPTER THIRTY-EIGHT

*Doral, FL*

"I'm really worried he's going to do something stupid," Agent Decker said, breaking the silence from the passenger seat of Baxter's BMW M3.

Baxter said nothing as he drove through the staggered barricades to the guard shack. He presented his credentials to the guard and was waved through after a brief vehicle walk around by an assisting officer.

"He just seemed like he had been pushed over the edge. I've seen that look before," she said, staring out the window.

"Well, he was pretty much completely discredited by the SECDEF. I would probably be a little upset too," Baxter replied as he pulled into a parking spot and shut off the engine.

"I know, but as much as the guy has been through, I don't want to see him do something that will ruin him," she said with a frown.

"You mean like going to the media?" Baxter asked as they walked toward the newly constructed building.

"Or trying to go get her himself," she replied, walking through the door the gentle Texan had opened for her.

Baxter frowned at her as he pulled out his credentials from his pocket and passed them through the bulletproof glass to the attendant in the lobby. Decker passed the attendant hers as well, and they waited for their credentials to be verified.

"Is this your first visit to SOUTHCOM?" the woman asked as she looked up their names in her computer.

"No, ma'am," Baxter replied. "I have been here a few times."

Located in Doral, Florida, United States Southern Command was one of nine combatant commands comprised of more than 1,200 military and civilian personnel representing the Army, Navy, Air Force, Marine Corps, Coast Guard, and several other federal agencies. Responsible for Central America, South America, and the Caribbean, it served as a command and control center for anti-terrorism, humanitarian, and other joint federal operations.

Completed in late 2010, SOUTHCOM's multi-million dollar facilities were state of the art and capable of processing high level classified information in various offices. The building served as the gateway to Latin America. If something were going on in Cuba, someone in this building would know about it.

At least that was what Baxter was hoping. After their theory had been completely blown off by the SECDEF and his aides, Baxter was determined to find conclusive evidence. The truth was always in the details. But if Martin was correct, he didn't have much time to get through them all.

Although it was late in the afternoon after their failed attempt to convince the SECDEF of the urgency of the matter, Baxter had been hoping his contact at the Joint Federal Task Force at USSOUTHCOM would still be working as he dialed her extension from his cell phone. He had worked with her a few times before, and knew she was probably still at work. She never seemed to leave the place or even sleep. She answered on the first ring and was more than willing to help. She was going to be at work anyway, so it was no trouble.

The woman handed them visitor badges and the large metal door buzzed as it released its magnetic lock. As they opened the door, a petite woman with dark brown hair and a pair of horn-rimmed glasses in a modest skirt and sweater was standing there to greet them.

"Agent Baxter, it's nice to see you again," she said, extending her pale hand.

Baxter gently took her hand with a smile.

"You too, Danielle," he replied. "Agent Decker, this is Danielle Warden, the NSA's smartest intel analyst, and best Call of Duty player I've ever met."

Agent Decker stepped forward to shake Warden's hand, but instead was greeted by an awkward wave as Warden quickly turned around and started walking.

"Come on! Let's not waste any time!" Warden said leading them to her work area.

Baxter shrugged apologetically as Decker looked at him in confusion. They did their best to keep up. Despite her short stature, she was relatively quick, leading them through the hallways and corridors lined with secure rooms and vaults.

As they reached Warden's Sensitive Compartmented Information Facility (SCIF), she paused momentarily before swiping her access badge.

"You guys don't have any cell phones, pagers, thumb drives, PDAs, or other personal media, right?"

"We locked up our phones in the lobby. My pager's there too, so I guess the crack deals will have to wait," Baxter said with a wink.

Warden rolled her eyes and swiped her badge. "I had to ask," she said as she typed in her PIN.

The magnetic lock clicked open and they were led into another door where she went through a similar procedure. A few moments later, they were walking into the relatively dark room filled with analysts steadily working in their cubicles. A large screen on the wall showed a map of what Baxter guessed to be all of the current operations in their area of responsibility. There were multicolored dots scattered around South America, Cuba, and Central America.

"You can close the door behind you," Warden said as she scurried into her office and sat down at her desk.

"That's a lot of monitors," Decker said, pointing to the four monitors that surrounded Warden's desk as they took their seats across from her desk.

"Being the boss has its perks. Besides, I have a lot of networks to keep track of at varying classification levels. Don't want to risk 'crossing the streams,'" she replied with air quotes.

Baxter pulled out a piece of paper from his pocket and handed it to her.

"What kind of imagery can you get for us with these coordinates?" he asked as Warden reviewed the handwritten coordinates.

"Cuba?" she asked. Baxter wasn't surprised that she recognized the coordinates. He wasn't sure what projects she was actually assigned to, but he knew her from his short time at the Joint Terrorism Task Force. She was considered an expert in satellite intelligence. Baxter had been amazed several times at how much information she could gather about suspects coming out of South America from a few high-resolution satellite images. He hoped her expertise would pay off again.

"Yes, it's very important to our investigation," Decker interjected.

Baxter had only explained that he needed help with a high-level investigation on the phone. He gave Warden the rundown from the information they had gained from Aalee's man and the investigation into Moss' disappearance and their theory about where she might be.

"Exciting stuff," she said as she typed away at her keyboard. "Unfortunately, at the time you gave me, the SBIRS-2 wasn't overhead, and with the cloud cover, the SPYGLASS-4 won't give you much."

"English, please," Baxter pleaded.

"The SBIRS-2 is a low Earth orbit Space Based Infrared Satellite. Officially, it's designed to detect infrared signatures for missile launches. Unofficially, well, let's just say that if it has a temperature delta, I can watch it. On the flip side of that, the SPYGLASS-4 is a high-resolution imagery satellite. Google Maps is advertised as one-meter resolution. The SG4 is measured in inches and if the environmentals are right, even better," she explained.

"When was the SBIRS last overhead?" Decker asked.

"The SBIRS-2 is in a geosynchronous orbit for this region, so once every twenty-three hours, fifty-six minutes, and four seconds," she said as she clicked through the screens on her computer. "And it looks like the last time was early this morning. Looks like 05:32:26 local time."

Warden turned her monitor to face Decker and Baxter. It was a monochrome infrared image of the airfield runway and hangars.

"Can you zoom in?" Baxter asked, pointing to the main hangar.

"Since the satellite wasn't tasked, I can't get you the really high-level stuff, but let me see what I can do," she said, busily typing away through a series of LINUX command prompts.

The on screen image shifted and rotated as Warden zoomed in. Soon the bird's eye view of the airfield was narrowed down to a single hangar with numerous white-hot dots scattered in and around it.

"Jesus, that's pretty impressive," said Decker. "I had no idea."

"That's Junior Varsity level for Danielle," Baxter said with a wink. "She can almost tell you what they had for breakfast."

"Stop it, you're making me blush," Warden replied. "But yeah, this is not that great. A little notice would have been nice."

As Warden continued to work, the image became clearer. "Ok, it looks like you have four to five individuals in the building itself, and seven individuals around the perimeter."

"Are there any isolated? As if being held captive?" Baxter asked.

"If we had tasked the satellite with its primary sensor, I could tell you. This is the secondary that's always on. You're lucky you even have this. The hangar appears to be two stories, so it's impossible to break it out like this," she explained.

"What about the other satellite you mentioned? When was it last overhead? Does it have the same limitations?" Decker asked.

"I can check, and no, the SG4 is always online," she replied.

"Wait! Before you close this, can you print that out for me?" Baxter asked.

"You realize this is Top Secret, right?" Warden replied incredulously.

"I am authorized as a TS courier, relax," Baxter replied with a sheepish grin.

Warden hit print, and the laser printer behind her whirred to life. "You're lucky you're cute," she said with a wry smile.

Baxter walked to the printer and grabbed the image. Warden handed him a folder marked TOP SECRET to put it in and went back to typing.

"The SG4 is a semi-synchronous satellite, so it's overhead every eleven hours and fifty-eight minutes," she said, bringing up another image of the airfield on her monitor. This time it was in color. Like the first, it was a bird's eye view, but the resolution was much sharper.

"Looks like it was overhead about two hours ago," she said as she zoomed in.

As the image resolved, she scrolled to the hangar bay. It was a huge hangar, seemingly capable of housing large aircraft. Baxter remembered the base's initial intent as a strategic bomber base for a looming second Cold War and figured that it must have been built to support bombers. The hangar doors were partially open, with men standing guard out front.

"Wait can you zoom in on that hangar door?" Baxter said, pointing to the partially open door on the monitor.

Without saying a word, Warden rotated the image and zoomed in on the hangar door. Baxter strained to pick out the detail. He could see a shadow on the hangar floor.

"Any chance you could tilt it and see what's inside?" Baxter asked as he sat on the edge of his chair trying to make out the contents of the hangar.

Warden frowned. "No, but I can advance the image. If the angle is right, we may be able to see what's inside."

With a few more keystrokes, the frames advanced and the image updated. Soon the shadow was replaced by something gray with a white panel open.

"Can you zoom in on that? Right there?" Baxter asked, pointing to the white panel.

Decker and Baxter both leaned forward in their chairs straining to see what it was.

"That's definitely a light of some sort," Decker said, pointing to the left of the open panel. "But that could be any kind of airplane."

"No, look!" Baxter said, pointing excitedly to the white panel. "That's the squadron patch for the Gators!"

"What? How can you tell?" Decker asked, straining to make it out.

"See that right there? It says 'World' and that's a Gator," he said pointing to the door. "This is a squadron sticker someone put in the access panel. 'World Famous Gators.'"

"I guess you want me to print this out too?" Warden asked as she hit print.

"Yes, please. You've been a great help! Thank you so much! I owe you," Baxter said as he picked up the image off the printer and shoved it into the folder with the other picture.

"Yes, you do. And don't think I won't collect," Warden replied.

Baxter gave her a big hug and Decker thanked her as Warden escorted them back out to the lobby.

"Let me know if you need anything else," Warden said.

Baxter thanked her again and they walked out into the lobby. It was completely dark as they walked out into the parking lot after retrieving their phones and turning in their badges.

Baxter stopped as they reached the car. "Hey, it's been a long day. Wanna grab dinner?"

Decker laughed at the awkward attempt to ask her out. "Why not? I'm sure Outback has a nice SCIF you can store that in while we eat." She chuckled as she pointed to the envelope containing the Top Secret folder in his hand.

"Oh, right," Baxter replied. "I almost forgot."

Decker laughed as she got in the car and he handed her the document to hold.

"Besides, I don't date agents," she said with a wink. "But that analyst seemed to have a thing for you."

# CHAPTER THIRTY-NINE

*Cutler Bay, FL*

S pectre had three missed calls on his phone when he reached his truck after dinner at the marina. He recognized the number from the first two calls immediately. It was the number Agent Baxter had called him from previously. The second number, however, was foreign to him.

Spectre played back the first voicemail. It was Agent Baxter. He simply asked if Spectre could call him as soon as possible. He had a distinct sense of urgency in his voice. The second voicemail was along the same lines and advised that Spectre could call back at any time as Baxter was planning on staying at the office late and urgently needed to speak with him.

Putting the truck in gear, Spectre pulled out of the marina parking lot toward home as he dialed Agent Baxter's number through his truck's Bluetooth connection. It rang once before being picked up.

"This is Special Agent Baxter," the voice through his truck's speakers said abruptly.

"Agent Baxter, this is Cal Martin, I'm just returning your call. Sorry it's so late," Spectre said apologetically as he drove down the narrow road past the sugar cane fields. It was nearing 9 PM and there were no other cars around him.

"Mr. Martin! I'm glad you called. Listen, I know it's late, but is there any chance you can meet me at my office tonight? It's very urgent."

Spectre considered the request. He was still angry with the levels of incompetence he had just witnessed hours earlier from his government and military leaders. Helping them after the way he had been treated didn't seem very appealing, especially with the work he now had to do.

"Can it wait until tomorrow? It's very late," Spectre finally replied.

"I understand that, Mr. Martin, and I'm sorry for what happened today, but I promise you, it will be well worth your time," Baxter pleaded.

Spectre let the request hang in the air as he continued driving. He liked Baxter. The guy seemed like a straight shooter and had been fair with him throughout it all. But Baxter was part of a bigger system that had failed him on numerous occasions. Whatever the man wanted could wait. Spectre had more important things to worry about than helping him with an investigation that none of the higher echelons even cared to hear about.

"I'm sorry, but if you'd like to set up an appointment tomorrow, I can see you then," Spectre finally said flatly. "I really have to go, please call me tomorrow at a reasonable hour."

The vehicle's Bluetooth announced "Call Ended" as Spectre hung up the phone without waiting for a response. Minutes later the phone rang again, this time it was the number he hadn't recognized.

"Hello," Spectre snapped.

"Mr. Martin?" the female voice asked. "It's Special Agent Decker, I'm so sorry to bother you."

Spectre was initially disarmed by her voice. Her tone had a calming influence, but he soon shook it aside.

"I already told Baxter I am done this evening," Spectre replied tersely.

"I don't blame you," she replied. "But we've made a huge breakthrough in the case that I think you're going to want to see, *before you do anything else.*"

Spectre took note of the emphasis she placed on "doing anything else." She couldn't possibly know what they were planning, but it was the second time she had warned him not to do anything. *How could she possibly know?*

"I'll be there in ten minutes," Spectre finally said.

Spectre's mind raced as he considered the possibilities of their discoveries. If they had proof of Chloe's capture, he was sure they wouldn't be consulting him. They wouldn't need to. They could easily take the information up to the SECDEF and Secretary of State and use official assets to recover Chloe. Decker's tone was pretty somber. She seemed to know that he was planning something and sounded intent on keeping him from making what she thought to be a huge mistake.

Spectre decided that he was thinking too far into it. He would just see what they had to say first. If it were another waste of his time, he would simply walk out. If they genuinely wanted his help, he would consider it.

Spectre pulled his truck into the OSI parking lot on the base and backed into a space. The lot was empty except for a BMW and another SUV. Spectre walked in and buzzed the doorbell. Moments later, the door opened and Agent Decker appeared. She looked tired, but beautiful as ever. Spectre caught himself wondering if there was something going on between Baxter and Decker to be hanging out together so late at night.

"Thanks for coming out on such short notice, we really appreciate it," she said, pushing a strand of blonde hair out of her face. "Agent Baxter is in the vault. We'd like your opinion on something."

Spectre nodded and followed Agent Decker down the hallway to the vault door. She entered a code and the magnetic steel door clicked open. Agent Baxter was sitting at a computer with files scattered about. He looked stressed.

"Mr. Martin, glad you changed your mind," Baxter said, rising to shake Spectre's hand.

"Try not to waste my time again," Spectre replied harshly.

Baxter handed Spectre a photo marked TOP SECRET. It was grainy, but Spectre immediately recognized it.

"Do you know what that is, Mr. Martin?" Baxter asked.

"Looks like the inlet and nav light on an F-16. That's the crew chief access panel."

"Do you recognize the logo?" Decker prodded.

"World Famous Gators," Spectre replied. "Holy shit, is this what I think it is?"

Spectre turned and leaned against a nearby desk. The realization hit him that this was Chloe's F-16. Until seeing the photo, it had all been speculation, theory, and conjecture. Now it was real. Staring him in the face was proof that he had been right. *She didn't crash.* She was in Cuba and in extreme danger. His resolve to act grew stronger.

"This is a high-resolution photo of a hangar on the air base you pointed us to," Baxter explained. "I was pretty sure what it was, but you just confirmed it."

"What do you mean I confirmed it? Why do you need a civilian to confirm it? How is this not being worked by DOD?" Spectre demanded.

Decker put her hand on Spectre's shoulder. "We forwarded this directly to Secretary Johnson's staff and had a fairly lengthy secure teleconference with his Chief of Staff. They consider it to be inconclusive."

"What the fuck do you mean, *inconclusive?*" Spectre snapped, standing back up and holding the photo up. "This is pretty goddamned obvious. An F-16 just happens to be in the hangar we thought it might be in, and they think it's inconclusive?"

Baxter sighed. "Believe me, I made the same argument, but their stance is that there's no proof of life or even that it's an American F-16, despite the sticker."

Spectre was beside himself. He wondered how the government ever managed to get anything done.

"Last I checked, the Cubans don't have F-16s, and – wait for it- we just lost one of ours!" Spectre's face was red and his eyes full of rage.

"They said it could be Venezuelan, and without any demands from anyone so far, if she is there, she's a defector," Baxter explained. "They're going to let the State Department make a formal inquiry."

"What about her family? That terrorist asshole Aalee?" Spectre asked.

"They said it was an unfortunate coincidence," Decker interjected.

"Copy, well thanks for nothing, I've got shit to do," Spectre said as he turned to walk out.

"Wait!" Baxter said fishing through his files. "There's one more thing."

Spectre turned around in disgust. If he had any doubts before, he didn't anymore. The only way to save Chloe would be to do it himself.

Baxter handed him another photo.

"I count twelve total, including your girlfriend," Baxter said, pointing at the white dots on the black and white picture.

"That's a pretty small force," Spectre said, looking at the infrared image.

"It would be for an intelligence operation," replied Baxter.

"Why are you showing me this?" Spectre asked.

"Because whatever it is you're planning, we're here to help," Baxter replied.

"What makes you think I'm planning anything?" Spectre asked suspiciously.

"Your eyes gave it away," Decker replied. "And we want to help in any way we can. *Unofficially*, of course."

# CHAPTER FORTY

*Redlands, FL*

The South Florida night air was thick and muggy. Even at three in the morning, it was still hot. Spectre guessed it was nearly 80 degrees without even the slightest breeze. The weather patterns in South Florida never seemed to change, regardless of the time of year.

They were all standing around Spectre's three quarter ton pickup in black tactical pants and black Army Combat Shirts. The shirts were designed to help wick away moisture with a fireproof mesh torso and thick abrasion-resistant sleeves, but it didn't seem to be helping in the humidity. Marcus and Carpenter were both going through gear in the bed of Spectre's truck as the others just stood and waited in silence.

Spectre was leaning against his truck bed when the silence was broken by the audible thump of what he recognized to be helicopter rotor blades. He tried to look out in the direction of the sound, but couldn't make out a helicopter in the horizon-less sky. There was no moon, and aside from the cab light illuminating the bed of his truck, it was completely dark.

They had been standing in the open field for only thirty minutes. There was nothing left to say. They had gone over the plan once more in Marcus's office before locking up the store and piling into Spectre's truck to make the drive out to the Redlands. Everyone knew what they had to do.

The noise grew louder as the blacked out helicopter cleared the tree line. There were no lights on and despite the yellow markings, its black paint job made it barely visible in the moonless sky. It appeared only as a silhouette before it briefly turned on its spotlight, coming in low and fast and landing in the open field in front of them.

Carpenter and Marcus grabbed their bags and body armor and took off at a jog toward the waiting Blackhawk. They had both seen this many times before in their careers. For Carpenter, it had only been six months since the last time he mounted up and rode into battle in Afghanistan. For Marcus, it had been years, but the sounds of the rotor blades and smells of jet fuel brought back a flood of memories. It seemed like only yesterday he had been running to the same helicopter in the desert of Iraq during Desert Storm.

Baxter and Spectre lingered behind with Agent Decker, who was standing at the back of the truck. She had been with them the entire day prior and was the first person to meet them at the store for their final briefing.

"You boys have fun," she said as Baxter and Spectre grabbed their gear. She had grudgingly agreed to stay back and provide top cover from the JTTF. She arranged a Sat phone for Baxter to carry, a last lifeline in case things really went bad to call in the cavalry. She would keep anyone from asking questions about Baxter's whereabouts for the next twenty-four hours while continuing to work with the Department of Defense for a tactical team to secure the facility and recover Chloe and the missing aircraft. Once Baxter called with confirmation, she would be their only hope to get things moving.

Baxter gave her a thumbs up as he grabbed his gear and headed for the waiting helicopter. Spectre was stopped as he turned to grab his gear.

"Cal, wait," Decker said, grabbing his arm as he reached to grab his bag out of the truck. "Listen, I know you're dead set on getting this girl home, but promise me you won't do anything stupid."

Spectre hesitated for a moment. It was the first time he had really picked up on her Georgian accent. She really was a southern belle underneath that hardened exterior.

"You mean more stupid than flying into a foreign country with a stolen helicopter just to get proof of life that we already have?" Spectre said with a grin.

"You know what I mean," Decker replied, rolling her eyes.

"I'll do my best," Spectre said as he slammed the tailgate shut on his truck and headed for the Blackhawk.

Spectre lowered his head to avoid the turning rotor blades and shielded his eyes from the dust and grass being kicked up as he entered the side door of the helicopter. With the four men on board, Elvis gave a thumbs up to Browning in the right seat and the twin turbine engines spooled up as the helicopter lifted off.

Decker watched as the helicopter gained altitude and turned toward the south. As it neared the tree line, its front spotlight extinguished, leaving only the silhouette moving across the dark night sky. She got in Spectre's truck and began the journey down the dark gravel road back to civilization. She had work to do.

Elvis and Browning leveled the Blackhawk just above the treetops and accelerated to its one hundred and thirty-five knot cruising speed. They were both wearing Night Vision Goggles attached to their helmets, but with the moonless night and low illumination, the threat of unseen towers or obstacles was still high. The two kept a constant scan as the helicopter cleared the farmlands and sped along the swamp toward the open waters of the Atlantic.

Spectre looked at his watch as he sat in the webbed seating next to the side door. In just over an hour, they would reach the landing zone and the real fun would begin.

He was still surprised at how quickly the plan came together. It helped that he was dealing with professionals. Marcus and Carpenter had been the tacticians behind the operation. Between them, they had over twenty years of experience with special operations missions. The hard part was getting Marcus to accept that technology had changed since he last put on the uniform.

Carpenter, Marcus, and Spectre met early at the range the previous morning and over coffee had come up with what they thought to be a pretty solid plan. Carpenter was dead set on assaulting the compound and taking no prisoners. Chloe would be taken out of there one way or another and they would at least stop the flow of secrets to foreign countries. It was also Carpenter that suggested that they bring C-4 Explosives and blow up the F-16 to ensure it too was safe from foreign intelligence.

But that plan didn't survive the two agents who showed up much later in the morning. Baxter had been through several more phone calls with the SECDEF's staff. They were still not budging on the proof issue, but on the third phone call at 7AM, one of the Marine Lieutenant Colonels on the staff admitted that if they could come up with definite proof that plane and pilot were both being held, he was sure the SECDEF would humor the idea of sending a Marine Fleet Anti-terrorism Security Team (FAST) from Guantanamo Bay Naval Air Station to secure the airfield and destroy the plane.

It was a debate that went on for the better part of an hour before the final plan was drafted. Spectre wanted to get Chloe out alive. He still believed that she was a victim and that time was being wasted discussing it. The SECDEF had already proven incapable of looking at the facts and more proof wouldn't sway his opinion. *They were just wasting time.*

Agent Decker, on the other hand, had come out from the back corner in defense of letting the system work for them. There was no way they could get in and out of the secured airfield alive. It was a suicide mission at best. At worst, they would all be captured and die in a Cuban prison. It was only a rescue mission if there was a chance of someone getting rescued, she argued. They just didn't have the logistical support.

To Spectre's surprise, Marcus was the first to agree with Agent Decker. He wasn't sure if Marcus had fallen victim to her southern charm or if the Marine Scout Sniper was coming out of him, but it was clear Marcus liked the recon plan. It was mostly survivable, as Marcus put it.

As the Blackhawk finally went feet wet and sped just fifty feet above the calm Atlantic seas, Spectre looked over his makeshift team. They were all deep in thought, probably going over their roles in the piecemealed operation they had come up with on a bar napkin. He could see calmness in Marcus and Carpenter. They were the real warriors. They had done this hundreds of times before. It was as natural as breathing to them.

Baxter sat quietly looking out over the mounted minigun into the starry sky. Spectre wondered if he had ever been part of any tactical operation before. He was still fairly young, but he had shown a great amount of maturity in their meetings. And he had been on target in every run through they had done.

After drawing up the plans and studying the satellite imagery that Baxter and his SOUTHCOM friend had provided, the newly formed team spent the morning and most of the afternoon running through drills in the store's configurable shoot house. They had tried to simulate as much of the airfield as they could, focusing equally on shooting in open areas and room clearing. Although their plan was not to directly engage anyone, they all agreed that if things went south, they needed to be able to work effectively as a team.

"You ok, buddy?" Marcus asked, tapping Spectre's leg and snapping him from his trance.

"I'm fine," Spectre replied over the intercom. They were all wearing David Clark headsets and tied in through the helicopter cabin intercom system. Baxter and Carpenter turned to look at the two talking.

"You're not going to get weak kneed on me are ya, fucking Air Force guy?" Marcus poked. Carpenter frowned and flipped off Marcus from across the cabin.

"Easy there old timer, you're outnumbered," Carpenter interjected.

Marcus turned with a devilish grin. "It's almost as bad as having a bunch of fucking Democrats with me!"

"Ten minutes," came the call from Elvis. They had just crossed into Cuban airspace and were nearing their designated landing zone.

The laughter ceased and the men went to work, unzipping their black tactical bags and pulling out their weapons. Spectre, Baxter, and Carpenter pulled out H&K 416s from their bags. Chambered in 5.56 NATO with semi-auto and automatic fire modes, it was a modified variant of the American M4 Carbine. They each had EOTech red dot sights with flip up magnifiers mounted to the flattop rails, as well as a flashlight and laser attachments.

Marcus had opted instead for his personal Knight's Armament M110 Semi-Automatic Sniper System rifle chambered in 7.62 x 51 with an AN/PVS-10 Sniper Night Sight scope. He had purchased it as a birthday present for himself when another nearby store had gone out of business. It had been a relative steal at $10,000 new in the box, but it made him as excited about shooting as the Red Ryder BB Gun he had as a kid. He never thought he would get to use it for real.

With their weapons ready, they each pulled out their body armor vests. They were equipped with Level III body armor with anti-trauma and anti-stab panels. While heavier than concealable vests, these black vests gave them both front and side protection from up to 7.62 caliber rounds and full stab protection. They each had MOLLE pouches for spare magazines and a knife on the left shoulder. Working at a military and police supply store had its perks, Spectre had mused earlier as they loaded up the equipment in his truck.

The helicopter cleared the shores and headed south over the sugar cane fields and farmlands. Elvis checked the map against their GPS. They were right on course and from their mission planning and imagery study, the landing zone would be off the nose soon.

Getting the helicopter had been the tricky part. As the Director of Air Operations, Browning had been used to significant leeway with air asset allocation in the past, but with the budget cuts and flying hour requirements, he had seen his freedom dwindle. A few months prior, it would have been easy. He and Elvis could have just signed out the helicopter on a cross country for hours and proficiency and no one would have blinked an eye.

But with the cutbacks, he had to be much more elaborate. So it took a little creative number crunching to find the helicopter in the fleet closest to needing depot level maintenance in Tucson and he signed it out as an early depot trip for operational necessity. He even had his maintenance team add two 230-gallon ESSS mounted fuel tanks for the trip, citing rising government contract fuel costs at civilian fields as justification for the extended range.

After repositioning the aircraft to nearby Homestead General Airport, the two met with the team at the store to discuss infiltration and exfiltration options and possible landing zones. They scoured the imagery and ran through various scenarios, finally settling on four possible landing zones. Two were directly north of the airfield, each about a mile from the perimeter fence, and the other two were due east about a half mile.

These LZs were adequately out of the line of sight of any possible roving patrols, and miles from the nearest farmhouses. At the predawn hours they had planned, they could easily get in under the cover of darkness without waking anyone to alert the Cuban authorities.

The Blackhawk continued over the sugar cane fields as it approached the primary landing zone. Under his Night Vision Goggles, Elvis kept a lookout for any people or animals that could pose a potential hazard. With the LZ cleared, he raised the helicopter's nose and began to slow for the landing.

Spectre chambered a round in his H&K 416 and checked the Kimber Ultra TLE 1911 handgun in his drop leg holster. He was hopeful that their intel had been correct, and no one would be anywhere near them when they landed, but he wasn't about to be caught off guard. His adrenaline started pumping as the tail wheel touched down followed by the main wheels and Carpenter opened the side door.

Carpenter and Marcus jumped out of the helicopter first and ran out twenty feet from the helicopter. In unison, they each dropped to a knee and established a perimeter. Spectre and Baxter followed suit from the opposite door and established a perimeter from the other side.

Carpenter keyed the throat mike on his Motorola radio and announced, "All clear."

With the perimeter secured, the Blackhawk's powerful turbine engines spooled down as the rotor blades slowed.

Despite the extended fuel tanks, they had decided it would draw the least attention to have the helo land and shut down versus risking being spotted on radar or someone seeing it flying around in a holding pattern and alerting the local authorities or the military.

As the rotors slowed to a stop, the men regrouped near the front of the helicopter and pulled their Night Vision Goggles from their bags. Their mission had finally begun.

# CHAPTER FORTY-ONE

*Castro Field, Cuba*

The team made their way through the narrow rows of the sugar cane fields as they progressed toward the preplanned observation position. Aside from the buzzing of cicadas and the occasional farm animal heard rustling in the distance, it was a fairly quiet night. The men had managed to move quietly through the fields despite their weapons, body armor, and additional gear they carried.

They kept their weapons low and ready, using their Night Vision Goggles to scan for patrols or farmers as they slowly crossed dirt roads and footpaths from field to field. Because they were only a mile away, they were able to move slowly and quietly using deliberate movements. Stealth was the only option for this mission.

Marcus and Carpenter still seemed right at home. They both were at the front of the column, navigating the team from the landing zone into their observation position, while Baxter and Spectre brought up the rear. Despite a seemingly endless amount of ribbing from Marcus as they packed their gear, Carpenter was using a Garmin handheld GPS receiver while Marcus stuck to his map and compass to navigate the route they had selected the day prior.

The men were on high alert, but despite the danger and fear of being discovered, Spectre's mind was wandering. He thought about Chloe and her captors. She was strong. He had always known her to be a strong woman, but surviving for this long with foreign interrogators would be tough for anyone. He wondered if they had even planned on keeping her alive. *Was her information more valuable than killing her and being done?*

He tried to push the thought out of his head. He wanted to believe she was still alive. He had to believe she was still alive. They had been through too much together. They had their own love story together.

He found himself reliving their proposal. It hadn't been anything creative or fancy. He had asked his father for the ring a few weeks prior. It had been his mother's before she died in a tragic car accident, and before that, her mother's. He thought Chloe would appreciate the significance. He wanted a simple, but meaningful, gesture.

She had flown up to Washington, D.C. to spend the Veterans Day weekend with Jack, Evan, and her mom. Congresswoman Ridley had been asked to speak at a Women Air Service Pilots function honoring the women who served as pilots in the Army at home during World War II. These women had been the pioneers of military aviation for women, and Chloe didn't want to miss the opportunity to meet them.

Chloe had asked Spectre to go with her, but Spectre used the store as a cover for declining, secretly buying a ticket to surprise her instead. His goal was to show up on Friday evening, propose in front of her family, and accompany her to the WASP function to watch her mom speak the next night. It wasn't the most romantic of plans, but he thought the surprise and the gesture of proposing in front of the people she cared about most would be well received.

Spectre had even coordinated with one of the Congresswoman's staffers, letting him in on the plan and using him for intel on where the family would be eating that evening. It was there he planned to pop the question and solidify their relationship.

He showed up with flowers in hand, just as they were ordering drinks. It was at this moment he realized his first tactical error. He had coordinated with the Congresswoman's aide, but had neglected to talk to the Congresswoman or Jack. So the woman that was barely fond of him in the beginning was now unpleasantly surprised by his sudden appearance.

"Cal? How'd you find me?" a surprised, wide-eyed Chloe asked, breaking the awkward silence.

Spectre immediately regretted his decision until a smiling Chloe stood and hugged him. "I mean, I'm so glad you came. I'm just really shocked you're here. I had no idea!"

The waiter took Spectre's coat and offered him a chair next to Chloe. It had been an awkward meal for Spectre. He could almost feel the disapproval from her mother hanging thick in the air. But the second tactical error was only realized at the end of the meal.

Spectre made his prepared speech to the table that recounted his time with Chloe and the love they shared, only to realize, as he reached for his jacket pocket, that his coat was in the coat check closet, along with the ring. Not wanting to ruin the moment, Spectre aborted the speech and instead thanked everyone for having him for dinner on such short notice. They had all been so confused.

It wasn't until much later in the evening, when they were alone and getting ready for bed in the spacious guest bedroom, that Spectre took the traditional one-knee approach and asked Chloe to marry him.

"Of course I will," she said as the tears began rolling down her cheeks. "You're my symbolon."

"I'm your what?" a confused Spectre asked as he put the ring on her finger.

"My symbolon," she repeated. "It means something broken into two parts that yearns to be whole again. Plato wrote about it as the origin of soul mates when Zeus was afraid humans were too powerful as a whole. He broke them up into two souls — man and woman. You are my soul mate — my other half. My symbolon!"

It had been the first time she had called him that, but it stuck from that point forward. She had called him that until they broke up, when his whole world seemed to fall apart.

Spectre shook off his daydreams as they neared the observation position. They were finally clearing the sugar cane fields and nearing the rice fields surrounding the perimeter fence. Spectre could see the glow of lights in the distance.

They spread out as they reached the levees of the rice field just outside the perimeter fence. Taking up prone positions, they used the levee for concealment in the dark early morning. There was no perimeter or runway lighting at the airfield. Aside from the lights from the open hangar, it was completely dark.

Baxter pulled out his satellite phone and digital camera with night optics while Carpenter set up his Toughbook Laptop. Marcus extended the bipod on his rifle and flipped open the dust cover on the scope, ready to snipe any possible threats.

"We're in position," Marcus radioed back to Elvis and Browning.

"Copy that," Elvis replied. "We'll have the bird ready to fly."

Spectre pulled out his binoculars and zoomed in on the hangar door. There were two men pacing around the outer perimeter of the ramp with AK-47s slung across their backs.

Based on the satellite photos, they had picked their observation point for the best viewing angle into the hangar, but it turned out not to be necessary as the large hangar door was more open than it had been in the photos. Spectre could clearly see an external power generator hooked up to an F-16 with what looked like technicians working around the jet. Spectre reasoned that they must have opened the hangar doors more to allow for the exhaust gases of the generator to escape.

"It's in there, let's make the call," Spectre said, handing the binoculars to Baxter as he picked up the camera.

# CHAPTER FORTY-TWO

*FBI Miami Field Office*

**D**ecker sat in her cubicle staring at the black satellite phone on her desk. The open area they called "Cube City" filled with cubicles for field agents was dark except for the glow of the hallway lights and Decker's desk lamp.

She had dropped off Spectre's truck at the range and made it into her office a few minutes after 5 AM. Except for the security guards and a few agents that had been working on field operations in another part of the building, she was alone. She was tired. She had only gone home for a few hours after the intense planning session the day prior before it was time to start their mission. It was enough time for a quick shower, an hour nap, and an early breakfast before heading back out. It wasn't much different than many of the other field operations she had been on, but she had never quite grown used to the lifestyle of a field agent.

Decker stared at the phone impatiently as she pushed a stray strand of golden blonde hair out of her face. She hated waiting. It was much easier to be in the action than waiting for a phone call. She still wasn't quite sure how she'd approach it though. As far as her bosses were concerned, she was still working the Aalee case with Special Agent Baxter. No one had any idea that Americans were in the process of infiltrating Cuban farmlands and spying on defunct Cuban airfields.

She wondered how she would even broach that subject. The Secretary of Defense had been adamant about letting the State Department handle the situation. It was only through the gentle prodding of an aide that she and Baxter had gotten an agreement to humor the idea of a Marine FAST team, but how the incontrovertible evidence would be acquired was never discussed.

Decker was just glad she had been able to talk Cal Martin down from going off alone on some half-cocked plan to get Moss out. She had seen the look in his eyes when they first realized she might still be alive, and again when he stormed out of the meeting with the SECDEF. Something in him had snapped. He had gone from looking defeated and depressed to hopeful and determined. She guessed love did that to people.

But Decker had never known such love. She had never had time for it with her busy career. She could only imagine what would drive a man to risk his life, freedom, and the lives of his friends for one person, especially when that person had ended the relationship weeks prior. She just hadn't been able to wrap her head around the motives in the case yet.

She still didn't trust Moss. She wasn't sure why an intelligent, successful fighter pilot would go to such great lengths if she were truly under duress. And if she were really a traitor, what caused a person who had everything to give it all up. And then there was Martin.

Martin had been the toughest to convince that a rescue operation was just too risky. He and Carpenter wanted to go in and take down the whole airfield like a Navy SEAL team. Martin had even said that as long as there was a chance Moss was still alive, he wasn't going to risk living with that hanging over his head the rest of his life. It was completely reckless.

At the same time, though, it was slightly romantic to Decker. Martin seemed to be very focused and intense. It was hard not to want to help him, despite the odds. He just had that about him. Decker just hoped this woman was worth it. It always seemed like the good ones were wasted on the worst women.

The satellite phone buzzed to life as Decker was deep in thought. Her heart leapt. They were finally calling, although she had been expecting it all along. She only hoped it was good news. She dreaded the phone call that they were in trouble and needed to be rescued, a very real possibility they had gone over in great detail.

"Baxter!" she said in a forced whisper, standing to look around to make sure no one else was around as she answered the phone.

"Is everything set on your end?" Baxter asked. His voice was slightly muffled, but seemed calm.

"Yes," she said, breathing a sigh of relief that they were still safe. "As soon as you upload the pictures, I'll print them out and send the secure fax to that Lieutenant Colonel."

"Uploading now," he replied. "I'll check back in twenty minutes. See ya."

Decker turned and logged into her computer as she hung up the satellite phone and put it back on her desk. Her heart was racing. She couldn't believe things were going so well. She had feared the worst. Now it was time for her to act.

She typed in her username and password and logged into the secure upload site they had set up to transfer the pictures. As she reached the main folder on the server, it was empty, but she knew with the delays of the satellite modem and the size of the high-resolution pictures, it could take a few minutes. She continuously hit refresh anxiously, willing the pictures to show up.

"You're here early, and a Sat phone?" a deep voice with a slight Spanish accent behind her asked.

Decker nearly jumped from her seat as she was still clicking the refresh button. She hadn't expected anyone in the office for at least another hour or two. She reached for her gun as she spun around in her chair.

"Easy there Agent Decker. Did I scare you?" the man asked, eyeing her hand on her Glock 19 in its holster. It was Special Agent Jay Leon, one of the Assistant Special Agents in Charge of the Miami Field Office of the FBI.

"Oh, Jay, it's you. I'm sorry, you startled me," she said, catching her breath.

"A little jumpy are we?" he said with a cheesy grin.

"Sorry, I just didn't expect anyone else to be here," she said.

Decker had never been fond of Leon. Although he was a supervisor, she hadn't worked with him much since she had been in Miami. He worked mainly foreign intelligence and espionage cases and spent most of his time behind a desk. She had only encountered him a few times, but the few times she had, he had come off sleazy and tried to hit on her. He had a reputation for trying to date agents in the office.

"It's quite alright," he said, moving closer. "Can I get you a cup of coffee?"

"No, I'm fine," she said. *He just wouldn't leave*, she thought.

"So what's up with the phone?" he said, nodding at the Sat phone sitting on her desk.

"Oh, it's for a case I'm working," she replied nervously.

"Yeah, I overheard you as I was walking by. I thought you were working with the JTTF on Thomas' old case. Aalee wasn't it?"

Decker blushed. She was mad at herself that he overheard. She thought she had done a decent job ensuring no one was around. It was a careless mistake, and now it was costing her time.

"Yeah, I'm just finishing up some loose ends on the case," she replied nervously.

"Did you guys figure out who he was working for?" Leon asked. He leaned against the cubicle with his cup of coffee in his left hand.

Decker shifted uneasily in her seat. She didn't like Leon asking so many questions. The case had nothing to do with him, and the tone of his voice seemed to indicate more than just a professional interest. The hair on the back of her neck was now standing up. *Something wasn't right.*

"I'm still working out the details. I just started on this case," she deflected.

"Ah, well if you find out anything, let me know. Thomas was a good friend of mine."

"Will do," she replied, letting her guard down. She decided that she was just being paranoid. She hadn't gotten enough sleep and the adrenaline from the operation was starting to make her see danger where it didn't exist.

"Thanks. Good luck on the case." Leon smiled and nodded as he turned to walk away. As he started toward the hallway, Decker's computer beeped. Decker froze as he stopped and turned back around.

"What is that?" he asked as he moved closer to look at her monitor.

Decker's heart stopped as she turned to look at the screen.

"Is that a hangar? And a fighter jet?" he asked ominously.

# CHAPTER FORTY-THREE

*Castro Field, Cuba*

"It's time," the voice said as the door swung open, letting in the blinding light from the hallway.

Chloe Moss groaned and squinted in the light as she tried to identify the person standing there. At first, she thought it was one of the guards that had been checking up on her. She wasn't sure how long she had been in the cell, but she guessed it had been at least twelve hours, maybe more. They had come in a few times, giving her bread and water and emptying her honey bucket. At first, she hadn't been hungry. Her appetite was completely gone from the interrogation, but by the third visit, she tried eating. She knew she'd need her strength for what was to come.

Within seconds of the door opening, it came to her. It was Ling, the man who had ripped off the nail of her right index finger. The sound of his voice made her tremble.

"Here, put these on, it's time for you to cooperate," he said, throwing a shirt and pants at her. It was the same loose fitting t-shirt and jeans she had been given when she first arrived.

Chloe groaned as she sat up on the floor and tried to pick up the clothes. Her whole body ached. Her face felt swollen and her whole right hand was hurting. She felt completely exhausted. She had been sleeping when Ling walked in, but it had only been a few minutes. She had only been able to manage thirty-minute sleep sessions maximum since she had been there.

"Where's Victor?" she asked as she pulled the shirt over her bruised body. Her voice was hoarse and weak.

"He will be there. For now, concern yourself only with getting dressed," he replied.

Chloe gingerly put on the pants and stood. Ling wasted no time, grabbing her arm and roughly ushering her out the door. His touch sent chills down her spine. She had never been so afraid of one person in her life. She only hoped her plan worked and she would never have to face him again.

Ling rushed her down the hallway and down a nearby stairwell. A man with an AK-47 followed close behind as Chloe stumbled, trying to keep pace. Her legs were weak. It was as if she had just run a marathon and could barely walk straight.

Ling pushed open the door at the bottom of the stairwell, revealing the hangar bay with several men standing around the F-16. Chloe saw the open hangar door and felt a sense of relief. She had never quite resolved how to fix that part of her long shot of a plan to get them free of their captors. It was still dark out beyond the hangar doors. It didn't make or break her plan, but it definitely helped and the door being open was exactly what she needed.

Chloe's heart leapt as Ling guided her closer to the jet. There she saw Victor. He was being held by an armed guard right next to the external power cart parked in front of the jet. It was a small jet fuel powered generator being used to power the F-16's avionics. The technicians in and around the jet worked feverishly to download software and data from the F-16's mission computers before they would eventually part it out for shipment to China.

The external power cart posed a small problem to Chloe's plan. While not her main plan, it made it impossible to use the aircraft as a secondary escape method, should something happen that she needed to fire up the jet and taxi out to create a diversion for Victor to escape. She would be forced to adhere to her primary plan and hope it worked.

Chloe winked at Victor as Ling guided her past him at the front of the jet. Victor nodded back and gave a forced smile as Ling continued to push her toward the left side of the cockpit where a small portable ladder had been hung from the side of the aircraft.

"If you try anything stupid, I will make you watch me kill him, and then I will continue our previous conversation," Ling said forebodingly. He nodded for the technician sitting in the cockpit to descend down the ladder and then pointed for Chloe to proceed.

"I already told you," she said as she began to climb up the ladder, "I just want to get us both out of here safely."

Chloe stopped as she reached the top of the ladder and looked into the cockpit. Everything was exactly as she left it, except for the addition of a small tablet computer attached by a fiber optic cable to a serial data bus on the center console display. *That must have been how they were attempting to hack into the software and get the data*, Chloe reasoned.

As she leaned over into the cockpit, she noticed her helmet bag was still stuffed in the back rear corner next to the F-16's reclined ejection seat. She hoped they had not searched her bag. If they had, the whole plan would fall apart instantly.

Chloe gingerly climbed into the cockpit and sat down, sweeping her left hand across her bag subtly as she settled in. She felt the hard mass she had been looking for as her hand swept across it. *Good. It was still there.* She and Victor still had a small chance of getting out of this alive.

Ling climbed the ladder behind her and leaned over the canopy rail to watch her.

"All of the systems have been booted up. Now, you will do exactly as you're told," he said.

Chloe nodded as she did a quick scan of the cockpit. Instantly she found the switch she had been looking for and returned her attention to the cockpit multifunction displays.

"First, bring up the aircraft's weapons systems and power up the Fire Control Computer," said Ling.

Her adrenaline started pumping. In the times she had gone over this scenario in her head, she thought he would make her power up the basic systems first. *They must have already gotten the data they needed,* she thought.

Turning on the aircraft's Fire Control Computer was perfect. The switch was on the panel her helmet bag was now resting on. *This was her chance.*

Chloe watched Ling's eyes as she reached for the red guarded switch by her thigh with her right hand and the switch under her helmet bag with her left. He was watching the data on the displays, not paying attention to her movements.

As she flipped the Fire Control Computer switch on with her left hand, she quickly flipped the red guard up with her right thumb and flicked the underlying MASTER ZEROIZE switch forward.

Ling's eyes widened as all three displays read "MASTER ZEROIZE." The aircraft had entered a mode to delete all classified data and sensitive information. Chloe had successfully declassified the aircraft.

"What are you doing!" he screamed as he reached in to grab her.

"Fuck you, asshole," she said defiantly as she pulled the trigger.

Chloe didn't really have a specific reason for sneaking her Smith and Wesson M&P 9C sub-compact 9MM handgun into her helmet bag. When she left the house that morning, she expected the reception in Cuba to be more of a hero's welcome than an interrogation, but something told her to bring it anyway.

It had been Spectre's voice in her head that pushed her over the edge as she debated bringing it with her. He never went anywhere without a gun, and when she asked him why he did it, he always said, "Better to have it and not need it than need it and not have it." He had been absolutely right. She was thankful for that. Spectre was a good man. She just wished he hadn't taken their relationship for granted and driven her away.

The sound of the gunshot was almost deafening to Chloe as the round hit Ling directly in the chest. He fell off the ladder, landing with a thud as Chloe jumped out of the cockpit and hustled down the ladder. The gunshot seemed muffled by the loud generator of the power cart, as the nearby technicians seemed concerned only that Ling had fallen off the ladder, not that he had been shot.

Chloe ran around to the front of the F-16 where Victor was standing with a guard and took aim. After all the years of being picked on as a kid for being left-handed, it was now of great use to her. There was no way she could have pulled the trigger with her right index finger.

Chloe fired, hitting the man to Victor's right in the torso.

"Let's go! We have to get out of here!" she yelled as the guard hit the ground.

She saw Victor bend over to pick up the man's rifle and she turned toward the open hangar door. She ran out into the darkness at a full sprint, her adrenaline forcing her through the pain and weakness she had faced earlier. She just had to make it to cover.

Gunfire erupted behind her as she sprinted out onto the ramp. She looked over her shoulder to see Victor running behind her. She wanted to go back and make sure he made it, but she knew she just had to trust that he would follow her. If she turned back, they would both certainly die.

She found a drainage ditch to her right between the ramp and the taxiway and turned toward it. If she could make it into the ditch, she could get enough cover to rendezvous with Victor and get a better escape route plan.

As she started toward it, she was startled by a guard approaching her from the left. She had missed him when she was in the cockpit. He must have been on a roving patrol outside. She raised her gun and fired in his direction, but both rounds missed wide.

She kept running, but as the man raised his rifle to fire, he was suddenly dropped. Someone had shot him. She looked back to see if it had been Victor, but couldn't find him.

Chloe slowed as she neared the drainage ditch and turned to look for Victor again. Her heart sank as she considered the possibility that he had been shot or recaptured as they made their escape.

As she swung around, she was suddenly knocked down. Her brain registered the signature pop-pop sound of an AK-47 as she hit the ground. Her lower back was suddenly in severe pain and the wind was knocked out of her. Regaining her senses, she tried to push through the pain. She had to get into the culvert for cover. She struggled to crawl forward.

The pain was immense, unlike anything she had ever felt. She couldn't feel her legs. Yet her biggest fear was still the fate of Victor. *Why hadn't he joined her yet? Was he dead?*

"Victor! My symbolon!" she cried out as she struggled to stay conscious.

※　※　※

Victor Alvarez stood patiently as Ling forced Chloe Moss past him. He tried his best to play the part of the beaten man as she walked by and winked at him. He still wasn't quite sure what her plan was, but he hoped it involved giving the Chinese what they wanted so they would be out of his hair and he could get his payday.

The whole operation had become more complicated than he had planned it to be. The original plan had been to give the F-16 to the Chinese, collect the money, and enjoy the promotion as his supervisors learned he had taken it upon himself to earn the trust of a rising superpower.

*But it was never simple.* The Chinese had to up the stakes with their insistence on using her as an intelligence asset. They couldn't just take the jet and do their reverse engineering magic at home. *That would have been too easy.* Instead, they wanted to work her and make her do their job for them. It was extra money, sure, but Alvarez had grown fond of the idea of using her for a few more weeks on the beach somewhere before ditching her. She had been great in bed.

The generator they were standing by was deafening. He could barely hear himself think. Ling had told him to stand there for effect so she could see him, but Alvarez wasn't sure why he couldn't stand farther away where his hearing wouldn't be permanently impaired.

Because of the generator, Alvarez never heard the gunshot that dropped Ling. To Alvarez, it looked like he had fallen off the ladder as technicians rushed to his aid. It was only when Chloe Moss popped around the corner with gun in hand that he realized the operation had gone horribly wrong.

Alvarez didn't have enough time to react as Moss dropped the guard next to him. He could only grab the man's rifle and give chase, hoping one of the guys on patrol outside could stop her.

Alvarez ran after her as she cleared the ramp. She was fast for someone who hadn't really eaten or slept in a few days. It was only after she dropped a second guard that Alvarez realized what he had to do before the situation got any worse.

Moss had become a liability, and the Chinese were going to be furious. It was time to cut his losses and move on. *Hopefully Zhang wouldn't hold her recklessness against him.*

Alvarez stopped and took aim as she took a hard right. It was dark, but the lighting from the hangar was enough to make out her silhouette as she sprinted past the taxiway. He took a deep breath, switched the AK-47 select fire switch from SAFE to FIRE and squeezed the trigger twice, hitting Moss in the back as she attempted to turn around.

Victor Alvarez sighed as Moss collapsed. It was sad to have to end it this way, but he knew it was part of the business. *There would be plenty of others.*

# CHAPTER FORTY-FOUR

*Castro Field, Cuba*

"Has it been twenty minutes, yet?" Spectre asked impatiently. They were still lying on the rice field levee, just a few feet from the perimeter fence of the secret Cuban airfield.

"Fifteen," Baxter replied, checking his watch.

"The sunrise is in another forty five minutes or so, we need to get things going if we're going to get out of here without drawing attention to ourselves," Marcus said, still lying prone behind the scope of his rifle.

"She should have the pictures by now, I uploaded them before you called," Carpenter interjected.

"Fine, I'll call again," said Baxter as he picked up the satellite phone.

Spectre returned to his binoculars. The hangar was still relatively motionless. Technicians were busy milling about near the F-16 inside the hangar. Outside, a lone guard patrolled the outer ramp. It seemed like it would be so much easier to just assault the airfield and get her himself versus waiting for the Marine FAST team to show up, but Spectre knew they had to stick to the plan. Going solo could get everyone killed, including Chloe.

"Anything yet?" Spectre asked impatiently as he put his binoculars down.

"She's not answering," Baxter replied.

"What do you mean, 'she's not answering?' You just talked to her. Call her back," Spectre demanded.

"I've tried three times," Baxter said, staring at the phone in his hand. "Something's not right."

"Maybe she's away from her desk and faxing it," Carpenter offered.

"And she left the phone? No fucking way," Spectre replied.

"Would you three ladies shut the fuck up," Marcus interrupted, looking up from his sniper scope. "There's movement in the hangar. Something's going on."

Spectre quickly picked up his binoculars and focused on the movement inside the hangar. He could see two men walking casually toward the nose of the F-16. One man had a rifle while the other was unarmed. They appeared to be talking.

Spectre watched as the two men took up positions near the external power cart. The two suddenly seemed to become serious and the man with the rifle grabbed the other's arm. Minutes later, two more people emerged into view. It was a man roughly pushing a woman forward toward the aircraft from the back of the hangar bay. She was wearing civilian clothes. Spectre's heart skipped a beat.

"It's Chloe!" Spectre said, trying not to yell. He was finally vindicated. *She was alive.* He had felt it all along, and now there she was, being forced across the hangar floor like a prisoner. It was all the proof he needed. He had been right about her being alive and right about her being in danger after being forced to steal the jet. He made up his mind. With or without the others, or a FAST team, he would bring her home or die trying.

Baxter picked up the camera and started taking pictures as Chloe was shuffled past the two men standing at the external power cart. When she was no longer in sight, he pulled out the SD card and handed it to Carpenter.

"Here, send these too. It's proof of life. This should seal the deal," Baxter said, holding out the card for Carpenter.

Carpenter took the card and inserted it into his Toughbook Laptop to be uploaded. Spectre watched as Chloe went out of sight momentarily and then reappeared climbing up the F-16's ladder. He watched as she worked her way into the seat as a man climbed up the ladder behind her and stopped near the top.

"They're making her access the weapons systems, we've gotta do something," Spectre said, pulling the bolt cutters out of his backpack.

"Cal, where are you going?" Baxter asked. "We need to stay put and wait for Agent Decker to get the FAST team mobilized."

"There's no time for that," Spectre replied, zipping his backpack with bolt cutters in hand. "You guys stay here, no need for all of us to get killed."

"That guy just fell off the ladder! Chloe is out of the jet, Cal, and she has a gun!" Marcus said, watching the events unfold from behind his rifle scope.

"Shit! Keep trying to call. Marcus, cover me!" Spectre said as he ran up the levee toward the fence.

"Wait! Cal, goddammit. I'm going with you," Carpenter said, handing the Toughbook to Baxter. "You stay here. Keep trying to call the hot blonde."

Carpenter grabbed his rifle and gave chase to Spectre who was already nearing the fence. As Spectre reached the fence, he started feverishly cutting the chain-links to give them enough room to pass through. Spectre could hear the sound of AK-47s coming from the hangar. A firefight had erupted. *He was running out of time.*

"She just cleared the hangar, running this direction," Marcus announced over their tactical radio.

"Elvis, do you copy? Get the chopper moving, we've got the package in sight. Be ready for a hot extraction," Carpenter said over his throat mike radio.

As Spectre cleared the last link and pushed the fence down, he heard the register of Marcus's rifle behind him.

"Tango down, she's still on the move, northwest taxiway," Marcus announced over the radio. He had just taken down a guard from the roving patrol that was approaching Chloe as she ran toward the runway.

"Keep her safe, Marcus," Spectre replied as he ran in a full sprint. The gear was weighing him down. He thought about ditching the body armor and backpack, but knew that if they had to dig in and protect Chloe, he'd need all of it. Carpenter was easily keeping pace with his rifle up, sweeping for nearby threats as they neared the western edge of the two hundred foot wide runway.

"There's someone chasing her, but I don't have a shot yet, Cal," Marcus replied.

Spectre willed himself to run faster. His legs were burning from the weight of the additional gear. He could see what looked to be Chloe running toward him through his Night Vision Goggles as they reached the middle of the runway. They were out in the open, completely exposed if anyone noticed them in the pitch-black runway, but Spectre didn't care. *He had to get to her before it was too late.*

As they reached the far edge of the runway, Spectre saw Chloe getting closer. She was running toward the drainage ditch between the taxiway and the runway. If she could just hold out a few more seconds, he could get to her.

Spectre finally found the man chasing her. He stopped to take aim. Spectre raised his rifle and tried getting a shot, but there was a parked vehicle between him and the man. He had no clean shot.

"Marcus, do you have a-" he stopped in horror as he heard the shots and watched Chloe drop face first. Carpenter returned fire while running, but only hit the side of the truck.

"She's down!" Marcus said over the radio. "Another tango approaching from the north side." Marcus took aim and fired again, dropping the second guard.

"Chloe! No!" Spectre screamed as he reached the edge of the drainage ditch. He heard Chloe yell out something, but he couldn't make out what she said. He could see her crawling into the ditch. She was still alive. Spectre prayed she could stay alive long enough for him to get her out.

Spectre dropped his rifle, letting it hang against its single point sling and jumped straight across the drainage ditch in stride. Carpenter followed suit, keeping his rifle up and shooting at the fleeing man who had just taken down Chloe.

"Chloe! Chloe!" Spectre screamed as he dropped to his knees next to her. She was on her back. Her face was badly bruised and swollen. She wasn't moving.

Spectre took off his backpack and dug for his first aid kit. Carpenter set up in a prone position next to them and covered Spectre while he started first aid.

Spectre checked Chloe's airway and breathing. She wasn't coughing up blood, and her breathing seemed labored, but she was at least breathing. Her pulse was weak. Spectre pulled up her blood soaked shirt. He could see an exit wound through her abdomen. She had been shot in the lower back.

"Chloe, can you hear me?" he said, trying to shake her awake.

"Elvis, what's your ETA? She's critical," Carpenter said over his radio as he looked over and saw Chloe's abdomen.

"We'll be there in five mikes, which LZ?" Elvis replied, indicating they would be on station in five minutes.

"Ditch between the main runway and taxiway," Spectre said as he tried to clean her wound.

"Main runway. I'll pop smoke, expect a hot extract," Carpenter added.

Chloe groaned in pain as Spectre tended to her wound. She started speaking, but Spectre couldn't make out what she was saying. It was mostly incoherent gibberish to Spectre.

"We're going to get you out of here, baby, don't worry," Spectre said.

"Baxter, any luck with the reinforcements?" Carpenter asked over

"Still trying, no answer," Baxter replied.

"But... V... Vic... Victor," she said weakly.

"He can't hurt you anymore. We're going to get you out of here," Spectre reassured her as he finished dressing the wound.

"Victor," she repeated, "he's..."

"Save your energy," Spectre said, grabbing her hand. He noticed the bandage around her right finger as he pulled her hand close to him.

"He's my symbolon," she said finally.

The words hit Spectre like a two thousand pound bomb. Spectre fell back and sat on his heels. He wasn't sure what he had just heard. *Was she delirious? Had he been wrong all along?* The clarity he thought he had finally achieved just moments before was gone.

"One minute," Elvis said over the radio.

Carpenter pulled out a smoke grenade from his backpack and pulled the pin, tossing it onto the grassy area between the ditch and the runway. The orange glow of the looming sunrise gave just enough light to make the green smoke visible.

"Cal, one of us will have to fireman's carry her on board so the other can cover," Carpenter said.

Spectre said nothing, staring aimlessly at the ground next to Chloe who was drifting in and out of consciousness.

"Cal?" Carpenter said, grabbing his arm and shaking him. "Do you want to do it or do you want me to carry her?"

Spectre shook off the confusion and turned to Carpenter. "I'll carry her."

Spectre could hear the distinct sound of the Blackhawk's rotors approaching. Despite the light from the slowly rising sun, it was still too dark to make out the blacked out helicopter as it neared.

Carpenter began firing as more armed men emerged from the hangar. One fell as the others took cover.

"Tango down," Marcus announced. "I count two more that just showed up."

"Ten seconds," Elvis announced as the sound of the Blackhawk grew closer. Spectre could see it nearing the fence line near the northern edge of the runway. He reached over and grabbed Chloe, hoisting her over his shoulder.

Spectre trudged through the muddy ditch as Carpenter laid down covering fire behind them. Spectre could hear the bullets zipping by him, but most were landing short of the ditch. She was heavy, but the adrenaline was more than enough to propel him across the mud and up the slope toward the smoke.

The Blackhawk came in low and fast, blowing up grass and dust as it landed in the thick grass next to the runway. As he hit the flat terrain, he picked up the pace, struggling to keep Chloe on his shoulders.

As he hit the Blackhawk's open side door, Spectre carefully laid Chloe down on the floor of the Blackhawk. He had no stretcher or gurney for her, so he could only lay her flat on the helicopter's floor and restrain her using cargo straps. Spectre climbed into the helicopter and squatted next to her.

"Joe, are you coming? The package is secure." Spectre asked over the radio. He could see Carpenter still lying prone in the ditch while laying down covering fire.

"I'll meet you at the secondary LZ, I'm going to secure the aircraft," Carpenter replied over the radio.

"When were you going to tell me about this plan?" Spectre asked, jumping out of the running Blackhawk.

"I've got this. You get Chloe out of here and pick up Marcus and Baxter. It will only take a few minutes to blow it with C4," Carpenter replied.

Spectre gave Elvis a thumbs up and swung his rifle around from behind his back.

"Bullshit. You're not doing this alone," Spectre said as he ran back toward Carpenter.

# CHAPTER FORTY FIVE

"What the fuck are you two doing now?" Marcus barked over the tactical radio as he watched the Blackhawk climb away while Spectre ran back to Carpenter near the drainage ditch.

"We're going to blow the jet and its secrets," Carpenter responded. His voice was slightly subdued by the sound of gunfire in the background.

Marcus returned to his scope, picking up two new targets coming from the south end of the hangar. He adjusted his aim, exhaled slowly, and pulled the trigger, hitting the first man in the temple.

"She's still not answering," Baxter announced. "It looks like we're on our own."

"Fucking Democrats," Marcus grumbled. "I'll bet they're figuring out how to surrender right now."

Marcus inserted a fresh magazine and looked for another target. Carpenter and Spectre had hit the second man as they ran toward the vehicle outside the hangar door.

"Elvis, can you pick up Marcus and Baxter and then meet us on the ramp for extraction?" Carpenter asked over the radio as he ran across the taxiway.

"Wilco, we'll pick them up at the north LZ," Elvis replied. "Heads up, Spectre, you've got multiple vehicles with troops approaching the hangar from the southeast road."

"Copy that," Spectre replied, his voice shaking over the radio as he ran across the large ramp with Carpenter.

Baxter grabbed the Toughbook that Carpenter had left with the Sat phone and shoved them into his backpack. He crouched next to Marcus and looked at his map as Marcus continued to pick off targets.

"The north LZ is 200 meters through that field," he said, pointing at the sugar cane field to his left.

"Let's go," Marcus replied, slinging his rifle over his shoulder and unholstering his Kimber Custom 1911 .45 ACP as he stood.

Marcus led the way as they jogged down the levee of the rice field and crossed a dirt path into the nearby sugar cane field. The dawn light was enough that they could easily navigate without the help of Night Vision Goggles.

"I've got another vehicle approaching from the northwest, Marcus," Elvis said over the radio. "Looks like a mounted patrol, what's your ETA?"

"We'll be there in three minutes," Marcus replied as they ran through the sugar cane field.

"Make it two, they're closing in pretty fast," Elvis replied.

"I'm too old for this shit," Marcus grumbled as he took off in full sprint.

Baxter followed closely, easily pacing the old Marine as they cleared the field and found the grassy opening they had designated as the north LZ. He looked up to see the Blackhawk swoop in and land fifty meters in front of them.

Bullets zipped by as they reached the clearing on the way to the waiting helicopter. Marcus turned back to see a jeep with a mounted gunner and two soldiers approaching their position. He fired two shots from his handgun and turned back, hoping to keep the enemy's heads down long enough for them to reach the helicopter.

Reaching the side door of the helicopter, Marcus turned around to wait for Baxter who had stopped to return fire with his rifle.

"Let's go, kid!" Marcus barked as he slid the side door open, revealing Chloe Moss strapped to the floor. She looked horrible. She didn't have much time.

"I'm on my-'"

Marcus watched in horror as Baxter stopped mid sentence and dropped to his knees just as he turned to run for the helicopter. He ran to Baxter's aid while firing at the approaching jeep, hitting the standing gunner in the right shoulder.

"Baxter!" he screamed as he reached his fallen comrade. "Get up, goddammit, we have to go!"

Baxter had been hit in the chest by a rifle round and was gasping for air. The body armor had successfully stopped the round, but Marcus was sure Baxter at least had a rib or two broken.

"We don't have time for you to lay here," Marcus said as he grabbed the drag handle on the back of Baxter's vest and pulled him to his feet. Using the handle as leverage, Marcus pulled Baxter as he stumbled toward the helicopter and pushed Baxter into the open door where he landed on his side, still trying to catch his breath.

As Marcus holstered his handgun and climbed into the helicopter, he suddenly felt a searing pain in his thigh. He looked down to see blood soaking his tactical pants.

"Goddammit, those fuckers shot me," Marcus said as he made it into the helicopter. "Baxter, get on that minigun!"

Marcus pulled himself up onto the webbed seat as the helicopter lifted off. He grabbed his rifle and took aim at the men in the jeep speeding toward them. Using his left forearm for support, he steadied his rifle and pulled the trigger, hitting the driver. The jeep coasted to a stop as the panicked passenger stopped shooting and grabbed the steering wheel.

Baxter willed himself up and tried to tend to Marcus's wound, only to be spun around and pushed toward the door-mounted minigun by Marcus.

"Shoot first, worry about me later," Marcus ordered.

Baxter stumbled into the door gunner's station and checked the six-barreled machine gun. It was loaded and ready to go. They had checked it before takeoff, and he was sure Elvis and Browning had pre-flighted it again during their downtime. He flicked off the safety and aimed for the jeep Marcus had just shot. Its occupants were now dismounted and shooting at the climbing Blackhawk.

Baxter squeezed the trigger, unleashing the fury of the M134 Minigun, shooting 7.62 x 51mm at two thousand rounds per minute. The two remaining men were obliterated as the rounds ripped through their bodies and the nearby jeep. It was both gruesome and strangely satisfying to Baxter.

Once it gained sufficient altitude, the Blackhawk circled back toward the airfield. Elvis again called out the convoy of vehicles approaching from a distance on the southeast hardball road leading into the hangar complex.

"Spectre, we're going to have the whole Cuban Army here soon if we don't get moving," Elvis said over the tactical frequency.

"Copy that, just hold them off for a few more minutes," Spectre replied over the radio.

The Blackhawk orbited over the main hangar as Baxter used the minigun to take out men approaching from all sides of the compound. Marcus was still firing using his rifle and scope to take out individuals, but Baxter could see he was starting to fade. He needed first aid soon.

"Can you get me closer to the lead vehicle? I might be able to buy them some time," Baxter asked Elvis.

Elvis gave him a thumbs up and banked the Blackhawk toward the road. The vehicles were now only a few hundred meters away.

Baxter sprayed the lead jeep with rounds, causing it to catch fire and spin out of control in front of the two troop carriers. The entire convoy screeched to a stop as the jeep blocked the narrow road. The men from the troop carriers dismounted and ran toward the hangar as the trucks stopped.

"They're on foot, Spectre, but you have to get out of there, maybe five minutes tops," Baxter said over the radio.

"Come get Joe now, I'll see you guys in Homestead," Spectre replied over the radio.

Baxter gave a confused look to Marcus.

"What... the fuck?" Marcus said before dropping his rifle. He slouched over onto the webbed seat.

"Marcus!" Baxter screamed, leaving his station to give Marcus first aid.

# CHAPTER FORTY-SIX

A s Carpenter and Spectre reached cover behind the vehicle outside the hangar, they took a second to inventory their gear. Spectre gave Carpenter two of his six remaining magazines since Carpenter had been doing most of the shooting that morning. They were both still catching their breath from the full sprint across the taxiway and ramp while Marcus provided sniper cover.

Spectre peered over into the open hangar. The technicians were all gone and the hangar bay seemed empty except for the F-16 sitting near the front.

"We'll stack up on the edge of the door," Carpenter said, pointing to the large hangar door. "I'll lead in and you cover, then I'll place the C4 charges in the cockpit and down the intake while you cover me."

"Wait," Spectre replied. "Let me do it."

Carpenter pulled the C4 bricks out of his backpack. There were four of them, each about six inches in length. They were all wired to a transmitter to be used with a remote detonator.

"You sure?" Carpenter asked, holding them out to Spectre.

Spectre grabbed them and put them into his open bag. "I've got this."

Carpenter nodded and visually cleared the north end of the building, while Spectre cleared the south side. Spectre fired off two shots, hitting a running guard who had just rounded the corner.

When they were satisfied that both flanks were clear, Spectre motioned for Carpenter to follow as he moved toward the hangar door. They both moved quickly, but smoothly, with their rifles up, sweeping left and right as they proceeded toward the hangar door. Carpenter stayed close by, covering the sides and rear.

Spectre motioned for them to stop as they formed a two-man column against the hangar door. He peered inside and cleared the room. There was a body still on the ground next to the ladder of the F-16, but aside from that, it was still completely empty.

Spectre gave the signal and the two men entered the hangar bay. Spectre turned right and cleared toward the F-16 while Carpenter turned left toward the empty space at the corner of the hangar bay.

Carpenter immediately took cover behind a large red tool cart as a lone technician wandered into the hangar. He was carrying a handgun, but didn't appear to have seen them as Spectre took cover behind the external power cart.

Carpenter watched the man in his sights for a few seconds and then squeezed the trigger as the man turned toward the F-16. The man dropped instantly and Carpenter flashed a thumbs up to Spectre, indicating that his side of the hangar was clear.

Spectre returned the thumbs up and reached into his bag for the C4 while slinging his rifle across his back. The F-16 was beautiful. He hadn't been this close to one since his last flight in Iraq. *It was such a shame to have to destroy a perfectly good aircraft.*

Spectre quickly climbed the ladder as Carpenter kept watch for any hostiles. He saw Chloe's helmet on the canopy rail and her G-suit and harness on the opposite wing as he reached the top of the ladder. It was his first time in the new Block 70 F-16. The all glass cockpit was slick looking. It looked like a brand new airplane, unlike what he had flown before.

Shaking off the nostalgia, he placed two of the C4 bricks in the cockpit. He put the first one behind the seat and then leaned forward on the ladder to place the second brick by the rudder pedals. The Fuel Quantity indicator caught his eye. Besides the standby instruments, it was the only analog gauge in the cockpit. Spectre thought it was odd that they would spend so much money upgrading the cockpit with LCD displays and electronic engine instrument displays, but leave an analog fuel gauge.

Spectre placed the second C4 brick and then started down the ladder. As he reached the bottom rung, Spectre suddenly stopped and started back up.

"What are you doing? We've got to go!" Carpenter yelled across the hangar.

"Just one second!" Spectre replied as he hustled back up the ladder.

Spectre reached the top of the ladder and looked back in the cockpit. The analog fuel gauge read 7,600 pounds. *The jet had plenty of fuel.*

It was something they had never even considered in the planning. His goal had always been to save Chloe first. He figured the jet would have been out of gas anyway, since she had flown half the sortie before landing, but he had never considered the big conformal fuel tanks on the spine of the jet. They alone added 3,000 pounds. *He had plenty of fuel to get in and fly it home.*

Spectre knew what he had to do. He had been wrong about Chloe, but he reasoned he could at least do something for the good of his country, and the fighter pilot in him knew there was no one better suited to fly it out, even if it had been over five years since he had flown anything.

Spectre reached in, grabbed the C4 charges, and stuck them back in his backpack. He descended down the ladder and headed back toward Carpenter. He could hear the Blackhawk circling overhead and its minigun firing in short bursts.

"Spectre, we're going to have the whole Cuban Army here soon if we don't get moving," Elvis said over the tactical frequency.

"Copy that, just hold them off for a few more minutes," Spectre replied over the radio.

"Joe, come help me," he said as he unplugged the long black power cable attached to the F-16's external power receptacle.

"Help you do what? I thought you said you had this?" Carpenter said as he jogged toward the external power cart while clearing with his rifle.

"I do. I'm not going to blow it though," Spectre replied as he finished and threw the cable onto the cart. "Help me push this thing out of the way. Hurry, we don't have much time."

"Dude, you're going to get yourself killed," Carpenter replied as he watched Spectre try to push the cart out of the way.

"I can think of worse ways to die," Spectre replied. "Now fucking help me!"

Carpenter slung his rifle around his back and took his place next to Spectre. The two pushed the cart toward the back of the hangar and away from the F-16's nose.

Spectre hustled around the airplane. As he reached the right side, he reached into a maintenance access panel with his right hand.

"What are you doing now?"

"Turning the rounds limiter off and setting the rounds counter to two hundred," Spectre replied. The rounds limiter had been set to 999 and had been left on, allowing the jet to be flown in air-to-air training missions without fear of accidentally shooting the gun.

"Why two hundred?" Carpenter asked.

"Because that's how many rounds they fly with in the jet when they're not actually shooting the gun. It's for weight in the nose when the conformal tanks are full," he replied as he continued doing his hurried preflight around the jet.

"What are you going to do with two hundred rounds? Dude, this is a horrible idea," Carpenter pleaded.

"Nothing, I hope. But I'd rather have it and not need it than need it and not have it. It's better than no weapons at all," Spectre replied as he threw the wheel chocks off to the side.

Spectre uninstalled the gun's hold-back tool designed to keep the Vulcan M61A cannon from spinning as he reached the left side. He now had at least some capability for self-protection with a fully armed gun. With the jet ready to go, he walked over to the right wingtip and looked at Chloe's G-suit and harness. He grabbed both and threw them to the side.

"You're not going to wear those?" Carpenter asked.

"She's five foot seven. Won't fit. I'll be fine," Spectre replied as he ran back over to Ling's body.

"Seriously man, I think you should reconsider this half-baked plan," Carpenter said helping Spectre drag Ling's lifeless body away from the airplane.

"They're on foot, Spectre, but you have to get out of there, maybe five minutes tops," Spectre heard Baxter say over the tactical radio.

"Come get Joe now, I'll see you guys in Homestead," Spectre replied over the radio.

"Say again?" Elvis asked over the radio.

Carpenter stood and watched Spectre as he finished pre-flighting the aircraft. He could see the look of determination on Spectre's face. There was no convincing him that he had chosen the path to certain death.

"I'll meet you for extract on the near ramp, I'll explain onboard," Carpenter replied over the radio.

"Copy that," Elvis replied. "One minute."

"Joe, it's been a pleasure, thanks for everything you've done," Spectre said holding out his hand.

"This is such a bad idea, but at least wear the harness so you'll have the ejection seat, you can loosen the straps to make it fit," Carpenter said as he shook Spectre's hand. "I had to do the same thing when they gave me that incentive flight at Nellis."

"Fine, help me get these doors open and then you get out of here," Spectre replied.

The two ran for the partially opened hangar doors. They each backed against their respective side and started pushing the massive hangar doors open. As they finished opening the door, they saw the Blackhawk swoop in and land on the ramp just fifty feet away.

Spectre flashed a thumbs up to Carpenter as he started back toward the F-16. Carpenter reciprocated and ran to the open door on the Blackhawk as Baxter waved him in.

Spectre decided to give the harness a try and ran to where he had thrown it just a few feet away from the right wingtip. He hung his rifle on the Captive Carry AIM-9 training missile on the wingtip and picked up the harness.

As Spectre loosened the straps on the harness, he suddenly felt something wrap around his neck. Someone had managed to surprise him as he struggled with the harness. Spectre reached up to his throat, feeling a rope against his neck. It burned as it dug into his neck and started to choke him.

Spectre twisted around as his attacker attempted to pull him back. The rope loosened under the leverage, and Spectre sent a knee directly into the man's midsection, knocking him back.

The man stumbled back and pulled out a switchblade knife. Spectre tossed aside the rope from his neck and took a deep breath. Spectre prepared himself for the next attack as the man extended the blade of the knife. He was well inside of twenty-one feet- too close to draw his holstered sidearm before the man would close the distance and stab him.

As the man charged Spectre, he instantly recognized him from the pictures in Baxter's office. It was the man that had sent his life into a tumbled chaos. *It was Victor Alvarez.*

# CHAPTER FORTY-SEVEN

Climbing aboard, Carpenter edged past Chloe and Marcus as they both clung to life on the floor of the Blackhawk. He grabbed a headset hanging from the ceiling as Baxter closed the side door and the Blackhawk climbed away.

Baxter returned to tending Marcus's wound. "What happened to him?" Carpenter asked, pointing to Marcus's leg. It was heavily wrapped in bandages and Baxter was still applying pressure.

"Shot in the thigh," Baxter replied.

"Femoral?" Carpenter asked as he grabbed the first aid kit and assisted.

"I don't know," said Baxter. "He's bleeding pretty badly. We need to get them both to a hospital."

Carpenter looked over at Chloe. She was unconscious but breathing. "How's she doing?"

"She's stable, but I think one of the bullets is still in there. If she doesn't get to surgery soon she might go into shock."

"I'll start IVs on both of them," Carpenter said, pulling open the helicopter's large combat first aid kit.

"What happened to Spectre?" Elvis asked over the intercom as they cleared the perimeter fence of the airfield.

"He wants to fly the jet out of there," Carpenter replied as he found a vein on Chloe's left arm.

"What the fuck, over?" Elvis replied, swinging his head back to look at Carpenter.

"I know, I tried to talk him out of it," he said, shaking his head, "but you know you fighter pilot types, there's no middle ground."

"I hope he gets out of there quick," Elvis said as he banked the helicopter low over the sugar cane fields toward the ocean. "If the Cuban Army gets to him first, it won't matter."

As the helicopter rolled out, Carpenter rushed to hold down Marcus, who was having a seizure.

"He's seizing! He's going into shock!" Carpenter yelled.

"We'll be in Key West in forty five minutes," Browning said from the left seat. "Let's hope they can both hang on long enough to make it."

\* \* \*

Spectre stood facing the reason he was in Cuba in the first place. The man had taken his fiancée from him, convinced her to steal an F-16, and nearly had him killed by Muslim terrorists. Spectre wanted nothing more than to crush the life out of him slowly and painfully.

But Spectre didn't have time. He knew the Cuban Army was rapidly approaching his position, and the thought of spending the rest of his life in a filthy Cuban jail was not worth extracting revenge on the knife-wielding piece of human excrement.

Victor shifted his weight as he prepared to attack. He rotated the blade around in his hand as he advanced, switching from a blade-up grip to a blade-down grip. Time seemed to slow down for Spectre as Victor lunged forward at him, trying to swing the blade across his body in a slicing motion. He was clearly aiming for Spectre's neck with the goal of slashing his throat first and then following up with a fatal stab to the back of the neck.

After years of Krav Maga training, Spectre's reaction was instinctive. His body moved instantly, blocking Victor with his left hand to stop the knife. He quickly closed the distance between them as his open right hand shot up to strike Victor in the face, sending fingers in both eyes to blind him. It was part of the mantra his Sensei had always drilled home to him in training – *attack your attacker, and always hit the face. A finger in the eye is nearly always effective.*

As Victor sent his left hand up to his eyes in response to the eye gouge, Spectre side stepped toward Victor's extended arm. He kicked low through Victor's right knee, tearing the tendons and ligaments as the man's fully extended knee buckled.

Using his right hand, Spectre grabbed Victor's right hand and swept it over his head, stepping behind the falling Victor and forcing Victor to stab himself in the side with his own knife. As he forced the knife as far as it would go, Spectre stepped back, allowing Victor to collapse as he gasped for air amidst his screams of pain.

"Who are you?" Victor said as he choked on his own blood.

"I was her fiancé, motherfucker," Spectre replied, kicking Victor in the head before turning toward the F-16.

Spectre grabbed the harness and his rifle and headed toward the jet. With no room inside for the rifle, Spectre unchambered the round and ejected the magazine, putting it back in his vest. He tossed the rifle next to Ling's lifeless body and attempted to put on the harness.

It was a snug fit even after significant adjustments, but it would do for the hour flight back to Homestead. Spectre raced up the ladder and climbed into the jet. He stood on the seat and turned, tossing the ladder to the side before shimmying down into the seat.

He grabbed Chloe's helmet and oxygen mask off the canopy rail and put it on. It was also a snug fit, but it was much better than the harness. He wasn't sure why he let Carpenter talk him into wearing it. *He didn't plan on ejecting.*

Spectre flipped on the battery switch on his left side as he finished strapping in. The Electronic Engine Management LCD powered on, giving him a digital read out for the engine on a display above his right knee. He found the Jet Fuel Starter switch and flipped it to JFS START 2. *So far, so good*, Spectre thought. All the switches were exactly as they were five years ago, even if the displays were completely new. The newer block F-16 hadn't changed the basics.

As the JFS whirred to life, Spectre watched the electronic readout of Engine RPM as it climbed through eighteen percent and up to twenty. He couldn't quite remember the operating limits, but guessed that twenty percent would be enough and rotated the throttle around the idle-cutoff position to initiate the main turbine start. He was just relieved the JFS accumulators were charged.

As the main engine RPM rose, Spectre lowered the canopy. As it reached idle, the main generator came online and Spectre lowered the seat and flipped the Fire Control Computer and Stores Management Computer switches to the ON position.

The screens flashed ZEROIZED across the screen as they booted up. Spectre cursed under his breath as he cleared the display. He at least had gun symbology if he needed it, but the jet would give him no indications if he were being locked onto by another aircraft and the radar would only work in its basic modes. He hoped he wouldn't need any of it.

Spectre turned on the Embedded GPS/Inertial Navigation System and moments later, the Head Up Display and navigation systems were online. He was ready to taxi. He had no idea how to set up any of the new weapons systems, but everything looked pretty familiar. The engineers had managed to keep the same interfaces while giving the jet enhanced capabilities.

His heart raced as he advanced the throttle and the jet rolled forward. He clicked on the nose wheel steering on the side stick with his right index finger and taxied the jet out of the hangar. He looked back. He could see Victor lying in his own blood as a group of soldiers flooded into the hangar. He advanced the throttle past eighty percent, knocking a few of them down with the big General Electric engine as they tried to take cover from the exhaust.

As Spectre taxied out of the hangar, he made a right on the ramp toward the taxiway. As Spectre passed the parallel taxiway, he saw the men running out toward his position, firing small arms in his direction. He advanced the throttle as he turned onto south-facing runway and selected the afterburner.

The familiar kick in the pants of the afterburner lighting gave Spectre goose bumps. It had been so long, but he felt right at home. *It was like being back with an old friend.* As the jet lifted off the runway, Spectre raised the gear and made a hard turn to the north.

Despite all that he had been through in the last couple of weeks, he felt strangely at peace with the world. He was back where he belonged. *He was home again.*

# CHAPTER FORTY-EIGHT

*Five Miles Off the Coast of Cuba*

**"M**ayday! Mayday! Mayday! We're being engaged by two MiGs!" the voice said on the emergency frequency of 243.0. It was the only frequency Spectre could monitor since all of the channelized frequencies had been erased by the MASTER ZEROIZE function.

Spectre was still climbing through ten thousand feet when he heard the call. His stomach turned as he recognized the voice. It was Elvis. *The Cuban Air Force must have launched two fighters to intercept them when the Army showed up at the airfield.*

"Elvis, it's Spectre, what's your posit?" Spectre said, keying the radio to ask Elvis his position.

"Spectre! Jesus Christ! You made it!" Elvis screamed over the radio. "We're being attacked by a flight of two Fulcrums. I'm not sure how much longer we can evade. We're about 20 miles off the coast right over the water."

Spectre pulled up his radar on his attack displays. Limited to the basic modes, he wasn't sure how much help it would be. He hoped it would be enough to get a lock. He put his cursors over the position in front of him and leveled off. He picked up two bricks on the radar screen and locked them. He wasn't sure which was which, but he was certain, based on the radar's reported airspeed of the targets, that he had found the location.

"I'm radar contact. I'm on my way," Spectre said. He checked his fuel. He was down to 6500 pounds. He had enough gas to get to the fight, but a prolonged fight would run him out of fuel pretty quickly. Right now it didn't matter, though. His friends were in trouble and, to Spectre, saving them was all that mattered.

Spectre reached forward with his left hand and pressed the emergency jettison button. The jet rocked as the two 370 gallon fuel tanks were jettisoned from the aircraft. They were empty anyway and would only hinder the maneuverability for the coming fight.

Spectre kept the throttle at military power as the jet rocketed through 500 knots. Without the tanks, it was relatively clean and accelerated effortlessly. As he neared the fight, he tried to find the aircraft through the Heads Up Display. Chloe's helmet had been just big enough to fit, but the Helmet Mounted Cueing System was completely unusable. *It was better that way anyway.* He had no idea how to even get the thing to turn on or align.

"Tally two," Spectre said as he picked up the two MiG-29 Fulcrums. At ten thousand feet, he was still five thousand feet above their altitude as they set up a racetrack pattern around the slow helicopter and were attempting to strafe it with their guns as Elvis banked and maneuvered to avoid their shots.

"We can't keep this up, Spectre!" Elvis screamed. "They almost hit us the last pass, and we've got to get to a hospital for Marcus and Chloe!"

"Copy that," Spectre replied as he rolled the jet on its back. As he pulled to point at the circling MiG-29, the realization hit him that he would have no G-force protection without the G-suit. The 9-G capable F-16 would be limited to whatever his body could withstand before he blacked out as the G-forces caused his blood to pool in his feet. His veins were pumping with adrenaline. He hoped it would be enough.

Spectre flipped the thumb switch on the throttle up to select the Dogfight mode and then moved the MASTER ARM switch to ARM with his left hand. He was glad he armed the gun on the ground. It was the only thing between the MiG-29 and his buddies.

As the lead MiG-29 rolled in on the helicopter, Spectre rolled in behind his wingman who was a few miles in trail. The second MiG noticed him and broke from the formation as the lead MiG made another unsuccessful attempt to strafe the maneuvering helicopter.

Spectre followed the second MiG through the hard left hand turn, using every muscle in his lower body to strain as the G-forces increased. His vision grayed slightly, but he was able to maintain sight of the MiG as it executed the left hand break turn and ejected self-protection flares.

With the MiG in a level turn, Spectre selected full afterburner and climbed. The MiG continued his level turn as Spectre gained vertical turning room in his climb. It was enough to give Spectre the angles to turn back in and end up in the MiG's control zone- a few thousand feet behind him with no ability to maneuver out of Spectre's sights.

Spectre lined up the jet's computed gun reticle on the massive twin engine, twin tail fighter as it continued its turn. Once he was in range, he squeezed the trigger for a second, sending one hundred rounds through the center of the jet's fuselage, creating a fireball as the jet broke apart, and the unspent jet fuel ignited.

Spectre broke away from the fireball to avoid ingesting the debris into the F-16's massive intake. He started searching for the other MiG. He had gotten so fixated on shooting the second MiG that he had neglected to keep sight of the first.

"Spectre, lead MiG is on you!" Elvis warned. "We're bugging out."

Spectre snapped his head back to look over his shoulder. He picked up the massive MiG-29 behind him maneuvering into a weapons employment zone.

Spectre executed a loaded barrel roll as he ripped the throttle to idle and extended the speed brakes. His goal was to get out of plane and defeat the impending gunshot while trying to force the MiG pilot to overshoot. Bullets flew by as the jink successfully defeated the first volley of shots.

As the MiG pilot pitched his nose up, Spectre recovered from the roll just three thousand feet above the water. It was much lower than he had ever performed such a maneuver in training. They had always practiced using a five thousand foot training floor. Today, the water would be the floor.

With the MiG struggling to maintain his position behind him, Spectre reversed his turn hard into the MiG causing him to collapse the range even further. They were now inside a few hundred feet of each other. The MiG-29 dwarfed the tiny F-16 as they jockeyed for position.

The MiG pilot overshot, allowing Spectre to retract the speed brakes and select full afterburner. He had managed to go from defensive to neutral.

The two pilots entered a flat scissors as they swapped flight paths, each trying to maneuver behind the other. Each time they passed each other, they reversed the direction of their turn into each other. It was a game of who could out power and outmaneuver the other. For the moment, they were staying relatively neutral.

As Spectre continued, the thrust of the Block 70 was enough to gain him a slight advantage, putting him behind the MiG-29 as they both climbed to try to stop their forward track across the ground. Once satisfied he had enough room, Spectre extended his speed brakes and deselected afterburner to descend without losing the ability to control the nose.

As his nose sliced through the MiG-29, he tried to get a fleeting gunshot, only to have the symbology in the Heads Up Display disappear as he ran out of bullets. His only option was to fight the MiG pilot until one of them ran out of gas, or hope he could cause him to run into the water.

Spectre checked his fuel momentarily as the MiG continued to squirm its way out of his sights. He had enough fuel left to fight for another minute before he wouldn't have enough to make it back home. He just hoped it was enough time for Elvis and the Blackhawk to get away.

As the two jets climbed through five thousand feet, the MiG pilot surprised Spectre when he rolled inverted and pulled into a split-S. Spectre started to follow, but as he saw the rapidly approaching water, shallowed out into a sliceback instead of a pure vertical split-s, allowing the brave MiG-29 pilot to go from defensive to neutral just feet off the churning Atlantic below.

As the MiG turned back for a head-to-head pass, Spectre saw a white plume of smoke as the pilot launched an air-to-air missile at his F-16.

Spectre ripped the throttle to idle and attempted to roll the jet around the missile's flight path to cause an overshoot as it screamed by. With such a short range, the missile had been unable to guide or fuse on his jet, but it had been enough to cause him to lose valuable energy at low altitude. The MiG was now offensive again, and Spectre had less than thirty seconds of fighting fuel left before he wouldn't have enough to make it to American soil.

# CHAPTER FORTY-NINE

*Alert Facility*
*Homestead ARB, FL*

**M**ajor Scott "Batman" Bane was on his fourth hour of Computer Based Training when the Klaxon sounded. He had just finished his Air Force mandated Sexual Assault Prevention training and was moving on to Cultural Sensitivity training when they got the call in the fifth hour of their twenty-four hour alert shift.

"Scramble, Scramble, Scramble," the voice on the loudspeaker said.

Batman grabbed his Common Access Card ID from the computer and headed for the door of the large recreation room as his wingman, Captain George "Tuna" Turner, put down his turkey sandwich and followed suit.

The two ran to their respective F-15 Eagles as their crew chiefs hustled to prepare the jets. Within minutes, they were both started and taxiing out onto the alert ramp located on the north end of the thirteen thousand foot runway.

Batman keyed the radio, checked in his wingman, and pushed the flight to the secure frequency for the Southeastern Air Defense Sector responsible for their tasking. After authenticating, the controller gave them their instructions.

"Sentry One-One, investigate Unknown Rider 180/95, possible Fulcrum," the female controller said, indicating an unknown aircraft was approaching the Air Defense Identification Zone without the appropriate flight plan, communications, or transponder codes.

"Confirm Fulcrum?" Batman asked as he scribbled the information onto his kneeboard data card.

"Sentry One-One, affirm, we've also received a distress call from the vicinity," the controller replied.

Batman switched the flight to the tower frequency and was cleared for an immediate takeoff. Once the two F-15s were rejoined and on the way, they were handed off to the tactical controller.

"Hunter, Sentry One-One checking in passing one five thousand," Batman said as they sped south toward the targeted area.

"Hunter copies, furball BRAA 190/80, 5000, four contacts, bogey," the male controller replied indicating that there was a group of unknown aircraft fighting eighty miles south of their position.

"Sentry One-One," Batman responded on their primary radio.

As they continued toward the last known location of the aircraft, Batman used his radar to search for the contacts. When they were within forty miles, he started to make out four radar contacts on his screen.

"Sentry One-One, radar contact 180/38, 5000, Hunter, declare," he said, attempting to get an identification of the group.

"Hunter unable, group 180/38 bogey," the controller replied.

"Confirm strength?" Batman replied. He could make out four aircraft in a tight orbit over the point. They were maneuvering within a few miles of each other.

"Strength four," the controller replied, indicating there were four contacts in the group.

Batman shook his head. If there were really four Fulcrums headed toward the US Mainland, he and his wingman were in for a bigger fight than they had prepared for, especially if they had to get in close and get visual identifications.

"One contact appears to be low and slow, possible helicopter," the controller added.

That made sense to Batman, given that they had been informed of a possible mayday call on guard earlier.

"Ok, Two, we'll bracket the group at ten miles for the ID," Batman said on the auxiliary radio.

"Two," Tuna responded as he flew a mile line abreast from Batman.

At fifteen miles, Batman descended to ten thousand feet. He could see one of the contacts separating at low altitude as the other three orbited on his radar screen. He looked out the canopy below to visually pick up the fight through his Joint Helmet Mounted Cueing System visor. He could see three dots maneuvering over the water as the sun was rising, but couldn't make out a type.

"Tally two, Sentry One-One is naked," Batman announced, indicating he was not being locked by any of the fighters' radars.

"Tally two, Sentry One-Two is naked," Tuna replied. The MiGs were not a threat to him.

"Ten miles, two, bracket," Batman directed. Tuna started a hard turn to the right as Batman offset left in an attempt to gain separation between himself and his flight lead. They would each take a side and meet at the group of fighters from separate avenues of approach, allowing one fighter an unobserved entry into the fight.

"Unknown Rider, Unknown Rider, position One-Two-Zero radial at seventy-six miles off Key West, five thousand feet, identify yourself on frequency 243.0 or 121.5, Hunter on guard," the male controller said, attempting to establish voice communications with the aircraft as the fight approached the ADIZ.

"Sentry One-One, cleared to engage," the controller said. In accordance with the rules of engagement, they were allowed to identify and intercept the targets. If they felt an imminent threat to themselves or the US, they were cleared to fire, but otherwise were to remain weapons tight.

"Sentry One-One," Batman replied.

"Holy shit!" Batman said to himself as he watched one of the dots explode in flight and plummet toward the water in a fireball.

"Sentry One-One has a fireball," Batman announced on the primary frequency.

"Hunter copies, do you have an ID yet?" the controller replied.

"Sentry One-One, negative," Batman said as he turned from his offset to face the fight at five miles.

"Hunter shows slow mover separating north squawking 7700," the controller said, indicating the slow contact was now indicating an emergency with its transponder code.

"Tally two only," Batman announced. At three miles, he saw the two aircraft, one much larger than the other. He could make out the distinct twin tails of the large MiG-29 as he watched it jockey for position with the other much smaller aircraft.

"Smoke in the air!" Tuna said, approaching the merge.

Batman was locked to the MiG-29 as he struggled to make out the type of the smaller aircraft. He watched as the missile left the rail of the MiG-29, sending a plume of smoke as it screamed past the smaller aircraft.

"Maintain ten thousand," Batman directed as the two fighters approached the merge. They set up a wide orbit over the fight.

"Looks like a MiG-29 and an... F-16?" Batman asked over the auxiliary radio.

"Concur," Tuna replied as the two jets circled above the fight.

Batman watched as the MiG-29 regained the advantage, rolling in behind the F-16. It jinked into a barrel roll as the MiG was in its control zone.

"Hunter, Sentry One-One IDs Fulcrum and Falcon, confirm friendly?" Batman said. He wasn't sure why a friendly F-16 would be this far away, but if it were, they needed to act fast. *It was obviously defensive.*

"Hunter unable," the controller responded.

He had to act quickly. The odds of a foreign F-16 being engaged by a known Cuban MiG-29 were slim in this part of the world. The nearest country with F-16s was Venezuela, and Batman doubted they would be fighting each other. He made the call.

"Sentry flight, green'em up, lead's in. Two, cover," Batman said over the primary frequency as he reached up and flipped the MASTER ARM switch to ARM.

As the F-16 rolled out in front of him, the MiG-29 maneuvered back into a firing solution. Batman selected the AIM-9, his most surgical air-to-air missile, checked for a good tone on the maneuvering MiG-29, and said a small prayer as he pressed the red "pickle button" on the control stick.

"Fox two!" he said as he maneuvered to maintain his offensive position behind the two aircraft.

The AIM-9 screamed across his canopy as it launched from the left inboard pylon toward the MiG, exploding as it hit the MiG's left engine. The pilot ejected just as the aircraft fell toward the water.

"Splash one!" Batman announced.

Batman rolled in behind the F-16 as it turned hard toward him. Batman breathed a sigh of relief as the aircraft rolled out and started rocking its wings.

\*    \*    \*

Spectre had lost the MiG-29 in the sun momentarily as he rolled out of the tuck under jink. He saw the pilot eject as the MiG exploded into a fireball behind him.

As he continued his turn to look for the shooter, he saw another set of twin tails in the rising sun and attempted another break turn. He had never seen the third aircraft enter the fight, but was relieved when he saw the light gray jet and realized it was an American F-15.

Spectre tried to key the radio and speak, but realized his radio cord had somehow been disconnected as he twisted and turned in the cockpit during the fight, so he rocked his wings – an indication in training to knock off the fight. He hoped the American F-15 pilot would recognize it.

As Spectre stopped rocking his wings and returned to level flight, he tried to maintain a non-threatening posture as the F-15 followed him in trail. He plugged in his comm. cord and attempted contact on the emergency UHF frequency.

"This is the F-16 squawking seven-seven-zero-zero, eighty miles southeast of Key West," he said. He couldn't think of a callsign to use. He thought about just using his name, but figured it would just be best to identify his position. He had never had that problem before.

"Aircraft squawking seventy-seven hundred, say intentions," the voice replied.

"Request a discreet frequency," Spectre replied, not wanting to broadcast what happened over an open, emergency channel.

"This is Hunter on Guard, change to my frequency three four three decimal seven," the male voice replied.

Spectre changed the frequency as the F-15 pulled alongside him in formation.

"This is the F-16 on three forty three seven," Spectre said.

"Say callsign," the controller replied.

"Uhh.... Spectre?" Spectre said, still unsure of what to call himself.

"Spectre this is Sentry One-One, you will be directed to Homestead Air Reserve Base," another voice said.

"Spectre copies," Spectre said, chuckling to himself at the idea of using his callsign as his flying callsign. "Request an escort for the Blackhawk off your nose for ten miles. It's an urgent medevac mission."

Spectre watched as a second F-15 descended in front of them in the direction of Elvis and the Blackhawk.

The F-15 escorted Spectre to Homestead ARB for a straight-in landing. It paced him until he was on short final to land, and then went around as Spectre touched down. Flying up the Keys, through Florida City, and past the racetrack brought back a flood of memories for Spectre. It was almost like the fini-flight he'd never been given.

As Spectre cleared the runway at the far end, the nostalgia ended. Two Air Force Security Forces Impalas and a Black Suburban met him at the end of the runway with weapons drawn. As soon as he stopped in the dearming area, his wheels were chocked. He was instructed to exit the aircraft with hands in sight as he shut down.

Spectre unstrapped and raised the canopy as the engine spooled down. A ladder was hung from the side of the aircraft as the men trained their guns on him. He was instructed to exit the aircraft and lie down on the hot ramp face down.

So much for the hero's welcome, Spectre thought.

# CHAPTER FIFTY

*Homestead, FL*

"Time to wake up, Special Agent, you're going to die a hero today," the man's voice said.

Decker awoke to a man standing over her waving something in her face. As she slowly regained her senses, she realized it was Leon waving an ammonia inhalant smelling salt in front of her nose.

Decker's eyes widened as she started to regain control of her faculties. Leon was standing over her with that same creepy grin he had earlier at her desk. Decker tried to take note of her surroundings. Her hands were bound to the old wooden chair she was sitting in. She had no idea where she was or what had happened. The last thing she remembered was downloading the image and trying to get the secure fax to work after Leon left her cubicle. Everything after that was a complete blank.

"Agent Leon? Where am I? What's going on?" Decker asked as she tried putting the pieces together. Her head was throbbing. It was scary to her that no matter how hard she tried, she couldn't remember anything.

"First, you are going to tell me everything you know about that picture and what you and that Air Force agent were working on," Leon replied as he sat in a chair next to her.

Decker took note of her surroundings. She was in the middle of what appeared to be a living room. There was a large flat screen TV surrounded by living room furniture. Her hands were bound by silk ties to the wooden chair she was sitting in. She felt the restraints loosen and the old wood flex as she wiggled her wrists. She was not well restrained.

"Tell you what?" Decker asked as she tilted her head to the side. "Is this some sort of sick joke?"

Leon leaned forward, resting his elbows on his knees. She could now see he was wearing latex gloves. "I'm afraid this is no joke, Agent Decker. You and the Air Force agent have gotten yourself mixed up with some very bad people, and I'm afraid it's going to bite you."

"What are you talking about?" she demanded.

"I read your case file, Agent Decker," he began, standing up from the chair. "You and Agent Baxter have been chasing wild leads about stolen airplanes concocted by jilted lovers. Unfortunately, that jilted lover will kill you in his own home. Tragic really, since we already lost Thomas in this case."

Decker watched Leon as he walked toward the rear of the room and picked something up. She tried to think of all the encounters she had with Leon, but came up blank. Other than being a sleaze ball, she had no idea what his angle was. The stolen F-16 had obviously struck a nerve with whomever he was working for.

"So you think kidnapping me and bringing me to Martin's home will somehow frame him? You know there were guards and surveillance tapes at the office, right? You can't expect to get away with this."

Leon walked back to the two chairs in the center of the room. He had picked up a carpenter's hammer on the other side of the room, and placed it on the chair next to her. He stood over her, staring with that same creepy grin.

"You really don't remember anything, do you?" he asked.

Leon seemed to savor the confused look on her face as she continued searching for answers in her blank memory.

"Let me help you. You walked right out of the office without so much as a word of protest. You even swiped your badge out and smiled at Frank as we passed the front desk. Sound familiar yet?"

Decker struggled to remember the details, but nothing was coming back to her. She only remembered standing at the secure fax, and even that was blurry.

Leon laughed. "Don't worry, the stuff is probably already out of your system by now. It only lasts an hour. No one will ever know."

"What did you do to me, asshole?" Decker snapped. The realization hit her that he had somehow managed to give her some form of a date rape drug. The thought of Leon touching her with his sleazy hands sent chills up her spine.

"Relax, it's just ketamine. You didn't even feel a thing. But I've answered enough of your questions, now you answer mine," he replied.

Decker thought back to the fax machine. He must have somehow injected her with it when she had her back turned. She cursed herself for dropping her guard after he walked off, seemingly satisfied with the explanation that the picture on her monitor was just something a friend had sent her unrelated to work. The ketamine explained her lack of memory though. She had heard of it a few times before, and she remembered it caused memory loss, compliance, a detached feeling, and sedation in victims. It was a very popular club drug in Miami.

"If you're just going to kill me, why bother?" Decker asked indignantly.

"Because I need to know just how much you actually know, and if you don't answer, I will make your death very painful and slow," Leon replied picking up the hammer. "It seems Mr. Martin learned some pretty ruthless stuff when he was in Iraq."

"What do you want to know?" Decker asked.

"Where did you get the picture?" Leon asked, taking his seat in the wooden chair across from her. He was still holding the hammer, spinning it in his hand as he waited for her response. The chairs seemed to be from the dining room set barely visible in the other room.

"I told you, they were just from a friend," she said, wiggling against the silk ties holding her in the chair. She guessed they must have been Martin's as well. Leon had been fairly thorough in building the evidence, but had been careless in choosing the restraints. She was slightly insulted.

Leon backhanded her with his gloved hand. "Is that really the way you want to go with this?"

"You don't scare me!" she screamed.

Leon put down the hammer and pulled a Gerber assisted-open field knife out of his pocket. He pressed the release and the blade clicked open.

"Good, then maybe we could have a little fun before we get back to business," he said, sliding the flat part of the cold steel blade across her cheek.

"Fuck you, you dirty piece of shit," Decker responded.

Leon let the blade drift down to her shirt. He slid it down to her chest and popped the top two buttons off, partially revealing her cleavage. He licked his lips.

"Ok!" she screamed. The thought of him touching her was worse than whatever sick, twisted plan he had for the hammer.

"Yeah, but I kind of like this idea," Leon replied, staring at her partially exposed breasts with his creepy grin.

Decker was horrified. She could see the guy was a psychopath. He had no idea Spectre wasn't even in the country, and didn't seem to care that if he did touch her, his entire framing operation would be out the window. She decided she had played along far too long.

"Don't you want to know what I know first?" she asked innocently.

"Good girl," he said, "but I was hoping you were going to be a bad girl. I've still got more ketamine in the car. Maybe later."

"Put the knife away, and I'll tell you whatever you want to know," she said as Leon took a step back and stared at her.

Leon took a step back and folded the knife against his thigh. He put it back in his pocket and sat down in the chair across from her.

"I'm listening," he said, motioning for her to explain.

Decker mumbled her response under her breath.

"I'm sorry?" he asked, leaning in.

Decker said it again, this time more softly as Leon stood and leaned in to hear her. He was within a foot of her. She could feel his disgusting hot breath on her face.

"I *said*, 'You're a fucking idiot,'" she said as she sent her right foot at high speed squarely into his testicles. He had restrained her hands, but had completely neglected her feet, leaving her a perfect opportunity as he stood before her.

As Leon leaned even further down toward her in pain, Decker leaned back and unleashed a devastating head butt into his nose. The blow had landed perfectly, sending blood gushing from his nose and face as he hit the floor. Decker ripped her right hand free of the wooden chair. She had noticed its right arm was not even glued down when she was testing the restraints, and the arm ripped right off as she twisted her body and pulled.

With one hand free, Decker turned and grabbed the chair as she stood. She picked up the chair and rotated, sending the chair crashing down on the doubled-over Leon. He collapsed as the chair shattered over his body, leaving Decker holding only the two wooden arms that her hands had been tied to.

Decker untied the silk ties from each hand and dropped the pieces of wood that had once been chair arms on the floor. Leon groaned and tried to get up, but a swift kick to the ribs was enough to make him stay down.

Decker noticed that Leon was still wearing his handcuffs on his belt, so she put a knee on the back of his neck and grabbed them out of his pouch. She handcuffed his hands behind his back and rolled him onto his back while pulling his knife out of his pocket and removing his gun from his holster.

She felt her forehead. It was tender, but she was in far less pain than Leon appeared to be. Being hard headed all her life had finally paid off. Her ex-boyfriends would be so proud to be vindicated.

"Snap out of it," she said, slapping his face. "I have more questions for you."

"I want a lawyer," he said, still groaning from the pain.

"Wrong answer," she said as she picked up the hammer from the ground. She wanted nothing more than to bash his face in.

Leon forced a laugh as he unsuccessfully tried to sit up. His ribs were bruised or broken, making it too painful.

"You aren't going to do anything, don't kid yourself," he said as he gave up his attempts to sit up. "You might as well call for backup, and then it's my word against yours."

Decker stared at him for a moment. Leon was smugly declaring victory in the face of defeat. She spun the hammer in her hand and squatted down next to him.

"Last chance," she said calmly. "Who are you working for?"

"Lawyer, bitch," Leon responded.

Without saying a word, Decker sent the hammer crashing down into his right knee, shattering his kneecap and causing him to scream in agony.

"What the fuck! What the fuck are you doing!" Leon cried as he rolled in pain.

"You've got one more and then I move on to testicles. You know, my word against yours and all that," she replied.

"Victor Alvarez!" he screamed, still rolling in pain.

"What was your involvement?" she asked, still spinning the hammer in her hand.

"I just gave him a heads up when his asset's name popped up on the wire and I fed him the stuff Thomas and you were working on," he replied.

"So why did you panic when you saw an F-16?" she asked.

"Because I knew he was trying to make some girl he got from another source steal one, and I figured if you were on to him, you would be on to me as well and everything would come crashing down."

"Who's the other source?" she asked.

"He never told me. Just some guy that works at the base. Gave him some files or something. Made fun of his shitty car with a busted muffler, but that's all I know. I really tried to stay out of it," he said, still reeling from the pain.

"And you were going to frame Martin?"

"Victor talked about flipping the girl right under the guy's nose. I read about the guy. He was kicked out of the Air Force. He flipped out on the Secretary of Defense. He seemed like a likely candidate to turn on you."

"Sure, if he were even in the country, dumbass," Decker said as she dropped the hammer and got up to walk out.

# CHAPTER FIFTY-ONE

*Operations Building*
*39th Fighter Squadron*
*Homestead ARB, FL*

Spectre sat alone in the small briefing room. It was a small area with a SMART Board electronic briefing board on one wall and a traditional dry erase whiteboard on the other. It had a small table in the middle with chairs all around for members of a flight to sit as the flight lead of whatever mission the pilots were on briefed the flight. It had been years since Spectre had been in a room like this, and although he had been a Gator, he had never been in this particular briefing room. The squadron had been completely renovated since he had left the Air Force.

Spectre was exhausted. His head was killing him. The adrenaline had finally worn off from the early morning events. Upon landing, he had been arrested, hauled to the squadron, and forced to tell his story in great detail by agents from AFOSI. It was the second time in less than a week he had been isolated and forced to justify his actions to law enforcement. Although this time, they were much more polite.

They had made him sign a Classified Information Nondisclosure Agreement before beginning the debrief. Under the threat of ten years in prison and ten thousand dollars, Spectre agreed never to speak of anything related to the recovery of the aircraft or Chloe Moss. Once that was complete, the agents allowed Spectre to tell his story.

He told them the story from the time he left the meeting with the SECDEF until landing at Homestead as they recorded the conversation and jotted down notes from his statement. When he was finished, the two agents thanked him for his time and left him to sit alone in the cold briefing room.

The door to the briefing room opened. Agent Decker walked in. Her blonde hair was in a ponytail and she was wearing a navy blue jacket with FBI stenciled in yellow letters across the left breast. She looked tired and her face was bruised.

"I was starting to wonder what happened to you," Spectre said looking at his watch. "You get lost on the way to the fax machine?"

Decker frowned as she sat across the table from Spectre. "It's good to see you too, Cal."

"I'm sorry. It's been a rough morning, what happened to you?" Spectre asked, eyeing the bruises on her wrists and face.

"Apparently you were going to kill me in your house," she replied.

Spectre's confused look launched Decker into a narrative of the past five hours. She explained how she had been drugged and walked out of the FBI field office with Agent Leon without being able to contact the SECDEF's staff.

As Spectre listened intently, she went on to describe how he intended to frame Spectre for murder, but underestimated her will to fight.

"Silk ties on a rickety chair?" she scoffed."Seriously? By the way, you're probably going to need a new dining room chair."

"They were Chloe's anyway," Spectre said somberly. "Have you heard anything about the helicopter yet? The last two guys knew nothing."

"They made it to Lower Keys Medical Center about thirty minutes after you landed," Decker replied.

"And?" Spectre asked impatiently.

"Marcus and Moss were both rushed to surgery. Carpenter, Agent Baxter, and the two Customs guys were detained until they can get this all sorted out. It's a real mess."

Spectre's head dropped. He still wasn't sure how to deal with what Chloe said as he tried to save her. It was obvious she had some relationship with Victor and had willingly taken the F-16. He was angry with himself for not seeing it sooner. Marcus had been right. *She had left him for another man.*

"Cal, there's something else," Decker said, trying to bring him back from his thousand yard stare.

"Yeah?" Spectre asked, looking up. His eyes were bloodshot. He looked like a defeated man.

"The agent working for Alvarez mentioned getting some files from someone on this base. Do you know what he could have been talking about?" Decker asked, pulling out her notepad.

"Files? Could mean anything. Was he more specific?"

"No, he just said that Alvarez picked the girl from another source. The source gave him files that he must have used to target her," she said as she reread her notes.

"Personnel files, flying schedules, and Emergency Data for next of kin, maybe," Spectre replied pensively.

"Is any of that information classified?" Decker asked

"Not that I know of. At worst, it's For Official Use Only, which basically means it's not classified, but it still should be protected. Do you really think you can find the person that gave him the information? It's a slap on the wrist at worst."

"If whoever did this is a source to a known intelligence operative in the United States, it's going to be a lot more than just a slap on the wrist," Decker said, leaning back in her chair. "And yes, I do think I can find him. He mentioned a beat up car with a bad muffler."

Spectre laughed dismissively. "Gee, that narrows it down. I guess you guys have your work cut out for you, staking out Pep Boys until someone shows up with a bad muffler."

Decker glared at Spectre.

"I'm sorry," he said, trying to backpedal out of the hole he was digging. "Did I mention it's been a long day? Can I go home now?"

"Oh yeah, that's why I'm here. You're being released under my care until the State Department and Department of Defense can get together and clear you of anything criminal," she said with a wry smile.

Spectre jumped up out of his chair and started for the door. "Sweet, I'll buy you breakfast. Let's get out of here."

Decker followed as Spectre led them out of the briefing room and down the main hallway of the large multi-million dollar Operations Building. The heat from the South Florida humidity hit him as he held the door open for Decker as she passed him.

Spectre followed, squinting in the morning sun. As they reached her black SUV, Spectre stopped dead in his tracks as a car pulled into the parking lot. It sounded like a bumblebee as it downshifted and pulled into the parking spot across from them.

He watched as a small man wearing a green flight suit hopped out of the car and put his blue officer's hat on as he headed toward the entrance.

Decker's phone rang as she reached the driver's door of her car. She fished for the phone in her jacket pocket as Spectre stood staring at the man walking toward the Operations Building.

As Spectre realized who it was, he took off in a sprint toward the man who was punching in his access code on the door's cipher lock. He reached the man just as he was turning the door handle.

"Coach Louhan!" Spectre yelled as he slammed the partially opened door back shut. The little man partially retreated in surprise.

"Cal!" Decker screamed from across the parking lot. "What's going on?"

"Cal Martin. I've heard you've been busy," Coach replied. "I would love to hear about it sometime, but, I'm very busy myself right now. Is there a problem?"

"You!" Spectre replied indignantly through his teeth as he moved into the man's face. He was just a few inches shorter than Spectre, but he cowered as Spectre stood in front of him.

"Excuse me?" Coach said timidly, backing up from Spectre.

"You fucking traitor!" Spectre barked, closing the small distance Coach had just gained. "You sold the documents to the Cuban."

Coach's eyes widened as his wrinkled face turned red. He tried to avoid eye contact. If the car hadn't been enough to confirm his suspicion, Coach's reaction had sealed the deal. The man standing before him who had ended his flying career was a traitor who sold information to foreign spies.

"I don't know what you're talking about, now get out of the way," Coach said, raising his right hand to push Spectre out of the way.

Spectre intercepted Coach's hand as it approached his chest. With both hands, he twisted Coach's wrist away from his body, snapping the ligaments and breaking Coach's wrist as he buckled under the pain.

"Get up," Spectre said, grabbing Coach's throat with his right hand and lifting him up into the wall. He slammed his head against the brick building.

"You can't do this," Coach grunted. "I am a colonel. I demand respect."

"Respect is earned, fuckstick," Spectre said, tightening his grip around Coach's throat and shoving his head into the wall again.

"Cal!" Decker said behind him as she ran toward the two men. "Cal, stop!"

"I had a family to think about! I had bills to pay! I owe people money!" Coach pleaded as he struggled to breathe under Spectre's grip.

"You ruined my career and took away the only thing I had left."

"It was either you or Pounder! He was going places! You made your bed when you chose the girl!"

"Cal! Enough!" Decker yelled as she tried to grab his shoulder. "Let the system work."

Spectre shifted his hand from Coach's throat to his left shoulder and pulled the man forward as he drove his right knee into Coach's sternum.

"Enjoy your new bed in prison, asshole," Spectre said angrily as Coach dropped to the ground gasping for air.

Decker pushed Spectre back as she dropped to a knee to cuff Coach as he rolled on the ground.

"That was the hospital in Key West calling," she said as she snapped the second cuff to Coach's broken wrist, causing him to scream in pain. "You're going to want to get down there soon."

# CHAPTER FIFTY-TWO

*Homestead, FL*

I t was raining. Spectre hated funerals, and it seemed like it was always raining at them. He was sure there was some old wives' tale that explained it, but for now, he stood in his trench coat and suit as the chaplain concluded the benediction in the light drizzle.

Spectre was standing near the back, behind the white chairs that had been set up for friends and family. He had been offered a seat near the front with family, but felt it best to stand in the back. He doubted any of the grieving family members actually considered him family anyway.

Despite everything that had gone on, Spectre felt responsible. He wondered if there was anything he could have done differently as the five-member rifle team executed the three-volley salute, firing three times in unison. As the last volley stopped, a bugler began playing "Taps."

Spectre stood with his hand over his heart while the military members in the crowd saluted the flag draped over the casket. When the bugler finished, two Honor Guard members removed the flag from the casket and began folding it as the crowd watched in silence.

Once folded, the flag was presented by the white gloved Honor Guard member to the chaplain who in turn presented it to the family seated in the front row. Spectre thought back to the chaplain that he'd driven with to Chloe's parents' house. He had just found out before the ceremony that the chaplain died in ICU a few days after the shooting. He regretted not being able to attend that funeral.

"She was a fucking whore! Why are we even here getting our asses wet?" Marcus grumbled from the wheelchair next to Spectre.

"Shut up, old man, before I release your parking brake and let you roll down this mostly shallow hill," Carpenter whispered behind him.

Spectre turned to Marcus and motioned for him to be quiet. The chaplain called for a moment of silence. A few moments later, a flight of four F-16s approached behind them in fingertip formation. As they flew over the gravesite, the number three aircraft went vertical, executing the missing man tribute.

Despite the sadness Spectre felt, he knew Marcus was right. She had betrayed her country and cheated on him. There was no justifying what she did anymore, but the official story would never reflect that.

After making the entire group sign Nondisclosure Agreements in exchange for immunity from prosecution, the official story was drafted. If Moss had lived, it would have been through a dramatic rescue effort in the Atlantic after days at sea. When she died, it just became the end to a tragic mishap.

Captain Chloe Moss had been killed on that fateful night when her F-16 crashed into the Atlantic Ocean. The cause was listed as Controlled Flight Into Terrain due to spatial disorientation. Her body had been recovered by a Coast Guard vessel, and the wreckage was never completely located.

Spectre brought up the inconvenient fact of the F-16 he had delivered to their doorstep with the tail number of the missing F-16 during their discussions. Not to worry, they told him, the aircraft would receive all new serial numbers as the latest delivery from the factory. As far as the Air Force was concerned, Chloe Moss' aircraft had officially been lost forever.

As the funeral ended, Carpenter pushed Marcus down the hill with Spectre as they headed for his truck. There was nothing more to say. That chapter of his life was over, and they still had a struggling store to deal with.

The rain stopped as Spectre and Carpenter helped Marcus into the front seat of Spectre's truck. He groaned in protest as they helped him with his injured leg. The doctors said it would be a few weeks before he would be able to start on crutches. He was just lucky to be alive, having nearly bled out in the back of the helicopter.

"Mr. Martin?" a man asked as Spectre started to close Marcus's door. Carpenter and Spectre turned to face the man. He looked like any one of the civilian attendees of the funeral. He was wearing a black suit with Ray Ban sunglasses.

"Can I help you?" Spectre asked cautiously.

"I was just wondering if you had a moment?" the man asked.

"Well, as you can see, we were about to leave," Spectre replied.

Carpenter took the hint and jumped in the back seat of Spectre's crew cab truck.

"Who's that guy?" Marcus asked as they watched the man walk away.

"Don't know, he just asked for a minute so I left them alone," Carpenter replied.

A few minutes later, Spectre hopped in the driver's seat and started the turbo diesel engine.

"Well, that was weird," Spectre said as he shifted from Park to Drive.

"You gonna fill us in?" Marcus asked impatiently.

"Guy said he had something he wanted to talk to me about in private and handed me his card," Spectre said, handing the card to Marcus.

Marcus pulled his reading glasses out of his coat pocket and studied the business card. It was all white except for the name CHARLES STEELE and a phone number below it.

Thanks for reading!

Turn the page for a sneak preview of C.W. Lemoine's second book in the *SPECTRE SERIES*:

# *AVOID. NEGOTIATE. KILL.*
SPECTRE SERIES: BOOK TWO

AVAILABLE IN EBOOK AND PAPERBACK NOW.

VISIT WWW.CWLEMOINE.COM FOR MORE INFORMATION ON RELEASE DATES, BOOK SIGNINGS, AND EXCLUSIVE SPECIAL OFFERS.

# PROLOGUE

**Key West Regional Hospital
Key West, FL
1500L**

I'm Jessica Kratzer," she said, handing her ID badge to the shift supervisor. "I'm here for the 3 PM shift."

The badge had a photo of her that looked exactly as she did standing in front of the older nurse. It identified her as a Registered Nurse with NextGen Nursing Solutions, Inc. Her light brown hair was held tightly in a bun and her burgundy scrubs fit tightly around her athletic body.

"You're a bit early," the older woman replied. She appeared to be in her late fifties, her hair almost completely white. She was several inches taller than the contract nurse standing before her. "But we can use the help. I'm Anne Millsaps. Have you worked ICU before?"

Kratzer shook her head as Millsaps returned the badge and motioned for her to follow through the automatic double doors and into the main area of the Key West Regional Intensive Care Unit. Kratzer trailed closely as the woman led her to the nurses station.

"It's not bad. There are eight rooms here, which usually means we generally have four nurses on staff. We're a bit short staffed right now, but luckily, there are only three patients right now. We just transferred one to the third floor."

"Who are those guys?" Kratzer asked, pointing to the men in suits standing outside the door of one the rooms. "They look serious."

"Protection detail. This morning we had two patients come in on some kind of military helicopter. No names, just Jane Doe and John Doe. Both had gunshot wounds. I've been in nursing thirty years. Never seen anything like it."

Kratzer watched as the men standing outside the room stopped talking and eyed her. They appeared to study her for a minute as she stood next to the older nurse. Seconds later, they seemed to relax and returned to their previous conversation.

"You'll get used to it," Millsaps reassured her. "Although, pretty little thing like you? You're probably already used to it."

Millsaps grabbed three charts from behind the desk and set them down in front of Kratzer as she watched a middle-aged male nurse exit the guarded room. "That's Tom," she said. "He's married, so don't get any ideas."

Kratzer frowned. *If this lady only knew.*

"Hey Tom, this is Jessica from the temp agency. I was just about to give her the run down. How's our Jane Doe doing?"

Tom smiled warmly at Jessica. He looked to be in his late thirties with dark brown hair and brown eyes. Like the other two nurses, he was wearing burgundy scrubs.

"She's doing better. Vitals are stable. I just hung that unit of blood for her," he said as he scribbled notes in the patient's chart.

"We also have Mrs. Mary Lee, seventy-seven, congestive heart failure and Mr. Gary Hall, seventy-four, who's just out of surgery with a hip replacement," Millsaps said. "Why don't you take Mr. Hall this evening?"

"What happened to the John Doe?" Kratzer asked.

"That was the one we transferred up to third floor about an hour ago," the older nurse replied, handing Kratzer the chart of Gary Hall.

Kratzer hesitated for a moment and then said, "Do you mind if I take the girl? I would feel more comfortable with the younger patient."

"Oh, honey," the woman said, taking off her glasses. "I've probably been nursing longer than you've been alive. Trust me, dear, they're all the same. Don't think that just because they're younger, they're easier patients to deal with."

"It's ok, Anne. If it makes her more comfortable, I don't mind switching," Tom interjected with another warm smile.

Kratzer smiled graciously as he handed her the younger woman's chart. "Thank you, Tom."

"Buy me a Coke later," he replied with wink as he grabbed the older man's chart and set off for his room.

"Like I said earlier, don't get any ideas," Millsaps warned. "It's probably about time to check on the blood transfusion on your patient. Have at it."

Kratzer quickly flipped through the chart as she gathered herself. The Jane Doe had spent nearly six hours in surgery earlier in the day having bullet and bone fragments removed. One of her kidneys had been hit and had to be removed, and she had nerve damage in her spine. Her vitals were fairly weak, but stable. She was in a medically-induced coma for the time being.

The two men standing outside the room eyed her as she approached the door. They appeared to be federal agents, but she couldn't pinpoint which branch of government. She guessed FBI, based on their suits and demeanor.

She smiled as she walked by them and opened the door. Another agent, this one female, sat in the chair at the edge of the bed. Kratzer walked in as the woman stood. Kratzer eyed the woman's badge clipped to her belt and handgun. The FBI shield and standard issue Glock 22 confirmed her previous guess.

"What happened to Tom?" the female agent asked.

"My name is Jessica," Kratzer responded with a disarming smile. "I'm going to be taking care of Mrs. Doe. Tom is with another patient. How is she?"

"She's still out," the dark haired agent replied, sitting back down. "But she's doing better than she was when she got here."

"Do you know what happened to her?" Kratzer asked as she walked over to the IV and blood transfusion unit. The girl's curly brown hair was still dirty and stuck together with blood. Her face was swollen and bruises covered her body.

"I can't discuss that," the woman said sternly.

"Sorry," Kratzer replied. "Just curious." That was all the information she needed. She was in the right room with the right patient. She pulled out a small bottle and packaged syringe from her pocket and unwrapped it.

"What's that? I thought she couldn't have anything while she's getting blood?"

"This is to prevent blood clots," Kratzer responded dismissively as she filled the syringe. "Big concern when getting blood."

Satisfied, the agent returned to her Sudoku puzzle as Kratzer stuck the needle in the IV line and injected her patient. When she was finished, she discarded the syringe and needle in the red SHARPS container on the wall and walked out.

"I'm not feeling very well," Kratzer said as she reached Millsaps at the nurses station. "Where's the nearest bathroom?"

"Just outside the double doors on the left. You ok, sweetie?" she asked.

"I don't know. Stomach bug has been going around and it may have just hit me," Kratzer replied, clutching her stomach.

"Well don't wait around here! Go!" Millsaps responded, shooing her away.

Kratzer nodded as she scurried out of the ICU and through the double doors.

"Those damned contract nurses," Millsaps said, shaking her head as she picked up the chart and headed for her patient's room.

Kratzer bypassed the bathroom and continued out toward the main corridor. As she reached the lobby, she entered the women's room and locked the door behind her. She found the backpack she had stuffed in the upper vent a few hours prior. She pulled out her jeans and jacket and pulled the blue Florida Marlins baseball cap low over her face as she balled up her scrubs and stuffed them into the backpack.

As she reached the door of the bathroom, she heard, "CODE BLUE, I-C-U, CODE BLUE, I-C-U," over the hospital public address system indicating a patient was coding and required a crash cart in the Intensive Care Unit.

She smiled as she unlocked the door and walked out. The Potassium Chloride she had injected into the girl's IV line was working, and within minutes, Chloe Moss would be dead.

She had only completed fifty percent of her objectives, but for Svetlana Mitchell, that's all that mattered. Her handler had been crystal clear – *kill the girl*. The secondary objective would only be a target of opportunity. It was unfortunate that they had moved him, but that was part of the game. She was sure her handler would understand, and she could always get him later if necessary.

She cleared the lobby, keeping her head low to avoid security cameras as she exited the large hospital. It was another beautiful South Florida day. She decided to spend the rest of her afternoon on the water after she collected her payout.

# CHAPTER ONE

**10 Miles Northeast of Al Hasakah, Syria**
**Present Day**
**2100L**

Avoid. Negotiate. Kill. They were the three basic tenets of Krav Maga that his Sensei had instilled in him since day one of his training.

First, he was to avoid confrontation. Some even called it the "Nike Defense." Running away was generally the preferred option. Living to fight another day was the highest priority, regardless of what his ego said. He had already spent the last two days practicing the art of avoidance by evading and hiding. It hadn't worked. The commandos of the al-Nusra Front captured him after he made initial contact with Iraqi Security Forces. He had exhausted that option.

His next priority was to negotiate. Sometimes a person could talk his way out of a situation. Maybe the attacker hadn't fully resolved his will to fight. Maybe the attacker wanted something that wasn't worth risking life and limb over. Or maybe a person could buy enough time for help to show up. As Cal "Spectre" Martin stared down the barrel of his own confiscated Beretta 92FS 9MM at point blank range, he realized that option was also no longer on the table. The man before him, in his torn and worn out camouflaged jacket and military pants, didn't appear to be willing to negotiate as he shouted for Spectre to read the paper the man had given him. All Spectre could do now was kill.

His ribs were sore and his face was swollen. They had not been gentle in transporting him from his holed up location in the desert of Iraq to their small village, although from what he had noticed, it wasn't much of a village. The locals had likely been driven out as the Syrian Opposition fighters had taken it over as a base of operations. It was mostly just a few small huts, war torn buildings and small trucks with bed-mounted machine guns.

"Read! Read!" the man holding the gun to his temple shouted from behind his black wiry beard. Spectre could feel the man's spit and hot breath hit him as he pushed the cold gun barrel into Spectre's temple.

Spectre picked up the piece of paper and looked into the tripod-mounted camera in front of him. He was kneeling in his desert khaki flight suit. His survival vest and radio had long since been stripped from him. The zippers of his flight suit pockets were starting to dig into his knees, adding to the pain.

"I can't read this chicken scratch," Spectre said, holding up the hand written piece of paper. He watched as the man sidestepped in front of him to see the paper. The hammer on his Beretta 92FS M9 wasn't cocked and the safety was still on. *Amateur.*

"What? What you say?" the man asked in broken English as he sidestepped again and repositioned the gun to Spectre's forehead. He was now standing between Spectre and the camera. "You read! No excuse! Or you die!"

Spectre brought the paper up to his face as if to get a better look. *It was time to kill.* As his hands reached his eye level, he dropped the paper and instantly grabbed the man's right wrist with his right hand and the barrel of the gun with his left. Falling to his side while securing the weapon, he flicked off the safety, squeezed through the double action of the fourteen-pound trigger, and fired at his shocked captor. The bullet struck the man in the throat and sent him stumbling back into the camera as he gasped through his last breaths.

Spectre reset his aim for the door. The small hut had only one door, and he remembered an armed guard standing watch as his captor, presumably a leader, had taken him in to make the propaganda video. Seconds later, the door flung open as a screaming attacker rushed in. Spectre sent two rounds to the man's chest and followed up with a round to the head as the lone man fell forward.

Scrambling to his feet, Spectre rushed to the guard's lifeless body. He grabbed the AK-47 from his hands and found two extra magazines and a fragmentation grenade in his pocket. Shooting his way out of the village had a low probability of success, but Spectre resolved to go down fighting. *He wouldn't make the mistake of being captured again.*

Spectre put the extra magazines in his flight suit along with the Beretta and readied the AK-47. He had no idea how many men were alerted by the sounds of his gunshots, but he assumed the worst. He took a deep breath and stepped out into the crisp night air. Taking cover behind a burned out car in front of him, he watched as a group of men advanced toward his position.

He tried to get a feel for his surroundings as he waited for a clear shot. He was still unclear of exactly where he was in the village and what the best route of escape was. They had kept a burlap sack over his head as they had walked him from his initial holding location to the small building where he had been held. The sack had been just worn out enough that he could barely make out guards as they shuffled him into the building. He knew he was roughly one hundred paces from his original location, but that was it.

He looked around as he crouched behind the car. He could see clear night air behind him and more huts to his left and in front of him. *Fight or flight.* Spectre had a decision to make. It was time to revert back to avoidance until that option was once again exhausted. He would never be able to hold his position with the combined one hundred rounds of 7.62 x 39 and 9MM for his AK-47 and Beretta 92FS.

Holding his rifle low and ready, he took off in a sprint toward the rear of the long building. As he reached the corner, rounds began peppering the walls as the men saw him. He took cover and assessed his new position. It was completely dark. *Desert.* He could tell by the dark abyss behind him that he had been held near the edge of the village.

Spectre held up his rifle as he peered around the corner. As one of the men reached the burned out car in front of the building, Spectre fired off two rounds that sent the man running for cover. Spectre sprinted to the opposite corner of the building. The other two men were attempting to flank his position from the opposite side. He pulled the pin on the grenade and tossed it in their direction. The grenade landed between the two men, sending shrapnel and debris everywhere as it exploded.

He sprinted back to the opposite corner and took aim at the man behind the burned out car. As the man peered around the rear bumper, Spectre fired a round, hitting the man in the forehead and instantly dropping him face first into the dirt.

Spectre could hear vehicles in the distance as more men approached. He took off into the darkness, his boots kicking up sand as he sprinted through the soft desert. He could hear the yells of the rebel fighters behind him as the vehicles got closer. At this rate, he would be overrun before he reached civilization.

Clearing the first sand dune, he turned around and dropped to a prone position while taking aim toward the village. He could see two vehicles with mounted machine guns and spotlights quickly approaching the edge of the village. They were firing wildly in his direction, but in the darkness, their un-aimed shots were in vain.

Spectre cleared his weapon and checked his magazine. *They would surely run him down if he kept running.* It was time to make his last stand and go down swinging. *At least he had made it this far.*

# ACKNOWLEDGMENTS

First and foremost, I'd like to thank you, the reader, for taking the time to join me in the story of Cal "Spectre" Martin. I hope you've enjoyed reading this story as much as I enjoyed writing it.

To my **Dad**, thank you for always being there for me and supporting me. I would not be where I am today without your constant encouragement and support. You've helped me become the man, officer, pilot, and now *writer* that I am today. I can only hope to one day be half as good of a father as you've been for me.

One thing about self-publishing is that you're pretty much on your own for the hardest part of writing – editing. For that, I am truly thankful for the help of **Doug Narby**. Thank you for putting up with my (often infrequent) chapters and rewrites. Your suggestions, edits, and feedback were invaluable in writing this book. I am truly grateful.

Along the same lines, I would like to thank my close friends who stood by me and listened while I went through idea after idea. Thanks for sticking it out with me.

**Charlie "TBear" Guarino**, your story was inspirational in writing Spectre's story. I hope one day I'll be reading your autobiography. It's a great story. You've been an outstanding friend, mentor, and colleague. Thank you for opening the door for me to fly fighters in the military.

At the risk of leaving anyone out, I'd like to thank those that took the time to read and make suggestions for the various drafts of this book – **Jack "Farley" Stewart** (and a special thanks for the back cover text), **Tonya Morrow**, and **Jim Holmes**.

Finally, to all my friends and family who have supported me along the way, thank you. Without you, I would not be the man I am today. I am truly fortunate to have you all in my life.

I hope you'll all join me as the Spectre series continues and evolves. Thanks for reading.

C.W. Lemoine is the author of **SPECTRE RISING**, **AVOID.**
**NEGOTIATE.      KILL.,      ARCHANGEL      FALLEN**,
**EXECUTIVE REACTION**, and **BRICK BY BRICK.**   He
graduated from the A.B. Freeman School of Business at Tulane
University in 2005 and Air Force Officer Training School in
2006. He is a military pilot that has flown the F-16 and F/A-18.
He is also a certified Survival Krav Maga Instructor and sheriff's
deputy.


www.cwlemoine.com

**Facebook**
http://www.facebook.com/cwlemoine/
**Twitter:**
@CWLemoine

Made in the USA
Coppell, TX
09 October 2020